Books in the NEVER SAY SPY series:

REACH FOR THE SPY

Book 3 of the NEVER SAY SPY series

Diane Henders

REACH FOR THE SPY

Published in paperback, November 2011 by PEBKAC Publishing v.2

Since You Asked...

People frequently ask if my protagonist, Aydan Kelly, is really me.

Yeah, you got me. These novels are an autobiography of my secret life as a government agent, working with highly-classified computer technology... Oh, wait, what's that? You want the *truth*? Um, you do realize fiction writers get paid to lie, don't you?

...well, shit, that's not nearly as much fun. It's also a long story.

I swore I'd never write fiction. "Too personal," I said. "People read novels and automatically assume the author is talking about him/herself."

Well, apparently I lied about the fiction-writing part. One day, a story sprang into my head and wouldn't leave. The only way to get it out was to write it down. So I did.

But when I wrote that first book, I never intended to show it to anyone, so I created a character that looked like me, just to thumb my nose at the stereotype. I've always had a defective sense of humour, and this time it turned around and bit me in the ass.

Because after I'd written the third novel, I realized I actually wanted to publish them. And when I went back to change my main character to *not* look like me, my beta readers wouldn't let me. They rose up against me and said, "No! Aydan is a tall woman with long red hair and brown eyes. End of discussion!"

Jeez, no wonder readers get the idea that authors write about themselves. So no, I'm not Aydan Kelly. I just look like her.

The town of Silverside and all secret technologies are products of my imagination. If I'm abducted by grim-faced men wearing dark glasses, or if I die in an unexplained fiery car crash, you'll know I accidentally came a little too close to the truth.

Thank you for respecting my hard work. If you're borrowing this book, I'd very much appreciate it if you would buy your own copy, or, if you wish, you can make a donation on my website at http://www.dianehenders.com/donate.

Thanks - I hope you enjoy the book!

For Phill

Much love.

To my beta readers, with gratitude: Many thanks for catching my spelling and grammar errors, telling me when I screwed up the plot or the characters' motivations, and generally keeping me honest.

To everyone else, respectfully:
If you find any spelling or typographical errors in this book, please send me an email at errors@dianehenders.com. Mistakes drive me nuts, and I'm sorry if any slipped through. If you let me know what the error is, and on which page, I'll make sure it gets fixed as soon as possible. Thanks!

CHAPTER 1

A faint noise woke me. My eyes flew open as I held my breath, listening. Had the sound come from outside the open window? I strained my ears, but heard only the usual quiet of a July night in the country.

A tiny, metallic click from the doorknob made me change the rhythm of my breathing, slow and deep. My eyelids drooped, and I watched the door through the fringe of my lashes.

I cursed the position of the shaft of moonlight. It fell directly across me in the bed, but the doorway itself was in shadow. The door swung open slowly and silently. A large, dark figure moved toward my bed.

I emitted a small snore, followed by a deep sigh, and rolled over. I let the bedsheet fall away as I reached under the opposite pillow and clenched my fist around the crowbar. The moonlight emphasized the curves and hollows of my naked body. The intruder froze, staring.

That's right, asshole. Take a good look. It'll be the last thing you ever see. Just come a little closer, now...

He turned away abruptly, and I was instantly in motion. The crowbar hurtled toward his temple in a flat, vicious arc with all my strength behind it.

"Aydan."

At the sound of his whisper, I let out a yelp of dismay. I tried desperately to slow and alter the trajectory of my weapon, but it connected solidly with his head. He fell.

Heart pounding, I floundered toward the huddled form on the floor. As I reached him, he sat up slowly. I flung myself on him from behind, one arm across his massive chest while my other hand clamped over his mouth.

"We're bugged," I breathed urgently in his ear.

His large hand closed around my wrist, and I let him pull my hand away from his mouth.

"I know," he said in normal tones. "I'm jamming them."

I collapsed onto the floor behind him, gasping. "Jesus fucking Christ, John! Don't ever fucking do that! I nearly fucking killed you, for chrissake!" If frequent use of obscenities indicated one's level of intellect, I'd apparently dropped about a hundred IQ points in the last couple of seconds.

"I noticed." He touched his head, and his fingers came away dark in the moonlight.

"Shit!" I started to scramble up, but he grabbed my arm.

"Don't turn on any lights."

"I need to look at that," I argued. "I was going for a home run until the last second. You're bleeding."

"I'll live. It just glanced off."

I blew out an irritated breath and knelt beside him. I ran my fingers through his hair, exploring the sticky area near the top of his head. At least I couldn't feel any squishiness that would indicate a fracture.

I stepped across him into my ensuite bathroom and came out with a clean washcloth. "Here."

He accepted it and pressed it against his head. He glanced up at me, and then looked away quickly. "Aydan…

Could you please put some clothes on? This is really... distracting."

"Oh!" I glanced down at my white skin, practically glowing in the moonlight. My forty-six-year-old body was in pretty good shape, except for the extra ten pounds or so around the middle. I'd never been shy about it. And getting naked with John Kane was near the top of my private list of things to do, but I was pretty sure braining him with a crowbar didn't qualify as foreplay.

Anyway, it didn't matter. Now was not the time. I stepped quickly to the chair in the corner where I kept my clothes laid out for quick access. I pulled on jeans and a sweatshirt and then turned back to him.

"Can you stand up?" I asked.

He rose. "I'm fine. We need to talk." He sat on the edge of the bed, and I perched beside him.

The moonlight made a dramatic study of his strong, square features. His silvered temples gleamed against his short, dark hair as he turned to eye me piercingly in the pale light.

"How did you find the bugs?" he demanded. "Do you have a scanner?"

"No. I found them the good old-fashioned way. Is Stemp monitoring them?"

"Yes. How did you know you were bugged?"

"I smelled them."

His dark brows snapped together. "What?"

I grinned. "Stemp needs to be more careful choosing his minions. Whoever he sent to install the bugs was a smoker who wore cologne. I smelled him the instant I came in the house. I checked everything over, and when I couldn't find anything missing, I started to look for things that had been added."

Kane nodded slowly. "You're good."

I peered at him in the moonlight. "What the hell are you doing here? Dammit, Stemp is going to notice that the bugs are jammed. I didn't want him to know that I knew about them."

"He won't know. I got Webb to generate a circular loop that will feed the monitor. We have an hour."

"You got Spider involved in this, too? What if you get caught?" I demanded. "It was bad enough when Stemp just thought you were sympathetic toward me. If he finds out about this, you're going to be next on his hit list, right after he whacks me."

He went still, watching me. "What makes you say that?"

"Come on, John. It's not rocket science. Stemp needs me right now, but he doesn't trust me because he can't manipulate me. The instant he's got an alternative, I'm going to get a lead suppository."

I sighed. "In fact, you'll probably be the one to get the order. That's what I'd do if I was Stemp. If you carry out the order to kill me, you keep your job. And live. If you refuse, he passes the order down the food chain to get rid of both of us. And on down the line to get rid of anybody else who isn't willing to follow orders. Get all the housecleaning done at once."

"That's the most paranoid, cynical thing I've ever heard you say."

"Yeah. Tell me I'm wrong."

He blew out a breath. "So that's what you were trying to tell me when you walked away from me last week. You were warning me to keep my distance. To protect me."

"Yeah. And here you are. Shit."

"Will you stop trying to protect everybody else and start looking out for yourself for a change? I'm a big boy. I can take care of myself."

I sighed inwardly. He sure was a big boy. In every sense of the word, from what I'd had the opportunity to observe. Too bad he had to be permanently off-limits to me if I wanted him to stay alive.

"I know you can take care of yourself," I told him. "But Stemp was watching us, and I wanted to make sure he didn't see anything that would make him mistrust you. He's your boss, after all. You'll still have to work with him long after I'm gone."

His brows drew together. "What you said last week... About how I'd follow orders no matter what. Do you really believe that? That I'm nothing more than a robot following orders?"

I hesitated, trying to find the right words. "No... But... that's what Stemp needs you to be. And that's the safest thing for you to be right now."

"You really think I'd kill you if he gave me the order." His voice was even, but I could hear the edge of suppressed hurt and anger.

"John..." I sighed and tugged my fingers through my long hair, yanking out the night's tangles. "You're one of our government's top agents. You've spent most of your life in military and law enforcement. That tells me that your top priority is doing the right thing for this country. Am I right?"

"Of course." He frowned at me in the shadows. "Where are you going with this?"

"What if it turns out that it's the right thing for you to kill me?"

He jerked back. "That's ridiculous."

"Is it? Think it through. Right now, I'm both incredibly valuable and incredibly dangerous. I can crack any data encryption, and I'm working for our government. Valuable. But I'm a civilian and Stemp doesn't trust me. As soon as he finds another way to break the encryption, I'll stop being valuable, and then all that's left is the danger that our enemies will scoop me up. He can't afford the risk."

"You'd never turn traitor," he said with certainty. "I've seen the sacrifices you've made."

"Thanks for the vote of confidence. But I know what groups like Fuzzy Bunny will do to get what they want. As long as I'm alive, there's the risk that I'll be captured." I looked him square in the eyes. "I'm no hero. I don't have any illusions about how long I'd withstand torture. So killing me might be the right thing for everybody, including me. Would you refuse that order?"

He sat silently, frowning. Finally, he said, "That's what you meant. When you said Stemp would be doing you a favour if he killed you."

"Yeah, something like that." I changed the subject. "So is Stemp actually evil, or is he just an asshole?"

"He's a ruthless bastard," Kane said slowly. "I can't always agree with his methods, but nobody can argue with his results. Since he took over as civilian director two years ago, we've had major improvements in our operations. You shouldn't have threatened him."

"That wasn't a threat. It was a sincere promise. If he does anything to harm anybody I care about, I will utterly destroy him. Or die trying."

He laughed suddenly. "Aydan, you're crazy."

I grinned at him. "You're just discovering that now?

What made you come to that conclusion after all this time?"

"Even when you can't possibly win, you fight anyway. Stemp has people and resources that you can't even imagine. And you're relying on your nose to sniff out bugs."

I raised a shoulder and gave him a half-smile. "I learned long ago that being willing to fight is sometimes enough to prevent the fight in the first place. Sometimes you win, just because anybody in their right mind would know that you can't possibly win."

He sobered. "Aydan, you can't possibly win this one."

"Ah. Victory will be mine, then. So why are you here? You thought it'd be nice to pop by and get your brains bashed in? You know damn well I keep a crowbar under my pillow. What the hell were you thinking?"

His lips twisted wryly. "Yes, I knew about the crowbar. But I thought you were asleep. No woman would intentionally throw off the sheets and lie there naked if she thought there was an intruder in the house."

"It worked, didn't it?" I smirked at him. "Someday that 'most women' stereotype is going to jump up and bite you. Or crush your skull with a crowbar. You knew I was armed and dangerous, and you still turned your back on me because of your preconceptions."

"I was trying to be a gentleman."

"And it nearly got you killed."

"What if I'd been a murderer or a rapist? What if I hadn't turned my back? Where's your clever strategy then?"

I shrugged. "Tell me you noticed when I reached under the pillow. You didn't, did you? Because you weren't looking at my hand."

He shifted uncomfortably on the bed. "True," he

admitted reluctantly.

"So it didn't really matter to me whether you turned away or not," I told him. "Either way, I got a weapon into my hand without you noticing. I might not have won the fight, but at least I had a chance."

"And you'd fight even if you couldn't win."

I patted him on the shoulder. "Now you're getting it. So why are you here? We're wasting our hour."

CHAPTER 2

Kane blew out a breath of frustration, or maybe resignation. "I wanted to make sure you knew about the bugs and cameras. And I didn't want to leave things the way we left them last week."

"Cameras? Shit! Please tell me he's set up a perimeter outside."

"Yes."

"But not inside anywhere?"

"No."

I let out the breath I'd been holding. "Good. I've been kind of creeped out about getting naked ever since I found the bugs. I figured cameras wouldn't be far behind. I went over this place with a fine-toothed comb, but I was afraid I'd missed something."

"Don't worry. So far, the only cameras are outside. If that changes, I'll let you know."

"Thanks. Where are they?"

"There's complete coverage of the exterior of your house, and about a twenty-five foot radius around it. One camera in the eaves of your garage, one in the tree at the back, one on the shed, and another on the back fence."

"Any blind spots?"

"No."

"So how did you get in?"

"Webb looped a thirty-second segment for the front

door camera, one segment at the beginning of the hour, and one at the end so I can get out again."

I sighed. "I really wish you hadn't involved Spider. You know Stemp intimidates him. And he's just a kid. He's just starting his career. I'd hate to see that jeopardized because of me."

"Aydan," Kane said. "He's twenty-six. He's old enough to make his own decisions. And he's the one who came up with the idea of looping the cameras and audio. He was furious that Stemp treated you that way after all you'd done for us."

"Oh." I thought about that for a moment. "Did I mention that I really appreciate you risking your life and your career to come here and warn me?"

"No."

"Sorry." I took his hand and squeezed it. "I really appreciate you coming here. Thanks. And I'm really sorry about bashing you in the head." I stood up and pulled him with me. "Come on."

He hung back warily. "Where are we going?"

"Into the closet."

"Because...?"

"Come on!" I tugged him toward the walk-in closet. "Because I can turn on the light in there without it being visible from outside. I need to look at your head."

"I told you, it's fine."

"Good. Then there's no reason to hide it from me." I pulled him inside the closet and reached past him to close the door and flip the light switch.

We blinked and squinted at each other in the sudden light. "Now, let me see." I reached up to the bloodied washcloth he still held against his head and gently pulled his hand away.

Even on my tiptoes, my five-foot-ten height wasn't enough to give me a clear view. "Get down here to my level," I commanded. "I can't see the top of your head when you're six inches taller than me."

He blew out an impatient sigh and stooped. I winced at the ugly wound on his scalp. "That's got to hurt."

He shrugged. "I'm still standing. Do I need stitches?"

"No, I don't think so. The bleeding's almost stopped. I'll go and get some peroxide. Lucky you've got thick hair. I don't think it'll be visible once it's cleaned up."

"I told you it was fine. It just glanced off."

"Yeah, yeah." I turned off the light and stumbled to the bathroom in the dark. I grabbed the peroxide bottle and gauze by feel and fumbled back into the closet.

The cleanup complete, I wrapped the blood-stained, peroxide-soaked gauze in the washcloth.

"I'll take that." He held out his hand. "Just in case," he answered my unasked question. "You don't want anything around here that might be hard to explain."

"Guess so." I handed it to him. "Thanks." I flipped off the light again, and we shuffled back to sit on the bed, waiting for our eyes to adjust.

"Where's the crowbar?" Kane asked.

"Why, are you afraid I'll hit you again?"

"No. We need to clean it."

I chuckled. "And this is why you're good at what you do. Details." I rummaged in the sheets until my hand connected with the crowbar. "Here you go."

My eyes still hadn't adjusted, and I heard rather than saw him wipe down the crowbar. I spoke into the darkness.

"So what should I expect tomorrow? I've never been a government asset before. Will Stemp have me monitored every minute I'm at Sirius Dynamics, too?"

His voice was wry. "I'm not exactly sure what you should expect. Being given an asset and told I'm a handler is new to me, too. I think it's a safe bet that Stemp will watch and record your every move. And mine. That's why I wanted to talk to you tonight."

I peered at him in the dimness. "Couldn't we have just gone for coffee or something, instead of the whole cloak and dagger thing?"

"Maybe." He shrugged. "Or maybe not. I won't really know until I see how things are set up tomorrow. I don't know how much control Stemp is going to exert, and I couldn't take a chance that you might say or do something without realizing that you were being watched."

He paused, then continued, "I really wish you hadn't lost your temper. You forced his hand. If you'd just gone along with it, I might have been able to do some damage control."

"He threatened me," I said flatly. "That was stupid. If he'd been smart, he would have talked to you first. He could have averted the whole fiasco. Maybe he's been doing great things for your department, but he's a shitty people manager."

Kane sighed. "He's good at what he does, but you're right, General Briggs is a better leader. Briggs would never have taken such a heavy-handed approach, but it's not his jurisdiction."

"But why do you have to listen to Stemp at all? Briggs is your direct superior, isn't he?"

"Yes, and no. Stemp is the director of our INSET

team, and my cover is as an RCMP officer with INSET. So I have to walk a fine line."

I sighed. "Bloody politics."

"Yes," he agreed with feeling.

"So do you think maybe we can work out a better way to communicate?" I asked. "Maybe one that doesn't involve panic on my part and personal injury for you? Because I'd really hate to have to explain to Stemp why I murdered you in my bedroom in the middle of the night."

He laughed. "That's a conversation I'd like to listen in on."

"Except you'd be dead."

"Well, there is that." I could still see the smile tugging at the corner of his mouth. "Best to keep it simple," he said, sobering. "If I need to talk to you, I'll hand you a black pen at some point during the day. If you need me to come here, you can give me a black pen. Then you can expect me that night. If it's urgent, use a red pen, and I'll figure out a way that we can meet sooner. You'll just have to stay alert for my signal."

"Okay, that works," I agreed.

He checked the illuminated display on his watch. "I have ten minutes left before I have to leave. Do you have any other questions?"

"No, I don't think..."

There was a sudden sharp report, and Kane pitched forward on top of me, the weight of his body pinning me to the bed.

CHAPTER 3

Kane's gun was already in his hand. He twisted around to search for the source of the sound as he sprawled across me, protecting me with his body.

"It's okay!" I freed one arm from under him with difficulty and gently covered his gun hand. "It's just the stupid roller blind. It fell off its mountings. It did that once before when the breeze got up and I had the window open."

I felt the tension leave him, and he drew in a deep breath as he stowed his gun again. "Get that damn thing fixed!"

"Roger that," I agreed. "Better still, as of this moment, it's garbage."

My heart was still pounding from the shock, but the feel of his muscular body on top of me wasn't doing anything to slow it down, either. Bedroom, moonlight, an incredibly hot guy, and we were already horizontal.

Jeez, somebody up there really hated me.

He gazed down at me for a long moment from inches away, his grey eyes completely black in the dim light.

Then we both sighed simultaneously, and he rolled off me and sat up. We caught each other's eyes and looked away quickly.

"Guess I'll go and get a snack," I said as casually as I could. I rolled off the bed and headed for the kitchen. "Do you want anything?" I asked over my shoulder as he trailed me out of the bedroom.

"Yes, but I can't have it," he replied. I glanced back at him, surprised at the uncharacteristic double entendre. He continued without missing a beat, "I've only got a few minutes before I have to go."

"Right." I pulled the cereal box out of the cupboard in the dark and reached for the fridge door.

His hand closed around my wrist. "Don't. The light will be visible from outside, and I don't want any hint of activity on the cameras."

"Hmmph," I agreed. I turned back toward the table and felt him stiffen as I brushed against him.

I gazed up at him and steadfastly resisted the urge to kiss him. I'd already done that last week. Then, he'd turned me down to protect me. Now, I had hold back to protect him, too.

I realized he was still holding my wrist and we were gazing into each other's eyes again. Shit.

I pulled away and stuffed a handful of the dry cereal into my mouth as I sat down at the table. Stay occupied, keep the mouth busy.

He stood wordlessly at the end of the table, watching me crunch my cereal. In a couple of minutes, he checked his watch again and sighed. "See you tomorrow. Lock the door behind me. And turn on your security system again. I disabled it when I came through."

"Okay." I followed him to the door and locked up behind him.

I tossed and turned for the rest of the night, and got up feeling tired and edgy at six o'clock. My mood was only marginally improved by a shower and breakfast, and I shuffled irritably to my desk to do some of the entries for one of my bookkeeping clients.

I kept looking at my watch, unable to concentrate. I wasn't due to see my clients at the Greenhorn Cafe until ten o'clock, and I was anxious about my first afternoon at Sirius Dynamics, the business that concealed the secret government defence research facility. Why hadn't I told them I'd be there in the morning instead of at one o'clock? The nervous anticipation was killing me.

The ring of the phone made me jump. When I answered it, a male voice spoke in my ear.

"You the bookkeeper?"

"Yes."

"Taking clients?"

"Yes."

"Bill Harks at the Silverside Hotel. When can you come?"

"I'll be in town this morning. How about nine-thirty?"

"Fine. Don't be late." The phone crashed down in my ear.

Well, that was short and sweet. I'd tacked up my business card in the post office, and I'd managed to get several clients since I'd moved there in March. So far, all my new clients had ranged from pleasant to downright delightful. Apparently the law of averages was about to kick in. I frowned thoughtfully at the phone.

Well, I didn't need to take his business if he was an asshole. But maybe he was just pressed for time. Heaven knew there were days when I'd have appreciated a concise conversation. I shrugged and went back to work.

By nine o'clock, the jitters drove me out of my chair and into my closet to change. I usually tried to overcome my natural slobbish tendencies when meeting a potential client for the first time, but I surveyed my neatly organized business clothes with distaste.

Already, the heat of the day was building in the light breeze that wafted through the window. I would have loved to just go in the baggy jeans and ratty T-shirt that I was wearing.

I sighed and selected a pair of beige dress pants and a cream-coloured sleeveless top that set off my red hair. I'd leave it loose for first impressions. Most guys liked long red hair, and the curt conversation I'd had with Bill Harks suggested that any advantage would be helpful.

I tossed the waist pouch that served as my purse into a larger, cream-coloured handbag, and headed out the door.

I had a brief moment of self-consciousness when I stepped outside and realized that I was on camera, but I pushed it aside. The bugs had been in place for a few days already, so undoubtedly the cameras had also been recording my comings and goings. I'd just have to remember not to scratch my ass or anything when I was outside the house. For most women, that wouldn't be a problem. Not so for me.

In my garage, I wistfully eyed my half-restored 1953 Chevy. Before Stemp had decided that I was the world's most dangerous weapon, I'd been looking forward to taking some time off this summer to tinker with my cars and suck back some cold suds.

Now I had a bad feeling that my summer was going to be filled with tedious computer work at best, and, at worst, danger and terror like I'd experienced the previous week. I shrugged as I made my way to my faithful '98 Saturn. At least I hadn't actually gotten tortured last week. And I hadn't had to kill anybody, either. My perception of silver linings had changed a bit in the past four months.

I hopped in the car and drove out my long lane, carefully locking the gate behind me. Fifteen minutes later, I was pulling into the tiny town of Silverside.

I arrived at the Silverside Hotel just a few minutes before nine-thirty. As I stepped into the dingy lobby, the deafening blare of a soccer game assaulted my ears from the sports bar that doubled as the hotel's restaurant. Already at that time of the morning, a couple of elderly patrons stared blankly at the giant TV screen in the dim room, but the place was mostly deserted.

I walked over to the reception desk and rang the bell on the counter. After a short wait, I rang it again. Nobody responded. I shrugged. Small town. They probably didn't get too many hotel guests on a Monday morning.

I wandered into the restaurant and headed for the girl behind the counter. She looked barely old enough to work in a licensed establishment. Her face was plastered with petulance and too much makeup. Her hair was dyed inky black, and piercings winked from her cheek, nose, eyebrow, and lip. Tattooed spiders crawled over her generous cleavage.

"Hi," I yelled over the noise. "I'm looking for Bill Harks."

She sneered. "If you find him, you can have him. He's a shithead."

Great. Just what I needed to hear.

"Where is he?"

"Door behind the reception desk. Knock before you go in. He's probably jerking off."

"Nice."

She shrugged. "Whatever."

I retreated from the din into the comparative quietness of the lobby and eyed the door behind the reception desk uneasily. It was closed. I'd rung the bell twice. This probably wasn't worth the trouble. I really prefer to avoid interrupting a man who's on a hot date with Rosy Palm and her five daughters.

My dilemma resolved itself when the door swung open. An enormous man shambled out, and I took an involuntary step back. He was at least six foot six, and he must have weighed well over three hundred pounds. His arms looked like hams. With no neck to speak of, his close-cropped hair gave him a troll-like appearance. His bullet head swivelled slowly toward me and he peered at me out of deep-set eyes.

I put on a noncommittal smile. "I'm looking for Bill Harks."

"You found him."

I stepped forward, trying to look confident. "I'm Aydan Kelly, the bookkeeper. We had an appointment for nine-thirty."

I reached out to shake his hand. Serious mistake. I've got big hands for a woman. My hand disappeared and he gave a thin smile as he crushed it in his. "You're late." My knuckles popped and agony shot through my hand as my arthritic thumb bent back.

I clenched my teeth and kept my face impassive.

He stared down at me for a long moment, and then released my hand. "Come on back to the office." He turned his back and trundled through the door behind the reception desk. I followed him with the distinct impression that this was a bad, bad idea.

Harks gestured to the chair behind the piled-up

desk. "Sit. It's all there."

I tried not to visibly detour around him as I walked past. The smell of stale beer and cigarettes overwhelmed me when I perched gingerly behind the desk. He came around behind my chair, and apprehension crawled up my spine. I hate having my back exposed.

The chair sank a couple of inches as he leaned his elbows on its back. He loomed over me, much too close for comfort, and gestured to the computer screen with his free hand. "There you go."

With an effort, I focused on the program, squeamishly moving the filthy mouse to view the entries. God only knew what was caked on that mouse. I sure as hell didn't want to know. I squinted at the smeared screen. The last entry was from December of the previous year.

"Is this the latest data entry?"

"Yeah."

"Do you have all your receipts and bank statements for the last seven months?"

"Yeah, I told you. It's all here." He stirred through the mess. A fossilized sandwich fell on the floor with a clunk, and he kicked it under the desk. "So how much do you charge?"

"That depends on what exactly you want me to do."

His cold smile came back, his eyes like pebbles. "What services do you offer?"

I ignored the innuendo. "What I meant was, once all the entries are caught up, will you want me to work once a week, or once a month, or quarterly? And can I take the work home with me, or do you need me to do it here?"

"Once a week. Here. Where I can keep an eye on you."

Marvellous.

I thought about it for a moment, and then quoted him a price twenty-five percent higher than my normal rates.

"You're expensive."

I stood and turned so I could look him in the eye. "Yes. And it'll cost you quite a bit up front until I get all the entries caught up. Once everything's up to date, it'll probably be a couple of hours a week."

He straightened and looked me up and down while I suppressed the urge to tell him I'd changed my mind, that I didn't have time for any new clients after all.

He nodded once. "Okay. You can start right away to get caught up. Then once a week after that."

"I can come by tomorrow at nine." I beat a hasty retreat without offering to shake his hand again.

Back in my car, I did a whole-body shudder and squeezed liberal amounts of hand sanitizer on my hands. When I arrived at the Greenhorn Cafe, I slipped into their tiny bathroom and washed my hands. Twice.

I greeted the owner, Jeff Latchford, as I stepped out of the washroom. His young, fine-featured face lit up in welcome.

"Hi, Aydan! How's it going?"

"Fine, how's the restaurant business this week?"

"Great," he beamed at me. "I'm so pumped that you're doing our books. Can I get you anything while you work?"

"No, thanks," I assured him. "But I'll come sniffing around the counter at lunch time, you can be sure of that."

"See you then." He waved me through the building, and I carefully mounted the rickety stairs at the back to knock on the door of their apartment above the cafe.

His wife, Donna, met me at the door and ushered me cheerfully through their spartan living room and into the converted bedroom that held the dilapidated computer desk. "We're so glad you're doing this," she smiled as she left me to my work.

I sat down at the computer with a smile of my own. Their enthusiasm and gratitude was the perfect antidote to Bill Harks.

About an hour later, a tap at the open door roused me from my concentration, and I glanced up to see Jeff hovering in the doorway.

"What's up, Jeff?" I inquired absently, still half-following my interrupted train of thought.

"We're doing another fundraiser for the volunteer firefighters," he said. "Would you like to buy a raffle ticket?"

"Sure, how much?" I mumbled, eyes on the computer screen.

"Twenty-five dollars."

What the hell, it was for a good cause. I knew Jeff and Donna had worked hard on the last fundraiser, and the firefighters had gotten some much-needed new equipment.

"Okay." I scrounged in my waist pouch for my wallet and managed to come up with twenty-five dollars in cash. He wrote my name on the ticket and handed me the stub, and I tucked it into my pouch without looking at it, already focused on the next entry.

I was thankful for the absorbing task of data entry, but nervousness set in again as lunchtime approached. At noon, I got up with a sigh and headed downstairs, locking the apartment door behind me.

Jeff and Donna were busy behind the lunch counter, and several people stood in line. I took my place in the queue and surveyed the menu board eagerly. When I'd finished the tasty meal, I dragged my feet out the door.

CHAPTER 4

I eyed the bland stucco facade of Sirius Dynamics despondently. Nothing good had ever happened to me here. It seemed highly unlikely that today would change that.

I shifted my weight from foot to foot, and then squared my shoulders and walked up the three steps into the main lobby. The guard looked up from his post behind bulletproof glass as I approached the security wicket.

"Ms. Kelly," he greeted me noncommittally, and spun the turntable around to disgorge my security fob and the sign-in sheet.

I duly signed my life away, and hovered anxiously in the tiny lobby, too tense to sit in one of the four chairs that were its only furnishings.

Promptly at one o'clock, Kane arrived. He greeted me pleasantly, and I did my best not to ogle the broad shoulders and bulging biceps that strained his black T-shirt.

The rear view was almost as good when he stepped up to the security wicket to claim his fob. As he turned back to face me, I determinedly tamped down the memory of the snug, firmly-packed black briefs I knew he wore under those dark jeans. I didn't know if I'd been successful in controlling my face or not, but if he noticed my glassy eyes, he gave no sign.

"Let's go on up," he said. "And you don't need to wait for me anymore. You can just go ahead whenever you get here. You work here now."

I sighed. "Don't remind me."

We waved our fobs at the security prox pad next to the doors, and they released to give us access to the office areas.

"Second floor?" I questioned, and Kane nodded. I felt some of the tension leak out of my shoulders. "At least we're above-ground."

He smiled down at me. "Yes. I know how hard it would have been for you to have to work in the secured area."

"I honestly don't know if I could do it," I admitted. "I can manage it for short stints, but if I had to be down there for days at a time..." I banished the thought as my heart sped up reflexively. Underground bunkers are not happy places for claustrophobics.

When we arrived at the meeting room, Stemp was already seated at the table, his reptilian features expressionless as always. Clyde Webb rose when I entered, his lanky arms and legs seeming only loosely attached to his skinny body. His youthful face split into a grin, and I greeted him with pleasure.

"Spider, how's it going?"

"Great," he responded. "Thanks to the IPs you gave me last week, we've already been able to track down those two Fuzzy Bunny sites. We've got them under surveillance now. I can hardly wait to see if you can track down any more."

"Guess we'll find out," I told him.

I gave Stemp a hard stare as I sat down. Nerves twitched in my stomach. We eyed each other for a few seconds before he spoke.

"You can begin immediately. You'll have an office on this floor. Your top priority is to decrypt the documents that we seized from Harchman's network last week. A close second priority is to see if you can recreate the virtual connections to Fuzzy Bunny's network and provide the IP addresses to Webb."

He paused, and I could tell he was struggling to make his next words non-confrontational. "We would appreciate as much time as you could provide for this."

I gave him a short nod, trying to stay focused on the importance of the work instead of my personal animosity toward the man. "I'll do my best. I have three clients to see tomorrow, but I have most of the rest of the week available."

"Very well." He stood. "Webb will show you to your office and brief you on his efforts to date. If you need anything, inform Kane, and he will make the necessary arrangements."

I gave him another short nod, which he returned brusquely before striding from the room.

Spider blew out a long breath. "Yikes. That was like watching somebody blowing up a balloon. I was starting to flinch, just waiting for the explosion." He turned to me. "You're... You look really scary when you're mad," he said hesitantly.

"I wasn't mad," I told him. "This time."

He gave a feeble chuckle. "If I ever see you as mad as you were last week, I'm going to hide under the table."

I patted him on the shoulder. "Don't worry, I don't think I could ever get that mad at you. Let's go find that office."

The three of us trooped down the hallway a few doors, into a pleasantly bright room containing a desk and chair, along with a small sofa and coffee table. I peeked out the window and took stock of the room with optimism. "This is nice. I can live with this. And I even get a couch."

Spider returned my smile. "Yes, it's nice to have the couch when you're going to be in the neural net for hours at a time. You stiffen up pretty badly when you're messing around in virtual reality without moving your real body."

"Good point," I said. "I never thought of that."

"Well, let's go in, and I'll point you to where the encrypted files are," Spider said. "You can have a quick peek, and then we can do some planning."

I sank onto the couch. "I'm so looking forward to doing this painlessly with a Sirius fob," I said. "You have no idea how tired I am of using that network key and getting my brain shredded every time I come out of the network."

Both men smiled down at me. "I'm glad you don't have to suffer any more, too," Spider assured me as he sat in the chair. "That was awful even to have to watch."

Kane pulled up a chair for himself. "I'll wait while you go in, and then we can do the planning session when you come out."

"Great," I told him, and mentally stepped into the white void of the virtual reality network.

Spider popped into existence beside me a second later, and a simulation of corridors and doorways sprang into existence around us. "The files are this way," he informed me, and we strode down the virtual hallway.

When we reached the doorway to the file room, he courteously opened the door for me, and I stepped through into the stacks of files.

"Holy crap, there's a lot in here," I said. "It didn't seem like this much when I saw it at Harchman's."

Spider shrugged. "I completely gutted their system. There's probably a lot of irrelevant stuff in here, but I couldn't decrypt it to find out. That's your job. Lucky you."

I sighed. "Yeah, lucky me. Where should I start?"

"How about here?" Spider picked up the nearest file and handed it to me.

I gave him a wry twist of my lips. "Thanks, Einstein." I flipped the file open and stared at the contents.

My heart sank to my toes. "Oh, shit."

"What?" Alarm flared in his voice.

"I can't read it."

"*What?*" he demanded. "But you could read everything at Harchman's."

"Well, I can't read this. Can you?" I showed him the file, and he shook his head, consternation written on his face.

"Could the files have been changed?" I asked.

"No. They're exactly as they were."

"Is it a problem with the network?"

"I doubt it. If there was a problem with the network, you wouldn't be able to access them at all."

I snapped the folder shut and flung it back onto the pile. "Goddammit, now what? What could it be?"

Spider stood silently for a few moments, and then turned an apprehensive face toward me. "I think I might know what the problem is."

"What?" I demanded. I looked more closely at his face. "Oh, shit, no. No. That would be just too... No."

"There's only one way to find out," he said.

I groaned.

CHAPTER 5

As I stepped painlessly through the virtual portal and returned my consciousness to my physical body, Kane smiled at me. "I think that's the first time I've ever seen you come out of the network without suffering."

I glowered. "Don't rub it in."

"What's wrong?" Tension stiffened his shoulders as he leaned forward, frowning. "What is it?"

Spider answered for me. "Aydan can't read the files. I don't know why. I'm afraid... I think she might have to use the network key after all."

"Dammit!" Kane's fist clenched by his side. "You can't read anything at all?" he demanded.

"Nothing. It's just gibberish."

"Dammit!"

I felt the same grim lines on my face as I saw on theirs. I sighed. "Let's go and get the bad news."

I dragged myself off the sofa and trailed down the hallway. They fell in behind me, and we made the trip back down to the lobby in dispirited silence.

I approached the heavy, steel-framed door reluctantly. I bent close to the small aperture that resembled a keyhole, and held still for the retinal scan. The featureless door unlatched with a muffled click, and I stepped into the cramped chamber beyond it, followed by Kane and Webb.

As the door closed and latched behind us, I stepped a

single pace forward to the door at the other side, and let it scan me, too. Then I compulsively counted down the thirty-second time delay, trying not to pay attention to the way the walls and ceiling seemed to close in. Both men stepped away from me to give me space, but it didn't help much. The room was only a few feet square. No one spoke.

When the latch released, I snatched the door open with a barely-suppressed gasp. As always, the enclosed concrete stairwell made my heart rate spike in momentary panic.

I walked down the stairs purposefully, trying to hide my shaking legs. At the bottom, I pulled the door open and stepped into the glassed-in corridor of the secured lab area.

The white walls and glass and the constant flow of cool, fresh air helped reassure me. I took several deep breaths, and deliberately pushed away the knowledge that I was locked underground.

Both Kane and Webb were watching me, looking concerned, and I avoided their eyes while we walked down the hallway to Spider's lab.

He unlocked the door with his prox card and retinal scan, and we all filed into the room. "Pull up a chair," he said tightly as he unlocked the compartment at the back of his desk drawer.

Kane and I both sat, and I scowled at the tiny circuitry inside the small box Spider handed me. Then I snapped the box closed and removed my security fob, looking from one frowning face to the other.

"Well, this isn't going to get any better for putting it off." I held the box in my hand and stepped into the network void.

This time, both Spider and Kane appeared beside

me. Our walk down the virtual hallway had the feeling of a march to execution. Or at least it did to me. I was too absorbed in my own misery to care what the other two were thinking.

When we reached the file room, I hovered unhappily beside the stack of files. Both men watched me, their faces sombre. I sighed and reached for the file I'd opened earlier.

"Son of a fucking bitch."

"What?" they demanded in ragged unison.

I sank to the floor and held my head in my hands. "I can read it just fine."

I rocked back and forth a couple of times as I jerked a couple of handfuls of hair. "What the hell did I ever do to the gods to make them this vindictive?" I whined.

Spider knelt beside me. "Aydan, I'm so sorry," he said wretchedly. He reached for my hand and squeezed it. "This totally sucks."

I looked into his troubled face and gave myself a mental shake. He was so tender-hearted, he was probably more upset about this than I was. My whining wasn't going to make things any better for me, but it was going to make him even unhappier.

I squared my shoulders and got up. "Never mind, Spider. Life goes on. And anyway, it's not like I'm going to be going in and out frequently. A couple of shots of pain a day won't kill me."

"But what if you get kicked out of the network again," he said fearfully as he stood, too. "That was... horrible."

I shrugged. "I can't see why that would happen. And you've still got the signalling device, haven't you? So you can signal me to come out whenever you need to."

He nodded, obviously unconvinced.

"Well, that's about as good as it's going to get, then. Let's go break the news to Stemp." I turned and headed for the virtual portal.

I braced myself as I stepped out of the neural net and back into my physical body. It didn't help.

Pain lanced through my head, and for Spider's sake, I managed not to cry out. I clenched my teeth on my reflexive profanity and took a few hissing breaths, holding my head and rocking until the pain subsided.

"I really fucking hate that," I muttered as I straightened up again.

I tucked the tiny box into my pocket and turned to the other two. "Let's go."

"Um," Spider said. "We can't."

"What? Why not?" I demanded, coldness slithering down my spine.

"Well, *we* can," he amended. "But we can't take the key with us. It has to stay down here in the secured facility. Stemp's orders."

"And Briggs's orders, too," Kane added. "Everyone is in agreement on this. It's too much of a risk to take it out of here unless it's absolutely necessary."

I took a deep, steadying breath. Then another. "You mean." I stopped and cleared my throat to keep my voice from squeaking. "You mean, I'm going to have to work down here?"

My voice came out shrilly despite my efforts, and Kane responded instantly, his voice deep and soothing. "Not necessarily. Don't worry, Aydan. Let's go upstairs and talk to Stemp. We'll see what we can work out."

I took another couple of deep breaths and jerkily

placed the box in Spider's hand. "I'm going up now. I'll wait
for you in the lobby." I grabbed my security fob and walked
out, suppressing the urge to flee pell-mell.

When the time-delayed door finally opened into the
lobby, my heart was pounding, and I controlled the need to
flail my arms frantically in the open space. I paced slowly
around the lobby, willing myself into yoga belly breathing.
Slow and steady. In. Out. Like ocean waves. I
surreptitiously wiped my sweaty palms on my pants.

By the time Webb and Kane reappeared, I'd regained
a semblance of calm. I met their worried gazes steadily, and
nobody said anything while we made our way up to Stemp's
office on the second floor.

Kane tapped on the door and stuck his head inside at
Stemp's terse, "Yes."

"We have a complication," Kane said without
preamble.

"Already?" Stemp's normally expressionless voice
sounded strained. "Come in, then. What is it?"

We stepped into his office and stood side by side,
like pupils summoned before the principal. I tried not to
fidget as something small and frightened skittered in my
stomach.

Kane stood at parade rest and addressed Stemp.
"The Sirius security fob works to get Aydan into the network,
but when she gets there, she can't decrypt the files."

Stemp turned a sceptical gaze on me. "Really."

My temper flared instantly, and Kane shot me a
warning glance. This time I heeded him and controlled my
anger with an effort of will.

"We've solved the problem, though," I said steadily.
"I can read the files if I use the network key to access the

network."

"I see." Stemp turned his impassive face to Spider. "Explanation."

Spider jerked his shoulders nervously. "I don't know for sure. My initial guess would be that the brainwave modulator that's built into the Sirius fobs alters Aydan's natural brainwave pattern in a way that prevents her from decrypting the files. The network key doesn't have a modulator, so she can do what she needs to do."

Stemp made an impatient gesture. "So why are you bringing this to me? You've already solved the problem. Get to work."

"We need your permission to bring the network key aboveground," Kane said.

"Absolutely not."

Kane took a breath and spoke steadily. His shuttered cop face and deliberately relaxed posture made his words seem conversational. "Aydan is claustrophobic. She has severe difficulty being in the secured facility for any significant length of time. She needs to work up here."

"I repeat, absolutely not," Stemp said flatly. "The risk is too great. If anything happens to that network key, we lose everything."

He turned to me, and I caught the almost-imperceptible glint of triumph in his snake-like eyes. "You will have to learn to tolerate working in the secured facility."

CHAPTER 6

I turned and walked stiffly out of the office. Fury suffused me, but I kept my hands loose and my shoulders as relaxed as possible while I walked down the hall and into the pleasant office that had been mine for a few short minutes. I lowered myself onto the sofa and stared into middle distance.

"Aydan?" Spider tapped timidly on the door frame.

I focused on his face, and he ducked his head as if expecting me to yell at him. I concentrated for a second on my facial expression, but I was pretty sure I wasn't glaring at him.

"What?" I was proud that my voice was even.

"Are you okay?"

"Yeah. Come on in."

He came cautiously through the door and sidled into a chair. A few seconds later, Kane stuck his head in the doorway. He scanned the pair of us and then came into the room, closing the door behind him. He strode to the other chair and sat.

If I hadn't known him, I might have thought he hadn't a care in the world. His body language was open and relaxed, his face composed, but I could read his anger in the flinty grey of his eyes.

"I'm sorry," he said evenly. "It seems there's to be no negotiation on this."

"Can't you talk to Briggs?" Spider exploded. "Couldn't we..."

"Don't worry about it," I told him. "I'll deal with it."

"But..."

I sighed and rolled my tense shoulders. "I hate to admit it, but I have to agree with Stemp. If I was him, I wouldn't let that network key aboveground, either."

"But... it's not fair. How can he expect you to do that? You can't even stand to be down there for a few minutes!" Spider's eyes were dark with distress.

I stood up. "I'll manage. When I'm in the network, it won't matter anyway. I was tied up hand and foot last week, and I managed to get through it. I can get through a few minutes in an underground bunker until my consciousness goes into the network. Once I'm in the network, I can make all the open space I need."

I squeezed his shoulder. "Come on. Let's go down and get to work." I headed for the door before I could change my mind.

Back in Spider's underground lab, I controlled my breathing with an effort. "Do you have the signalling device?" I asked Kane.

"Right here," he nodded reassurance.

"Good. I'd hate to be hanging around in the network not knowing there's a fire alarm blaring in real life." I tried to make a joke of it, but it didn't come out sounding funny at all.

Kane reached for my hand and squeezed it gently. "Don't worry. I have the signalling device, and Webb's going to be in the network with you anyway. Between the two of us, we'll make sure that you get out if you have to."

"Thanks," I said awkwardly. "I'm sorry I'm being

such a chickenshit about this."

"You're not."

I stepped quickly into the virtual void of the network and immediately created a simulation. By the time Spider's avatar popped into existence beside me, we were standing on a mountain peak. Far below us, a glittering lake reflected the vividly blue sky. Across the deep valley, a range of mountains marched into the misty distance. Echoing silence surrounded us, underscored by the constant whisper of the breeze sifting through the stunted spruce trees.

"Wow!" He turned in a circle, gaping. "This is amazing! I've never seen a sim with so much detail. And it's so realistic! I can even smell the pine trees."

"They're spruce," I ribbed him.

"Picky, picky. Is this a real place?"

"Yeah. Mount Indefatigable, in Kananaskis Country. This trail is closed now. Too many grizzly bears. Which I've conveniently omitted from the sim," I hastened to reassure him as he glanced anxiously around.

"I'm pretty much a city boy," Spider admitted sheepishly. "Wilderness makes me nervous."

We stood in silence for a few moments, and then I stretched and sighed. "Well, I guess I'd better get to work." I let the simulation go, and we stood again in the network's white void. A few minutes later, I was absorbed in files.

Spider and I worked steadily, decrypting and recording the data. The files we'd selected at random were of little importance, but I had to go through the documents completely to make sure we weren't missing anything.

The back of my neck was beginning to ache when there was a sudden blip in the network, and a small stab of pain knifed behind my eyes.

I sprang up. "Time to get out."

Spider frowned up at me in confusion. "Okay. Do you need a break?"

"No, Kane just signalled me. Didn't you... Oh, no, I guess you wouldn't have noticed it. That's just me and the network key."

"You'd better go, then. I'll come, too."

We made our way rapidly back to the virtual portal. "You go first," I told him. "I'm going to step through nice and slow."

"Good," he agreed. "I don't want to see you thrash around in agony ever again."

He vanished through the portal, and I stepped unhurriedly through it behind him.

The usual pain crashed through my head, and I grunted and jerked into a ball, wrapping my arms over my throbbing skull. I breathed slowly and deeply until I could open my eyes without wincing.

I straightened up. "You rang?" I inquired.

"Quitting time," Kane said cheerfully.

"Really?" I peered at my watch. "Holy crap, it's nearly six o'clock. Time flies when you're having fun." I turned to Spider. "See, I told you it wouldn't bother me to be underground as long as I was in the network."

"We'll need to come up with a more efficient solution than this, though," Kane said. "It's not a productive use of time for me to sit here doing nothing but holding the signalling device."

"Right. I didn't think of that." Spider frowned for a second, and then his face cleared. "No problem. Aydan can go into the network, and I'll work externally. We can still communicate through the network interface, but I'll be here with her physical body so I can signal her if necessary."

"That'll work," Kane agreed. "Aydan, what are your plans for tomorrow?"

"I have to be at the Silverside Hotel at nine, at Blue Eddy's at eleven, and then I'm due at Up & Coming at one. I could be here by two-thirty."

"Does that work for you?" Kane addressed Spider.

"Fine. I can work with that," he agreed.

"Okay, then, I'm out of here. See you tomorrow." I made a beeline for the door, feeling the oppressive weight of tons of concrete hovering over my head again. This time I made it into the lobby without hyperventilating. I turned in my security fob at the desk and went out outside, blinking in the sudden glare of sunshine and heat.

As I slid into the oven-like interior of my car, I felt the tension begin to unwind from my shoulders. I pressed my back into the dark upholstery and closed my eyes while the heat seeped into my bones.

My body spasmed with shock at the sound of Kane's voice. "Are you okay?"

My eyes flew open to meet his concerned gaze as he leaned in the open driver's door. "I was, before you gave me a heart attack," I stammered.

"Sorry." He met my eyes seriously. "I just wanted to tell you that you did a great job today. I know what it took for you to do that."

I felt a flush on my face that wasn't related to the heat of the car. "Thanks."

"You're welcome. See you tomorrow."

He strode away, and I listlessly reached for the ignition. With the strain of the day lifted, my muscles felt like wet dishrags. I drove home on autopilot and stumbled into my overheated house with my stomach growling.

I opened all the windows while I ate some leftovers, and then made a feeble effort to work at my desk for a couple of hours. I fell into bed early and tossed and turned while I ran endlessly with leaden feet.

CHAPTER 7

I crept out of bed and into the shower the next morning feeling only marginally refreshed. At the breakfast table, I marshalled my shrinking courage with a brisk pep talk about positive attitude. I could do this. Claustrophobia was all in my head.

This time, I made no effort to dress up beyond a well-fitting pair of jeans and a flattering T-shirt. Even so, I was over-dressed for the grimy office at the Silverside Hotel. I made my unwilling way to Harks's chaotic desk, and began to sort through the heaps of stained and wrinkled receipts.

Harks's aversion to tidiness actually worked in his favour in a few cases, as I harvested slips of paper from where they'd drifted onto the floor and into the corners. I tried not to think about the nameless objects that lurked in the dingy cavern under the desk.

Harks made a short appearance, again leaning heavily on the back of my chair. The faint wheezing of his breath from a few inches behind my head made my skin crawl, and a dull headache bloomed as my neck and shoulders tensed.

After an hour and a half, I'd sorted and stacked the papers in orderly piles, ready for me to tackle the next time. As I left the office, Harks looked up from the reception desk.

"You leaving already?"

"Yes, I have another client."

"I need this done right away, you know. For what I'm paying you, I should come first in line."

Yeah, right. He'd ignored it for at least six months, and now he needed it right away. I left without comment.

I stepped gratefully out into the blazing sun and stumbled to my car. After another liberal application of hand sanitizer, I slumped in the seat for a few seconds, massaging my headache, and then drove over to Blue Eddy's.

My spirits lifted immediately at the sound of the piano when I let myself in the back door. Rollicking boogie-woogie made me grin as I poked my head into the bar. Doing the books for Eddy was the bright spot of my week.

He glanced up and returned my smile while the music continued to pour effortlessly through his nimble fingers. I knew I couldn't resist the temptation anyway, so I didn't try. Instead of going directly to the office to get started, I wandered over and leaned against the piano, watching him play. He walked the bass home and grinned up at me.

"You're still my all-time favourite client, Eddy," I told him sincerely.

"Ah, you're just sucking up because you love my burgers," he teased.

"True, but I'm also sucking up because I love your piano playing. And your bar. And the blues. And your beer." I sighed. "Man, I could sure use a beer right now."

He hopped up from the piano stool. "Do you want one?"

I shook my head regretfully. "I'd love one, but I can't. I'm driving. And anyway, beer and bookkeeping probably isn't a good combination."

His observant eyes narrowed searchingly. "Are you

okay? You look a little pale."

"Yeah, I'm fine. I've just been really busy lately. I've gotten a couple of new clients."

"What, more dens of iniquity like mine?" he joked.

I laughed. The only other bookkeeper in town had strong religious convictions, so she wouldn't work with any business that didn't meet her moral standards. That left all the good stuff for me.

"One of them is a den of iniquity," I agreed. "Or a den of disgusting filth, anyway."

"Do tell. I didn't know we had disgusting filth here in Silverside."

"Then you've never been in the office at the Silverside Hotel."

Eddy sobered, a faint line appearing between his eyebrows. "Bill Harks? Are you sure you want him for a client?"

"No," I said truthfully, trying to make it sound like a joke. "His office is so gross and dirty, I needed a shower by the time I left. He had a sandwich lying on his desk that was older than I am."

Eddy stood in silence for a moment, his face troubled. "Aydan... be careful over there."

"Why?" I joked. "Will the cooties crawl out of the carpet and eat me?"

"No. At least I don't think so," he said with a half-smile. "It's just... You don't want to be around Bill when he's drinking."

"Thanks, Eddy," I said seriously. "That's good to know. I'll be careful. Thanks for being my guardian angel." I began to drift reluctantly toward the office. "Guess I'd better get to work." I raised an eyebrow at him. "Then you could go back to playing the piano," I hinted heavily.

He laughed. "I could, indeed."

The merry sound of the piano waltzed me into his tiny office.

At twelve-fifteen, I was just putting away the books when a movement from the open doorway caught my eye. I glanced up and chuckled at the sight of a disembodied hand holding a big burger and home-cut fries on a generous platter.

Eddy's smiling face popped into the doorway above it. "Can I tempt you?"

"Eddy, you can tempt me any day, any time," I assured him. "Thanks!" I rummaged in my waist pouch for cash.

"On the house," he demurred.

"No, I can't. You're always feeding me." I pushed a twenty at him, but he backed away.

"No, really. A customer ordered it and then changed his mind. I can't legally sell it to you."

I regarded him for a moment. "Okay. Thanks, Eddy." I returned his grin and bit into the hot, juicy burger. He was a lousy liar, but I didn't see how I could tell him that. If the man wanted to feed me enough to lie about it, who was I to argue?

I finished my excellent lunch and stepped out into the bar, soaking up the classic blues from the sound system. Eddy was occupied with filling glasses at the bar, and I returned his jaunty wave as I left.

I stepped into Up & Coming on the dot of one o'clock, feeling as though life was worth living after all. Amazing what some good food and good music will do. I recoiled theatrically at the sight of the enormous black silicone penis on display at the front of the shop.

"Lola!" I called. "You left Big John the Wonder Horse out again!"

Her smirking, wrinkled face bounced up from behind the counter. "Hi, Aydan! I'm just rearranging the shop."

I eyed her with amusement. "Purple? I love it!"

She ran her hands through her spiky hair. "Yeah. I got tired of blonde. And this is such a bright, happy colour."

It was. In fact, her hair practically glowed purple. Combined with the low-cut, body-hugging purple dress she wore, it made her look like a wrinkled neon pixie. She stepped out from behind the counter. Okay, a wrinkled neon dominatrix pixie.

"Whoa, killer shoes," I kidded her. "I didn't think they could cram that many straps and buckles on shoes that tiny." The outfit should have been wildly inappropriate on a woman of her age, but it worked for her.

She struck a sexy pose and grinned up at me. Even wearing four-inch heels, she was still a good seven inches shorter than I. "These are from the same manufacturer as those thigh-high boots that you tried on a couple of weeks ago," she said.

"You mean, the ones you forced me to try on. Don't remind me," I groaned. "You still owe me for that. That guy who peeked in the window and saw me? I saw him on the street yesterday, and he stared at me like I was a sideshow."

"Good. I'll just tape one of our business cards to your butt."

"If you do, I'll charge you extra for the advertising space," I threatened.

The door chimed, and I turned to meet Linda's

smile. "Granny, I thought we agreed that we'd try to play up the lingerie and couples toys," she chided Lola. "I think you should put Big John somewhere different. He's kind of hardcore."

"I know, honey," Lola agreed impishly. "But it's so much fun to see folks' faces when they walk in."

"You're hopeless." Linda walked over to hug her grandmother, and I chuckled at the two diminutive women standing side by side. Lola's outrageous outfit and artful makeup contrasted violently with her granddaughter's practical nurse's scrubs and cosmetic-free complexion, but the family resemblance was unmistakeable.

I shook my head at them. "I'm going to leave you two midgets to your sordid plots." I headed for the back office and settled in at the desk.

At a quarter after two, I closed the books and emerged into the store.

"Aydan, come here," Lola commanded. "Try this on."

"No chance." I kept moving and didn't look too closely at the garment she was holding up. "I have another client. Gotta go. See you."

I fled.

CHAPTER 8

As I approached Sirius Dynamics, I repeated my mantra. I could do this. My heart thumped as I signed for my fob and approached the heavy steel door.

I stepped into the time-delayed chamber and stood straight and tall while I counted down the seconds. I could do this.

Wobbling down the dreaded concrete stairwell, I gave my knees another brisk pep talk. I could do this.

I managed to greet Spider in nonchalant tones as I stuck my head into his lab. He looked up with a smile.

"Hi, Aydan, how's it going?"

"Fine," I lied. "Ready to roll?"

"Sure." He held up the signalling device. "All set."

He handed me the box containing the network key, and I propped myself in a chair. "I'm going in. I'll let you know when I'm at the files."

"I'll monitor you from here," Spider assured me. "I'll keep the data record running in real-time so I can see what you're doing."

"So you're saying I shouldn't pick my nose," I said dryly.

He blushed. "No."

I was chuckling as I stepped into the simulation. He was such a nice kid. And so easily embarrassed.

The blip came so quickly that it startled me. I

addressed Spider directly through the network interface. "Are we done already?"

"Yes," he replied. "It's five-thirty. I spoke to you through the interface, but I guess you didn't hear me."

"No, I was buried in this file," I admitted. "Lucky you've got the signalling device."

I got up and stretched, then realized it was a pointless activity since my avatar was only a virtual body anyway. No point in stretching it when it was a creation of my own mind. I shook my head at my own silliness, and stepped carefully out the portal.

When I'd recovered enough to straighten up, I met Spider's sympathetic eyes. "I really wish there was another way," he said.

"Thanks, Spider. Me, too."

I stood and stretched. My body had stiffened considerably after being propped motionless in the chair for three hours. God, and I needed to pee so badly my back teeth were floating. I creaked and groaned my way carefully to the door. "Tomorrow, signal me to come out every couple of hours or so."

Spider gave me a cheerful salute. "Will do. See you then," he agreed.

The next several days blurred into a tedious round. Each morning, I worked a couple of hours at the Silverside Hotel, followed by a long day of intense concentration at Sirius Dynamics. At night, nightmares stalked my sleep while I ran with frantic slowness from faceless assailants.

By Friday, my head was aching more or less constantly.

I hissed through clenched teeth and pounded my fist on my knee, eyes screwed shut. Despite my best efforts, some creative obscenities leaked out. As the pain subsided, I gradually squinted my eyes open and pushed myself up, hands braced on my knees.

"Are you okay?" Spider's anxious face hovered in front of me.

"Fine." I rolled my stiff shoulders and got up. "I'm out of here. I'm going over to the Greenhorn for lunch. Do you want to come?"

"No, I have to get some other work done, so I'm heading over to the shared office. Kane will meet you back here and take over the signalling device for the afternoon."

"Okay. Are you working tomorrow?"

"Usually not on weekends," he said. "But if you want to come in, I could, too."

"No, it's okay. I could use a break." I shuffled toward the door, massaging my head.

"I think that'd be a good idea," Spider agreed.

I turned away from the concern in his eyes. "Okay, have a good weekend."

I climbed the stairs, envying him chance to work in natural light and real air. By the time I escaped the confines of the time-delayed room, my hands were shaking, and I gulped the outside air hungrily.

At the Greenhorn, the trembling didn't seem to want to subside while I stood in the lineup waiting my turn to order. When I reached the head of the line, Jeff's face lit up.

"Aydan, hi! Good news, you won!"

I smiled at him uncertainly, racking my tired brain. "Hi, Jeff. Um... won what?"

"The raffle for the firefighters."

"Oh!" The previous Monday seemed aeons in the past. I'd forgotten I'd even bought a ticket. "What did I win?"

"A firefighter."

"What?" I stared at his grinning face, nonplussed.

He laughed. "I told you, it was a raffle for the firefighters."

"Yeah, but…"

I realized I was holding up the line while I gaped at him. "Um, let's talk about this later. I should order." I gave him my food order and wandered dazedly over to my usual corner table. I kicked myself mentally. I knew better than to sign up for something without reading the fine print.

As I stared into space, my eyes gradually focused on a colourful poster pinned to the bulletin board next to the door. 'Firefighters Raffle', said the headline.

I got up and drifted over to read the smaller print below. 'Win a date with a firefighter'. Oh, shit. What the hell had I gotten myself into? I couldn't back out now. Jeff and Donna would be disappointed if I did.

I relaxed a little as I read further down the poster. A ticket had been drawn corresponding to each of the local volunteer firemen, and the 'date' was a dinner sponsored by the Greenhorn and Blue Eddy's. All the firemen and their dates would attend together. Thank God.

I went back to my chair and sank into it with relief. Jeff and Donna had a knack for organizing successful events, and it seemed this would be no exception. Jeff had already told me that the local volunteer firefighters were a motley crew of all ages and shapes and sizes. This would be good clean fun, nothing more.

I looked up as Donna placed my plate in front of me.

"So who did I win?"

"Tom Rossburn."

I shook my head. "I don't know him."

"He's a good guy. You'll like him."

"So what do I have to do?"

"Just come here tomorrow at five-thirty. Unless you want him to pick you up?" I shook my head, and she continued. "We're doing the dinner here. Dress western. It's Stampede time down in Calgary, so we're going with that theme."

I breathed a sigh of relief. This wasn't going to be so bad after all. I hate making conversation with strangers, but I could get through a dinner. I wouldn't even have to dress up. Life was good.

I finished my delicious meal and hoisted myself out of the chair. Usually food made everything better, but I still felt weak and shaky when I headed for the door.

Back at Sirius, the hand tremor intensified while I waited in the time-delay. I switched to belly breathing, willing calm. A muscle jumped in my cheek as I walked down the sterile hallway to Spider's lab.

Kane looked up when I tapped on the door. "Hi, Aydan." He searched my face. "You look like you've had a tough week."

I shrugged. "Same old, same old. I'd better get used to it. Are you ready for an afternoon of paralyzing boredom, waiting to press the button on that signalling device?"

He laughed. "In my life, paralyzing boredom is a nice change. I've brought some paperwork, so I'll be able to entertain myself."

"You sure know how to have a good time." I flopped into my chair. "Could you signal me in about an hour and half? I tend to lose track of time when I'm in there."

"All right." I caught the tail end of his nod as I closed my eyes and stepped into the network void.

It took me a few seconds to summon up the virtual corridor. Even in the sim, my avatar body felt sore and exhausted, and my brain responded sluggishly to my efforts to control the sim.

When the blip that signalled the end of my day finally came, I crept wearily out the virtual portal.

Pain slammed through my head, and it took all my willpower not to curl into a ball and weep helplessly. I squelched the impulse and belted out a few good solid profanities instead. The last curse ended with a bit of a whimper, so I shut up and rocked back and forth instead.

The strong, warm hands massaging my head and neck brought tears anyway. I wiped them away under the guise of rubbing my aching eyes while I slumped forward, relaxing under Kane's ministrations.

Finally, I groaned relief and sat up. "Thanks."

"You're welcome." He squatted in front of my chair and looked into my face. "You need to get some rest. Don't push so hard."

"I'll get a break this weekend. I'm just tired because I haven't been sleeping well."

He eyed me dubiously. "Okay. Let's get you out of here."

"You don't have to tell me twice."

We headed for the door, and after turning in my fob, I drove gratefully home. When I arrived, I walked out past the house, up the hill to the high land. I lowered myself into the rustling grass at the edge of the hay field and blew out a long breath.

The wide vista of farmland opened below me, the big Alberta sky arching above. The breeze carried the warm, sweet scent of alfalfa to me while the sun scorched my back. I let the song of the insects lull me into a trance, easing the week's tension out of my muscles.

A movement on the distant hill caught my eye as a lone horseman rode silhouetted against the sky. He moved purposefully along his fence line, and I smiled. I'd seen him a couple of times before, when I took the time to sit up here. He could probably see me, too, but we'd never acknowledged each other's presence. I appreciated his respect for my privacy. Or his indifference. Either way, it worked for me.

When my growling stomach finally drove me down from my perch, I was feeling much better. A good supper and the knowledge that I didn't have to go to Sirius the next day made my spirits rise even more. I puttered away the evening in my garden and slept reasonably well for the first time all week.

I spent a leisurely Saturday morning and afternoon doing a few easy chores around the house. By the time five o'clock rolled around, I was heartily regretting my commitment to Jeff and Donna's fundraiser. After a week of stress, all I wanted to do was stay home and be alone.

I sighed and shrugged as I headed for my closet. Thank God I could wear comfortable clothes. I slid into a pair of my better blue jeans and topped them with a soft brown plaid sleeveless shirt with western detailing. I brushed my hair out and left it loose, then eyed my cowboy hat. Nah. No need to go overboard. I slid my feet into my battered, comfortable western boots and headed for the door.

When I arrived at the Greenhorn, I sidled in the door

and took stock of the people packed into the tiny cafe. I wasn't sure how many volunteer firefighters a small town like this normally had, but apparently there were at least a dozen or so, along with the women who would be their dates.

I felt a little underdressed as I surveyed the other chattering women. Their outfits ranged from bright western shirts and elaborately beaded jeans to full skirts and dangling jewellery. My hand went reflexively to my ear. Shit, I hadn't even changed out of the plain stainless steel studs I usually wore. And the only makeup I had on was lip balm.

Oh well, story of my life. At least this wasn't a real date. No pressure. I sighed, wondering how long I'd have to stay before I could make a graceful exit.

"Aydan!" Linda waved to me from across the room.

I made my way over. "Another lucky winner," I greeted her. "I'm glad there's somebody here I know."

"You don't know anybody?" She grabbed my hand. "Come and meet everybody, then." A few minutes later, I was surrounded by a jovial crowd while I struggled to remember the barrage of names.

Everyone seemed in high spirits, and I relaxed as the jokes flew. This might turn out to be fun after all.

CHAPTER 9

At six o'clock, a shrill whistle split the babble of voices. The group quieted and turned to Jeff, who stood on a chair near the counter. Donna and Blue Eddy stood beside him, all of them incongruously attired in dark formalwear.

I realized that while we had been laughing and chatting, the Greenhorn's tiny tables had been draped in white linen, and sparkling plates and stemware had been set out. Each table sported a single red rose in a tall vase. Once again, Jeff and Donna had outdone themselves.

"Welcome, everyone," Jeff declaimed. "We're going to get this show on the road, so it's time to pair up the dates. And now for our first firefighter: Chief Wally Nodell!"

A grinning white-haired man with a spectacular handlebar moustache strode to the front of the room and turned to face the crowd, which promptly erupted in cheers and shouts of friendly abuse.

His western wear was of the authentic variety, faded and scuffed from long hours of daily use. He slapped his hands against his keg-like gut. "What lucky lady wants some of this?" he bellowed good-naturedly. The crowd roared and stomped its approval, and Jeff whistled again to get our attention.

"And Wally's lucky date is... Linda Burton!"

Linda bounced up to the front amid laughter and cheers, and Wally swept her a magnificent bow. "I'd say it's like dating my daughter, but you're not quite old enough," he laughed.   The crowd whooped and applauded as they proceeded arm in arm to their table.

The next several firefighters were introduced, to somewhat more decorous applause, but everyone was clearly there for fun. Laughter and friendly insults abounded as each man was matched up with his date, or mismatched, as was more frequently the case. Jeff hadn't been kidding. They really were all ages and shapes and sizes.

"Tom Rossburn!"

I scanned the crowd, wondering who I'd be paired with. A tall, lean figure detached itself from the wall and strode unhurriedly to the front. I caught a glimpse of short brown hair and a blue denim shirt as he made his way through the crowd. When he reached the front, he turned and hooked his thumbs in his belt loops while he surveyed the room with a crooked smile.

I felt my eyebrows go up at the realization that he was one of the better-looking men there.   Not killer handsome, but a lean, good-natured face, with blue eyes framed by the kind of wrinkles you only get from long hours squinting into sun and wind. His shoulders were broad without being bulky, and his rolled-up shirtsleeves showed tanned, sinewy forearms. Working muscle, not gym muscle. His jeans and boots were pleasantly faded and well-worn.

"Aydan Kelly!"

I started at the sound of my name and tried for a pleasant expression as I made my way up to the front. The crowd applauded politely as he stuck out his hand with a smile.   I took it and accepted a firm handshake as his callused palm rasped against mine. He offered his arm, and we paraded ceremoniously off to our table in the corner.

"Nice to finally meet you, Aydan," he said as we settled ourselves in the chairs.

"Nice to meet you, too, Tom," I replied. "Um... what do you mean, finally?"

He leaned back comfortably in his chair and smiled. "I think we're neighbours."

"Oh? Where do you live?"

"Six miles west and two miles north of the stoplight."

Like small towns everywhere, directions originated at the town's single stoplight. I did the math.

"Oh, we are neighbours, then. I'm three miles north."

"I thought so. I've seen you sitting out on the edge of the field a few times. I couldn't see your face at that distance, but your hair's easy to spot. It streams out like a copper banner when the wind blows."

The poetic phrase was incongruous with his down-home appearance, and I hesitated, distracted, before I made the connection. "Oh, you ride your fence line on horseback sometimes."

"That's me. You just moved in the spring, didn't you? How do you like your new place?"

"Yes, I came in March. And I absolutely love it. I lived far too many years in the city. It's so good to be out in the country again."

"You're a country girl at heart?"

"I grew up on a farm. I lived in the city the whole time I was married, but when my husband died two years ago, I was ready to get out. There was nothing there for me anymore."

He nodded slowly. "I'm sorry for your loss. It's a little unusual for a woman to move out to the country alone, though, if you don't mind my saying so."

I grinned at him. "I'm a freak."

He laughed. "I'd say 'interesting'," he contradicted. He eyed me for a few seconds, and then seemed to come to a decision. "I heard you had some troubles back in March," he said.

Shit. Damn small towns.

"Yeah."

"I must have heard the rumour wrong," he said slowly. "I heard you'd had some trouble with your ex-husband, and you ended up in the hospital. But you said just now that you're widowed."

I shifted uncomfortably in my seat. The psycho ex-husband had been my cover story back in March, when I'd run afoul of Fuzzy Bunny for the first time. I really didn't want to repeat the lie, but I didn't see that I had much choice.

"Unfortunately, widowed and divorced are not mutually exclusive. The problems were with my first husband. They're all taken care of now. He won't bother me again. I'm widowed from my second husband."

His face cleared. "That explains it. Well, I'm sorry you had a problem. If you ever need any help, don't forget you have neighbours."

"Thanks, Tom. That's another thing I missed about living in the country."

Our conversation meandered easily over farming life while Jeff, Donna, and Eddy served a delicious four-course meal, dessert, and coffee. We discovered a common love of cars, and we were deep in a discussion of Chevy big-blocks when Jeff's whistle pierced the air again.

"Folks, thanks for coming," he addressed the crowd.

"This is the end of the official part of our fundraiser, but you're welcome to stay as long as you like and visit. Or if you're interested, there's a dance out at the community hall, and Eddy here has generously covered your admission. So go, enjoy, and thanks again for supporting our firefighters."

The murmur of conversation started again, accompanied by the sound of chairs being pushed back as a few people began to drift toward the exit.

Tom gave me his attractively crooked smile again. "What do you say? Do you want to go to the dance?"

"I'm not much of a dancer," I told him regretfully. "I enjoy it, but I don't know any dances besides a waltz and a polka."

"You don't know how to two-step?" He regarded me with mock horror. "Ma'am, ya cain't live in the country if ya cain't two-step," he drawled.

"Damn. So you're telling me I'm going to get ridden out on a rail?"

The weathered skin around his eyes crinkled into the kind of laugh lines that never failed to captivate me. "Your only escape is if you come to the dance with me. I'll teach you."

"You don't know what you're getting into. I'm a dangerous woman around unprotected toes."

He laughed and rose. "I'll take the chance."

I shrugged and got up with him. "Your loss. I hope your insurance is paid up."

He ushered me out the door. "Do you know where the community hall is?"

"I think so."

"If you want, I could drive us over, and then bring you back here to pick up your car afterward. It'd save us taking two vehicles."

I considered that for a moment. I've never been particularly trusting, and the last several months had made me even more cautious.

But it wasn't like I was going off with a stranger into the middle of nowhere. The community hall was only a few minutes' drive away, and everyone at the fundraiser had seen us together. He'd have to be downright stupid to attack me. And despite his laid-back country-boy appearance, our dinner conversation had proven that he was definitely not stupid.

I looked up at him in the long rays of the evening sun, realizing that he was watching me quietly. "Okay, that sounds good," I told him.

His crooked smile came back as he guided me to a four-wheel-drive pickup truck and opened the door for me.

We arrived at the hall without incident, and I duly learned to two-step, amid much laughter and teasing from the friendly group. I even allowed myself a single beer early in the evening. I was pretty sure I'd burn it off before it was time to drive home.

The hours flew by while we laughed and danced to the music of the talented local band. Finally, the lights came up and the band began to pack away their instruments.

"I guess we've closed it down," Tom chuckled. "Come on, I'll take you back to your car."

Our conversation flowed easily on the short drive. Back in the deserted parking lot at the Greenhorn, I turned to him in the dimness.

"Tom, thank you. I had so much fun," I said sincerely. And it was true. I couldn't remember the last time I'd relaxed and enjoyed an evening on the town. No pressure, no agenda, no spying, no threat of torture or death.

I sighed inwardly at the realization that those threats were likely to be part of my life for the foreseeable future, but I put the thought away and smiled at him. "More fun than I've had in a long time."

"What's wrong?" he asked quietly. "You looked so sad for a second there," he explained when I raised a puzzled eyebrow.

"Oh." I waved a dismissive hand. "Nothing. I really had a great time. Thanks again."

I was turning to get out of the truck when he took my hand in his callused one. "I had more fun tonight than I've had in a long time, too," he said. "I couldn't believe how lucky I was to be with the most beautiful woman there. All the guys envied me."

And he leaned over and kissed me.

His lips were gentle and unhurried. As he pulled back a few inches to look into my eyes, I sat in stunned confusion. This was more than I'd bargained for.

His mouth curved in that crooked smile, and he leaned in and kissed me again, stroking his fingers through my hair. This time the kiss lingered, and I found my hands sliding over his corded shoulders. His denim shirt was soft over the hard, lean muscle, and I felt a shiver of heat start low.

He pulled me closer, and warning bells went off in my brain as my body responded hungrily.

This was such a bad idea. We were neighbours. Too close for comfort. I was deeply involved in dangerous activities that would undoubtedly cost me my life sooner rather than later. And he could be in danger, too, if he was anywhere close to me.

Shit, shit, shit! This was such a bad idea!

I pulled away breathlessly, and he let me go, watching me in the soft light from the dashboard.

"Tom," I began. I sighed. Better to get it over with cleanly. "I had fun tonight, and I like you. But I don't think this is a good idea. Good night."

I got out of his truck and headed for my car before I could change my mind.

CHAPTER 10

The next day, I was just finishing my lunch when I heard the unmistakeable rumble of a Harley.

I sprang up from the table and dashed as soundlessly as possible for the front door, mindful of the bugs. At the front door, I slowed to a more casual pace as I stepped out onto my front porch and into camera range.

The bike pulled to a stop in front of the house, and I stepped briskly forward to confront the burly, tattooed biker grinning at me.

I took a challenging stance, one fist on my hip, and raised my hand as if to shade my eyes. I was pretty sure my raised arm would block the camera's view of my lips from that angle.

I spoke softly but clearly. "Don't look too friendly. I have a situation."

His ugly, pockmarked face hardened as his keen eyes darted around, checking out the house and surrounding area.

I pointed forcefully down the lane for the benefit of the cameras. "Turn your bike around and drive halfway down the lane. Wait for me there. I'll be a few minutes."

I blessed his quick mind and private investigator's instincts as he turned the bike around without comment and rode away. I turned on my heel and marched back into the house, listening to the receding rumble. It stopped, and I hoped the bugs had registered it as fading in the distance rather than as a cessation of sound.

I waited for a few minutes, and then strode through the house and stepped nonchalantly out onto my back porch. I picked up my hoe and wandered in the direction of my garden.

Out of camera range, I turned and circled the house, being sure to stay outside the effective radius of the surveillance. As I walked up to him, Hellhound swung off his motorcycle. He warily scanned the yard and house, then gave me a teasing grin.

"Ya said ya got a situation? This the kinda situation where ya got a man in your bed an' ya don't want him to see the competition? Guess I shoulda called first," he rasped.

I laughed and snuggled up. "I wish it was that kind of situation."

"It could be, darlin'." He bounced his eyebrows suggestively. "I was just out cruisin' an' thought I'd drop in. See if ya wanted some company."

"Oh, yeah, I definitely want your kind of company," I assured him as I slid my hands under his jacket, stroking his bulky, solid chest.

He pulled me closer and kissed me. Lust poured through me at the touch of his tongue. If there was a hall of fame for tongues, his would be in it. Deep. I was starting to pant by the time he broke the kiss.

"So what's this situation?" he asked.

"Huh?" I shook my head and refocused with difficulty. "Oh. Um. I'm under surveillance. My house is bugged and there are cameras all around the exterior."

"*What?*" He jerked upright, scanning the area again. "Aydan, what's goin' on? Are ya in danger again?"

I sighed. "More like 'still'. And don't worry, the bugs and cameras are being monitored by the good guys. Well, kind of good guys. I guess. But I don't want them to know that I know they're monitoring me."

"What the hell's that s'posed to mean?" he demanded.

"Can't tell you. Classified. As usual. But it's more of the same shit with that technology I was using last week."

"But you're safe, right? Kane's watchin' out for ya?"

"Yeah, no problem. It's just going to put a bit of a damper on my love life for a while."

"No shit. But why're ya worried about me bein' on camera outside the house?"

I scuffed at the gravel with the toe of my shoe while I thought about my reply. "Um... it's complicated." I looked up at his frown. "You know how you got caught in the crossfire last week because Fuzzy Bunny saw us getting friendly?"

He nodded, his face darkening. I took his hand and stroked it, trying to erase the memories. He closed his hands around mine.

"Ya are in danger," he said flatly. "An' you're tryin' to keep me out of it."

"Well... yeah, kind of," I admitted. Too bad his dumb-biker image was just a facade. I couldn't slip anything by him.

"Aydan, what d'ya need me to do?" He studied my face, and I suppressed a shudder at the thought of what he'd already done for me. And what it had cost him.

"Nothing. Just don't get friendly with me within camera range. Or in public."

"Okay," he said slowly. His head jerked up as he

glanced over my shoulder. "Speakin' a' situations, ya got one comin' for ya right now, I'd say."

"Shit, what?" I wheeled around to follow his gaze. My heart sank at the sight of the approaching figure.

"Looks like a cowboy carryin' a bouquet of flowers," Hellhound observed with a chuckle. "Ya been busy, darlin'?"

"Shit!" I turned back to him desperately. "You've got to help me."

"I dunno, I think ya can take him. Save a horse, ride a cowboy, ain't that the sayin'?"

"Very funny. He's the type to get attached. You know how I feel about getting attached."

His face softened, and he stroked the hair back from my face. "Darlin', maybe ya should think about gettin' attached again. Ya been alone a long time."

I put my fists on my hips. "Are you proposing?" I challenged.

"Christ, no!" The consternation on his face made me laugh despite the gravity of the situation.

"I feel the same way about getting attached as you do. I like being alone. Help me out here. You know I'd do the same for you," I begged.

"Hey, I know you're different, darlin', but most chicks wanna settle down in the end. I just thought ya might be gettin' soft or somethin'," he teased.

I smacked him on the chest. "No, goddammit! Stop messing around!"

I heard the soft thump of approaching hooves behind me as Hellhound chuckled. "Okay, darlin', I can throw myself on this grenade for ya," he whispered.

He grabbed my ass and yanked me against him. The abrupt contact shocked an involuntary cry out of me, quickly muffled by his lips. His fist knotted in my hair as he kissed me hard and hungrily, his magical tongue teasing me.

Instant fire flared through me. His hand slid intimately around my ass and between my legs, and I gasped and shuddered with the sudden intensity of my need.

"She said no, dirtbag! Get your hands off her!"

Through a haze of lust, I mentally replayed my last words and gestures. I suddenly realized how badly this could backfire when I heard the thump of Tom's boots hitting the ground as he dismounted.

I pulled away from Hellhound and spun to face Tom's furious scowl and clenched fists.

"Tom, it's okay. You just misunderstood. Arnie's a friend," I gasped.

He looked slowly from me to Hellhound's ugly, bearded face and badass leathers. "Looks like I misunderstood something. I just don't know what, exactly."

I sighed. The horse was eagerly devouring the bouquet Tom had dropped. Might as well make equally short work of this situation.

"Tom, I told you last night that I didn't want to take things any further with you. This is Arnie Helmand. He's my good friend. He's also my lover, from time to time. Now is one of those times."

"Oh." Tom frowned, searching my eyes.

I heard the crunch of tires on gravel. Shit, now what?

I turned to see Kane's black Expedition pull to a stop in front of Hellhound's Harley Fatboy.

Jesus, my yard was starting to feel like a Village People reunion. So far I had the cop, the biker, and the cowboy. My overstressed brain temporarily disengaged as I glanced toward the road, half-expecting to see a musclebound construction worker approaching.

Thank God, none appeared.

I dragged my attention back to the situation at hand as Kane strode up. His eyes flicked across the tableau.

"Hellhound?" he inquired.

"Cap," Arnie greeted him noncommittally.

Kane frowned at me.

"John, this is Tom Rossburn, my neighbour," I said weakly. "Tom, I'd like you to meet John Kane."

The two men measured each other with their eyes as they shook hands. Kane returned his attention to me. "Aydan, I need you. Now." He turned to the other two. "Sorry."

Hellhound swung astride his bike. He regarded Tom seriously. "Ya might wanna move your horse away. This beast's loud."

Tom nodded brusquely. Then he mounted and rode away without a backward glance.

Hellhound gave him some distance before firing up the Fatboy. "See ya later, darlin'," he rasped over the din. He lifted a hand to Kane and me, and rode down the lane.

Kane turned to me. "Anything I need to know about this?"

"Nope."

CHAPTER 11

"I'm sorry to bother you on a Sunday," Kane said. "But I urgently need you to check a document over at Sirius. Can we leave right away?"

"Um. I have a bit of a continuity issue. I have to circle around outside the cameras and put the hoe back on my back porch. As if I was coming from the garden." I gazed up at him. "Why did you drive all the way out here? Why didn't you just call me?"

"I tried. You didn't pick up. I ran the surveillance footage back, so I knew you were here, working outside. I expected you to be out back."

He frowned down at me, and I suspected he was resisting the urge to ask me what the hell had been going on. I relaxed as he apparently let it go.

"I need you to carry your phone with you at all times," he said. "Just in case. Especially if you're going to play hide and seek with the cameras."

I sighed, feeling the noose tightening. "Okay."

"What's the story with your neighbour? Does he suspect anything?"

"No. This was the first time he's ever been in the yard. But I told Hellhound about the bugs and cameras."

"All right. Hurry up and get rid of your hoe. You can follow me into town, and I'll meet you at Sirius."

I arrived at Sirius Dynamics twenty minutes later

and navigated the depressing security with a sense of impending doom. I'd been so looking forward to having two full days up in the daylight and open air. My hands started to tremble again as I opened the door at the bottom of the concrete stairwell.

Kane and Webb looked up from Spider's desk in the lab as I came in. "Good, you're here," Spider said. "We just intercepted this communication, and we think it may be important."

"That'd be a nice change from all the tedious crap we've been wading through," I muttered as I slouched into my chair. "Where is it?"

"In the usual file room," Spider said.

I nodded morosely and stepped into the network.

The digital file was enormous. After the first fifty pages, my brain ceased to process any of the information, and I simply decrypted the document word for word without comprehension.

At long last, I spoke into the network interface. "That's it. Is there anything else you need here?"

Spider's voice vibrated with excitement. "No. That was excellent. That document was a game-changer. Come on out."

I heaved my aching avatar up from its chair and stumbled toward the portal. When I stepped through, my fatigue made the pain seem worse than usual, and I caught myself whimpering while I beat my throbbing head against the nearest solid surface.

A few seconds later, I recognized that the solid surface was Kane's chest when he held my head firmly against him. "Aydan, stop," he said urgently.

I groaned and made an effort to unclench my teeth.

"I'm okay. You can let go now."

He released me and raised my chin to look into my eyes. "Are you sure you're okay?"

"Yeah. Just tired. What time..." I raised a shaking arm to glance at my watch and suppressed another whimper. Eight o'clock. I was starving.

Kane looked at his watch, too, and his expression darkened. "Aydan, I'm so sorry. We did it to you again. Can you make it upstairs?"

"Yeah. I can manage without regular meals as long as I don't have to run any marathons."

I hauled my trembling body out of the chair and staggered for the door.

Kane's hand was under my elbow as he turned back. "Webb, get that document sent out ASAP."

"I will." Spider turned back to his keyboard, fingers flying.

I straightened up and did my best to approximate a normal stride down the hallway. Kane paced beside me, watching me closely. He put his hand under my elbow again while I dragged myself up the stairs and into the time-delay chamber.

When the heavy door finally released, he guided me to one of the lobby chairs. "Stay here. I've got some orange juice upstairs."

I put out a hand to stop him. "It's okay. I only have a problem if I exert myself. I'll just swing into the burger joint on the way home and grab something."

He eyed my trembling hands. "I'll follow you."

I really wasn't in the mood for company, but I was too tired to argue. I sighed and headed for the door.

The burger was greasy, and nowhere near as good as

Eddy's. I nibbled it half-heartedly while Kane devoured his meal. When I couldn't force myself to swallow any more of it, I laid the remains back into the basket and sank my aching head into my hands.

I started out of my semi-conscious doze at the sound of Kane's voice. "You didn't eat much."

"No. Eddy's spoiled me," I mumbled.

"Are you okay to drive?"

I straightened up and shook myself. "Yeah. Good night. See you tomorrow."

The fifteen-minute drive home seemed interminable.

When I arrived at the farm, I parked the car and climbed the hill above the house again, unable to face the thought of being enclosed even by my own house. I stood for a long time on the brow of the hill, soaking up the open space and letting the wild wind tear at my clothes and hair.

I glanced over as movement caught my eye, and saw Tom silhouetted on his horse again. I sighed, feeling sorry for myself and for him. That had been a shitty way to end things. He seemed like a nice guy.

I sat down and rested my head on my drawn-up knees in the long red beams of the sunset, feeling melancholy and still unwilling to go indoors.

"Aydan." The soft voice jerked me awake. "Are you okay?"

A gentle hand lifted the hair away from my face, and I rolled over to peer up at Tom's frown in the twilight.

"What...?" I frowned back at him, disoriented.

"Are you okay? Do you know where you are?" he asked anxiously.

I sat up as he squatted on his heels beside me. His horse snuffled placidly a few yards away.

"Can you tell me your name? Do you know what day it is?"

I shook my head vigorously, my brain gradually rebooting as I recognized classic first-responder orientation questions.

"Sorry. I'm fine. Yes, I know where I am. I just fell asleep."

"Tell me your name," he repeated patiently.

I laughed. "It's okay. My name is Aydan Kelly. It's Sunday evening. I'm sitting on the hillside above my farm, outside Silverside, Alberta, and I really just fell asleep."

The tension eased from his shoulders and he gave me his crooked smile as he sat down on the ground beside me, stretching out one long leg. "You scared me."

"Sorry. What are you doing here?"

"I was out riding. Just... thinking things over. I saw you up here, so I went the other way. I didn't want to intrude. But you were out here so long, and when I looked over, I saw you kind of collapse onto the ground and lie still. I was afraid something was wrong."

"Thanks for watching out for me. I just had too long a day, I guess."

"Aydan... since I'm here anyway, I owe you an apology. I was out of line last night. You said you were widowed, and I never thought to ask if you were involved with someone. I'm sorry. I owe your boyfriend an apology, too. I didn't mean to poach."

I drew up my knees and rested my chin on them while I stared out over the long vista fading in the twilight. "It's okay. And Arnie's not my boyfriend. He wouldn't care one way or the other."

"But... you said he was your lover."

I sighed and glanced over at him. He really deserved the truth. Or at least as much of it as I could tell him. "Can I be really blunt?"

He nodded. "Might as well be, I'd say. You don't owe me any tact."

I stared out over the fields again. "Arnie and I are good friends. Neither of us wants to get involved. With anybody. Including each other. We get together from time to time. We have a few laughs. We have sex. If he walked in and found me in bed with another man, he'd probably apologize for not calling first. I'd do the same for him if I walked in on him with another woman. I know it might seem weird, but it's what I want right now."

"Oh." He sat in silence for a while. "You don't pull any punches, do you?"

"I try not to."

After another short silence, he spoke again. "I don't think your relationship is weird," he said quietly. "After my wife died, I went through a time like that."

I turned to him in the half-light. "I'm sorry. I was so absorbed in my own drama, I didn't even think to ask if you'd been married."

He shrugged. "It's okay. It was twenty-five years ago. It's old news."

"Twenty-five years?" I peered at him. "Jeez, how old were you?"

"I was twenty. She was nineteen." He sighed. "We had to rush the wedding a bit because she was pregnant, but I would've married that girl no matter what. I was crazy about her."

"What happened?" I asked softly.

"She died in childbirth."

"I'm so sorry."

He shrugged again. "I spent a lot of years afraid to get attached. I just found a warm body and took a little comfort now and then. But now, I'm okay with whatever happens." He took my hand gently. "So I know where you're coming from. If you just need a warm body some night, I can be that for you. No attachment."

I sat and stared out over the darkening fields. I still felt fragile after the strain of the day. I could lie back right now on this warm, grass-scented hillside, and let Tom Rossburn soothe my aching body under the big sky. Just a short chance to forget everything and take a little comfort.

Not counting my late husband, Hellhound was the only man I'd been to bed with in... Jesus, nearly two decades. I deserved a chance to sample the herd, dammit. There was nothing stopping me. A nice, willing man was sitting right beside me. No strings attached.

I sighed. There were always strings. It was too complicated. It was too dangerous for him. And I had a sneaking suspicion that despite his past, or maybe because of it, he was ready to get attached again.

"Thanks, Tom. I'll keep that in mind. But I don't think it'll happen."

"Why not?" He wasn't demanding, just asking.

"I just... can't."

"Why are you being faithful to him when you know he won't be faithful to you? You deserve better than that."

"I'm not being faithful to him. I just... there are other reasons."

"Aydan." He leaned forward to meet my eyes. "Are you afraid of him? Is he abusing you?"

"No!" I stared at him in shock. "Arnie would never

hurt me. He's the gentlest man I know." I realized how implausible that sounded as the words left my mouth. With his ugly bearded face, tattoos, and biking leathers, Hellhound made a frightening first impression. 'Gentle' was not the first adjective that came to mind.

"If he's the gentlest man you know, then you need to get to know more men. He was rough with you today. If that's what he's like in public, what's he like in private?"

"No, no, he was just horsing around. He's not like that." I threw up my hands. I knew I was sounding just like every abused woman on the planet, defending her abuser.

"Tom, thanks for being concerned. I wouldn't put up with abuse. And I don't believe Arnie would ever hurt me. Or any woman."

"Okay." He rose. "I have to get back."

I stood, too. "Me, too. It's going to be another long week." I peered through the falling darkness at him and hesitated. "Can we just... be friends?"

He squeezed my hand. "Friends, for sure. With benefits, if you want that."

"Thanks. Good night," I said awkwardly.

"Good night." He swung easily into the saddle and I listened to the receding thud of hooves.

CHAPTER 12

I dragged myself into the shower in the morning. After another night of desperately trying to run away while my dream feet refused to move, I was exhausted and edgy. Despite my determined effort at a positive attitude, dull dread of the day weighed down my body like lead chains.

I caught myself at the breakfast table with my head propped in one hand, inches over my bowl while I mindlessly shovelled cereal into my mouth. I shook myself and sat up straight. Get a grip.

Hoping for a boost, I brewed myself a cup of caffeinated tea instead of my usual herbal, and headed out the door.

At the Silverside Hotel, I perched reluctantly in the grubby chair. After organizing the papers the previous week, I'd cleaned the desk and computer, so at least that was an improvement. On the downside, Bill Harks had taken to leaning on the back of my chair and breathing down my neck for extended periods of time.

As he lumbered into the office yet again, I squelched my irritation and concentrated on my entries. Even at nine o'clock in the morning, I caught a whiff of alcohol on his breath when he loomed over me from behind. I'd been working and trying to ignore the sound of his breathing for about ten minutes when I felt the touch on my hair.

It wasn't noticeable enough for me to comment, and

in fact, I thought I'd imagined it the first time. A couple of minutes later, though, there was no mistaking the feel of his hand stroking down my back.

I stood immediately and turned to face him, Eddy's warning ringing in my head. "Don't touch me."

"Geez, you're uptight. Relax."

"Get away from me. I don't work until you leave."

"I'm paying you." His hard little eyes squinted even smaller. "Sit your ass down in this chair and give me what I'm paying for."

"I am giving you what you're paying for. You're not paying for the privilege of touching me."

"Well, I'm paying more than anybody else in town. Seems to me I should get some extra services for that."

Shit, I'd had a bad feeling that extra charge was going to come back and bite me. But I was exhausted and on edge, and I was feeling distinctly threatened. My temper flared despite my best efforts to control it.

"You're paying extra because your working conditions are disgusting. If you want to pay regular price, you'll have to let me take the work home."

His enormous hand shot out, remarkably fast for such a big man. He crushed my wrist in his grip and yanked me toward him. "You're gonna work here. And I'm gonna get what I'm paying for."

Adrenaline flooded through me as I glared up at him from close range. "You have exactly three seconds to let go of me."

"Or what?" He grabbed my breast and squeezed. Hard.

Pain and fear turned into violent rage in a split second. I didn't even consciously aim the vicious kick that connected solidly with his crotch.

In the second that it took for the impact to register in his brain, I was already jerking my arm out of his grasp. As he started to fold, I locked my fists together and used my coiled-up momentum to unwind into a whistling two-handed blow that caught him in the side of the face.

The desk rattled as he hit the floor. Completely out of control, I snatched up the ledger book and flung it savagely at his head.

"*I quit, asshole!*" My voice was harsh and unrecognizable even to my own ears. I stood panting, fists clenched, for a few long seconds, using all my willpower not to kick him into a bloody pulp while he lay there clutching himself.

At last, control won by a tiny margin, and I let out a wild roar of frustrated fury and stamped from the room.

I shoved past the two incoming staff members and forged straight out to my car. I burned rubber out of the parking lot, mindlessly heading for the highway.

Common sense whispered that I was far too upset to be driving.

I pulled the car over at the small community park and got out, shaking all over. Still driven by a massive overdose of adrenaline, I launched myself into a berserk sprint, circling the park until my heart threatened to burst from my chest.

My knees suddenly gave out between paces, and the jolt of my body hitting the ground knocked some sanity back into me. I lay sprawled where I'd fallen. My pounding heart darkened the edges of my vision while I gasped helplessly for air.

The ground vibrated with the rapid thudding of feet

approaching at a run.

For shit's sake, could this day get any worse? I'd thought I was completely alone, and the park was surrounded by trees. Nobody should have been able to see me.

I groaned with the sheer injustice of it all and resisted the urge to pound my head against the ground. For one thing, it would be embarrassing to get caught doing that. For another thing, I couldn't lift my head yet.

"Aydan!" Kane's voice. "*Aydan!*" What the hell was he doing here? I concentrated instead on the more urgent question of how to drag more air into my burning lungs.

Then his large hands were rolling me over and brushing my tangled hair back, his tense face hovering above me.

"I'm fine," I gasped.

He whipped out his phone and punched a button. "I've got her."

He hung up and stared down at me, his fingers on my pulse. "What happened?"

"In... a minute," I panted. "Gotta catch... my breath." I sucked air for a little while longer while he frowned down at me intently, still holding my wrist.

Finally, I took a deep, unsteady breath and shoved myself into sitting position. My T-shirt was stained with sweat and coated with prickly grass clippings from the freshly mown lawn. Apparently I'd scraped my elbow when I fell, and I noticed a small bloodstain on the shirt, too. Great.

"Aydan, what the hell?" Kane demanded. "Your heart rate was up over two hundred. What happened?"

"Long story." I was still a little breathless.

"I've got time," he assured me grimly. "Can you walk

to the truck?"

"In a minute."

I brushed the grass off my shirt front and jeans while he did the same for my back. He started to pick the grass out of my hair, but I stopped him. "Never mind." I delved into my trusty waist pouch and pulled out my hairbrush.

When I'd divested myself of most of the grass, I heaved myself up onto trembling legs and let him escort me to his Expedition. At least we had no audience. Gotta love a small town on a Monday morning.

Kane settled me into the passenger seat and then went around the vehicle to swing into the driver's side. He fixed me with a stern eye. "Now. Everything. Start to finish."

I sighed. "I had a bit of a disagreement with one of my clients."

"So I heard. From the RCMP."

"Oh. Shit." If I'd had any adrenaline left in my body, I'd have panicked. Fortunately, I'd used up the year's supply, so I achieved faint dismay.

"What happened?" he asked again, his cop voice firmly in place.

"Bill Harks at the Silverside Hotel hired me last week. He decided he wasn't getting all he was paying for and decided to help himself. He grabbed my boob and hurt me. I kicked him in the nuts and hit him in the face and left. Oh, and I threw a book at his head, too. Is he dead?"

"No," Kane said, his expression unreadable. "But he's mad. He wants to press charges."

I slumped forward and beat my forehead gently against the dashboard. "Please, shoot me now."

"I don't think that will be necessary. It was clearly

self-defence on your part. A sexual assault charge will settle him right down. I'll deal with it."

I left my forehead on the dashboard as I mumbled, "Thanks," to the floor.

"But, Aydan, what were you doing here? Why were you lying there in the middle of the park? I thought you'd been shot or something." This time, the cop voice couldn't conceal the edge in his tone.

I sighed and stared at the floor some more. "John, I've never been so close to beating somebody to death in my life. I just couldn't... could barely control it."

I realized my fists were clenched when he took one in his hand and stroked it until I released my fingers.

I took a deep breath. "I just had to blow off some steam. I wasn't even safe to drive. I don't know what I would've done if anybody had gotten in my way. So I just came here and ran in circles."

I spoke into his silence. "I know. Pathetic. Sorry. I've just been on edge lately."

"Aydan." His hand tightened on mine. "You've had the week from hell. You were attacked, and you reacted. You took out a man twice your size. You are absolutely not pathetic. You're amazing."

I was grateful for the curtain of hair that hid my flaming face. "Thanks," I mumbled to the floor.

He held my hand for a few moments longer. "Do you need help to sit up, or is that just a comfortable position?"

I groaned. "Both, actually. Kidding," I added as he reached for my shoulders. "I can manage."

I heaved myself upright and slumped against the passenger door. "How the heck did you find me? Better question, why did you even know you should look?"

"I'm a spy." His mouth quirked.

"Funny man."

"One of the employees at the Silverside Hotel called the RCMP. Witnesses placed you charging out of the hotel looking furious, leaving Harks lying beaten semi-conscious in the office. They knew who you were, obviously. You're easy to identify." He gave me a wry look.

"The closest officer was down at the detachment in Drumheller," he continued. "So they called me, since I was in their records as the officer in charge when you were abducted in March. As soon as I got the message, I fired up the tracking system and locked onto your cell phone."

"Thanks for rescuing me again," I told him. "Do I have to go and talk to the RCMP now?"

"No, I've taken your statement, and I'll straighten it out with them. I don't think there will be any problem, under the circumstances."

I sighed. At least there were some advantages to working with spies. The ability to make assault charges go away, for one thing.

I looked at my watch. "Guess I'd better get over to the Greenhorn."

"Are you sure you're okay? Why don't you take the rest of the day off?"

"I don't want to skip Jeff and Donna's work. And I need to get back into that sim this afternoon. I swear that pile of files is breeding and multiplying."

Kane eyed me seriously. "Don't push it. We need you for the long haul. Don't burn out in the beginning."

The thought of the long haul sent a cold chill down my spine as my stomach clenched. I pushed away the dark cloud of dread and straightened up. "I'll be fine. See you this afternoon. And thanks again."

I got out and headed for my car.

CHAPTER 13

The Greenhorn was pleasantly quiet and predictable. My huge expenditure of energy had left me so drained that even moving the mouse was an effort. I kept my eyes open with difficulty, and made a mental promise to recheck all my entries when I came back the following week.

I barely tasted the delicious lunch, and dragged myself back out to my car. By the time I parked at Sirius Dynamics, I had to bite back the whine that threatened to escape.

I shook my head vigorously and briskly patted my cheeks, trying to awaken some initiative. Apparently initiative was heavily drugged and refusing to answer the door. Or maybe it had packed up and headed out for a quick vacation in Rio. I compromised, and awakened dumb stubbornness instead.

Down in the lab, I clasped my hands together so the tremor wouldn't be so noticeable and turned to Kane. "Any emergencies today?"

"No, you can go back to the files from Harchman's. I'll stay here until two, and then Webb will take over with you for the rest of the afternoon."

"Okay. Signal me when you do the shift change. I'll be ready for a break by then."

I propped myself up in the chair again and stepped into the network.

Bill Harks lunged at me, his face contorted with rage.

I let out an involuntary shriek and leaped backward through the network portal.

Uncontrollable screams wrenched from me as my body convulsed, flailing wildly to escape the torture. Fire burned my skin and boiled inside my veins. A maelstrom of colours churned around me as I fell. Nausea ripped through my gut. The endless screams lacerated my throat.

An eternity later, the suffering began to abate. The swirling colours faded, and my screams trailed off into raw whimpering. As awareness returned, I silenced myself and concentrated on opening my eyes.

Kane's voice called my name again and again, and I finally summoned up the strength for a hoarse whisper. "I'm okay."

I felt a cessation of tension, and realized he was holding my tightly curled body while he alternately stroked my hair and massaged my head and neck.

One by one, I relaxed my clenched muscles until I was sprawled on the floor. I'd managed to squint one eye partway open, and I finally achieved both eyes simultaneously as he rubbed the pain away from my temples.

I groaned and tried to sit up. His strong arm supported me, and I managed a semi-vertical position slumped against his broad chest.

"Aydan, what happened?" he demanded. "Did you get kicked out of the network?"

I breathed deeply for a few seconds while I tried to force my brain to formulate an answer. It reluctantly began to function again as I sat up a little straighter and rubbed my hands over my aching face.

"No, I didn't get kicked out," I croaked. "I was just

stupid. I came through the portal too fast again."

He peered down at me. "Why? You just went in. It was literally seconds before you started screaming. What happened?"

"I wasn't paying attention to where my thoughts were going. All of a sudden, Bill Harks was there, and I forgot it was a sim and jumped back through the portal. I just wasn't thinking. My fault."

He held me close and stroked my hair wordlessly for a few moments. Then he stood, lifting me to my feet. "Come on. You're done for the day."

I rolled my sore shoulders and cracked my neck. "I'm okay now. I'll just be more careful with my thoughts this time."

He pried the network key's small box out of my hand and put it in the drawer. "I'm your handler. And I say you're done for the day." He ushered me firmly out the door and up the stairs.

In the lobby, he stood beside me while I turned in my security fob, and then walked with me out into the hot sun. At my car, he gazed down at me sternly. "Go home. Have a nap. Work in your garden. Play some music. Anything you want as long as you aren't overtaxing yourself. That's an order."

I slithered weakly into the driver's seat. "Roger that." I looked up at his concerned face. "Thanks. See you tomorrow."

"Not until three o'clock," he warned. "And then, only for a couple of hours."

"Okay."

I drove home, feeling as though I'd been beaten from head to toe with a baseball bat. I crept into the house, and did my best to follow his orders for the rest of the day.

I had another crummy sleep. I squinted apathetically at the hag in the bathroom mirror before groaning my way to the breakfast table.

After breakfast, I shambled down the hall and contemplated my desk.

"Fuck it." I spoke aloud before remembering I was bugged. Well, tough. If you listen in where you're not wanted, you're bound to hear something you don't like. I hoped sardonically that my audience had appreciated the resounding fart I'd let go earlier.

I snickered at the thought. That was enough to boost my spirits a bit. I hadn't remembered the bugs at the time, but it was still nice to know somebody else was suffering, too.

Feeling a little more cheerful, I went out onto the back porch and grabbed a folding chair as I headed out of camera range. I set up the chair in a sheltered corner of the yard and slouched into it, stretching my legs out in the early sun. I let my mind clear, and listened to the quiet of the country morning.

I jerked awake with an aborted snore. Slowly and carefully, I straightened my stiff neck enough to look at my watch. God, ten-thirty. I had just enough time to get changed and get to Blue Eddy's by eleven.

I levered myself out of the chair and hobbled around for a few minutes, trying to shake out the pins and needles in my legs. Then I made for the house as briskly as I could manage.

When I let myself in the back door at Blue Eddy's, the piano was disappointingly silent. I felt my shoulders sag. I really could have used some happy music this morning.

I dragged down the hall and into the office to start

on the week's entries. About twenty minutes later, Eddy poked his head around the door frame.

"Oh, you're here. I didn't hear you come in."

I glanced up from my work. "Never trust a sneaky bookkeeper," I joked.

He laughed, but sobered quickly. "Aydan, are you feeling all right? You're really pale." He hesitated. "I heard you had a bit of a problem over at the hotel."

I shrugged. Small town. Probably everybody knew by now.

"Yeah. I'm glad you warned me about Harks earlier."

He stepped into the room and perched on the edge of the desk. "I didn't actually expect you this morning. Are you really okay?"

"Yeah, I'm fine."

His mouth quirked up, but his eyes were serious. "Word has it that Bill was down for the count."

I sighed. I really didn't want to talk about it. As if reading my mind, Eddy straightened. "I know you probably don't want to talk about this, but I wanted to give you another heads-up. This isn't the first time rumours have gone around about Bill assaulting a woman, but nothing ever sticks. The women always seem to change their minds about pressing charges, and it all gets swept under the table. And none of them ever did a number on him like you did. You should watch your back."

I gazed up at him wearily. "Jesus, Eddy, this is one of the things I hate about small towns. Everybody knows who the bad apples are, and nothing ever gets done about it."

"I know." He sighed. "Just... be careful, okay?"

"I will. Thanks, Eddy."

He turned to go, and I sank my head into my hands. "Aydan?"

I jerked my head up, startled. He was hovering in the doorway, and his eyes were kind. "Remember, you have friends here. You're not alone."

I cleared the sudden huskiness from my throat. "Thanks, Eddy."

He nodded and vanished, and a few minutes later, the sound of the piano made me smile.

I enjoyed another delicious free meal that had been mysteriously ordered and declined by a customer, and made my way to Up & Coming feeling comforted by Eddy's care and friendship.

Some off-colour banter with Lola heartened me almost as much as her flagrant approval of what she referred to as 'a good dose of whup-ass' for Bill Harks. I arrived at Sirius Dynamics feeling almost human again.

I grudgingly approached the secured door, and gave myself a determined attitude adjustment while I waited for the time delay. I only had to control my thoughts for a few moments until I got into the simulated file room and began my decryptions. Once I was absorbed in the documents, time would pass easily.

I squared my shoulders and marched down to Spider's lab. My hands were hardly shaking at all.

A couple of hours later, my positive attitude was slightly frayed around the edges as I held my skull together with both hands and swore. I straightened slowly. Two sets of eyes regarded me uneasily.

"I'm fine." I answered the unasked question.

"Good," Kane said with obvious relief. "That's it for today then. Get out of here."

"I could probably do another stint. It was a pretty short day today."

"No." He plucked the network key out of my hand and passed it to Spider, who secured it in his desk drawer as if afraid I'd arm-wrestle him for it.

"Okay. You don't have to tell me twice." I rose with relief and headed for the door. "See you tomorrow morning. Nine o'clock?"

Both men nodded, and I scooted for the stairs. I made it through the time delay with more ease than usual, and patted myself on the back for my progress.

Then I drove home and sat on my hillside for a long, long time.

CHAPTER 14

Nine o'clock came far too early the next morning. I glowered up at the Sirius Dynamics building as I dragged my reluctant feet up the stairs.

It was another beautiful, sunny day. A sprinkle of rain overnight had washed the sky to a clear, translucent blue, and the scent of grass and flowers filled the air. Birds twittered a carefree symphony. Little bastards.

Inside Spider's lab, the fluorescent lights glared and the flat scent of filtered air filled my nose. It could have been morning, afternoon, or midnight. No sense of time passing. Like a prison.

"Are you okay?" Spider eyed my trembling hands as he passed me the network key.

"Fine." I flopped into my chair and closed my eyes to step into the network. Even the white void seemed confining. I skipped the corridor simulation entirely and folded sim-space to step directly into the file room. I snatched up the nearest file and started to decrypt.

When noon finally rolled around, I pried myself out of my chair and stumbled for the door, still trying to massage away the pain of exiting the network.

"Aydan, wait!"

"What, Spider?" I did my best not to snarl as I turned to face him.

"You have to leave the network key here."

"Oh. Right." I tossed him the box. "See you after lunch."

He fumbled the catch, frantically juggling the tiny cube. It bounced off his hands and rebounded onto the desk, where it skittered across the top as he swatted at it.

With a shock of horror, I saw the top begin to open, and I pounced for it at the same time as Spider. Our four hands locked over top of the small object, and we stared into each other's wide eyes from close range.

"Shit," I breathed. "Shit, shit, shit."

I carefully removed my hand from the top of the pile, scrutinizing the palm to make sure nothing was stuck to it. Spider did the same, and then I repeated the motion with my other hand.

White-faced, he lifted his hand from the desk, and our breath whooshed out simultaneously when we spotted the tiny circuitry stuck to his thumb. With shaking hands, he poised it over the box and dropped it back in, closing the lid securely.

I sank to the floor, clutching my chest. "Jesus, Spider, I'm sorry! I wasn't thinking. Jesus, son of a bitch." I sucked a few deep breaths. My hands shook violently.

Spider collapsed back in his chair and did some deep breathing of his own. "That was close."

"If I'd lost that, we'd be completely fucked. Jesus."

He hauled himself out of the chair. "We didn't lose it. It's okay. Come on, let's get out of here. I think we both need a break." He reached down to give me a hand up, and I tottered down the hallway beside him, my heart still pounding.

As we stepped out of the time-delayed door into the lobby, we came face to face with Stemp. He regarded our ashen faces and my pronounced trembling with his usual expressionless face. "Is everything all right?"

"Fine," we chorused. We looked at each other and then looked away again hurriedly.

His eyes bored into us, and I turned away to hand in my security fob. "I'm going to the Melted Spoon, Spider, want to come?"

"Okay," he said faintly, and we made a hasty exit.

A savoury grilled panini and a cup of herbal tea later, I gazed wistfully around us as we walked back to Sirius. The early freshness of the air had gone, and the sun burned down. Another scorcher of a day. Too bad I wouldn't get to enjoy it.

We signed for our fobs again and made our way back into the dungeon. Spider gingerly handed me the tiny box, and I clutched it convulsively. "Can we tape it shut or something?"

"Good plan." He put a couple of wraps of tape around it, and we both relaxed.

I looked around at the cell-like walls and shuddered involuntarily.

"Okay, signal me in a couple of hours," I told him, and stepped into the void.

A barred cage immediately closed around me, and I let out a squeak of reflexive terror before jerking my mind back under my conscious control. My mountain top opened around me, and I breathed carefully.

"Aydan, what was that?" Spider's voice was tight with alarm.

"Sorry, it's okay, my mind just wandered for a second. I'm fine now." I took a few more breaths. I couldn't smell the spruce anymore. Even in my sim, the air smelled flat and stale.

I sighed, dissolved the mountains, and went back to work.

I stepped out the portal and swore violently and continuously, waiting for the pain to subside. When I finally succeeded in focusing, Spider was wide-eyed.

"Sorry," I mumbled insincerely. "I really should do something about this potty mouth."

"It's okay," he said. "I've learned a lot since I met you. I didn't realize what a sheltered life I'd led."

I snorted. "Too bad you never met my Uncle Roger. He could peel the paint off an aircraft carrier at fifty paces. People's ears were known to bleed when he really got going." I smiled wistfully. "He was such a nice man."

Spider laughed. "Only you would say that in the same breath."

I gave him a half-hearted grin and heaved myself to my feet. "I'm out of here. See you tomorrow."

Outside, I sagged against my car and tried to force my exhausted brain to make a decision about supper. I'd eaten all the leftovers in the house, and I just couldn't face the thought of going home and cooking.

I swung by Fiorenza's and waited for them to build me one of their fabulous take-out pizzas. Lucky I was getting paid for all my hours at Sirius.

I carried the pizza up my hill and ate it while I watched the wind sweep in waves across the fields below. I sat for a long time before I trailed into the house to get ready for bed.

I jerked awake, my heart pounding. The insistent ring of the phone bored into my addled brain. I fumbled a nerveless hand in the general direction of the cordless. My eyes wouldn't focus on the call display, so I jabbed blindly at the talk button.

"Wha...?"

There was silence on the other end of the line.

"Hello?"

Nothing.

"Fuck!" I slammed the phone down and collapsed back onto the bed, waiting for my heart to regain its normal rhythm.

I glanced over at the clock. Two fifteen. Jesus.

I practiced my yoga breathing. In. Out. Slow like ocean waves. Warm. Comfortable.

I levitated off the bed with a yelp as the phone rang again. This time, I glared at the call display. Private number. I looked at the clock. Four thirty-five.

I groaned and shoved the pillow over my head while I waited out the rings so that the answering machine could pick up. No message. Seconds later, the phone rang again. Private number.

I snatched up the phone. "Listen, you cock-sucking son of a bitch, you've got the wrong fucking number! Fuck off, already!"

Silence on the other end.

With the last remnants of my self-control, I resisted the urge to hurl the handset against the wall and watch its little plastic guts spray out across the room. I laid it gently back in the cradle and unplugged the phone.

It took a long time to get back to sleep.

CHAPTER 15

I groaned at the sight of my haggard face in the mirror. I must have managed several hours of sleep, but it sure as hell didn't feel like it. I plodded out to my car and snivelled my way into Silverside.

The hand tremor seemed to have spread. I wobbled down into the lab and fell into my chair. Spider regarded me with worried eyes.

"Aydan, you look awful. Sorry," he added quickly. "I didn't mean you look awful, I just meant..."

"I look like shit. I feel like shit. Hell, I feel worse than shit. I feel like shit after a dog's eaten it and then shit it out again. Some fucking moron decided to phone me in the middle of the night. Twice. Two hours apart. If I find out who it was, I'm going rip his fucking nuts off and feed them to him. On crackers."

Spider blanched slightly.

"Sorry." I reached over and patted him on the shoulder. "I didn't mean to take that out on you."

"It's okay," he said faintly.

Kane strode in and gave my face a searching glance. "Are you all right?"

"Fine."

He held my eyes for a few seconds more. "Okay." He handed me a red pen as he turned away to sit down. "You dropped this on the way in."

"Thanks." I took it from him as casually as I could. "I wondered where I'd lost that." I eyed him for a second. "I was just getting ready to go into the network."

"Fine," he said. "We'll signal you in about an hour and a half, as usual."

I shrugged and concentrated on the network's white void. I navigated the virtual corridor without incident and buried myself in the files.

When the blip came, I stepped out into the usual pain. Heat and pressure surrounded my head while I groaned through clenched teeth. The pain subsided, but the pressure continued as I pried my eyes open.

"You can let go now," I told Kane.

He removed his large hands from around my head. "Just making sure you didn't try to beat your brains out again."

"Nah. I only do that at the end of the day," I joked feebly. I dragged myself to my feet. "Pit stop. Back in five."

The short walk down to the bathroom helped me regain some circulation. When I got back to the lab, I sank into the chair again. "Any special requests?"

"Same old, same old," Spider said wryly.

"Hmmph." I slouched down and closed my eyes.

This time, the cage shrank quickly. Wild panic flashed through me as the heavy bars squeezed against my chest and back. I struggled desperately against the ties on my hands, wailing without thought.

Thought.

I burst out onto the mountain peak again, gasping.

"*Aydan!*" Spider sounded almost as panicked as I felt.

"Fine. I'm fine." I breathed deeply. The long

mountain vista had lost its depth. It looked more like a painting on a wall. A close wall.

"Aydan, Kane says to come out now."

"No, I'm fine. I'm in here, I'll make it worthwhile." I dissolved the mountains and picked up the next file.

When the signalling blip flashed through the sim, I dragged my gaze up from my tedious reading. The file room was lined with iron bars. As I sucked in a breath, they advanced slowly, eating up the space.

"Back off," I muttered, and banished them with an effort. I pushed through the virtual door and headed for the portal.

"Okay, I'll live," I grated. "You can let go now."

Kane released me and stooped to look into my face. "Lunch time. Let's go."

The three of us trekked back upstairs. When the heavy door finally released, I took a couple of rapid steps into the lobby. I stared into middle distance, trying to control my breathing while my heart raced like a frightened gerbil.

I jerked and yelped involuntarily when Kane's face appeared in my field of view. "Aydan?" he asked carefully. "Are you all right?"

"Fine." I turned toward the security booth, fumbling to unclip my security fob with cold, quivering fingers.

I stepped gratefully out into the blazing sun, squinting in the heat and brightness. My legs twitched with the urge to run.

"Come on, we'll take the Expedition." Kane's voice broke into my reverie, and I unsteadily followed him and Spider toward the parking lot.

We buckled in wordlessly, and Kane put the vehicle in motion. We'd driven for a block or two when Kane gave a brisk nod. "Webb?"

Spider extracted a small device from his pocket and waved it around the interior of the SUV, then up and down close to me.

"Clear."

I relaxed. "I'd love to have one of those," I told him.

"Take this one." He offered it to me.

"I can't. Too hard to explain if it was found." I sighed and turned to Kane. "What's up?"

"I was going to ask you the same thing. You were screaming last night. You just about blew the audio on the bugs. What happened?"

"Nothing." I squirmed in embarrassment. "Shit. I was dreaming. That's all. Sorry."

"It's okay." He shot a glance over at me. "I got a frantic call from the analyst who was monitoring. I called you, but of course I couldn't say anything. Your phone's tapped, too, did I mention that?"

"I figured." I put two and two together. "Oh!" I felt a flush rising on my cheeks. "I'm sorry I was so rude."

He gave me a puzzled frown. "You weren't particularly, considering."

"Then you've got an amazingly high tolerance for rudeness."

Spider gulped. "Actually. That was probably me you were talking to. I made the second call."

"Oh, Spider, I'm so sorry! I was just so tired, and I thought it was a crank call."

"It's okay," he assured me hesitantly. "So what you said this morning in the lab..."

"No, no, I'm sorry! If I'd known it was you, I never would have said that."

"Said what?" Kane asked.

"I said if I caught the fucking moron who'd phoned me, I was going to rip his nuts off and feed them to him," I told him sheepishly.

"On crackers," Spider added with obvious dismay.

Kane burst out laughing. After a few seconds, Spider and I joined in, and I laughed until tears came. Finally, I clutched my aching stomach. "That bit about the crackers really got to you, didn't it," I wheezed.

"Yeah," Spider gasped. "Please don't ever say that to me again."

"I promise."

Kane sobered as we parked in front of Fiorenza's. "I'm sorry it has to be this way, Aydan, but we'll have to respond the same way if you keep screaming at night. We have to make sure you're all right. That means that you have to answer the phone and say something."

I sighed. "It's okay. If I'm screaming, you'll be doing me a favour by waking me up anyway. I'll try not to be so obscene in the future."

Back in the lab after lunch, I breathed deeply in my chair while I clutched the network key.

"Just stay focused," Kane encouraged.

I nodded and stepped carefully into the void. It wavered around me, ghostly bars drifting toward me, but I marched forward and they parted along my path. I made my way to the file room and grabbed the next file.

Unlike the others, this one looked like gibberish. Letters and numbers swam on the page in random combinations. I shook my head and refocused. The text stabilized, but it was still incomprehensible. I frowned and put it down, rubbing my eyes. Then I slapped my cheeks gently and tried again.

"Aydan? What's wrong?" Spider inquired through the network interface.

"I'm not sure. Hold on." I squinted at the page again. The groups of numbers and letters remained adamantly cryptic. My tired brain seized on the joke, and I giggled before I could stop myself. Cryptic. No shit.

"Aydan...?"

"Hang on." I laid aside the troublesome file and picked up the one I'd finished before lunch. It was still completely clear and understandable. I grabbed the next one off the pile. Equally easy to decipher.

"What the hell?" I muttered, and picked up the page again. Still random letters and numbers.

"Okay, this is weird," I told them. "This one is just a bunch of random letters and numbers. I'm not sure whether I can't decrypt it, or whether it's really just numbers and letters."

"Just a second," Spider said. There was a short pause. "Kane says to get started and give us what you're seeing," he told me. "It might mean something to us."

"Okay." I frowned at the document and started to transcribe. It was laborious work as I double-checked each line, getting lost and starting over again in frustration. I finished the first page and sat back with a groan. "What do you think?"

"Hold on again."

I squeezed my eyes shut and rolled my shoulders. When I opened my eyes again, the sim wavered and vibrated around me. I saw movement in my peripheral vision and quickly whipped my head around, but nothing was there.

I groaned and rubbed my eyes. A surreptitious movement to my left made me jerk around again, staring at the wall of the file room. A wraith-like body slipped through the wall away from me, its skeletal limbs rippling the surface of the wall like water.

I blinked and stared as more apparitions began to drift through the room. One swooped at my head, and I ducked involuntarily. They gained form and substance. They had teeth...

"Aydan."

I started, and the file room solidified around me. I shook my head. Jeez. I must be more tired than I realized.

"Aydan!"

"Sorry, what?" I refocused on the task at hand.

"Aydan, this is gold! Keep going!"

"Okay." I bent to my task.

My eyes burned. A small flame licked across the page, and I snatched my hand away before I realized I'd created it out of my own metaphor. I sighed and visualized cool water.

I swore and put down the dripping document as I got up and shook myself like a dog.

"Aydan? Is everything okay? What was that?"

"Fine. I'm just getting tired, I guess." A large tire rolled toward me, and I snickered in spite of myself. Puns. The lowest form of humour.

"Maybe you'd better come out now."

"I think you're right." I stood up and stretched, and then shook my head at my own idiocy. Stretch in the real world, dummy.

I shoved the mannequin aside and headed for the portal. Mannequin. Dummy. Get it?

A large board hurtled toward my head, and I ducked in the nick of time. Yeah, yeah, subtle as a two-by-four to the head.

I tried to clear my mind as I skirted the pink hippopotamus twirling in its tutu and ballet slippers. Flying pigs fluttered gracefully overhead. Don't look up. Don't look...

I dodged the plummeting clumps of pig shit.

"Fuck this," I muttered. "*Yikes!*"

I frantically folded sim-space to avoid the truly impressive construct that had been summoned up by my unfortunate choice of obscenities, and stepped carefully out of the portal.

By the time I straightened, clutching my raging headache, Spider was still scarlet. Kane's impassive cop face showed signs of cracking.

"Sorry about that," I addressed Spider. "Next time I'll be more careful with my language."

He blushed even more furiously. "No big deal," he said with a heavy attempt at nonchalance. He turned away, and I carefully avoided looking at Kane as I scrubbed my hand over my face to wipe away my smile.

A few seconds later, I thought I had it under control. I caught Kane's eye. An explosive snicker burst out of me. He quickly turned away, his broad shoulders quaking with suppressed laughter.

"Bless you," Spider said without turning.

"Thanks," I choked. "Back in a flash." I scurried out of the lab and down the hall to the ladies' room before I lost it completely. Inside, I propped myself against the counter and wheezed silent laughter until tears poured down my cheeks.

It took longer than it should have to regain my composure. Every time I stopped laughing, I glanced at my flushed, tear-stained reflection in the mirror and started all over again. Poor Spider. I really wasn't laughing at him. I just couldn't seem to pull myself together.

Finally the pain in my sides made me sober up. A few last giggles escaped me as I dabbed at my eyes and patted cool water on my face. I took some deep breaths and avoided looking in the mirror as I left the bathroom.

When I returned to the lab, Kane's eyes were still dancing, but his face showed nothing but his usual calm composure. I managed a straight face with an effort.

Spider met my eyes and turned pink all over again. "This document is going to be really valuable," he said quickly. "How much more of it is there?"

My urge to laugh vanished without a trace. "Lots. Probably another five pages." I sighed. "I guess I'd better get started."

"No, I don't think so," Kane countered. His eyes were serious again, too. "You need a rest. You weren't controlling the sim at all at the end."

As he spoke, an immense weight settled on my shoulders, and I staggered back a step to drop into my chair. I realized that my hands were still trembling, and my overworked core muscles vibrated finely.

"Okay," I agreed. My eyes drifted shut.

"Aydan!"

"What?" I mumbled.

"Come on." I cracked an eyelid open as Kane took

the network key from my hand and pulled me to my feet. "Let's get you upstairs."

I let him tow me down the corridor. He half-carried me up the stairs, and I leaned heavily on him in the time-delay chamber. Then there was another flight of stairs, and a blessedly soft horizontal surface.

My eyes snapped open.

Kane halted in the doorway. "Oh, I didn't think you were awake."

I sat up groggily from the sofa in my office. "Just woke up." I squinted at my watch. "Crap! It's five o'clock!" I stood up and stretched, yawning. "I'll get back on that document now. If it's important, I want to get it done today."

"It's not important enough for you to drive yourself into the ground."

I read his tone behind the words. "It's really important, isn't it?" I asked.

He sighed. "Yes."

"Let's go."

CHAPTER 16

"Wait." Kane put a restraining hand on my arm as we passed the small employee lounge at the end of the hall. He ducked into the room and returned momentarily, carrying a bottle of orange juice and a couple of cereal bars.

I gazed up him, touched. "Thanks!" He'd even gotten the brands that I usually bought.

"You're welcome."

I followed him down the stairs, smiling.

At the entrance to the secured area, my smile drained from my face while I stood still for the retinal scan. By the time we reached the bottom of the stairs, my heart was pounding, and I strode forward briskly to hide my shaking knees.

In the lab, I gulped down a cereal bar and half the juice, and then propped myself in the chair once more.

I stepped into the white void and determinedly shoved my way through the constricting bars. They refused to vanish, so I clamped my hands on them and bent them apart as I stepped through. I shoved and kicked my way to the file room. In the doorway, I braced my hands on my knees, gasping with exertion.

Stupid. It was just a sim. I slapped myself in the head and held the image of the file room hard. Guttural laughter growled behind me as I closed the door.

"Aydan, is everything okay?"

I shook my head vigorously and picked up the file. "Fine."

The nap had helped a little. I concentrated fiercely on the contents of the file, refusing the urge to look around. After an endless time, I laid the document down. "That's it."

The sickening smell of burning hair filled the room.

"Aydan! Your back's on fire!"

I sighed. "Yeah. I know." I flopped backward into the convenient plastic wading pool. A theatrical sizzle and cloud of steam arose. A cartoon coyote strode over and gazed down at me as I lay on my back.

"Yeah, right." I didn't waste any time folding the sim-space to get to the portal. I really didn't want to know what my subconscious mind was planning to serve up this time.

It took a long time for the pain to subside. Kane's strong hands slowly crushed out the tiny fires at the ends of my nerves while I groaned and whimpered.

Finally I shut up and straightened. "Thanks." I clutched at my head with both hands when it attempted to float away.

"Here." Kane handed me the other cereal bar.

I squinted at my watch. Eight o'clock. My exhausted brain responded wearily. I squinted up at Kane. "It's Thursday, isn't it?"

"Yes." He returned my gaze with concern. "You knew that, didn't you? It was just a rhetorical question?"

"Yeah. I was just checking."

I hauled myself out of the chair. "Forget cereal bars. I'm going over to Eddy's to get a decent meal and listen to some blues. Tonight's open jam. Anybody else interested?"

Kane shook his head regretfully. "I'd love to, but this

document that you just decrypted is vital. We have to deal with it tonight."

I stared at them in horror. "You mean you guys have to stay here even longer?"

Kane shrugged. "You know how it goes."

I shuddered. "You have my undying respect. But sadly, my loyalty is all used up for tonight. I'm out of here."

"Good, because I was going to order you out anyway," Kane joked. "Good night. Have a beer for me."

"Can't, I'm driving."

We exchanged a shrug, and I made a beeline for the exit.

Blue Eddy's was packed as usual on a Thursday night. I hovered at the edge of the bar, hoping against hope to find a vacant table where I could put my back against the wall.

The musicians were just finishing a song, and as I scanned the stage, I spotted Hellhound with his beloved guitar. A few seconds later, he caught sight of me in the crowd. The corner of his mouth quirked up, and he cocked an eyebrow at my usual table.

I grinned and made my way over to the table to find his lurid jacket slung over a chair. The slavering black beast glared up at me from the leather, and I patted it affectionately as I sat down. I stretched out my legs with a sigh of pure contentment and let the superb blues music wash over me.

The waitress hurried by. "You want your usual?"

"Yeah, thanks, Darlene."

"Beer?"

"Love to, but I'm driving."

She raised an understanding shoulder and wove her

way back to the bar. As she punched my order into the computer, Eddy looked up from his frenetic bartending and tossed me a cheerful wave and a smile.

I moved happily to the beat, watching Hellhound's gifted hands on his guitar and shivering privately at his sexy, raspy voice while he sang.

When my meal arrived, I tore into the delicious food. As I was finishing, the musicians took a break.

I watched Hellhound obliquely as he wandered down from the stage. He took his time meandering through the crowd, stopping to greet people as he went. He paused by another table and shook hands with its occupants, laughing and joking for a few minutes before he turned toward our table.

When he arrived, he greeted me nonchalantly and swigged from the beer bottle that had occupied the table when I arrived. His eyes roved over the crowd, and he nodded across the room when he spotted someone else he knew. He turned back to me as he replaced his bottle on the table, and clasped my hand in a friendly handshake. "See ya later," he rasped, and strode away.

I sipped my drink for a few moments before I opened my hand. The note was scribbled on a scrap of paper. "Come see my new tattoo." I slipped his room key into my pocket with a secret smile.

A couple of sets later, he stepped down from the stage and made his way through the crowd again. He smiled, picked up his jacket, and disappeared out the door.

I slouched comfortably in my chair and tried to hide my impatience while I waited for the next set to begin. As the musicians began again, I unhurriedly signalled Darlene for my bill. A few minutes later, I was on my way.

I cursed my bad luck. There was only one hotel in town. I sincerely hoped Bill Harks wouldn't be working tonight. That was a confrontation I could do without.

Heart thumping, I sneaked into the lobby, trying to look invisible. I sighed relief at the sight of the young man on duty behind the reception desk, and hurried across the open space to the stairs. On the second floor, I tapped on the door to 218 and turned the key.

I smiled as I stepped inside and closed it behind me. Hellhound was shirtless, and the light of the single lamp emphasized his bulky, tattooed muscles. He rolled off the bed and pulled me into his arms. His lean musician's fingers stroked through my hair as he found my lips. The kiss lingered, and the touch of his tongue sent heat rolling through me.

I pressed closer and ran my hands over his chest while I kissed him back hungrily. "What's this about a new tattoo?" I mumbled against his lips. "Should I go looking?" I unfastened the button on his jeans and started to slowly slide the zipper down.

He chuckled. "Ya can look at anythin' ya want down there, darlin', any time. But ya ain't gonna find my new ink if ya do."

"Mmmm." I trailed my lips over his chest. "Where should I look?"

"Down an' to the left."

I kissed my way south. "Am I getting warmer?"

"Aaah... Darlin'... Yeah... You're gettin' warmer for sure. But ya ain't gettin' any closer to this." He held up his left arm, and I studied the new artwork on the inside of his bulging bicep.

He leaned down to kiss me. "D'ya like it?"

I smiled as I regarded the shapely black-clad woman crouched on the footpegs of a black motorcycle, long red hair billowing behind her. "I like it. I'm flattered. But I think your tattoo artist got a little carried away with the boob size."

"I know what I saw, darlin'." He grinned. "I get a hard-on every time I remember ya ridin' over that hill."

I let my hand drift down. "Well, anything that gives you a hard-on makes me happy."

He growled and locked his hands on my ass as he pulled me against him.

"Ow!"

He let go instantly. "What, Aydan? Are ya okay?" He gazed down at me worriedly.

"Fine, I just caught my hand on your zipper." I showed him the small scratch.

He kissed the spot tenderly. "Sorry, darlin'. I didn't mean to hurt ya."

"You didn't. Didn't even break the skin."

He looked into my face seriously. "I thought I might've hurt ya when I grabbed ya on Sunday, the way ya yelled out."

"No, you just startled me. Definitely didn't hurt me." I grinned and linked my arms around his neck. "Turned me on like a gas barbeque, if you want to know the truth."

"Ya always turn on like a gas barbeque." He ran strong hands down my back and pulled me closer.

"Mmmm..." I circled my hips against him, relishing the feel of the hard bulge in his jeans. "You must really, really like that tattoo."

"It ain't the tattoo that's doin' it for me, darlin'," he rasped. He leaned down to growl in my ear. "Want me to play big, bad biker for ya tonight? I bet a big, bad biker can make ya come in two minutes or less."

His hand circled my ass and slipped between my legs from behind. The heat of his touch burned through my jeans and set fire to a certain piece of tropical real estate.

The tropics got hotter and wetter as his lips and whiskers trailed down my neck. The contrast of smooth and rough made the small hairs stand up on the back of my neck. Other things stood to attention, too. Hellhound grinned as he stroked a thumb over one of my nipples.

I gasped as his fingers moved dexterously in two places at the same time. "The big, bad biker is definitely on my list of things to do." I sucked in an unsteady breath as the exquisite combination threatened to steal my ability for speech. "But... you know what I really want tonight?"

"What, darlin'?"

I brushed my lips against his ear. "I want that hot, sexy musician I saw onstage. Playing his guitar with those fabulous hands."

The hands in question slid under my T-shirt and lifted it over my head, then drifted down to unfasten my jeans.

"Playing his harmonica with those yummy lips. And that amazing tongue."

He knelt as he slid my jeans down my legs. When I stepped out of them, I got the full benefit of the lips and tongue combo when he traced up the inside of my thigh. I gasped, eyes half-closing, but he stood and kissed me deeply and unhurriedly. "Ya wanna have a musician tonight, darlin', ya gotta take time to listen to the music. I'm gonna give it to ya slow an' easy."

The exhausted stress eased from my body as we moved gradually toward the bed, shedding clothes. He lowered me onto the bed, and I reached to pull him down to me. "You have the sexiest voice. Sing to me."

He stretched out beside me. His gifted hands played my body lazily while he leaned close to sing. I shivered when I recognized Bob Seger's 'Fine Memory'. His rough-edged voice caressed my ear while his sensuous stroking melted my aching muscles into warm honey.

He finished the song and gazed down at me for a few seconds, his face softened by the mellow light. He kissed me again, and his lips trailed down my throat to my breast. I gave myself to his hands and mouth, feeling the hot, sweet tension build.

I caught my breath and arched against him as one of his hands glided downward. His adept fingers stroked and circled. The light of the lamp took on a rosy glow. My body began to move of its own volition against his touch while my mind emptied of everything but blissful sensation. Breathless little moans escaped me while I poised luxuriously on the edge, taking my time, deliciously anticipating...

My phone rang.

I let out a despairing cry. "Oh, Jesus, no!"

"Ignore it," Arnie rasped.

"Fuck, I can't." I whimpered and reached for the phone. "If it's Kane, I have to pick up."

Hellhound's lips trailed down my body, and I shuddered with desperate need as I checked the call display. Kane.

"Shit!" I pressed the Talk button. "Hello?"

"Aydan, how quickly can you get to Sirius?"

I did a quick mental calculation. "Seven minutes."

"Do it. Sooner if you can."

"On my way."

Hellhound was already gathering up my clothes and handing them to me. "I'm sorry," I panted miserably as I pulled on my underwear.

"It's okay, darlin'. I know ya gotta go."

I yanked on my jeans and T-shirt. "Next time, I want the big, bad biker. And I want that orgasm in two minutes or less. Screw this leisurely shit. Goddammit."

He laughed and kissed me as I shoved my feet into my shoes. "Ya got it, darlin'." He held my face in his hands for a second. "Be safe."

"Thanks." I kissed him quickly and slipped out the door.

CHAPTER 17

I ran down the stairs and finished tucking in my T-shirt as I arrived in the lobby. Striding across the open space, I snatched my hairbrush out of my waist pouch and yanked it through my tousled hair, glancing at my watch. I might make it to Sirius in less than seven minutes.

As I shoved the brush back into my pouch, I caught a glimpse of Bill Harks in the office. Shit!

I was moving fast, though, and I shot out the front door before he could make his way around the reception desk. I jumped in my car and hit the gas.

My mind raced wildly on the short drive. My shoulders tensed up around my ears, and I blew out a long breath and tried to calm down. Silver linings. Thank God I'd been with Hellhound. I couldn't imagine trying to explain to Tom, or any other man for that matter, why I would leap out of bed and run away seconds before achieving orgasm. Screaming, head-banging orgasm. Goddamn it to hell!

I charged up the stairs at Sirius, and the security guard had my fob ready before I was half-way across the lobby. "Go," he said. "I'll fill in the sign-up sheet."

"Thanks."

I jittered in the time-delay chamber while my breath came too fast. My muscles quivered in knots. I had to remind myself yet again to unclench my fists when my fingers started to ache.

When the door released, I flew down the stairs, too wound up to even notice the claustrophobia. I hurtled down the hallway and skidded to a halt at Spider's lab.

"What is it? What's wrong?" I demanded at the sight of two strained faces.

Kane's normally even voice was tight. "We need you to decrypt another document as fast as you can. We think one of our agents has been captured."

Agent captured. Nightmare memories flooded my mind. Kane handed me the network key, and I flung myself into the chair. "Where's the file?"

"Same file room," Spider said tensely.

I closed my eyes on the sight of his white face and dove into the void.

My feet slithered in the blood that coated the virtual corridor. A battered, unidentifiable man dangled from chained wrists, gurgling blood from a ravaged face. The stench of burned human flesh filled the air. A barrage of bullets shredded a naked man, tissue and body fluids spraying out in slow motion. Mangled, partially dissected hands reached for me in crippled supplication.

I ignored Spider's strangled cry and skated through the gore to the file room.

I slammed the door shut on the hell outside and tracked bloody footprints over to the desk.

"Aydan?" Kane's voice was cautious.

"Yeah." I dropped into the chair, already reading the first few lines of the file.

"Are you okay?"

"This is another one of those letters and numbers things. Here's the first of it."

"Sorry, you'll have to go a little slower. I can't work

as fast as Webb."

I looked up from the file. "Where's Spider? He was just there a second ago."

Kane's voice was grim. "He just ran down the hall puking his guts out."

My heart smote me. "Oh, no, poor Spider. I'm so sorry! Nobody should have to see that shit."

"You had to." His voice sounded weary and angry.

I took a deep, unsteady breath. "Yeah. Just tell him it was a sim, that it wasn't real."

"I'll tell him. Are you really okay?"

I gulped down the nausea and horror and focused on the file in my violently trembling hands. "Here's the next line."

When I reached the end of the document at last, I paused. "Spider, go for a walk."

"What?" he quavered. He'd returned to take over the transcription duties from Kane, but he was clearly still in a fragile state. I intended to get out of the network as quickly as possible, but I didn't want to take a chance on the memories or monsters my brain might offer up on the way.

"Go for a walk. Now. Don't come back until Kane tells you." I kept my burning eyes focused on the document, reading and re-reading the last line.

Kane's voice. "He's gone."

"Thank God. Here's the last line."

I laid the document down and immediately folded sim-space to get to the portal.

I wasn't quite fast enough.

The cage clamped around me with brutal efficiency as the horrors of the corridor surrounded me again. I jerked and twisted in animal terror as my screams rose above the other sounds of torment. The bars thickened, blotting out light while they squeezed more and more tightly. My heartbeat thudded impossibly fast in my ears. My cries faded to shallow wheezing as the iron coffin crushed the air from my lungs.

Blindness and deafening noise overtook me, and I ceased to comprehend anything but agony.

CHAPTER 18

I had air in my lungs again. The better to scream with, my dear. My throat tore as my body convulsed with unspeakable pain. I flailed blindly and helplessly, trying without thought to batter my head against something, anything to end the torment.

At last, the pain abated enough for awareness to return. I felt Kane's arms around me, but their strength recalled the constricting cage. I cried out and began to struggle anew. I still couldn't open my eyes, and hysteria erupted when his arms tightened around me.

Speech and vision returned simultaneously. I thrashed impotently in Kane's grip, shrieking, "Let-me-go-let-me-go-let-me-go!"

His eyes widened in comprehension as his arms flew open. I scrambled wildly across the floor away from him on hands and knees, my too-fast panting whistling in my throat.

"Aydan, calm down. Breathe." Kane's voice was deep and reassuring, and he made no attempt to approach me. "Slow down. Breathe with me. In. Out. Nice and slow."

I gasped a few more breaths and then clamped down hard, imposing my yoga breathing. It helped, but adrenaline pumped unabated into my bloodstream from a full-blown panic attack. I hadn't had one of those in years. I grappled for control.

"I have to get out." The harsh voice sounded nothing like me.

"Go." Kane stepped back to give me a clear shot at the door, and I took it like a sprinter off the blocks. I heard his feet pounding behind me as I took the stairs two at a time.

In the time-delay chamber, he flattened himself unmoving against the opposite wall to give me space. My knuckles glowed incandescent as I gripped the door handle. I realized I was rocking compulsively in time to my whimpers, and I managed to shut up and stand still just before the door finally released.

I strode jerkily to the security wicket, fumbling with my fob. Kane's warm hands gently pushed my stiff, shaking fingers aside as he unfastened it and laid it in the tray at the security wicket along with his own. "Sign us out," he said briefly, and the guard nodded as we turned away.

I stepped outside onto the deserted sidewalk and took a deep breath. I stood rigid and trembling, fighting my internal battle for a few seconds before the panic won out.

I launched myself into crazed flight. My feet pounded on the sidewalk, the rapid footfalls echoing back from the silent storefronts. I heard Kane shout my name, and then the sound of his running feet behind me.

I ran for the tiny park again, sobbing for air. I felt the tears on my face, but I couldn't stop them. At the edge of the park, Kane caught up to run beside me as I began to falter. He was breathing hard, but with the deep, even rhythm of a conditioned athlete. "Aydan, slow down," he commanded.

With the remains of my rational mind, I tried to obey, but my body was driven beyond reason. My breath wailed in my throat. My feet wouldn't stop.

A few yards into the park, Kane's arms wrapped around me and we crashed to the ground. He released me immediately, and we lay gasping. I couldn't suck air into my lungs quickly enough. My body jerked with the desperate struggle for oxygen. My head throbbed with the triphammer beat of my heart.

I dimly realized that Kane was holding my wrist again. A distant part of my mind laughed through my tears. Good luck with that. Unless he kept an electronic defibrillator in his back pocket, taking my pulse wasn't going to help anything.

Maybe I passed out, or I might have just lost track of time while I lay in the grass. Eventually, my battle for air eased into helpless sobs. Unable to summon the energy to stop them, or even to move, I sprawled on the ground, weeping uncontrollably and utterly humiliated. In the darkness, Kane's hand gently stroked my hair, over and over.

Eventually, I regained enough control to gulp back the mortifying tears. I blessed the darkness. At least he hadn't actually seen me bawling my eyes out. Maybe I could pretend I'd just been struggling to regain my breath.

"Aydan." His voice was soft. "Can you sit up?"

I groaned. "Just leave me here. Maybe by morning I'll be ready to move."

"You have two choices," he told me firmly. "You can try to sit up now, or else I'll call the ambulance."

I groaned again and flopped over onto my back. "You're a cruel man." I tried to drag my trembling body upright.

"Is it all right if I help you?" His voice was cautious.

"Yeah, it's okay. I'm done freaking out now." God,

this was embarrassing.

He put a strong arm behind my shoulders and half-lifted me into sitting position. I sighed. To hell with pride. I slumped against his chest and put my arms around him. Just taking a little comfort.

After a second, his arms closed around me and he held me gently. I felt his lips move against my hair. "I'll talk to Stemp again. We'll figure something out. It'll be okay." We sat in silence for a time.

Finally, I took a deep breath. "Sorry about that." I pushed myself away from him and tottered to my feet, heading back the way we'd come.

Kane stood with me. As my knees wobbled, he wrapped an arm around my waist to steady me. "You have nothing to apologize for," he said firmly as we trudged together back to the sidewalk. "I'm sorry that I had to yank you out of the network again and cause you so much pain."

"It's okay. I'm not sure if I would have made it out on my own. I'm glad you did."

I tripped over my leaden feet, and he caught me again. Then he scooped me up in his arms and carried me along the sidewalk.

"Put me down," I hissed. "You can't carry me all the way back to Sirius."

"Is that a bet?"

"No! It's a command. Put me down!"

He set my feet on the ground. "Okay. But someday you should learn to accept help."

I sighed and concentrated on putting one foot in front of the other. "Please leave me with an illusion of competence, here. I'm feeling a little inadequate at the moment."

"No one will think less of you if you're not under complete control every second."

"I will."

He blew out a breath. "Aydan, don't drive yourself so hard!"

"I had to. Have to. If one of your agents has been captured..." My voice wobbled in time with my knees, and I concentrated on holding them both steady.

Kane put a gentle arm around my shoulders. "You've done all you can. More than anybody has a right to expect from you." He steered me to my car. "Are you okay to drive home?"

"Yeah." I delved into my waist pouch for my keys.

As I slid shakily into the driver's seat, Kane rested his forearm on the top of the open door and leaned in. "Get some sleep. Don't come in until at least one tomorrow."

"But what about your agent? What if you get another document?" He started to shake his head, and I gripped his wrist. "John, promise you'll call me if you need something else decrypted. Don't make me responsible for..." My throat closed up, and I swallowed hard. "...For whatever might happen to that agent."

"Aydan, you wouldn't be responsible..."

I shook his arm. "Promise me! Don't put that on my conscience! If you don't promise, I swear to God I'll go back into Sirius right now and sleep in the lobby until somebody retrieves that agent!"

His face softened, and he gently pried my hand off his wrist and placed it on the steering wheel. "You're a good person, Aydan. I'll call you if we need you. Go home. Get some sleep."

I searched his face. He was a spy. I'd seen him lie

easily and convincingly before.   He met my eyes.   "I promise."

"Okay. Thanks. Good night."

"Good night."

I drove slowly down the silent street, thinking.   I glanced at my watch and groaned.   After one A.M.   Every inch of my body hurt.   I was so exhausted it was an effort even to grip the steering wheel.

I could go back to the hotel and try to salvage the evening.   I knew Hellhound would welcome me regardless of the hour.   And I knew he'd make it worth my while.   That man could give an orgasm to a dead woman.   And I could really use a little comfort tonight.

I sighed.   If I ran into Bill Harks again, I might be a dead woman.   I couldn't summon up the courage to go through the lobby again, and I couldn't phone Hellhound to come and meet me because my phone was tapped.   I whimpered self-pity as I drove on past the hotel and hit the highway.

I had to stop twice for fresh air to keep me alert on the fifteen-minute drive home.   Parked in my yard, I jerked awake when my forehead thumped against the steering wheel.   I groaned and hauled myself out of the driver's seat.

When I stepped into the house, the stuffy heat closed around me, and I gasped with a momentary return of claustrophobia.   I quickly opened all the windows, and then grabbed a blanket and stepped outside again.   I'd just go and sit on the hill while the house cooled down.

Perched again on my hill, I watched the stillness of the long silver vista in the light of the full moon.   Even though the house held the heat of the day, the evening air was cool, and I wrapped the blanket around me while I let the wide-open silence soothe my ravelled nerves.

A sudden sense of foreboding made me jerk around to confront the dark figure behind me. Terror flashed through me, and I sprang to my feet to run frantically, my leaden feet too slow. I glanced fearfully behind me as I fled over the uneven ground. He was gaining.

The earth disappeared under my feet and I tumbled into the pit I hadn't seen. Lying in the cold, damp dirt, I tried to scramble to my feet, but my legs wouldn't move. Wordless wails of dread escaped me as he grinned over the edge. I clawed at the dirt wall, sharp stones tearing my fingers. Clods of dirt rained down on me as he began to bury me alive.

Screams ripped from my throat as the weight of the earth crushed me. Airless blackness surrounded me. My mouth filled with dirt.

The last scream tore through me as I bolted upright on the hillside. I flailed free of the blanket and crouched gasping in the grass. When full awareness returned, I whimpered and collapsed back onto the blanket. The cold moon poured its indifferent light over me while I lay still, catching my breath. After a few minutes, I shivered and dragged myself to my feet.

I heard my phone ring through the open windows of my house below. I sighed and made my quivering way down the hill and inside. I didn't rush. I was sure they'd call back.

Sure enough, as I was closing the windows, the phone rang again. I picked up without bothering to check the call display.

"Hello?" I mumbled.

"Aydan? It's Tom Rossburn. Is everything okay over there?"

"Huh?" I'd been expecting silence on the other end of the line. "Uh, yeah, everything's fine. Why?"

"I'm up tonight with a colicky horse, and I thought I heard screaming."

"Oh."

I thumped my head with my free hand. Jeez, as if the bloody bugs weren't enough. Now the neighbours had me under surveillance, too. "Thanks for checking up on me, but everything's fine."

"Okay, sorry to bother you. Guess it must have been a wild animal."

"It's okay. I hope your horse gets better soon."

"Thanks. Bye."

"Bye."

I dragged myself into the bedroom and fell into bed.

The phone rang.

"Unnnggghh!" I flopped over to check the illuminated clock. Three thirty. I groaned and pressed my face into the pillow as the phone rang again.

"Hello?"

"Hey, you hot bitch. Wanna party?"

"Wha...? No! Who is this?"

"Come on, I got good money. How much for a little party?"

"You've got the wrong number." I slammed the phone down. Seconds later, it rang again.

I picked up. "What!"

"You gonna be nice to me, bitch. I know where you live. I'm gonna come over, and we'll have ourselves a party. Just you and me."

Fear turned to fury so quickly I barely registered the transition. "Listen, you bag of shit, if you come anywhere near here, I'll blow your fucking nuts off with a twelve-gauge. So come on over. Right now, asshole. Right fucking now!"

My only response was a click as the caller disconnected. I slammed the phone back into its cradle and collapsed onto the bed, trembling and hyperventilating. I was so mad and scared that the threat about the twelve-gauge was probably superfluous. I'd rip his nuts off with my bare hands.

I gradually brought my breathing under control and willed my shaking muscles to relax. I was never going to be safer than I was right now. Thanks to the bugs and the phone tap, I was relatively certain that Stemp's minions would have a guard on my house faster than my unknown caller could get here, and the guard would probably stick around for the rest of the night. I almost hoped the stupid asshole caller did show up. Wouldn't he get a hell of a surprise.

CHAPTER 19

I groaned and buried my head in the pillow. Normally, I'm a morning person. Not so this morning. I swore at the cheery clamour of birdsong from outside and stomped over to slam the window shut. Then I burrowed back into the bed and clamped the pillow over my head.

Several hours later, I emerged, feeling less than refreshed. I scowled at my baggy-eyed reflection in the mirror and bitched my way into the shower. I rested my forehead on the shower wall and let the water pour down my back for a long time, trying to ease muscles stiffened from my wild run.

After breakfast, I glared at the clock, irritated that half my morning was gone. I creaked my way out of my chair and headed for the garden.

A couple of hours of pleasantly mindless work in the warm sun eased my tense muscles and my frazzled nerves. If Stemp had put a guard on me last night, the guard was either really good, or else he was gone. Nobody disturbed my peaceful solitude.

I ate a late lunch, and then dragged myself reluctantly out to the car again. This time, my heart started to thump before I was even inside the Sirius Dynamics building. I leaned against my car and concentrating on breathing deeply and evenly.

As I stood there, Kane emerged from the building

and strode across the street toward me. He stopped a couple of paces away, and activated a small electronic device, apparently scanning for bugs again. After a second, he looked up. "Walk with me."

I fell in beside him as we ambled down the sidewalk. Anything that postponed going back into Sirius was fine with me.

When we were out of visual range of the building, he finally spoke. "You had some excitement at your place last night."

I sighed. "Yeah."

"We traced the call. It came from the pay phone in the lobby of the Silverside Hotel."

"Gee, there's a surprise. I don't think it was Harks, though. His voice is wheezier."

Kane lifted a shoulder in irritation. "We have no way of knowing who it was. I questioned the desk clerk, but he said he didn't notice anybody using the phone last night. Either he was lying, or he has the intellectual capacity of a flea. I'm leaning toward the latter."

I looked up at him. "You look as tired as I feel."

"Probably because I spent half of last night skulking around your yard."

"I wondered about that. Doesn't Stemp realize that you do actually need to sleep at times?"

"Actually, yes. He's pulling Germain up from Calgary today. It seems like a waste of resources to me, but Stemp says he's not sparing any expense to make sure you're protected."

"I'm flattered."

Kane snorted. "Too bad he won't give you what you really need."

I gazed up at him uncertainly.

"I talked to Stemp again this morning," Kane said. "He's still not willing to compromise with the network key. I'm sorry. He insists it has to stay below-ground."

I gave him my best nonchalant shrug. "No surprise."

I felt his eyes on me, and I kept my face composed. "Aydan..." he hesitated. "I know you have reasons for hiding your emotions. But if you keep hiding how much this is bothering you, Stemp will never budge. And we both know that your problems in the network are getting worse, not better."

"I won't go whining to him."

"Aydan!" He blew out a frustrated breath. "For once in your life, will you just..."

"Just what?" I spun to face him. "Just show weakness to the one person who's most likely to exploit it? I don't think so. Come on." I turned and started walking back toward Sirius.

He paced beside me in silence for a block or so. Then he turned to me again. "Aydan?"

"Yeah."

"Just... let yourself bend a little. So you don't break."

I sighed. "I'll try. Thanks for being concerned."

Buried in the lab again, I blew out a long breath, trying to ease my shoulders down from around my ears. I regarded Spider's pale, worried face with remorse.

"Spider, I'm so sorry about yesterday. It was just a sim, remember. No different than the movies that you watch all the time."

He gulped. "I know. It was just so... sudden. And so

real. But... I think what bothered me most was that it came from you. That it's inside your head." He shuddered, his eyes darkening.

I took his hand. "Hey, Spider, don't forget, you've got awful-looking things inside your head, too. You watch all those Terminator and Diehard and slasher movies. All that stuff's inside your head. If it suddenly came out in a sim, it would shock everybody else, but you'd know where it came from. You'd know it wasn't real."

His shoulders eased a fraction as his face cleared. "Yeah, I guess you're right. Thanks, Aydan."

I patted his hand. "No problem. It's just context, that's all." I changed the subject. "Am I looking for anything specific today?"

"No, back to the regular files today."

Spider surveyed my trembling hands. "Aydan," he said hesitantly. "Are you sure you should be doing this today? Maybe you should take the day off." He shot Kane a questioning glance. "Shouldn't she?"

Kane scowled. "If you can convince her, you're a better man than I am."

"Aydan..." Spider entreated.

"How about if we compromise. I'll make it a short day."

"Okay," he agreed.

I closed my eyes and drifted into the void. All was inky darkness. With an effort of will, I resisted the urge to give in to fear and step back out the portal. "Hey, Spider, what's going on?" I asked, holding my voice determinedly steady.

"I don't know," his puzzled voice came back. "Nothing's changed in the network."

I waved my arms blindly, and stifled a small shriek when I touched something warm. I jumped away, flailing my arms. More things touched me in the dark. I bit down on rising whimpers.

The darkness was as thick as used motor oil. As the thought occurred to me, my breath stopped and acrid, suffocating pressure filled my nose and mouth. Unable to speak, I churned desperately through the blackness with the last oxygen in my lungs.

I couldn't see the portal.

I circled wildly, lungs bursting while I swung my arms, hoping to make contact.

I couldn't escape.

Trapped!

Strangling...

"Aydan! Aydan! What's happening?"

Blackness filled me as I collapsed to my hands and knees. My body heaved with the effort to inhale. No air. My hammering heart began to slow. I floated weightlessly as the last beats faded.

CHAPTER 20

Kane's lips pressed hard against mine. I gasped, breathless. Then he started crushing his fist into my chest. My eyes snapped into focus. "Ow!"

"Aydan!" Kane's tense face loomed over me as he pressed his fingers against the pulse in my neck.

"What? Ow," I whimpered as my breath lifted my bruised chest.

"Thank God." He brushed my face with his fingertips, his touch feather-light. "I'm sorry," he murmured inexplicably.

I shook my head vigorously, trying to comprehend what was happening. I was lying on the floor of the lab again. That was getting old. I tried to sit up, but Kane gently restrained me. "No, lie still for a while." His fingers still pressed against my pulse.

Spider skidded around the corner, white-faced. "It's open. Ambulance is on the way."

"Good." Kane picked me up off the floor and carried me toward the door.

"What did I tell you about carrying me?" I demanded. "Put me down, for crying out loud."

"Oh, thank God," Spider quavered.

"Aydan, shut up," Kane said. I opened my mouth to express outrage. "Please," he added quietly. Something in his face made me subside. I clearly didn't have the whole story here. I lay passively in his arms while he carried me up the stairs and through the open time-delay chamber.

"What happened?" I asked, trying to distract myself from the stares of the bystanders as we passed through the lobby.

He laid me carefully onto the stretcher. "We'll talk later." The paramedics wheeled me to the ambulance.

When they brought me into the hospital, I recognized Wing B, the area reserved for Sirius Dynamics covert personnel. Déjà vu. After my repeated visits in the spring, I'd hoped not to see it again for a while. A long while.

Dr. Roth's piercing eyes raked me as she strode along beside the stretcher. "Are you causing trouble again?"

"Apparently," I grimaced.

She briefly checked the IV that the paramedics had inserted in my hand on the way over, and eyed the digital display on the monitors. "Take her straight to the MRI," she told the porter, and he nodded and wheeled me away.

Outside the MRI, I successfully persuaded her that I was able to get off the stretcher and change into a gown instead of having my clothing cut off. Little victories.

"I'm fine, really," I assured her. "Nothing hurts. Well, except my chest."

"That happens when you get CPR," the doctor responded wryly. "Are you claustrophobic?"

I frowned at her in confusion. "Yes, but what does that have to do with CPR?"

"Nothing. It has to do with the MRI. I'll give you a sedative, and then we can get started."

"Can we skip the sedative?"

She frowned at me. "Why? If you're claustrophobic, I think you should have it."

"I hate being sedated. And I want to be able to drive home."

"Okay," she agreed dubiously. "We'll see how it goes."

She wedged my body in place on the table of the MRI, and my heart began to pound when I eyed the opening. It looked really small.

Dr. Roth glanced at the monitors and gave me a sharp look. "Your heart rate is increasing. Do you want that sedative now?"

"No, I'm fine." I took a deep breath and reassured myself that the MRI was just a hollow tube. Open at both ends. I could get out if I had to. No worries.

The doctor pressed a soft object into my hand. "If you feel panicky during the procedure, don't move, just squeeze this."

I took a deep breath as the table slid smoothly into the body of the machine. The inner curve of the opening was only a couple of inches above my face. My heart leapt with instinctive panic, and I breathed slowly and deeply as I reassured myself. Just a hollow tube. Nice fresh air moving across my face. I closed my eyes so I couldn't see the closeness. No problem.

"Aydan, are you okay? Your heart rate is still climbing."

"I'm fine." Breathe. In. Out. Ocean waves.

This was taking forever. I lay rigidly. Don't move. Breathe.

"Aydan? Do you want the sedative? We'll just run it into your IV line. It'll be working in a few seconds."

"No. I'm fine." Breathe.

A second voice. "Doctor, her heart rate just hit 165.

Still climbing."

"Sedate."

"No..." I muttered as the warm fuzziness drowned me.

When I opened my eyes, Kane was sitting beside my bed. I fought my way through the haze. "I really hate sedatives," I mumbled.

He chuckled. "You hate anything that might make you sacrifice your independence."

"Well, duh." I pawed at the oxygen mask and struggled to sit up.

"Stay." He held me down with a heavy hand on my shoulder.

I sighed, and my eyes closed again without my permission.

When I opened them again, the oxygen mask was gone. Dr. Roth stood at the foot of the bed. "Everything looks fine. We're just going to keep you here for another half hour or so while you recover from the sedative, and then you can go."

I squirmed, and she pointed out the controls on the bed. "If you want to sit up a bit, you can use these buttons. But stay in bed," she added severely. "Until I give you the all-clear."

I nodded obediently and used the controls to raise the head of the bed while Kane watched, his eyes twinkling.

"I should get some of that sedative," he joked. "It makes you very cooperative."

"Don't even think about it," I growled. I glanced around to make sure there was nobody within earshot.

"What the hell happened?"

"I was going to ask you the same thing."

"Everything was black, and then I couldn't breathe."

He frowned. "We saw the blackness on the monitor. We couldn't see you, and you weren't saying anything. Then all of a sudden, your body just fell off the chair. I thought you were trapped in the network again, so I slapped you to try to get you out as fast as possible. I knew you wouldn't wake to anything but a pain stimulus, so I hit you pretty hard." His hand reached for my cheek again, but stopped without touching me. "I'm sorry."

I shrugged. "It's okay, I didn't feel it."

"I know." His eyes were troubled. "You didn't feel it because you were dead."

"Say what?"

"You weren't breathing. Your heart wasn't beating. You were dead."

"Oh. Yeah. I guess I did hear my heart stop."

"Dammit, why didn't you come out of the sim?" he demanded. "Why do you have to be so damn stubborn? I keep trying to tell you, this isn't worth it!"

I leaned my head back and closed my eyes, fighting sleep. "I actually was trying to come out. But I couldn't see. I couldn't find the portal, and I couldn't breathe. I tried. Believe me, I tried. Suffocation is not a nice way to go."

His hand closed around mine. "I'm sorry."

I sighed. "It's okay. Natural assumption. Stubborn is my best thing. So that's why you were beating up on me when I woke up. CPR."

"Yes. I started CPR right away, and Webb got the ambulance and opened up the time-delay." He frowned at me. "What do you think happened? You can't go back into the sim until we figure this out."

I struggled to stay coherent. This is why I hate sedatives. "Nothing happened. It's a sim. I just wasn't concentrating. I panicked. It was my own stupid fault."

"Aydan, don't be so hard on yourself. Let's think about this constructively for a minute. Is there anything else besides the claustrophobia that's making harder for you to concentrate?"

I blinked slowly. God, I was tired. Oh. Duh. "I haven't been sleeping. I think I'm just too tired to concentrate properly."

"Can you find a way to sleep better?"

"Yeah, if I can stop being claustrophobic."

He shook his head in puzzlement. "What do you mean?"

"I mean it's a vicious circle. The worse things get during the day, the worse I sleep at night. Then I'm more tired than ever, and the next day gets worse. And the next night. And so on."

"I'll talk to Stemp again," Kane said. "If he sees that this is literally killing you, he might rethink his decision. In the mean time, you're going home today, and you're not coming back to Sirius until Monday. Not for anything."

I clutched his arm. "But what about your agent? What if..."

"Oh!" He smiled suddenly. "I meant to tell you, and then all this happened. We retrieved the agent. He's going to be okay."

I slumped back against the pillow. "Oh, thank goodness!" The relief was so intense that I had to turn away for a second and blink back tears. "That's so good. Thank goodness."

"No, thank *you*," Kane corrected. "If you hadn't decrypted that document, we wouldn't have gotten there in time. You saved him."

I squeezed his hand. "We saved him."

Dr. Roth cleared her throat from the foot of the bed, and I suddenly realized that Kane and I were holding hands and beaming at each other. I resisted the urge to snatch my hand back like a guilty child, and casually let go as I turned to her. "Can I leave now?"

"Yes. The MRI came back fine. You don't seem to have suffered any ill effects. But take it easy for the rest of the day, and don't drive or operate dangerous equipment for twenty-four hours. You're considered legally impaired until then."

"This is why I didn't want the sedative," I growled.

She shrugged, unfazed. "The wellbeing of my patients comes before their convenience. You might not have wanted the sedative, but you needed it."

"Hmmph."

The doctor turned to Kane with a smile. "Get this grumpy patient out of here."

"With pleasure," he agreed.

CHAPTER 21

They both withdrew while I got dressed. When I pulled the curtain aside, Kane was waiting with a wheelchair. "Aw, come on, you've got to be kidding me," I complained. "I'll walk. Never mind the wheelchair."

"You have two choices," Kane said severely. "You can sit in the wheelchair like a good little patient, or I can carry you out. Which would you prefer?"

"Now you're just showing off," I ribbed him.

The corner of his mouth quirked up. "If that's the way you want it."

"No, I'll behave." I sat in the wheelchair, feeling foolish while he wheeled me to the hospital doors.

On the sidewalk, he deftly manoeuvred the chair into a shady spot and locked the brakes. "I'll go and get the Expedition," he said. "I'll pick you up from here."

"I can walk to the parking lot," I protested.

"Or I could carry you."

"All right, all right," I grumbled as he strode away, grinning.

The warm, fresh-smelling breeze wrapped gently around me, and I let my eyes drift closed. I leaned slowly back in the chair, moving carefully to avoid pulling the painful bruise.

"Aydan!"

My eyes flew open, and I jerked upright with an

involuntary grunt of pain as I clutched my chest.

Tom squatted down beside my chair, looking into my face with horrified eyes. "Aydan, what happened? What..." His eyes narrowed as he surveyed my face. "He beat you. That lousy dirtbag was beating you last night, wasn't he? That was you screaming. I'm going to find him and kick his sorry butt from here to-"

"Tom," I interrupted. "Stop. Nobody was beating me."

"Aydan." He placed his hand gently on my cheek, his callused palm barely touching my skin. "You have a huge red handprint across your face. A handprint that's bigger than my hand. And I have big hands."

"Oh."

Shit.

I went for damage control.

"Tom, it's not what it looks like. I swear to you, Arnie never hit me."

"Then who did?" His face was hard with anger, his normally sky-blue eyes the colour of arctic ice. "Tell me, Aydan. You're not doing anyone any favours by protecting him."

I sighed. My brain waded sluggishly through the remains of the sedative. "It wasn't... I was at work, and I fainted. Kane was trying to wake me by patting my face."

"Kane? John Kane? The guy who showed up in your driveway and commanded you to come with him like he owned you? That's a heck of a pat."

I sighed again and squeezed my eyes shut, trying to focus. "It only looks bad. I have very sensitive skin, and the slightest touch makes it go red. In a couple of hours, you'll never know there was ever a mark on my face. Here, I'll show you."

I turned my wrist up and scraped my fingernails across it. As we watched, the scratches turned white, then bloomed into livid red in a few seconds. "See? I barely touched the skin." I held it up for his inspection.

He frowned at me, unconvinced. "When I startled you, you flinched like it hurt you. Do you have an explanation for that, too?"

I was saved from replying when the Expedition pulled up at the curb. Kane got out and came around to stand beside me. Tom rose from his crouch beside the wheelchair and stood to his full height, only a couple of inches shorter than Kane. He locked eyes with Kane.

"Do you care to explain this?" he inquired mildly, gesturing toward my face. His tone reminded me of the way his soft denim shirt had felt over those lean, hard muscles. Only soft on the surface.

Kane's posture stayed relaxed, though I knew he'd caught the subtle threat. His eyes flicked to me, and I gave him a tiny nod.

He met Tom's gaze squarely. "Aydan collapsed at work. I was trying to revive her. I guess I was more scared than I realized, and I patted her face harder than I intended to. I feel terrible about this."

Tom held his eyes for a few seconds longer, and Kane returned his look levelly. "What else did you do?" Tom asked in the same quiet voice. "Why is she moving like somebody's beaten her up?"

"Probably because she's badly bruised. Her heart stopped, and I had to give her CPR."

"*What?*" Tom swung a worried gaze back to me. "Your heart just stopped?"

"No," Kane lied smoothly. "She got an electrical shock, enough to stop her heart for a few seconds. She's been fully checked out, and she'll be fine. We have to go now. She's been sedated, and I have to get her home."

I let my eyes drift closed again as I swayed a little.

"Do you need help?" Tom asked.

"No, that's fine, I can manage," Kane replied. He helped me into the Expedition and buckled me in, and then closed the door and went around to the driver's side. I slumped against the door and lifted a listless hand to Tom as we drove away.

When we turned the corner, I straightened and scrubbed my hands over my face, wincing slightly at the ache in my left cheek. "Dammit. He's becoming a serious problem."

"I had a feeling there was more to this than you were telling me. Fill me in," Kane commanded.

I sighed and slouched back in the seat. "Tom seems to think I have a habit of getting into abusive relationships. And being the nice guy that he is, he's decided that I need rescuing. And in the process, he's going to get himself caught in the crossfire. Dammit."

"Why would he think you have abusive relationships?"

"Well, first that damn cover story from March came back and bit me. Small town, rumours, you know. So he thinks I have an abusive ex-husband for starters."

Kane shrugged. "That should be old news."

"Yeah, it should have been. Except he also thinks that Hellhound's beating me. And now you."

Kane's eyes bored into me. "Why would he think Hellhound is beating you?" he asked.

I sighed again and stared out the window. "Bad timing, that's all. Last weekend when Arnie and I were standing in the driveway, Tom came over. He just happened to show up just as we were horsing around, and he got the wrong impression."

"What exactly happened?"

At the sound of his carefully controlled cop voice, I glanced over to see his impassive cop profile. Shit.

"We were just joking around, but from a distance, I guess it would have looked like I was mad. I had my hands on my hips, and then I yelled and smacked Arnie, and he grabbed me."

"That's pretty hard to misinterpret," Kane said dangerously. "What did he do to you?"

I threw up my hands. "Jeez! You're his best friend, and you're still misinterpreting it."

"Then enlighten me." The steering wheel creaked faintly under his grip.

"Hellhound saw Tom coming across the yard, and he was bugging me about making time with cowboys. And then he made some comment about how maybe I should think about settling down with somebody. You know how I feel about that."

"I don't, actually." His voice was neutral.

"Oh. Well, I have no intention of having any kind of a committed relationship in the foreseeable future. Arnie knows that damn well. And I know he feels the same way, so I put my hands on my hips and asked him if he was proposing."

A snort of laughter escaped Kane, and I grinned. "That was the first time I've ever seen him scared. It was funny as hell."

"I would have paid good money to see that," Kane agreed. "So then what happened?"

"Well, then, of course, Hellhound had to start teasing me. He was asking me if I was going to settle down and get attached, and that's when I smacked him and yelled 'No, goddammit'. Tom arrived just then and completely got the wrong idea."

I looked over and saw with relief that the cop face was gone. "So what do you plan to do about Rossburn?" he asked.

I tugged a couple of fistfuls of hair. "I don't have a clue. I already told him plainly that I wasn't interested in a relationship with him."

"You did?"

I glanced over at his unreadable expression. "Well, yeah, of course. In the first place, I don't want a relationship at all. In the second place, even if I did want one, it would be far too complicated and dangerous to have one with him. There's just too much about my life that can't be explained right now. And hell, Stemp made it abundantly clear that anybody who's close to me is at risk. I'd feel terrible if something happened to Tom because of me."

Kane braked at my gate, and I got out to open it before he could protest. A scrap of paper was pushed through the shackle of the lock, and I unfolded it while I stood waiting for Kane to drive through the gate. 'Sorry I missed you. Call me when you got a couple minutes.' I recognized Hellhound's scrawl. "You promised me you could do it in less than two minutes, buddy," I muttered, grinning.

I stuffed the paper into my pocket and got back into the truck. Kane glanced over. "What was that?"

"Just a note. I missed a visitor."

"Mm. So do you want any help dealing with Rossburn?"

"No, not at the moment. I don't know what you could do anyway. If I think of anything, I'll let you know."

He parked in front of the house. "Do you want a hand getting into the house?"

"No, I'm fine." I reached for the door handle.

"Aydan? Take it easy this weekend. Get some sleep."

"I will. Assuming my nocturnal callers let me. Maybe I'll sleep outside."

He eyed me doubtfully. "Are you serious?"

"Possibly. Depends on whether I get any more calls like last night."

"You shouldn't..." He stopped and blew out a breath. "Carry your phone with you if you do."

"I will."

CHAPTER 22

I wandered lethargically into the hot house and opened all the windows. The outside temperature wasn't much cooler, but at least a breeze blew through. I flopped down on the sofa to think. What the hell was I going to do about Tom?

I jerked awake when the phone rang. I squinted at my watch as I stumbled toward the noise. Seven o'clock. I must have been more tired than I'd realized.

I didn't recognize the number on the call display, and I picked up the receiver with trepidation. "Hello?"

"Hi, Aydan!" The sound of Lola's throaty voice made me smile.

"Hi, Lola, what's up?"

"Girls' night out is what's up. I'm getting a bunch of the girls together, and thought you might like to join us. Are you free tomorrow night?"

I was pleased and flattered that she'd ask me, but the thought of going out made my head ache. All I wanted to do was stay home and hibernate.

"Thanks, Lola, that's nice of you to ask. But I haven't been feeling well lately, and I think I'll just stay home and rest up."

"I thought you were looking a little peaked on Tuesday," she said. "A little pick-me-up would do you good."

"You're probably right. But right now, what I want

more than anything is a decent night's sleep."

"Well, I hope you feel better in the morning, then. Give me a call if you change your mind, honey."

"Thanks, Lola, I will."

I hung up the phone smiling. I was so lucky to have such nice clients. I headed for the kitchen in search of supper, feeling better about life in general.

I was just about to drag my full belly out to the garden for a therapeutic weeding session when the phone rang again. I picked up hesitantly, not recognizing the number.

"Hi, Aydan, how are you feeling?" Tom's voice. Shit.

"Fine, thanks, Tom. How's your horse? I forgot to ask you this afternoon."

"Oh, he's fine. The grandkids fed him a bunch of green apples yesterday, that's all."

"You have grandkids?"

"Emily is three, and Jackson is four and a half. My son and daughter-in-law are out from the city for a holiday."

"Well, that should keep you hopping."

He laughed. "That's for sure. Actually, that's part of the reason why I'm calling. Every year around this time, David brings the family out, and my folks and I get together and invite all the neighbours over for a potluck. I wondered if you'd like to come tomorrow night."

"Um." I thought furiously. Any other time, I would have appreciated the neighbourly invitation. If things had been different, I might have even appreciated the neighbour himself. In more ways than one. I shook my head and refocused.

"Thanks, Tom, I really appreciate the invitation. Ordinarily, I'd love to, but I'm busy tomorrow night," I lied uncomfortably.

"Oh, what are you up to? You could come by for a little while before or after if you wanted. People come and go all evening."

Nnngh! I grasped frantically at the first straw that came to mind. "I'm doing a girls' night out with some friends. It sounds like it's going to take up most of the evening. Sorry about that."

"That's okay, I should have asked you sooner. Have a good time, then."

"Thanks. You, too."

I hung up and groaned frustration. Lies always came back to bite me in the ass. There was no help for it. I called Lola and told her I'd be there.

After a pleasant evening outside, I crept into bed early. For the first time in days, my muscles weren't vibrating with tension. I eased myself into a comfortable position that didn't hurt my bruised chest, and was asleep instantly.

Until the phone rang. At two A.M. I pried open my gummy eyes to peer at the call display. Private caller.

"Hello?"

"How much for a blowjob?"

"Blow yourself. Or get your mother to do it for you. She's probably good at it." I slammed the phone down. It immediately rang again, and I ignored it.

"Fuck this," I said out loud for the benefit of the bugs. "I'll sleep in the fucking garage."

I got dressed and gathered up my pillow, sleeping bag, and ancient air mattress, stuffing my cell phone in my pocket. I trailed out to my garage and made a cozy nest in the corner of the smooth concrete floor. Soothed by the happy smells of engine oil and warm rubber, I drifted off almost immediately.

I woke once when I rapped my knuckles sharply against the wall in the throes of a violent nightmare, but I managed to get back to sleep again. When I finally opened my eyes, the garage was bright with the beams of the mid-morning sun.

I rolled over slowly and stretched. That was the best sleep I'd had in a week. I yawned my way into the house and headed for the bathroom. The phone rang again as I stepped out of the shower, and I ignored it. I hadn't been screaming. No need to pick up.

It rang twice more while I sat at the breakfast table. I saw 'private caller' on the display, and resisted the urge to answer the phone and make the caller's ear bleed. Instead, I took a deep breath and wandered out to my beloved garden again.

After a pleasant day of solitude outside, I faced the prospect of an evening out with moderate good humour, even though I was going to have to make an attempt to dress up a bit. I wasn't sure what girls' night out involved, exactly, but I probably needed to be wearing something better than a sweat-stained T-shirt and baggy, dirt-encrusted jeans.

As I changed my clothes, I recalled that my car was still in Silverside, parked at Sirius Dynamics. I debated for a few seconds, and then grinned and headed for the garage.

A few minutes later, I fired up my '66 Corvette convertible and let its throaty rumble carry me down the road. On the highway, I nobly resisted the urge to let my horses run. The warm wind lifted my hair, and the heavy vibration of the big 427 soothed my body like a massaging chair.

As I drove into Silverside, the single stoplight turned red at my approach. As usual.

I pulled to a stop and let the 'Vette wind down into a lolloping idle. The car shuddered with suppressed power as the lumpy cam churned out its brute-force rhythm, and I beamed with the pure joy that only excessive horsepower can bring.

A movement caught my eye, and I glanced over to see a tall, broad-shouldered figure astride a black BMW K1300R as he pulled up beside me at the light. His teeth gleamed behind his helmet's face shield as he revved his engine.

I gave him a feral grin and goosed the accelerator. The big engine let out an equally feral roar. You wanna play, baby?

We gunned our engines a couple more times, grinning at each other until the light changed. I knew I didn't have a chance in hell of taking a motorcycle off the line, so I didn't even try.

Instead, I smoked the tires in a short but satisfying brakestand. Then I drove sedately past Kane, who had pulled up about a half a block further on. I tossed him an innocent wave, and rumbled on down the street toward Up & Coming.

As I parked, he pulled in behind me and swung off his bike. "That the best you've got?" he kidded as he strode over.

"You're just sorry you don't have a sexy car like mine."

"I've got a sexy bike."

I grinned up at him. "Yeah, but you can't beat the sound of a muscle-car. Your little sewing machine engine just can't compete with that."

"True. That's not the stock cam, is it?"

"Hell, no."

We leaned comfortably over the open hood, discussing tuning and trading good-natured insults until I spied Lola crossing the street. She waved and appraised Kane's black riding chaps and broad, leather-clad shoulders with frank appreciation as she drew up to us.

"Nice!" she commented, looking him up and down.

The corner of his mouth quirked up. "Thanks." The sexy laugh lines around his eyes crinkled as he regarded her vivid purple hair and stiletto heels.

I hastened to introduce them. "Lola, this is John Kane. He's one of my clients. John, this is Lola Ives. She runs Up & Coming along with Linda Burton, her granddaughter."

Kane stooped slightly and gently engulfed her tiny hand in his. "Pleasure to meet you."

"You, too, Big John," she winked.

I used the excuse of closing the hood to turn away and hide my grin as I recognized the reference. The way those riding chaps focused attention on the good stuff, I definitely knew where she was coming from. I'd been trying not to look. Really trying.

Well, maybe not really.

I determinedly herded my mind out of the gutter as Lola turned to me. "Come on, Aydan. Let's get this show on the road."

"Okay." I turned to Kane. "Enjoy your ride."

"I will. Oh, do you want me to swing by and pick you up Monday morning so you can take your car home Monday night? Your other, boring car."

"Watch your mouth. I love that car!"

He laughed. "I know."

"I'd appreciate the ride. Thanks. See you then." I waved and followed Lola's diminutive figure toward the shop.

Close to midnight, I staggered away exhausted, my sides aching from an evening of laughter. I'd come in for my fair share of teasing about Big John the Wonder Horse, but I'd given as good as I'd gotten. The party was still in full swing behind me, and I wondered when they'd finally pack it in. I'd had fun, but I was definitely ready for some silence, solitude, and my bed.

I was humming the last tune from the movie we'd watched when the scrape of a footfall made me jerk around to look behind me. A man in a red plaid shirt stood a few yards behind me, weaving slightly as he stared. With chagrin, I recognized the man who'd peeked in and caught me vamping in the sex shop wearing the thigh-high boots.

Shit.

As I quickly turned to head for the car, Bill Harks stepped out from between the buildings to confront me. I recoiled and backpedalled a couple of steps before realizing the first man was closing in from behind. Before I could even formulate the idea of running, they had executed a pincer movement that left me with my back to one of the buildings, all escape routes cut off.

CHAPTER 23

My mind frantically sorted and discarded options while I watched them, my heart pounding. The streets were deserted. The music was still blaring at Lola's party. Nobody would hear me if I screamed. They were both big men with long arms. The way they'd closed me in, I likely wouldn't be able to dodge past them.

"Hey, you hot bitch," Red-shirt slurred. "Let's party. How much?"

"Fuck off," I snarled.

He frowned and staggered. "What, I got money. How much for half an hour?"

"I'm not a hooker."

Harks sneered down at me. "Oh, yeah? Saw you night before last using my hotel for one of your johns."

I drew myself up. "I was visiting my boyfriend. He was staying there."

Harks laughed. "Yeah, and you were in and out of there in half an hour, putting your clothes on and looking at your watch. What, your boyfriend couldn't get it up?"

I glared at him as he continued. "Yeah, and my buddy here saw you later with your next boyfriend after you fucked him in the park."

Red-shirt chimed in. "All sweaty and covered with grass. You like it kinky, don't you? What's it cost to be your boyfriend for half an hour?" He grinned and staggered. "I want you to wear those whore boots while I fuck you."

"Go fuck yourself! I'm not a hooker!" I retorted. He made a grab for me, and I dodged his hand. Fear and anger made me reckless. "And even if I was, there's not enough money in the world to make me do a sack of shit like you."

Harks and Red-shirt closed in a pace. "You're gonna learn some respect," Harks snarled. "And you're gonna drop those assault charges, too."

"Not a fucking chance in hell. You're going to rot in jail, along with your bum-buddy here. Which one of you is the wide receiver?"

Jesus, I'm a moron. Start with two dangerous guys. Piss them off thoroughly. Mix lightly and bake in hell. My heart pounded so hard I could feel the front of my T-shirt vibrating.

Harks's face contorted with rage. "You won't be so fuckin' mouthy with my cock shoved down your throat."

I bared my teeth at him. "You're going to look really fucking stupid without a dick."

He lunged, and I sidestepped in the nick of time. His knuckles connected with the wall behind me as I dove forward under his outstretched arm. He caught me with a glancing blow on my back, and I hit the pavement hard and rolled.

I scrambled to my feet and turned to run, but Red-shirt tripped me. I sprawled on the pavement, twisting frantically. Thank God, he didn't try to kick me. Instead, he launched himself at me, trying to pin me to the ground. In pure panicked reflex, I drew up my knee at the last second.

There was an unpleasant crunch as the immovable object met his balls with irresistible force. He let out a high-pitched squeak and collapsed on top of me. His forehead smashed against my mouth as his weight crushed me.

The pain galvanized me into berserk terror and rage. A wild roar ripped from my throat as I bucked his limp body off and scrambled to my feet.

Harks was already lunging at me, his hand reaching. I grabbed his wrist and yanked with all my strength, using the momentum to propel myself past him.

Run like hell. It was my only hope. If he connected with even one solid hit, it'd be all over for me.

I'd only managed a couple of steps when my head snapped back. Harks yanked me toward him by my hair. I dimly realized that I was roaring and shrieking like a wild animal as I spun under his grip. Thank God my hair was long enough to allow me some movement.

I aimed a knee at his crotch, but he was too fast for me. My attack thudded into his thigh instead. I swung a fist in a hammer-blow at his nose and felt a solid crack. My head wrenched sideways as he jerked my hair, and I had to let my body follow or have my neck broken.

I sprawled on the sidewalk again, rolling wildly. At least he'd let go of my hair. I scuffled my feet under me for another attempt at flight. Too slow. Harks bellowed and swung like a windmill. I ducked and dodged frantically, and the blow aimed at my head connected with my shoulder instead.

God, he was strong. Pain and cold fear shot through me as the glancing blow drove me back against the side of the building. My breath slammed out of me. I was saved from a punch to the face simply because my knees buckled and I dropped like a stone.

Harks yelled again when his fist hit the wall where my head had been seconds before. I managed to suck a breath into my lungs and took another shot upward at his nuts. It was a bad angle, and there wasn't much strength in my blow, but it slowed him down. I floundered away on hands and knees as he gasped.

My chest and back were crushed in thorny bands of agony. I panted hysterically, dragging myself to my feet for another try at running away. I hadn't even managed a step before a tremendous blow to my back flung me to the ground again. I barely managed to get my hands in front of my face before the pavement rushed up and smacked my forehead.

Time stopped. Slow despair coursed through me while lights exploded behind my eyes. I tried to roll, but my body wouldn't cooperate. I managed to flop over onto my back, but I could only lie helplessly gasping.

So this is how it ends. Beaten to death by some brainless monster. Shit. I'd been hoping for a bullet to the brain. Tidier.

Harks's foot drew back languidly, a freeze-frame of his bruised, bloodied face grinning down at me. Kick me when I'm down. Really fucking brave, Harks. This was going to hurt. My heartbeat drummed slowly in my ears.

Just before his kick landed, I heard a shout that sounded like "Melee!"

An elf leaped on Harks's back just before his foot hit my ribs. The blow didn't have as much force as it could have, but it still folded me into a ball. My tortured breath wailed in my throat.

Have to get up. Have to run. I forced myself to uncurl.

Harks was overrun by elves.

I squeezed my eyes shut and shook my pounding head violently. This wasn't a sim. I was sure of it. If it had been, I would have conjured up something a lot more lethal than elves to attack him.

I looked again. Pointy ears. Elvish costumes. Little hats. Six of them. Or maybe seven. Hard to say.

I groaned and swiped my hand across my face. The elves bore Harks to the ground, uttering yells of triumph.

I slumped down on the hard sidewalk and closed my eyes. I must have sustained a massive brain injury. Please God, don't let me hallucinate elves for the rest of my life.

"Aydan! Oh my God, Aydan!" I cracked an eye open. One of the elves was kneeling beside me. I squeezed my eye shut again and groaned. Please, not elves.

"*Aydan!*" The voice sounded familiar. My brain slowly engaged.

"Spider?" I mumbled.

"Aydan, hang on! The police and ambulance are coming!"

I groaned. God. Not another friggin' ambulance ride. I opened my eyes. "Spider, please tell me you're dressed like an elf."

"What?"

"Oh, God. I'm so fucked."

"What? No! I mean, yeah, I'm dressed like an elf."

I let out a whimper of relief. "I'm not even going to ask why. Cancel the ambulance, Spider, I'm fine."

"No, I don't think you are," he quavered.

I rolled over and sat up painfully, despite Spider's attempts to convince me to lie still. The remaining elves had distributed themselves between sitting on Bill Harks and his still-moaning buddy. They were doing a pretty good job of restraining them. Considering they were elves...

Two of the elves were texting furiously. Another

stood apart from the group, holding his phone at arms' length as he recorded the scene on video.

"Okay, no, I have to know. Why are you dressed like an elf?" I demanded.

The skidding of tires on asphalt interrupted his reply as Kane's black Expedition rocked to a halt beside us. I recognized Kane's smooth, fast combat mode as he bailed out and reached my side in a few quick steps. He spared a brief, incredulous glance at Spider's costume before focusing on me.

"What happened." Flat, expressionless cop voice.

I sighed and leaned over to dribble a bit of blood from the cut inside my mouth. "Harks and his buddy decided to tune me up a bit." I surveyed the bloodstains and ground-in dirt on the torn remains of one of my nicer blouses. "I'm never fucking dressing up again," I mumbled.

The elf who'd been recording the video bounded up to Spider. "Dude, this is mad cool! I got just about the whole fight scene! Watch this... She ducks, she nuts him, bam! Sweet! And then our guys come in. Swarm the troll! AWESOME!"

Kane's large hand closed around the elf's phone.

"Hey, dude, that's my phone," the elf protested.

"No, it's evidence." Kane's flat stare and expressionless voice made the kid step back a pace.

"But, man..." He subsided and trailed away disconsolately as Spider made shooing motions.

The ambulance pulled up, sirens blaring. The rest of the women from Lola's party tumbled out of the building to form a gasping, exclaiming ring around the scene. Elves chattered, Harks swore and blustered, and Red-shirt threw up.

"Get me out of here," I muttered to Kane.

"Right." He picked me up and carried me to the ambulance.

"You're showing off again."

"Stay at the hospital until I come for you. That's an order."

"Roger that." I sighed and let the stretcher roll me into the ambulance for the second time in two days.

CHAPTER 24

This time, the doctor on call was a hard-looking middle-aged man. He eyed me with barely concealed resignation as I was wheeled in. "What happened?"

"A couple of guys attacked me. It's just minor scrapes and bruises. I just have to wait here until Kane collects me. Sorry."

His eyebrows went up. "A couple of guys? Who?"

"Bill Harks and one of his buddies."

"And you have minor scrapes and bruises." He shook his head. "Now I've seen everything."

The paramedic grinned. "You should see the other guys."

"I'd love to." The doctor's savage smile made me think that perhaps the Hippocratic Oath wasn't uppermost in his mind. He turned to me. "Let's get those abrasions cleaned up. Where did you get hit?"

I slouched tiredly as the doctor picked the last of the gravel out of the road rash on my shoulder. My entire body throbbed slowly. Kane's voice broke my dull reverie. "How's it going?"

"Dandy."

The doctor taped on the last dressing. "You're done. Next time you're going to roll around on gravel, try wearing riding leathers."

"I'll keep that in mind." I groaned my way off the examining table and turned to Kane. "Please tell me I can go home to bed now."

He eyed me with sympathy. "Soon. Come on out to the truck. I need to get your statement."

I plodded beside him. "Aren't you going to carry me?"

He laughed. "I wouldn't want to show off."

"Yeah, now you get all modest."

He paused in the lobby. "You sit here. I'll bring the truck around."

"No, it's okay. I'm just bitching because I can. I'd rather walk so I don't stiffen up so much."

We made our way slowly out to the Expedition, and I hoisted myself into the passenger's seat with a grunt. I really hadn't taken that many hits. I hated to think what would have happened if not for the onslaught of elves. Come to think of it, I never did find out about the elves. Maybe I didn't want to know.

"Aydan."

I jerked upright and managed to muffle my yelp of pain. "Sorry. Did you ask me something?"

"Tell me what happened. Start to finish."

I explained the whole sordid story while we drove back to where I'd left the Corvette. Kane parked and raised an eyebrow at me. "You're just a magnet for trouble, aren't you?"

"Tell me about it. I lived forty-five years without the slightest hint of trouble. Then I move out to the country to live the quiet life, and I turn into a punching bag for the entire friggin' universe."

"Well, you won't need to worry about Harks for a while. He won't be released again before his trial. Thanks to that stupid kid, there's a video record of most of the fight. At least he called the police right away, but it's too bad he didn't have the brains to help you sooner."

I shrugged. "He's an elf. What can you do?" I glanced over at his profile in the dark. "Dare I ask why Spider was dressed up as an elf?"

Kane lifted a shoulder. "It's some World of Warcraft thing. They were over at the internet cafe, gaming."

"Thank God. I took a hit, and when I opened my eyes, I saw elves. I thought I had a head injury for sure."

"If not for those elves, you'd have more than a head injury."

I sighed. "Yeah. Can I go home now? Oh, did they arrest Red-shirt, too?"

"Yes."

"Good. I'm pretty sure he was the one who was harassing me with the phone calls. Maybe I'll get some sleep tonight."

Kane took my abraded hand gently in his. "Go home. Get some sleep. Drive carefully."

"Don't worry. I wouldn't take a chance on cracking up my baby."

He chuckled. "Whatever keeps you safe."

I rumbled home without enjoying the ride as much as I could have under other circumstances. I took a couple of ibuprofens and eased myself carefully into bed. It took a long time to fall asleep.

The peal of the phone made me moan and squint blearily at the clock. Three forty-five. I'd slept for less than two hours. The phone rang again.

"Noooo." I buried my face in the pillow.

I fumbled the phone off the hook on the third ring. "What."

Silence on the other end.

I groaned and hung up. Guess I'd been screaming again. I briefly considered dragging myself out to the garage, but the effort was too much for me. I pulled the covers over my head.

Morning came too early, so I ignored it. By eleven, the aching stiffness of lying in bed outweighed my apathy, and I crept painfully into the shower. The hot water seared my raw skin, but soothed the sore muscles underneath. By the time I stepped out, I could almost turn my head without whimpering.

I eased myself into shorts and a tank top, preferring to leave my damaged skin uncovered in the open air instead of replacing the dressings with their itchy adhesive. Then I shuffled into the kitchen and ate a bowl of cereal. It wasn't much of a lunch, but I was out of leftovers, and I didn't feel like making anything.

The warm breeze beckoned through the open window, and I answered the call. Out of range of the exterior cameras, I sank into my chair in the warm shade and slowly stretched out my legs.

I really wasn't hurt that badly. A few scrapes and bruises and sore muscles weren't really a big deal. But after the stress and fatigue of the past few weeks, I couldn't seem to shake off the urge to just curl up and cry. I took a deep breath and determinedly rerouted my mind to my bookkeeping clients. I'd have to do a little desk work today, just to be ready for next week.

My eyes were welling up in spite of myself when

Tom's half-ton pulled up at the gate. A small moan escaped me. If I'd been sitting around the back of the house, I could have ignored him, and he'd never have even known I was here. But I was in plain sight, so I hauled myself stiffly to my feet and did my best to hide my limp while I trod carefully across the lawn. Apparently, I'd landed on my butt at some point last night, too.

He swung out of the truck as I approached. His smile vanished when I got close enough for him to see my injuries. I cursed myself for not putting on a T-shirt and jeans to hide the scrapes. I looked like I'd gone a couple of rounds with a renegade belt sander.

"Aydan, what happened?" he demanded. "Were you in an accident?"

I grunted as I unlocked the gate and swung it open. "Accident for me. On purpose for the other guys."

"Who did this to you?" His eyes blazed with blue fury.

"Bill Harks and his buddy. And don't worry, they're in jail. Where they'll stay for a while."

"Two of them? Two of them attacked you?" His fists clenched into hard knots.

"Yeah, brave guys. They cornered me last night in town." I really didn't feel like going into it, so I changed the subject. "What's up?"

"Shouldn't you be in the hospital?"

I sighed. "I got cleaned up there last night. I've just got a few bruises and some scrapes from rolling around on the pavement. It's nothing serious."

"Aydan, you can hardly move." His tanned face was creased with worry.

I shrugged slowly and carefully. "Harks decided to

sling me around by my hair, so my neck's pretty stiff today. It'll settle down in a couple of days."

Anger blazed from his eyes again, and I held up a restraining hand. "It's no big deal. They're in jail. It's all good." I tried again. "So what's up?"

I could tell he didn't want to let it go, but after a few seconds, he sighed and turned back toward the truck. "We had far too much food at the potluck last night, as usual. I thought if you were still feeling under the weather from yesterday, you might appreciate some of it." He frowned again. "I didn't realize how under the weather you were going to be."

"Food?" My stomach emitted an eager growl. I clapped a hand over it. "Sorry. Comments from the peanut gallery."

He gave me his crooked smile as he indicated the cardboard box on the seat. "Where do you want it?"

I considered. I didn't really want him near the house, but I also didn't really feel like carrying a heavy box of food today, either. Fuck it. He was just a neighbour. As long as Stemp didn't see him too frequently, he should be safe.

"Why don't you just drive on up to the house with it, and I'll put it in the fridge."

"Okay, hop in. It'll save you the walk." That seemed like a fine idea. I climbed carefully into the passenger seat.

He pulled up in front of the house, and I held the door for him while he brought the box inside. As I unpacked the food on the kitchen counter, my stomach growled again.

Tom gave me a quizzical look. "Maybe you should eat some of this right now."

I grinned at him. "I was trying to be polite and not stuff my face in front of you."

"Forget that." I got the crooked smile again. "Where are your plates?"

I loaded up a plate, exclaiming over the variety of food while my stomach roared its eagerness. I packed the remainder of the food into the fridge and made for the front door, carrying my plate. The sooner he was out of the house and away from the bugs and cameras, the better.

"I'm going to eat this outside," I told him. "I've been cooped up inside buildings all week."

He got the door for me and followed me out. I'd half-hoped he'd leave, but instead, he followed me out to my chair in the shade. I sat carefully, and he lowered himself to the grass, leaning back on his elbows with his long, denim-clad legs stretched out.

I dug into the food enthusiastically, and he squinted up at me from the ground, the lines crimping around his eyes. "You were starving. And your fridge was completely empty. Don't you have any food in the house?"

"I've got tons of food in the freezer," I told him. "I've just been too lazy to cook lately."

He gave me a piercing look. "I wouldn't say lazy. I'd say you've had a tough week."

Uncharacteristic tears threatened again. I hate sympathy. I swallowed hard and looked away. "Yeah, not one of my better weeks," I agreed lightly. "Hey, I meant to ask you. Or somebody who knows more about hay than I do, anyway. What's up with my hay field up there?"

He glanced up the hill. "What do you mean?"

"It looks pretty sad to me. Should I be doing something with it?"

The conversation veered to farming, and I relaxed into the comfortable topic while I finished the excellent food.

I scraped the plate clean, and leaned over slowly and stiffly to put it on the ground.

Tom turned a troubled face to me. "I wish there was something I could do to make you feel better."

"Not unless you can recommend a massage therapist." I eased my aching neck around to give him a rueful smile. "I know a good guy in Calgary, but I'm not up to driving two hours to see him."

"There's one in Silverside, but I know she's on vacation this week." He frowned. "If you'd like, I could probably help a bit. I don't have any training, but one of the women I dated for a while was a registered massage therapist, and she taught me a lot."

I threw caution to the winds at the glorious thought of somebody, anybody, doing something to ease my screaming neck and shoulders. "Would you? That would be wonderful."

"Sure." He rose and looked down at me dubiously. "You should lie down."

"I don't think I can. I'm too sore." Also, I had no intention of bringing him anywhere near the house.

"Tell me if I hurt you, then." He stepped behind me and stroked my hair away from my back. His firm, gentle hands started to work my shoulders and neck.

I slouched forward and propped my head in my hands as the heavenly touch eased my stiffened muscles. A small moan escaped me, and he stopped instantly. "Did I hurt you?"

"No. That feels amazing."

He started again, and I blinked back tears of gratitude. Even if he'd been doing a lousy job, the caring touch of his hands would have been worth it. And he wasn't doing a lousy job. Far from it.

I lost track of time while I floated mindlessly. Finally, he stopped, and I did my best not to whimper a complaint.

"I have to get going now. Sorry," he said.

I straightened slowly in the chair, and then dragged myself to my feet. "Thank you. I feel so much better now."

He smiled, his eyes soft as the summer sky. "Good." He hesitated. "Aydan... I hope you'll call me if you ever need help. I'm here for you if you do."

I blinked and swallowed. "Thanks, Tom." I cursed the quiver in my voice. Suck it up, for chrissake.

He surveyed my face for a second, and then stepped forward and put his arms around me. I gulped hard. I really didn't want to get involved with him. And I do not cry in public.

I managed to hold out for a couple of seconds before I slid my arms around his lean body and hid my face in his shoulder. We stood in silence while I struggled for composure. His corded arms held my aching body as softly as if I might break.

And I might.

I took a deep breath and pulled away.

He let me go immediately, and took my hand gently instead. "Call me if you need me."

I didn't meet his eyes. "I will."

CHAPTER 25

I heard the phone ring through the open window, and trailed back into the house. The message on the machine was from Lola, worrying about me. I called her back and chatted for a few minutes, reassuring her.

I blinked heavy eyes at my heaped-up desk in the stuffy office. I was trying to motivate myself when the phone rang again, and I picked up to another of the women from the previous evening, expressing concern.

I hung up after the short conversation and sighed. Then I tucked my cell phone in my pocket and made for the garage. I opened the main door to let in the breeze and curled up in my comfortable nest in the corner.

A couple of hours later, I finally roused myself and creaked back into the house. My body still hurt, but the urge to cry was gone. I headed for my desk, feeling much more positive, and immersed myself in the pleasantly predictable world of bookkeeping.

The phone rang frequently as several more of my new friends from the previous evening called to check on me, along with Spider, Blue Eddy, Jeff Latchford, and Kane.

By suppertime, I was feeling thoroughly loved, my bookkeeping work was caught up, and my fridge was still full of delicious food. The phone rang again, and I smiled as I picked up.

"Hello?"

"Watch your back, bitch. I'll be waiting for you."

A lump of ice formed in the pit of my stomach. "Who is this?"

"You'll find out." Click.

I sat and regarded the receiver as it trembled in my hand for a moment. Then I laid it carefully back in the cradle. My newfound optimism somewhat dented, I headed for the kitchen and consoled myself with potluck leftovers.

With my belly filled, the world looked rosier. I put the dishes into the dishwasher with a shrug. Whatever. I was in no more danger than before. Stemp's analysts would be busily tracing that call.

I got to bed early and managed to sleep most of the night. Only one call with silence on the other end, which I chose to regard as comforting. Somebody was looking out for me. And only one more nocturnal threat. Could have been worse.

I crept stiffly out of bed and made a point of being showered, dressed, and ready to go when Kane arrived at eight-thirty. "How are you feeling?" he asked sympathetically as I climbed carefully into the Expedition.

"Pretty good today, actually. Still stiff and sore, but it's better already."

"Good."

"Did your guys get a trace on those calls?"

"Public phone at the Silverside Hotel again. But we couldn't find anyone who could tell us who'd been using it. Everything is in chaos over there now that Harks is in custody. The owners are trying to find a replacement for him, and nobody knows what's going on."

"Harks wasn't the owner?"

"No, just general manager."

I snorted. "Well, anybody they hire will be an improvement."

As we pulled up outside Sirius, my heart sank. Kane turned to study my face. "Are you okay?"

I sighed. The hand tremor was back. "All in all, I think I prefer taking a shit-kicking in the open air to living unscathed underground. As long as I'm outside, I have the illusion that I might be able to escape."

He regarded me in silence, his face troubled. I lifted a painful shoulder. "Let's go do it."

I made it into Spider's lab without panicking. I sank slowly into my usual chair, breathing deeply and carefully.

"We're going to do things a little differently today," Kane informed me. "Webb will monitor from the lab as usual, but I'm going to come into the network with you. If you're incapacitated for any reason, I'll be able to get you out."

"Or we'll both die in there."

"No." Kane shook his head. "That won't happen. Don't forget, I can be woken from the network easily from outside the sim. It's only dangerous for you because you can't be roused from your trance externally when you use the key."

I gave him a wry look. "Are you sure you want to come in with me? How are your pigshit-dodging skills?"

He laughed. "My job in the sim is to create virtual umbrellas."

"Yeah, that would have worked. Too bad I didn't think of it."

"You were doing more important work. Speaking of

which, Stemp wants you to take a new direction today. He wants you to leave the files for today and get into the network traffic to see if you can track down some more IPs for Fuzzy Bunny's sites."

I frowned at Spider. "Any suggestions? I really don't know what I'm doing."

He returned a shrug. "Whatever you did before worked. I know how I'd do it if I was working externally, but your sim visualized things entirely differently than I would have. Just go with what you did before. If that doesn't work, we can collaborate on an approach."

"Okay," I sighed. "Wish me luck." I closed my eyes and concentrated on stepping into the network void.

My heart lurched as I entered, but there was only familiar whiteness this time. Just as Kane popped into existence beside me, a wisp of black mist drifted by, carrying the faint reek of burned flesh.

"What was that?" he demanded.

"Sorry. I just..." I took a deep breath, and stood on the mountain top. It still looked flat and two-dimensional, and I struggled to open the long vista. I sagged with sudden relief when the scent of spruce came to my nose. The crisp, fresh breeze sighed across the deep valley. I flopped onto the ground before my wobbling knees could drop me.

Kane sat down beside me. I gave him a quick sideways glance. "Thanks. Nice umbrella."

His mouth quirked up, but his eyes were grave. "You're welcome."

I sighed. "Well, I guess I'll start poking around. I don't really know what this is going to look like to you. Last time I did this, it was kind of like... being sentient Silly Putty. Or something. I kind of stretched in all different directions.

And I need to be invisible."

"This is going to be complicated." Kane frowned. "I don't dare try to follow you. The key makes you undetectable, but I'd stick out like a sore thumb with my fob. But if I can't see you, I won't know if you need help."

"Spider? Any ideas?" I asked the virtual sky.

"I haven't a clue," he admitted. "I don't even know how you did it the first time. I don't know what your rules would be."

"Shit!" I churned my hands in my hair. After a couple of minutes of thought, I turned to Kane. "Okay, let's try this." I took his hand. "I'll turn invisible and stretch wherever I need to go, but I won't let go of your hand. If I squeeze your hand, or if you need to bring me back, just start pulling."

I gave him a wry grimace. "It might take a while to reel me in. I might be on the other side of the globe."

He scowled and took a firmer grip on my hand. "Okay."

I faded into invisibility, and felt Kane's hand tighten reflexively around mine. Then I let the sim dissolve around me, and floated my consciousness up into the tunnels and corridors of the network.

I effortlessly intercepted and opened data packets, snooping on network messages and services. My invisible self was infinitely flexible, and I stretched into multiple channels simultaneously, sniffing my way along. Vast amounts of data rushed by me, and I absorbed it as easily as a dark cloth absorbs sunlight.

I found the files in the virtual file room, and poured my attention like water over and around them. I didn't bother to interpret their content. Instead, I touched and smelled and tasted, listening to the faint echoes of electronic signatures. I needed to find a path that felt like these files.

Casting down infinite corridors, I caught a sudden whiff. My consciousness snapped into focus, burrowing down the corridor. Yes, this was definitely the right one. I methodically backtracked, holding the scent.

Kane jerked in shock when I snapped back into existence beside him. He was clutching my hand painfully, and I gave our clasped hands a little shake. "Go easy, Superman."

"Sorry." His grip loosened a bit. "Your hand just… shrank. To almost nothing. I could barely feel it."

"Mm. Oh well. Hey, Spider, I've got some IPs."

"Great, shoot!"

I passed the first batch over to him. "I'll go and get the rest. Hang tight."

I quested down the tunnel again, snapping back to report IP addresses as I discovered them. Finally, the scent led me to a firewall. I poked my virtual head cautiously through, sampling the data packets. Triumph flowed through my attenuated body.

Gotcha!

I laid a careful trail of virtual breadcrumbs on my way back.

I flopped on my back on the mountain-top, gasping and grinning.

"What?" Kane demanded.

"I got one. Found one of Fuzzy Bunny's sites."

"Are you sure?"

"If it smells like a bunny and tastes like a bunny, it must be a bunny. Hey, Spider, can you see my breadcrumbs?"

I heard his laugh through the network interface. "You have the most bizarre sim imagery. But yes, I can track the markers you left. It'll just take me a while."

"Good, then we'll take a break," Kane said. "It's past lunch time."

I gazed up at him from my supine position. "That explains why I feel like I can see through my stomach."

He glanced over, and then looked away. "I *can* see through your stomach. Let's get out of this stupid sim."

"Sorry." I tried to pull myself together. Literally. My body oozed like tar over the warm rocks.

"Stop," Kane said firmly. "Come on, let's dance."

Vertigo whirled through my head as the mountain top changed to a ballroom. A waltz played, and I stepped into his arms. He waltzed me expertly over the portal, and we went through together.

I moaned and swore as the pain ripped through my head. The aches and bruises of my real-world body pounded me again, and I keened miserably for a few moments.

Straightening up was a punishing effort. My body had stiffened considerably after being immobile in the chair for so long. When I finally groaned my way upright, Kane and Webb were both watching me with worried eyes.

I bit back the last of the obscenities. "Thanks for getting me out. That was smart."

Kane grimaced. "I was hoping a complete change of context would shock you into concentrating again. I'm glad it worked. The only other idea I had was to try to pour you into a pail."

"That would have been... disturbing."

"It was disturbing enough as it was, thanks," he replied. "Come on, let's get lunch."

At the Melted Spoon, turned heads and whispers greeted me. Apparently the rumour mill had been in full swing. I shifted uncomfortably and stared at the menu board while I waited in line. Beside me, Kane stood impassive.

A small, elderly man rose from his table and was making his way to the door when he spotted me standing in the lineup. He veered over and patted my arm gently on the way by. "Good job, honey."

I was gazing after him open-mouthed when Kane nudged me. "You're up."

"Oh." I turned to give my order to the woman behind the counter. When I reached for my wallet, she smiled and shook her head. "On the house. You did what a lot of us have wanted to do for a long time."

I shook my head, baffled. "What, get beaten up by a couple of losers? You can have it."

"No. Stood up to a couple of bullies." She handed me my sandwich. "Enjoy."

"Thanks..." I drifted away to a corner table, bemused.

Harks wasn't a popular guy. By the time I'd finished my lunch, several other people had dropped by the table to congratulate me, though I couldn't imagine why. I tried to explain that I hadn't done anything except failed to run away, but nobody seemed to want to hear the facts. After the third attempt, Kane leaned over. "Don't bother. They want a hero, and you're it."

I grimaced and gulped the last of my sandwich. "Let's get out of here."

A pale, thin young woman stopped me on my way out. "I'm so glad you fought back," she whispered. "I wish I had."

Something in her face stopped me in my tracks. I cut my eyes to Kane, and he stepped casually outside the restaurant to wait. "Did he assault you?" I asked quietly.

"Yes." She hung her head. "But I was too scared to tell anybody. He said if I told, he'd... do terrible things to me."

I took her hands. "Tell the police now. He can't hurt you anymore, and every woman who comes forward will strengthen the case against him."

She backed away. "No, I couldn't. I'm not brave enough."

I sighed. "I know how scary it is. But you're not the only one, I know it. Just think how much good it would do if every woman he'd attacked went to the police now."

She met my eyes timidly, and I smiled at her. "Just think about it, okay?"

"I will." She turned away quickly, and I went outside to join Kane.

He paced easily beside me as I marched along the sidewalk. "What's wrong?" he asked. I took a deep breath and unclenched my fists.

"That asshole Harks has been assaulting women all over town. And then he threatens them to keep them quiet."

"Was that woman one of his victims?"

"Yes. And she's still too scared to come forward. I tried to encourage her, but... Jesus, I wish I could have kicked his ass the way he deserved!"

"You did something better. You made sure he'll get punished for what he's done."

I felt my lips twist as I looked up at him. "You really believe that? He'll get a slap on the wrist, and come out even meaner and uglier than he is now."

Kane sighed. "Maybe. Maybe not, if more women come forward."

"Well, I'll start spreading the word, then. Maybe some good can come out of this after all." I looked up as Sirius Dynamics loomed in front of me again. "Godforsaken hellhole."

"Please get that thought out of your mind before you go into the sim again," Kane said seriously.

CHAPTER 26

I took a deep breath and clasped my hands together. They trembled visibly anyway. Along with the rest of my body. I closed my eyes and leaned back in my chair, belly breathing and doing my best to clear my mind. The trip down the stairs had been like being slowly buried alive. Breeze and sun blotted out, replaced with canned air and canned light.

I tried to refocus. That imagery wasn't helping. I opened my eyes again, and the institutional grey of the walls advanced on me. Prison walls.

Jesus!

Spider and Kane were watching me worriedly. I swiped my hand over my aching face. "Just trying to get focused before I go in."

I clamped my eyes shut again and imagined my hillside. I clung to the warm, sweet alfalfa smell, the buzzing of the insects in the grass, the long stretch of fields locked in their wild dance with the wind. The sun baked down on my back, and I stretched my pain-free body.

Kane smiled over at me. "That's better."

I sucked in a breath and the vista contracted rapidly around me when I realized I'd stepped into the sim.

"No, stay with it," Kane encouraged. I wrapped my arms around myself and repressed a whimper. Bars sprang up around me, but Kane was instantly on his feet, holding them back. "No," he said firmly. "You control this. It doesn't control you."

I held onto his words and held onto the sight of him holding back the bars. They slowly dissolved, and the sun came out again. I took a deep breath. "Okay. I'm okay now. Thanks."

I breathed some more. "Okay. I'm going to go and see if I can put a bug on that Fuzzy Bunny server." Kane reached for my hand, and I stretched my invisible body along my path of breadcrumbs.

I seeped through the firewall and floated through the enemy network, stealthy as air. I sniffed through their files and noted their automated synchronization routines with satisfaction. I'd be back another day to sneak along the tunnels to their other facilities. Today, I had something different in mind.

I teased delicate tendrils into their services and applications, and created miniscule pinholes in firewalls. I built a tiny, invisible bug to skitter along my gossamer pathways, listening and learning. And then I stretched an infinitesimally fine thread behind me as I eased my way back into the sim.

Back in the home network, I carefully constructed the ear that would listen to my new little creation. Ever so gently, I connected the thread, and breathed life into the system. The tiny thread vibrated as the data began to stream down it, and I smiled. Yes, this was good.

At last, I turned my attention to the tugging on my virtual arm. I snapped into existence in front of Kane, stumbling into him as he yanked my hand.

"Aydan!" His eyes were dark with worry. "What happened? Where were you? I've been pulling on your hand, and it just... stretched. I couldn't get a grip on you."

My knees wobbled, and I sat hurriedly on the ground. My head spun. "Sorry. I was setting up a surveillance system," I said distantly. The hillside spun faster. Like a tornado.

"Stop!" Kane's voice was powerful over the roaring of the wind. "You control this." He stood in the eye of the storm, his reality unaffected by the chaos around us. He reached out a hand, and I took it, letting him pull me inside the circle of calm.

He looked into my eyes. "Aydan, focus. Let's go to the portal."

I tried. God help me, I tried.

The wave crashed over me, ripping my hand out of Kane's and slamming me into the ocean floor. Helpless as a rag doll, I rolled and tumbled as rocks gouged my flesh. Flailing wildly, I tried to gulp a mouthful of air, but choked on sand and water instead.

Drowning. My heart thundered in my ears.

Suffocating.

Mindless panic took me as I thrashed and struggled against the merciless bars. They squeezed tighter as I sank into the darkening depths. My lungs couldn't expand. There was no air for them anyway. My racing heart began to slow.

Through the twilit green, my last sight was of Kane as he parted the water and lifted me, cage and all.

Then his lips were on mine, and I knew nothing but pain.

The pain began to subside, but Kane was still kissing me. That was nice. First good thing today. I lay passively.

Maybe I should respond. Most guys appreciate that.
It seemed like a lot of effort, though.

I lay still a while longer, enjoying the sensation in a
detached sort of way. Yeah, just keep doing that. That's
nice.

He pulled away, his face rigid as he cradled my head
in his hands. "Come on, Aydan! Breathe!"

And suddenly, I desperately needed air. I sucked in
a long, wheezing breath, then another, gasping and panting
as my body jerked with my struggle.

"That's it," he encouraged. "Keep breathing."

As I finally achieved a ragged rhythm and began to
register my surroundings, Spider dashed in the door,
followed by Mike Connor, the security analyst who did
double-duty as a paramedic for Sirius staff. Mike stopped
short.

"Aydan!" he stammered. "My God... Thank God...
you're alive." He quickly knelt beside me and hooked up a
portable oxygen cylinder. He worked in silent concentration,
checking monitors and watching me closely.

At last, I caught my breath. "Hi, Mike. Long time no
see."

He squeezed my hand. "I missed you. It's been,
what, four months since the last time I peeled you off the
ground?"

I chuckled weakly. He was such a nice young guy.
"Yeah. I thought I'd see you sooner. Have you been away?"

"Vacation. Don't talk so much just yet. Just breathe
for a little while."

I nodded and concentrated on inflating my lungs.
The oxygen seemed to be helping.

Finally, he checked the monitor. "Okay, your sats

are back up to normal. Let's try it without the mask for a bit."

I let him slip the mask off. "Sats?"

"Oxygen saturation in your blood. You were down really low."

"Oh."

Everybody stood around and watched me breathe for a while longer. "Can I get up now?" I begged. "I feel fine."

"Okay, why don't you get up and sit in the chair for a few minutes?" Mike agreed.

I rose unsteadily as Kane hovered. I took the few steps to the chair, and sat stiffly. Connor consulted his monitors. "That's fine. I think you'll be okay now. You should probably go over to the hospital and get checked out thoroughly, though."

"Do I really have to? I was just there. Twice. In two days. Three times in a row just seems a little much."

Connor chuckled. "If you really don't want to, I don't think there's any pressing need. If you start to feel faint, though, call the ambulance right away." He turned to Spider. "Keep an eye on her for a little longer. I have to get back to work. World of Warcraft tonight?"

"It's a plan. See you then," Spider told him.

"I really need to get out of here," I said, holding onto calm with both hands. Or maybe clinging to it with my fingernails. My heart rate increased again at the sight of the prison-grey walls. Definitely fingernails.

"Okay, let's go," Kane said soothingly. He stayed close as I rose carefully from the chair and made my way stiffly down the hall. By the time I reached the top of the stairs, my heart was pounding and I was panting shallow, rapid breaths. Kane took a firm hold on my elbow as we reached the top of the stairs.

I shook him off when we stepped into the time-delayed chamber, and he understandingly flattened himself against the wall again. When the door released at last, I stumbled light-headedly out into the lobby. "Outside," I mumbled as I wove my way toward the door.

"Hold on." Kane quickly unclipped my security fob and dropped it at the desk along with his. In a couple of quick strides, he was by my side again, his hand under my elbow.

I tottered outside and leaned against the scorching wall. Sweat sprang out all over me. Kane peered down at me in concern, still holding my arm firmly. "Aydan, sit. You look like you're going to faint."

He dragged me to the steps and lowered me onto the top one. I got my breathing under control again. "No, I'm okay. Just hyperventilated a bit, I think."

"Nice change from not breathing at all."

I lifted a painful shoulder. "What can I say. I like variety."

We sat for a few more minutes, and then I stood up. "Let's go back inside. I need to talk to Spider."

"No," Kane said flatly. "You're done. That's the second time you've nearly died in the sim. No more."

"I won't argue," I promised him. "I have no intention of going back into the secured area. But I absolutely have to talk to Spider right away. Can we go up to the second floor?"

He eyed me dubiously. "All right. But just a short meeting. Then you need to eat, and go home."

I glanced at my watch. Five o'clock. No wonder I was so hungry. "Deal. In fact, if you've still got some of that orange juice upstairs, I'll have some of that."

"Fine." He followed me in. "You go on up. Webb and I will meet you in a few minutes."

I retrieved my fob from the security wicket and made my way up to the second-floor employee lounge, where I collected a bottle of orange juice. Then I slipped into the office that should have been mine, and leaned back on the small sofa, sipping.

In a few minutes, Kane and Spider arrived. Kane swung the door shut behind him, and they sat. Spider leaned forward eagerly. "What did you do in the sim? I found a very interesting little piece of software."

I grinned at him. "I've bugged their server. Kind of. I don't know what the right word for it would be. But for every email that goes through, for every new file that's created, a copy will get dumped to our network."

"Sweet!" Spider beamed at me. "I can hardly wait to see what comes through. Are you stealing their whole system?"

"No. It's only going to collect anything that's active. I plan to sneak back in there and check over their files later. And I'll be able to tunnel into their synch sites, too."

"That assumes that you go in again," Kane said. "As of right now, you're grounded. No more network access at all. Not unless we can figure out a way to make sure that you won't die in there."

"But I need to..."

"You need to stay alive. I barely got you out in time. We can't risk that again."

"Hmm." I tugged a lock of hair. "Let me think about it. There has to be a way."

"Maybe, but not tonight. Go over your software

setup with Webb, and then go home. That's an order."

"Aren't you the bossy one?" I grinned at his frown.
"For once in my life, I'll obey willingly. I can hardly wait to
get out of here."

It was well after six by the time I staggered out the
door. But my little pet software program was humming
along beautifully, and Spider and his team of analysts would
monitor it 'round the clock. I went home feeling I'd truly
accomplished something.

CHAPTER 27

I pulled up in front of my house smiling. Yeah, I'd almost died. Again. Yeah, my entire body still hurt. But I'd kicked Fuzzy Bunny's furry ass today. And I still had good food in the fridge. And it was still daylight. And I didn't have to go back underground tomorrow.

I grinned from ear to ear and did fist-pump on my way to the house, before recalling with chagrin that a) I was on camera; and b) a fist-pump hurt like hell. I scuttled into the house and repressed the urge to sing while I assembled a plate for supper. No need to torture the poor sucker who'd gotten stuck with bug duty tonight.

I gobbled my meal with more enthusiasm than I'd had in a couple of weeks. I did a few chores around the house, and then headed out to my garden. I was glad I'd done some hoeing before my dance with Harks and his buddy, so I didn't have to overtax my sore body. I puttered happily along the rows, hand-weeding here and nibbling fresh peas there. I had just crouched down to examine the blossoms on my beans when I heard a thud, and a small fountain of dirt kicked up about six feet to my left.

I barely had time to register surprise before the echoing crack of a high-powered rifle reached my ears. All my muscles convulsed simultaneously as the electric shock of adrenaline hit. I sprang up with a yelp and ran flat out for the house, ducking and dodging. My muscles screamed protest, but I wasn't inclined to listen to the complaints as several more shots rang out.

I only saw one of them hit the ground, ahead and several yards to my right. I rocketed up the front steps two at a time and burst into the house.

"Somebody's shooting at me, rifle from the northwest," I gasped as I pounded toward the basement stairs. "Going to the basement. I'm armed. Identify yourselves before you come in."

I plunged down the stairs and jerked around the corner to my gun locker, my breath sobbing in my chest. Goddamn gun laws! I scrabbled frantically at the lock with violently shaking hands.

Finally, it gave, and I snatched my 12-gauge shotgun and .22-250 rifle out of the case. I realized I was cursing loudly between gasps as I grabbed my ammo box. Stored separately. Just like a good little citizen. If I got shot because I couldn't get armed fast enough, I was going to come back and haunt whoever made up these laws.

I flung myself into a corner, two solid concrete walls at my back, and fumbled the shells into the shotgun first. I spilled the rifle shells in my wild haste. My swearing ratcheted up a notch. Scrambling on hands and knees, I scooped up a handful of bullets and stuffed four into the magazine, cursing my clumsy hands.

I jammed my back into the corner and looped the strap of the shotgun over my shoulder for easy access while I held the rifle. And then I waited.

My entire body shook uncontrollably, and I wedged myself more tightly into the corner, hoping my knees wouldn't give way. All was silent except for the pounding of my heart and the sound of my panting. I stared at the base of the stairs until my eyes watered. Blink. Right. I could do that.

Minutes ticked by, and I spared a quick glance at my watch. I had no sense of how much time had passed. How long would it take for Stemp's analysts to raise the alarm, and how long would it take for help to arrive after that? Please, please, let them come quickly.

And while I was at it, I added a plea that they'd remember to identify themselves before they came downstairs. God, what if I shot one of the good guys by mistake? I gulped hard as the trembling redoubled.

My ass vibrated, and I almost leaped out of my skin. Christ, I'd forgotten I'd put my cell phone in my back pocket before heading out to the garden. I fumbled it out of my pocket. Kane. Thank God.

I juggled the rifle and the phone. The phone lost.

"Goddammit!"

It hit the concrete floor and sprayed pieces in all directions.

"Goddamn snot-gobbling sonuvabitch fuck-pig..." I carefully set the loaded guns down and floundered across the floor, retrieving the battery pack, case, and backing. I jammed them back together and held my breath as I powered it back on.

A creak sounded from the main floor overhead, and I wedged myself frantically back into the corner. I snatched up the rifle and damn near dropped the phone again. Too frightened to even swear, I stuffed the phone back in my pocket and pressed the rifle butt against my shoulder, my chest heaving. I'd be lucky if I could hit the side of a barn at this rate.

The unmistakeable sound of my front door opening

made me jerk the gun up into ready position. The floor creaked again as someone moved stealthily across it.

My phone vibrated again. A tiny, silly part of my mind noted that I should have put in my front pocket instead. At least I could've gotten a cheap thrill before I died. I blinked hard and refocused while the vibration in my back pocket continued.

It was probably Kane, but I couldn't spare a hand to answer. The rifle was heavy. There was no way I could one-hand it. And there was no way I was going die of stupidity, talking on my cell phone instead of pointing my gun.

The quiet movement above continued. Somebody was methodically searching the house. Very soon, they'd come downstairs.

At the sound of a creak from the top of the stairs, I nestled my cheek into the stock. Show time.

The crosshairs bounced crazily as I trained them on the base of the stairs. With any luck, the intruder wouldn't see me immediately. He'd have to turn at the bottom of the stairs before he did. My overused muscles screamed with pain and fatigue from the weight of the rifle. Come on, asshole. Hurry up. Before I fall down from sheer exhaustion.

Slow, careful footsteps on the stairs.

"Aydan."

I gasped desperate relief at the sound of the whisper.

"I'm here. All clear," I quavered.

I straightened out of my crouch and let the muzzle drop as Kane spoke aloud. "I'm coming down. Don't shoot."

I gave a shaky laugh as he came around the corner. "Don't worry, you're safe. I can't hold the friggin' gun up any longer." Then my trembling knees gave out, and I slithered down the wall to sit on the floor.

He closed the distance between us fast and knelt beside me. "Are you all right?"

"Fine. What's happening up top?"

"We're securing the area. The house is clear. Germain's upstairs standing guard. We'll stay down here until we get the all-clear from JTF2."

I gaped at him. "You brought in JTF2? How the hell am I going to explain helicopters and army guys with assault rifles to my neighbours?"

Kane scowled. "That's the least of our worries. Did you get a look at the shooter?"

"Hell, no. I was too busy running. But I'm pretty sure the shots came from the northwest. And the guy had to be a lousy shot. I was a sitting duck in the garden, not even moving, and he missed me by at least six feet."

"Either that or it was extreme range."

"Could be. Somebody smart could probably do the math. The bullet hit, and then about a half-second later, I heard the shot."

"It would depend on the muzzle velocity of the rifle."

"It sounded a lot like my .22-250," I told him.

He shrugged. "Okay. Let's take that as a wild guess. Muzzle velocity on those is around thirty-five hundred to four thousand feet per second." He considered for a few seconds. "Somewhere around a thousand feet away, then. That's an easy shot, so your gunman wasn't a professional."

I gaped at him. "Okay, I'm impressed."

Kane chuckled. "Don't be. Remember, it's just a wild guess. I could be out by fifty percent or more."

"Still. You know the muzzle velocity of a .22-250 off the top of your head?"

As he shrugged, Germain's voice floated down the stairs. "All clear. Come on up."

"You go ahead," I told Kane. "I need to unload everything and put it away."

He frowned at my arsenal. "Not exactly convenient defensive weapons."

"No kidding. The guy could have strolled in and shot me before I even got the stupid gun locker open." I sighed. "I understand why we have gun laws, really I do. But I sure could've done without them today."

"Mm," he agreed, and went up the stairs.

I hunted out all the shells I'd scattered during my wild loading spree, and stowed everything carefully away again.

When I poked my head around the top of the stairs, I grinned at the sight of the blocky man cradling a sub-machine gun easily in the crook of his elbow. "Carl! Hi again!"

"Hi, Aydan." His good-natured square face crinkled into a smile. "We have to stop meeting like this."

"No kidding. Hey, you finally got your hair cut."

He laughed and ran his fingers through his crisp black curls. "Yeah. Finally. This is so much better."

"I don't know. I liked the rock-star ringlets on you."

"Very funny." His two-way radio crackled, and he turned away to reply.

The ring of the phone made me jump. Kane held up a hand and leaned over to check the call display. "It's Rossburn. You'd better pick up."

"Shit!" I reached for the receiver. "What should I tell him?"

The phone rang again. Kane made a frustrated

gesture. "Stall him. Make something up. Just answer, or he'll be coming over here wondering what's wrong."

I snatched up the receiver just before the machine picked up. "Hello?"

"Aydan, it's Tom. Is everything okay over there?"

"Everything's fine, thanks, Tom."

"Aydan," he said hesitantly. "I'm not trying to butt in, but I saw a military helicopter landing at your place."

I bared my teeth at Kane and thudded my free hand against my forehead. He rotated his hand in a 'string him along' gesture. I glared at him and tried again.

"Don't worry, it's fine." Inspiration hit me. "I have a friend who's in the military, and I offered to let them use my place for a training exercise. Nothing to worry about."

"Oh." The relief was palpable in his voice. "That explains the gunfire earlier, then, too."

"Yeah. I'm sorry, I should have let you know in advance."

"That's okay. It's none of my business, anyway. I just wanted to make sure you're all right."

"I'm fine. Thanks for checking."

I hung up the phone and made fists in my hair. "Jesus Christ. I might as well live in a fucking fish bowl."

"You handled that well," Kane said with satisfaction. "It's a good cover story, and it will explain away a lot of activity over here. Nice work, Aydan."

I shrugged to hide my pleasure at the compliment. "Thanks."

Germain hooked his radio back into its holster. "They found shell casings up on the northwest hill, about three hundred and fifty yards from the garden. Looks like .22-250. There were tire tracks leading away that look like a regular recreational quad ATV."

"Can you trace any of that?" I asked.

Kane shrugged. "The .22-250 is a pretty common rifle in rural areas, and there are lots of quads out here, too. We'll be able to trace it eventually, but it'll take time." He turned to Germain. "Which way did the tracks go?"

"Out to the road." Germain grimaced. "They could have just run along the road, or else they could have loaded it onto a trailer and driven away. No way to tell."

"Did you hear the quad?" Kane asked me.

I thought hard. "I should have been able to," I said slowly. "If it was less than a quarter mile away. Hell, I should have been able to see it if he was riding along north of my fence line."

"But you don't remember."

"No." I made a face. "I was absorbed in my garden, and the wind is from the south today. It must have carried the sound away. Or else I was a lot more tired than I realized."

I sank shakily into a chair as the truth of that statement became clear to me.

Kane regarded me with sympathy. "Why don't you go and lie down? There's nothing you can do here, and it'll take us quite a while to get everything buttoned up. You need to stay in the house until we're done anyway."

That sounded like heaven. I nodded gratefully and shuffled off to the bedroom. The sound of male voices and the noise of the helicopter floated through the open window. I smiled and fell asleep instantly.

I opened my eyes to Kane as he bent over me in the

silver moonlight. He smiled as I reached to pull him down.
He lowered himself on top of me, and my breath caught at
the sensation of his hard body against mine. His fingers
stroked through my hair while he kissed me slowly. I
moaned against his lips, running my hands down his broad,
muscular back.

"Aydan," he whispered.

I kissed him hungrily.

"Aydan."

I moaned again, feeling his touch on my shoulders,
wanting him desperately.

"Aydan." He was shaking my shoulders gently.

I frowned. That was annoying. "Stop that," I told
him.

"Aydan."

I jerked awake. Kane was stooped over the bed,
gently shaking me. "Aydan, it's okay, it was just a dream."

"I know!" I snapped. "Dammit!"

"Aydan, wake up. You were moaning in your sleep.
It was just a dream."

I sighed. "I'm awake. Thanks. I'm fine." I squinted
over at the clock. "Why are you still here? It's almost two
A.M."

"You've got a twenty-four hour guard now. Stemp's
orders. Germain is taking over at two. I'll be back to pick
you up at eight tomorrow morning. We have a meeting with
Stemp at eight thirty."

I groaned. "Yeah, I could see that coming."

"Go back to sleep," he advised. His phone buzzed in
his pocket. "That'll be Germain arriving. See you in the
morning."

"Okay. Thanks. Tell Germain not to worry if I start

screaming."

"He'll come in and wake you if you do."

I groaned. Guess I'd be sleeping in my clothes for the foreseeable future. I didn't own any nightwear.

I heard the brief rumble of male voices in the kitchen, and then tires crunched on gravel as Kane departed. I rolled over and buried my face in the pillow, not sure whether to feel comforted or smothered by the guard. Before I could decide, sunlight and birdsong woke me.

CHAPTER 28

Six thirty. I lay lethargically for a few minutes until my brain spun up to speed and reminded me that I could look forward to a major confrontation with Stemp this morning. Shit, he was going to be pissed that I'd known about the bugs all along.

I rolled stiffly out of bed and shuffled to the shower, trying to formulate a strategy for the meeting. I wondered how Stemp would react. He'd better not push me again. Tension wound up in my stomach.

By the time I entered the kitchen, my hands were quivering.

"Good morning," Germain greeted me cheerfully. His sharp brown eyes gave me a quick once-over, noting my tremors. "Everything okay?"

"Fine," I lied. No way I was going to say anything in front of the bugs. "I'm just hungry. Do you want some breakfast?"

"I wouldn't say no," he agreed. "Have you got coffee?"

"That's not my area of expertise," I admitted. "Do it however you like it. The coffee pot's over there."

When Kane arrived a little before eight, we were just finishing off the last of our toast. He stuck his head in the door, sniffing. "Is that some of your homemade bread?" he inquired hopefully.

"Sure is. Want some?"

He nodded, and I pointed him toward the breadboard. "Help yourself."

He sawed off a couple of generous slabs and slapped on some butter. "I'll take these with me. We need to head out."

Kane stepped casually out the front door, sweeping the yard with his eyes. Germain brought up the rear. Kane raised a hand, and I was startled to notice the man in camouflage concealed in the band of trees that formed my windbreak. I hadn't even seen him until he returned Kane's salute.

"How many of those are there?" I asked.

"Two. They'll trade off during the day so that your house and yard stays secure."

I climbed into the Expedition with a sinking sensation in my chest. "This is a huge expenditure of manpower just to keep me safe."

"Yes," Kane said carefully.

"Shit, this isn't going to work for the long haul, is it?" I clasped my hands together firmly.

Kane apparently wasn't fooled. He glanced at my shaking hands and then met my eyes. "We'll figure something out. Don't worry. One thing at a time."

I sighed. "Yeah. Stemp might just shoot me today anyway. That'd solve all my problems right there."

"Except for the problem of being dead."

I shrugged. "Not my problem. I won't be here to worry about it."

Kane eyed me with concern. "You say that like you don't care."

"At this point, I don't."

At Sirius Dynamics, I struggled to fasten my security fob. My perfidious hands shook, and I breathed deeply, trying to calm down. I honestly didn't know whether I'd leave the building alive. Despite my words to Kane, I kind of hoped I'd survive. The idea of being dead didn't scare me at all, but the dying part didn't sound like much fun.

I gave a mental shrug as I followed Kane's broad shoulders down the hallway. What the hell, I'd died a couple of times already in the sim. Same old, same old.

I marched into the meeting room and took a seat beside Kane with my back to the wall. I made my body language open and casual, and repressed the urge to fidget. Slow, even breathing. Calm.

My heart sped up when Stemp appeared in the doorway, his face impassive as always. He took a seat facing us and we locked eyes for a few seconds. Stemp spoke first.

"How long have you known about the bugs?"

"Since the day you put them in."

"Who told you?" He shot a flat glance at Kane. Fear rushed through me. Keep Kane out of it.

"Nobody told me. I smelled the guy you sent to install them, so I went looking."

Stemp's expressionless face faltered. "You *smelled* him?"

"Yes. He was a smoker who wore cologne."

"Oh." The mask was back in place. "And how did you know that the bugs were ours?"

"I didn't. But the timing was just too coincidental."

"That was a stupid risk to take," Stemp said. "You should have reported them right away. What if they hadn't been ours?"

I shrugged, refusing to let him get under my skin.

"Then whoever it was would've heard exactly what you heard. Which was nothing."

"Until last night. What if Fuzzy Bunny had showed up instead of us?"

"If Fuzzy Bunny knew about me, they wouldn't be wasting time bugging my house. They'd just walk in and snatch me."

"How can I trust you to keep your word when you deliberately conceal knowledge from me?"

I swallowed the wave of rage that flooded me. He was accusing me of being untrustworthy? That was the funniest fucking thing I'd heard in a long time. I breathed deeply.

"Actually, speaking of deception, you do realize that as soon as you placed those bugs, you were in breach of our agreement," I said calmly.

Kane shifted suddenly in the chair beside me, and Stemp's eyes darted sideways. "Nonsense."

"Not nonsense at all. Our agreement was that I would have the final say in any and all measures you used to protect me. And I'm being generous in allowing you the benefit of the doubt that the bugs were installed to protect me. You failed to inform me. You deliberately breached our agreement."

I let the silence lengthen.

Stemp was too good a poker player to squirm, but his eyes twitched sideways again. "So what do you intend to do?" he asked finally.

"We had an agreement. You clearly understood the consequences of breaching the agreement. And you breached it less than twenty-four hours later."

"Aydan..." Kane began. I glanced over to see the

warning clear in his eyes.

I swung my gaze back to Stemp. "If you were in my place, what would you do?"

He leaned back in his chair, watching me. "I'd balance the seriousness of the breach against my loyalty to the other party in the agreement," he said.

I snorted. "Sadly, there is no loyalty to the other party in the agreement. The agreement existed solely because I can't trust the other party. So in my place, what would you do?"

Stemp went still, and I could see the wheels turning. There was a short silence before he spoke again. "In your place, I'd consider my loyalty to the team and to the country, and balance that against the importance of making sure that the agreement was followed to the letter."

"Really." I stared into his snake-like eyes. "And, in my place, do you think it would be a good strategic decision to ignore a blatant breach of the contract, thereby giving the other party reason to believe that the agreement had no teeth? How long do you think it would take before the other party decided to test the agreement again?"

"Aydan," Kane said urgently.

I didn't look at him. "Shut up, John."

It took a long time before Stemp dropped his eyes. "In your place, I'd be forced to take a zero-tolerance approach," he said bitterly. "Very well. I see we understand each other."

"No," I told him. "You don't understand me at all. You're a spy. I'm not. In your world, honour is bought and sold and coerced. In mine, it's not negotiable."

I blew out a long breath. "So I'm going to do the stupid, honourable thing, and balance my loyalty to the team and the country against the relative seriousness of the breach. I'm doing good work here. I'll keep doing it, if you promise to honour our agreement going forward."

"I will," Stemp said smoothly.

I frowned at him. "I'm going to pretend I didn't hear that. I want you to think for a while about what you're really promising. And realize that you're getting a second chance only because I believe in my team, and in the work we're doing."

I stood up and turned to leave, rubbing my aching forehead. "The sad part is, I know for a fact that you'll lie to me about this anyway. But I have to give you the chance. Stupid honour. Let me know when you've thought it over."

I was almost out the door when Stemp spoke. "Wait."

I turned wearily to face him. "What?"

"You're right," he said quietly. "I will lie to you. I will do whatever it takes to manipulate you into doing this work, and I will do whatever it takes to keep our operations secure. No matter who or what gets damaged in the process." We met each other's eyes, and for an instant, I saw a tired man fighting a desperate battle.

The mask flicked up again as he continued. "All I can promise is that I'll keep you informed as long as it doesn't compromise our operations. And I won't try to manipulate you with threats."

"Pretty lousy promises."

He raised a shoulder, his face impassive. "You wanted the truth. That's what I can truthfully promise."

I held his eyes for a few moments, feeling incredibly old. The man had told me the truth. It wasn't his fault that I didn't like it.

"Thanks for being honest," I told him finally. "Just remember that if you cause harm to someone I care about in the process of manipulating me, you will pay the price."

"Understood." His expression never wavered.

I gave him a nod and left.

CHAPTER 29

I strode down the hall, wondering what the hell I should do. I could hardly hover indecisively after making my exit. That would definitely spoil the effect.

But Kane had driven us in, so I couldn't go home. I'd thought he'd follow me out of the room, but he hadn't. Shit.

I let my feet carry me down to the employee lounge, where I brewed myself a cup of tea, stalling. I went into my office and plopped into the desk chair, staring blankly at the phone, the only thing on the desk.

Hmmm. Maybe Spider had some news from my snoopy little program. I dialled his extension.

"Hi, Spider, how's it going?"

"Fine, as far as I can see. Your program is gathering some data, but it's all encrypted. I'd love to know what's in it."

"Me, too. Maybe I'll just pop down for a few minutes." Going into the secured area was the last thing I wanted to do, but hanging around here like an idiot was the second-last. I'd make it quick.

"Aydan..." Spider said hesitantly. "Didn't Kane ground you yesterday? I thought he said no more network access."

"Yeah, but I won't be in for long. You know I usually don't have a problem unless I'm tired, and I slept pretty well last night."

"No..." he said uncertainly. "I don't think I should give you the key. We shouldn't take a chance."

"Oh, come on, Spider. Only for a few minutes." I couldn't believe I was begging to do this. But I really, really wanted to see what was in those new files.

Resolve firmed his voice. "No. Sorry. Not until you clear it with Kane."

I briefly considered bullying him into it, but I didn't have the heart. Besides, I had a better idea. "Okay. Talk to you later."

I hung up and headed downstairs. I knew he was as curious as I was about those files. I'd just go and hang around the lab for a while until he weakened.

When I got down to the lobby, though, I started to lose my nerve. My heart pounded as I eyed the heavy steel door. It was the time delay that got me. If I could go through without being shut into that damn coffin...

I blew out an impatient breath. Suck it up. I was just bending close for the retinal scan when a large hand closed on my wrist.

"What the hell do you think you're doing?" Kane hissed.

I managed to smother my cry of shock as I jerked upright. "Jeez, you scared the shit out of me."

"Come on." He didn't exactly drag me to the security wicket, but I was definitely being firmly guided.

We turned in our security fobs, and he steered me out the door. "Walk with me."

I frowned up at him as we marched down the sidewalk. He looked relaxed, his face composed, but his eyes were the colour of frosted iron. And he hadn't let go of my wrist yet. He wasn't holding me hard. But still...

"You can let go of me now."

He kept walking. I stopped and tugged. "Hey. I said you can let go now."

Across the street, I identified Tom's pickup with a sinking feeling. Perfect timing, as always. Thank God, he didn't seem to be looking in our direction.

I jerked my arm. "Kane!" I hissed. "Let go. People are watching."

He released his grip instantly and spun to face me. "Dammit!" He stared down at me, his cop face unreadable. "Come on." He turned and strode on.

"Where are we going?" Even with my long legs, I had to pick up the pace to stay beside him.

"Just walking."

Okay. I was still a little stiff and sore, but a brisk walk might help loosen me up. Not that I had a choice. Brisk was the only option available if I wanted to keep up.

We marched along in silence. Asking questions seemed like a bad idea. He'd wanted me to walk with him, so presumably he'd reveal his purpose eventually. After another glance at his arctic eyes, I wasn't in a hurry to find out what it was.

My body rebelled as we reached the park. "I have to stop," I gasped. "Sorry." I collapsed onto a park bench.

He sat down beside me wordlessly. I slouched for a few minutes catching my breath, and then turned to him. "Okay, what's wrong?"

He crossed his arms over his massive chest and stared into middle distance. Just when I thought he wouldn't answer at all, he spoke.

"Tell me about this death wish of yours."

"Say what?"

He jerked around to face me. "What the hell, Aydan?" he demanded. "What the hell was that?"

I clamped down my reflexive urge to flinch at his tone. Defensive anger gushed into my veins, and I felt my eyes narrow. "What do you mean?" I inquired evenly.

He stared at me for a moment, and then surged to his feet and took a couple of steps away. He stood briefly with his back to me. When he turned, his face and voice were controlled. "Why did you push Stemp like that? And why were you going into the secured facility?"

I willed my fists to unclench, and kept my voice as controlled as his. "Stemp has to know he can't push me around. And you may recall that I work in the secured facility now."

"Dammit, Aydan…" He took a deep breath. It didn't seem to help. His impassive cop face vanished. "I'm busting my butt trying to keep you alive, and you just… you just… it's like you're deliberately trying to get killed! You just keep pushing the limits. If you want to commit suicide, that's your business, but tell me now so I don't…"

He stopped and drew in another deep breath.

I rocketed to my feet, fists clenched. "So you don't what? Get caught in the crossfire? I've been trying to keep you out of the fucking crossfire! You think I want this? You think I asked for this? I'm just goddamn well trying to stay alive and do the right thing here. You really think I wanted to see all the shit that's inside my head and will never, ever fucking go away? You really think I wanted to get beaten and tortured and damn near raped and shot and scared out of my fucking mind…"

I stopped to gasp a few furious breaths that sounded almost like sobs. "…And see good people, people I care

about, getting maimed and tortured because of me and...
and... be in a prison where I'll never see the light of day..."

I turned and strode away on shaking legs before I
lost it completely.

He caught up to me a few yards down the sidewalk.
"Aydan."

I kept walking.

"Aydan, where are you going?"

"Walking." I stared straight ahead and kept moving.

"Stop." He caught my wrist gently. "Come back and
sit down for a while. Let's talk."

I spun to face him with clenched fists, holding onto
anger to keep back the tears. "Let me go. I need to be alone
for a while."

A sense of inevitability filled me as Tom's pickup
pulled over to the curb beside us. "Let go!" I hissed.
"Dammit, just leave me alone for a bit."

Kane made a frustrated gesture as he let go of me.
"You know I can't do that right now. You're under twenty-
four hour guard."

I wasn't in a sim, but I could feel the bars closing
around me. The trembling spread from my hands to the rest
of my body. I was trapped. The urge to run pounded at me.
I breathed deeply. It didn't help. I was going to run. Or cry.
Or explode.

Tom rolled down the passenger window. "Hi,
Aydan. John." He gave Kane a hard look. "Everything okay,
Aydan?"

I forced my voice into the best semblance of casual I
could manage. "Fine, thanks, Tom." The quaver wasn't too
noticeable. I took a shallow breath.

Run.

"Hey, Tom, can you give me a ride home?"

"Sure, no problem. Hop in." He leaned over to unlatch the door.

Kane grabbed my wrist again and leaned close to whisper fiercely. "Aydan, don't do this. I can't let you out of my sight. You know that."

I stood shaking in his grasp. I knew he was right.

Run.

"Aydan?"

I glanced over at Tom, trying to control my face. "Just a minute. Sorry." I turned back to face Kane.

"Aydan! I'm not kidding. I can't let you out of my sight. Don't make me force this."

Rage flooded through me as I jerked my arm out of his grip. "Force it how? What are you going to do, beat me into submission?"

His hands darted out, and I flinched in spite of myself. He held my face between his palms and looked down into my eyes as he spoke softly but clearly. "In two seconds, Rossburn's going to get out of that truck. He will fight me. He will lose. It will be your fault."

I heard the click of the door latch and the slam of the door. Kane let go, and I stepped past him to face Tom as he came around the back of the truck.

"Thanks anyway, Tom, but never mind. John will give me a ride home." The harsh voice didn't sound anything like me.

Ice-blue eyes raked over Kane, then swung back to me. "Aydan," Tom said quietly. "Get in the truck. Stay there."

I took both his callused hands in mine, feeling the tension in him. "No, I can't. I'm sorry."

I glanced back at Kane. He stood motionless, calm and utterly lethal. I knew how much power was coiled up in those massive arms and shoulders. I didn't know what type of martial art he used, but I'd seen him take on three men at once with nothing more than his bare hands. And leave three bodies behind.

I turned back to Tom. "Thanks anyway. John and I have a little disagreement over work, and I think I'll stay so we can work it out."

"Aydan." He searched my face. "If you're afraid of him, just get in the truck now. You don't have to live like this."

"I'm not afraid of him." I tugged gently at his hands until he followed me reluctantly. I towed him around to the driver's side. "Thanks for stopping, but I don't want to hold you up any longer."

"Aydan..."

"Thanks. See you later." I squeezed his hands, and walked away without looking back. I'd gone at least half a block before I heard the truck door close and the engine start.

CHAPTER 30

Kane wisely trailed me at a distance while I strode back to the park, holding onto composure with every fibre of my being. At the park, I kept my pace to a brisk walk. I knew if I started to run, I'd never stop.

I circled the park, around and around. Kane leaned against a tree near the edge of the park, but I avoided looking at him. If he as much as spoke to me, there was a good chance I'd attack him physically.

The increasing pain in my tired muscles drove me harder. Trapped. Hurt. No way to get home. No privacy at home, either. My sanctuary invaded by strangers. No way out.

I was panting shallowly, and I forced myself into belly breathing. Stay calm. These were the good guys. The good guys who were trying to protect me. I was outside, not underground. Sunshine. Fresh air. Stay calm.

I circled several more times, slowing as my strength faded and the pain nagged insistently. My hands ached, and I reminded myself to unclench my fists.

Finally, I couldn't do it anymore. I trudged to the far side of the park and sank down on the grass with my back to Kane. I rested my forehead on my knees and panted pain and tension and exhaustion.

I stiffened at the sound of someone approaching behind me. My back was exposed. Unable to control the urge, I twisted around.

Kane.

I turned away and stared into the distance as he sat down beside me, facing the opposite direction. Watching my back, I realized with grudging appreciation.

We sat in silence. My muscles tightened expectantly, but after several minutes, it seemed he intended to wait me out. I rolled my shoulders and laid my head on my knees again, trying to dissipate my agitation before I spoke to him.

Finally, the words burst out of me. "Way to push my buttons." I didn't actually add 'asshole' out loud, but I was pretty sure he heard it anyway.

Kane sighed. "I'm sorry. I only had a few seconds, and I had to get through to you."

"Yeah, sorry is real nice. When you pull shit like that, saying sorry afterward is a fucking insult."

"What do you want me to say?"

"Nothing." I stared off into the distance. "You were bugging me earlier about showing my emotions. As soon as I do, you use it to attack me."

"Aydan, I wouldn't..."

"Yes, you would. You just did. You knew how upset I was over you and Arnie getting tortured because of me. And you used it to manipulate me. Made it my fault that another good person was going to get hurt."

Kane blew out a breath between his teeth. "Aydan, you pulled Rossburn into it. Like it or not, that makes him your responsibility. My job is to keep you safe. Your feelings have to take a backseat to that."

He frowned over at me in obvious frustration. "I know how tough you are. I've always been able to count on you to do what needs to be done. Why are you suddenly so..." He paused, apparently trying to find the right word.

"Fucked up?" I supplied in a small voice. I buried my face in my hands and rested my forehead on my knees. God, I was so damn tired.

"Aydan..." I felt his hesitant touch on my shoulder. "I'm sorry. Don't cry."

I straightened up and turned to face him. "I'm not crying! I'm just tired and pissed off."

The relief on his face was almost comical. "Then talk to me," he said after a moment. "Why are you fighting me? Why do you keep putting yourself at risk for no reason?"

He looked into my eyes. "A couple of weeks ago, you said Stemp would be doing you a favour if he killed you. In the sim, I've seen the kind of images you're living with. Are you having suicidal thoughts?"

I groaned.   "You mean other than right now? Because I'm ready to chew my own wrists open just to avoid this conversation."

"Aydan, I'm not joking."

"Okay, fine," I sighed. I scrubbed my hands through my hair and yanked out a couple of tangles. "No, I am not suicidal. I am not deliberately putting myself at risk. It might look like that to you because I'm willing to do whatever it takes to avoid being trapped."

I met his eyes squarely. "I thought I could get over the claustrophobia if I wanted to badly enough. I was wrong. Now I'm not just freaking out when I'm underground, I'm freaking out at the slightest hint that somebody is trying to control me. I've been trying to figure out a way to fix it, and I can't. It's just getting worse."

I rolled my head carefully from side to side, trying to loosen the locked muscles.   No success.

I sighed and continued. "Stemp has managed to bury me underground as surely as if he'd gone ahead with his original plan. And it's having exactly the result I expected. I've been down this road before. It starts with the screaming in my sleep. Next the anxiety attacks start. It's downhill from there. I figure I've got another week, tops, and then I'm going to be totally useless to everybody, including myself."

"So it's really just the claustrophobia. Being trapped underground is what's causing all these problems."

"Yes."

He blew out a long breath. "Good. Because that's what I told Stemp this morning. I laid it on the line to him. I told him that he was in danger of losing his precious weapon, because you'd nearly died in the sim twice already. And he agreed to let you work upstairs."

I'm pretty sure I didn't faint, but I collapsed backward into the grass, hyperventilating. "Oh Jesus. Oh thank God." I swiped shaking hands over my face, because this time I actually was close to crying. "Oh thank God."

I pulled myself together with an effort. "Thank you. You just saved my life again." I thought about it for a few seconds. "No wonder you were mad, after you went to bat for me. I'm sorry."

Kane smiled down at me, sexy laugh lines crinkling around his eyes. "It's okay. You didn't know. I'm glad you think it'll solve the problem." He stood, and reached down a hand to pull me up.

He sobered as I brushed off grass clippings. "But, Aydan, don't charge in like that again without checking with me first. That could have gone very badly."

"I'll try. I'm just not used to reporting to anybody else."

He eyed me speculatively as we walked across the grass. "This must be making it hard for you to deal with your... other operations."

"John, I have no other operations. I'm just a civilian. You know that." I sighed inwardly. I'd thought he'd abandoned the idea that I was an undercover secret agent.

"Of course," he agreed.

We made our way back to Sirius Dynamics in silence. Outside the building, I leaned my aching body against the wall. "So, how do you feel about going to Eddy's?"

He shrugged. "It's only a quarter to eleven. He's not even open yet. Are you hungry already?"

"No, I'm due there at eleven to do his books. And if you're not letting me out of your sight, then you'll have to come, too."

"Well, let me see. That's tough. Go to the pub and eat lunch and listen to blues. On department expense." He grinned. "I think I can force myself to do that."

"Good, because you're driving. And I'm having a beer for lunch."

In the parking lot at Eddy's, I turned to look at Kane. "So why exactly are you following me around?"

He frowned, looking a little concerned. "You're under twenty-four hour guard. Remember?"

I laughed. "I remember. I meant, what should we tell Eddy? And Lola. I have to be over at Up & Coming at one. What's our cover story for why you'd be tagging along with me?"

"Oh."

"I think Eddy will believe that you're just there for lunch." I couldn't resist stirring the pot. "But exactly why would you visit a sex shop with me? And stay there for an hour and half?"

He gave me a devilish look. "What makes you think I'm not a regular customer there?"

Gulp. I realized how badly the tease had backfired as I felt the flush spread up my face. I did my best nonchalant shrug. "Well, if that's the case, I'm sure you'll be able to find something to keep yourself entertained."

"I'm sure I will."

I got out of the truck and headed for Eddy's back door with perhaps a little more haste than was absolutely necessary.

At a quarter to one, I finished my beer with a distinct sense of discomfiture. Up to now, I'd been sufficiently distracted by my struggles in the sim to keep my mind off lusting after Kane. Now I seemed to be making up for lost time.

Jesus, I hoped Lola had put that chocolate-scented leather thong away somewhere. Ever since she'd mentioned it a few weeks ago, I'd been harbouring a particularly tasty fantasy involving it and Kane. He definitely had the body to show it off to maximum effect, with those broad shoulders tapering to six-pack abs, narrow hips, and perfect ass. Not to mention the way he'd amply fill that yummy package of chocolate-scented heaven...

"Aydan?"

I jerked out of my glassy-eyed reverie at the sound of his voice. "We'd better get going. You said we needed to be at Up & Coming at one?"

"Yeah." I drained the last few drops from my glass and tossed some cash on the table.

"Don't worry, Stemp can pick this one up," Kane

grinned as he handed the money back to me.

I made an effort to act normal. Or what passes for normal for me, anyway. "Yeah, probably easier to expense a purchase here than at the sex shop."

He laughed. "True. Though it might be fun to try."

"I think Stemp would fail to see the humour."

"Probably."

CHAPTER 31

When we walked into Up & Coming, Lola and Linda were behind the counter with their heads together.

"Duck," I said to Kane. "When these two get together, the results are deadly."

They laughed, and Lola brightened visibly as she looked Kane up and down again. "Hi again, Big John. Looking for something special?"

I beat a hasty retreat into the back office as he gazed down at her, eyes twinkling. "Can you show me something fun for couples?"

Don't think about it. Just don't think about it. I buried my head in the books.

Despite my best efforts, I couldn't help eavesdropping on the conversation while I did my entries. Lola flirted shamelessly, and Kane teased her back good-naturedly. I tried to close my ears to Lola's enthusiastic account of their products, but I failed. Great. Now I had a whole new set of tempting mental images to overcome.

I heard Kane excuse himself as he apparently picked up a phone call. "Yes. Fine. No, I'm here for another hour or so. If you don't mind, I'd appreciate it. I want to get it done today. Thanks."

He hung up, and Lola launched into another detailed description. I refocused with difficulty.

A few minutes later, I heard Lola's voice raised.

"Aydan! Can you come out here for a second?"

"Why?" I inquired warily.

"Big John needs you."

Ha. I wish.

"It's okay, Aydan, don't bother." Kane's voice held the hint of a chuckle.

"Come on!" Lola popped into the doorway and seized me by the arm. "This'll just take a minute."

Despite my better judgement, I let her drag me out into the shop. "Here, put these on," she ordered, and handed me the thigh-high boots. Again.

"No. Once was enough." I turned to go back into the office.

"You've already worn them once?" Kane sounded amused. And possibly intrigued.

I sighed. "Yes. Thanks to merciless coercion by this imp of evil. That's how Harks's shit-for-brains buddy got the idea that I was a hooker. Thanks but no thanks."

"Come on," Lola cajoled. "Big John really wants to see what they look like on you."

"No, he doesn't. He's just humouring you." I turned to go back into the office.

"Aaay-daaan..." Lola sang. A chill of foreboding ran down my spine as I turned slowly. "Look," she carolled as she held up the boots in one hand and the chocolate-scented thong in the other. "You wear something nice for him, he'll wear something nice for you..."

A choking noise made us all turn. Spider stood framed in the doorway, a piece of paper crumpled in his hand. His face apparently couldn't get any redder, so he turned an unbecoming shade of purple instead.

"Lola," I said hastily. "Just because we came

through the door at the same time doesn't mean we're together. I don't know who the other half of John's couple is, but it isn't me."

"Oh." She looked abashed only for a second. "Well, then, put on the boots so he can see what they'll look like on his girlfriend."

"I really don't think that's appropriate," I mumbled, and scuttled back into the office.

When I dared to raise my head a few minutes later, Kane and Spider were discussing Spider's paper, and Lola was looking disappointed. Linda hovered nearby, her eyes sparkling with interest. I ducked back into my paperwork and tried to concentrate.

By the time I emerged cautiously at two-thirty, Lola was the only one left in the shop. She pounced on me.

"Aydan, you're kidding me. You're not making a play for that fine specimen of a man?"

I shrugged. "That would be cheesy. He's got a girlfriend."

"Well..." She looked unconvinced. "Maybe they're not serious."

I patted her shoulder. "And maybe they are. I'm not about to ask the question. See you."

I went out the door with a confident stride, but my mind was elsewhere. I hadn't really thought about it before, but I wondered what Kane did for female companionship. I knew he'd been divorced years ago, and he'd never mentioned a girlfriend. But I sure as hell didn't get the impression that he suffered from a low sex drive.

Then again, he was a spy. He was probably capable of keeping multiple girlfriends, and never letting them find out about one another. And a guy like him could have his pick of women.

I realized I'd trailed to a halt on the sidewalk, and I scoped out the street casually. After his insistence about keeping me guarded, I found it hard to believe that Kane would have just vanished.

Sure enough, I spotted the Expedition parked a half-block down the street, just out of the direct sight line of anybody inside the sex shop. I strolled toward it, noticing Spider's custom-painted lime green Smart car parked behind it.

I made sure nobody was watching me as I slid into the passenger seat. Kane glanced over and punched a speed dial button on his phone. "Pull out. Meet us at Sirius."

At my raised eyebrow, he explained. "Lola was a little too eager to put us together as a couple, so I thought it would be better if we left separately. I took surveillance of the front entrance. Webb was watching the back."

"Was that a good idea?" I asked. "Seems to me the last time you put Spider at the back door of a shop, somebody ploughed into him and nearly ruptured his spleen."

Kane grinned. "You weren't even close to his spleen. And anyway, he volunteered. Eagerly. That little brunette might have had something to do with it."

"Ooh." I bounced my eyebrows. "The kid who blushes if anyone even utters the word 'sex', and the owner of a sex shop. Sounds like a match made in heaven."

"For one of them, anyway," Kane commented with a wicked grin.

I laughed. "Not to be inappropriate here, but I'm sure that Spider would prove to be a quick study if properly motivated."

Kane shook his head. "I'm not even going to go there." He pulled out and steered the truck back toward Sirius Dynamics.

Inside the building, Kane waved me toward the glass doors. "You go on up. I'll be there in a few minutes."

I swiped my fob past the prox pad and let myself into the office area with a buoyant sense of relief. In my office, I resisted the urge to do a quick happy-dance. Probably Stemp had surveillance here, too. Despite evidence to the contrary, I did actually attempt to preserve my dignity at times.

I sank onto the couch and leaned my head back. I started when Kane tapped on the open door. He frowned. "Webb's not here yet?"

"Haven't seen him."

"Hm." He came in and handed me the tiny box containing the network key. "Keep this concealed at all times. There are only a couple of people here who have a high enough security clearance to know about it. I'll bring it up for you every day and take it back down again when you're finished."

I gazed up at him. "Did I say thank you for this?"

"Yes."

"Thank you. Again. I can't tell you how much this means to me."

He smiled. "I have an inkling."

Spider rushed through the door, his cheeks flushed pink. "Sorry I'm late. I got... um... tied up."

I bit my tongue. It didn't stop me. "Kinky," I teased him.

He blushed scarlet. "Um. I brought my laptop up so I can monitor your session." He bustled over to the desk and busied himself setting up the computer, his cheeks still flaming. Kane's lips twitched, and I hid a smile of my own.

"Okay, I'm ready," Spider said a few minutes later, his eyes still riveted to his screen in an almost-convincing display of concentration.

"All right." I grinned. "Let's see what my little toy has given us to play with."

I bowed my head and stepped confidently into the clean, white void. Kane popped into existence beside me just as I took a deep, satisfied virtual breath. He smiled. "Better?"

"You have no idea."

I folded sim-space effortlessly and stepped into the file room. A neat stack of files waited for me in the location I'd designated for my listening device, and I grinned as I picked up the top one. "Come to Mommy."

A thought struck me as I flipped it open. "Hey, John, can you read this?" I stuck the file under his nose.

He frowned down at it for a moment. "No."

"Mmm. Too bad. I'm going to look through these files first, and then I have an idea I'd like to try. It would be great if I could build my little device so that it decrypted the files as they came in."

Spider spoke up from the external network connection. "Aydan, if you could do that, it would be incredibly valuable."

"Well, I'll give it a try as soon as I'm through these files, then." I plopped down at the virtual desk and started translating.

I got through the first half-dozen or so and took a break, rubbing the back of my neck. I glanced over at Kane.

"What?" I asked.

"This is a gold mine," he replied, and I could hear the

edge of excitement in his voice.

I realized that while I'd been absorbed in my decryption, he'd been working through another network interface. His face held the intent, predatory focus that I'd seen on a few other occasions, the age-old expression of a hunter stalking his prey. I grinned and dove back into the pile of documents.

A blip in the sim and a small stab of pain behind my eyes made me look up at last. "What, Spider?"

"I said, it's five o'clock. Are you ready for a break?"

"Oh, sorry, Spider, I didn't hear you. Did you?" I turned to Kane.

"What?" He looked up, obviously interrupted in the middle of a train of thought.

"That'll be a 'no', then," I chuckled. "Spider says it's time for a break."

"Oh." His eyes were still far away. "I just need a minute here..." His voice trailed off as he concentrated on his virtual terminal.

"We'll be out in a few minutes, Spider," I said. "Signal me again if it goes over half an hour, okay?"

"Okay."

I picked up the next file and began decrypting. Panic drove through me, and I wildly scanned for the date/time stamp.

"SHIT!" I bellowed, and sprang invisibly into the data stream.

I rocketed crazily down the virtual tunnel, a wild roller-coaster ride that careened through IPs and blasted through firewalls. I held onto invisibility with all my concentration. If I betrayed my presence now...

I screeched to a halt outside the last firewall, my

attenuated consciousness snapping back into me like a rubber band. I knew my virtual body didn't even need a heart, but the drumming in my ears hammered on unabated while I panted.

Now came the tricky part. I seeped through the firewall, swift but stealthy. Burrowing into the heart of the enemy network, I sniffed undetectably through data packets as I made for my goal.

At last, I identified the file I sought. Dread suffused me as I wrapped my feelers around it. Too afraid to hope, I narrowed my concentration to infinitesimal detail, feeling and smelling and tasting and sensing.

I gulped overwhelming relief. Still intact. Untouched.

I destroyed it without a trace.

How many others were there? I slithered into the network services, checking synch routines. Six other sites. This was going to take some time. Time that might have already run out for me.

I chose a tunnel at random and propelled myself down it. I had to make a clean sweep, or I'd be doomed. Dead woman walking.

I found no evidence of the file at the first synch site. That was the good news. The bad news was that I found another web of connections. I'd have to explore them, too, just to be sure. But first I needed to check the main sites. I snapped back to the original site, and took the next tunnel.

An eternity later, I crept along the last tiny strand of connection. I'd found and eradicated two other copies of the file, neither of which appeared to have been viewed. My luck was holding.

I found nothing, and I let the connection end,

leaving me floating in a limbo of unidentifiable tunnels. For a few seconds, I let my exhausted consciousness drift, washed along by streams of data. Then I sighed and turned for home.

Which was... where, exactly?

The fear that had driven me forward swelled into a shock of panic. I'd stretched myself so far, along so many convoluted routes, I couldn't feel anything anchoring me anymore.

For the first time, I stopped to wonder what would happen if one of the connections I'd used was severed. Would I float forever, unable to coalesce back into myself?

I twisted wildly, searching for anything that felt like me, but I'd spread myself so thinly, I could only find traces here and there. I clamped down on terror and calmed my mind as best I could.

Just go one step at a time. Like a droplet of water gathering raindrops. I held the image and seeped backward with sluggish desperation.

I lost all sense of time as I slowly gathered myself. Wending my way through infinite corridors, I held the panic at bay. Collect one drop at a time.

At last, I recognized the server where I'd originally started. I tried to marshal my consciousness into the rubber-band form I'd used before, but I couldn't manage it. All I could do was dribble formlessly back down the data tunnel toward Sirius Dynamics.

With the last of my sentient thought, I hoped that Kane had brought his bucket. He was going to need it.

CHAPTER 32

I trickled lethargically into the corner of the familiar virtual file room and lay in a stagnant puddle. With no eyes to see and no ears to hear, I sensed Kane pacing the room.

"Aydan!" His voice was hoarse, and I wondered how long he'd been calling. I tried to form words. Nothing happened.

One of his large shoes splashed through me, and I involuntarily recoiled, ripples running through me. "Ow!"

"Aydan?" His voice sounded closer as he fell to his knees beside me. "Is that you?" he asked hesitantly. I could see him now, his image undulating as if I was looking up from below the surface of water. He reached out a careful hand.

His touch was startlingly personal, as if he'd touched my entire body all at once. I let out an involuntary gasp, and tried to divert my mind from sudden prurient curiosity about what it would be like to have sex inside the sim.

Fortunately, my concentration was too weakened to give form to that thought, but it provided enough focus to let me form a word. "Help."

"Don't worry," Kane reassured me. "We'll get you out."

Too exhausted to deal with the logistics, I lay in my torpid puddle. He'd said he'd rescue me. I knew he'd get me out somehow.

"Aydan."

I made an attempt to rouse myself. I managed the faintest of whispers. "I'm here."

"Can you take my hand?" He laid his palm on my surface again. His heat radiated, and the intimacy of the touch sent ripples racing through me.

Goddamn. If I managed to create any corporeal form at all, it wouldn't be my hand he was holding. Wouldn't that make Spider blush.

I concentrated on the sensation of his hand in mine. What did it feel like to hold his hand? Big, broad, hard palm. Strong fingers.

"Good, keep going," he encouraged. "I'm going to help you get up now."

I felt the pressure of his hand as he gently pulled upward, but I couldn't sustain my grip. I trickled through his fingers and back onto the floor.

"Dammit!"

"Sorry," I whispered mouthlessly.

"It's okay. All right, we'll do this the hard way." The floor tilted and rolled crazily as he sluiced me into a bucket.

"Aaaah! Goddammit!" I clasped my pounding head in both hands, then quickly reconsidered and clapped one hand over my eyes to keep them from exploding. I rocked painfully and swore until I was certain I could open my eyes without having them rupture.

"Jesus *Christ*!" My eyeballs weren't the only thing in danger of rupturing. I tottered to my feet as soon as I could see. "Gotta go. Back in a flash."

I caught a glimpse of two worried faces as I

staggered rapidly from the office and made a beeline for the ladies' room. I clenched my teeth and whimpered as I scuttled into one of the stalls, knees locked together.

I didn't even dare to think about how long it had been since I'd finished that beer at lunch time. I studiously avoided looking at my watch until the pressure dissipated enough that I wasn't actually in pain. Finally, I breathed a deep sigh and slumped against the toilet paper holder, shaking. God, another couple of minutes in the sim, and I wouldn't have made it.

There was a tap at the door, and Kane's voice floated in from the corridor outside. "Aydan? Are you all right?"

"Fine. I'll be out in a minute."

I dragged myself to my feet and propped my quivering body against the counter while I washed my hands. When I wobbled out the door, Kane immediately handed me a bottle of orange juice. I took it from him gratefully, and promptly spilled it down my chin as my trembling hands made me miss my mouth.

I swore and lurched, swiping my chin in an attempt to keep the dribbles off my T-shirt.

"Sit." Kane pried the bottle out of my hand and lowered me to the floor with my back against the corridor wall. "Try it now." He handed me the bottle again, and I managed to drink some, steadying it with both hands this time.

"Thanks." I sipped a bit more, and he slid down the wall to sit companionably beside me on the floor.

Spider emerged from the men's room and surveyed us quizzically for a few seconds before taking a seat on the floor across the corridor from us.

We sat in silence while I drank my juice. We all

glanced up at the sound of a door closing, and Stemp stepped out of his office. He hesitated at the sight of us sitting in the hallway, then walked down toward us, his face unreadable as always.

He stopped in front of Kane. "Your requisition is approved, and the equipment is ready downstairs. You can pick it up whenever you want it." He eyed Kane expressionlessly for a few seconds. "I hope your judgement is sound." He turned and vanished into the stairwell. The steel door clanged behind him.

Kane offered no explanation, and I frankly didn't care that much. The tremors were starting to subside as my blood sugar equalized, but I was still starving. I finally summoned up the courage to look at my watch. After eight o'clock. Jeez. My stomach growled.

I heaved myself to my feet, and the other two followed suit. "Sorry, Aydan, but we still need to debrief," Kane said.

"Yeah." I sighed. "I'm going to go wash off the orange juice, and grab a cereal bar. And then I have to go back into the sim again."

Kane was already shaking his head, and I held up a hand to forestall his objection. "We'll talk about it in a minute," I told him firmly, and ducked back into the bathroom.

When I returned to the office, Spider and Kane were snacking, too. I tore the wrapper off my bar and bit into it ravenously as Kane looked up.

"So what the hell was that?" he demanded.

"Sorry, I panicked," I mumbled. "Hang on." I gulped down the too-large mouthful and chased it with a swig of orange juice. I sank into the couch, and took another, smaller bite. "Just let me get this down."

We all munched in silence for a few minutes. I swallowed the last of the bar and leaned back on the couch.

"Okay," I sighed. "Sorry I vanished like that. I should have let you know what was happening, but I read that document and freaked out."

"What was it?" Kane demanded.

"Somebody was notifying Fuzzy Bunny that I'm still alive, and that I have network access."

Both men jerked forward in their chairs. "Who? How far did it go?" Kane snapped.

"I don't know who it was. I found it in three separate locations and destroyed it. I had to search every single path on every single synched site. That's why it took so long, and that's why I didn't dare waste any time. I'm pretty sure I got all the copies, and I'm pretty sure nobody had read the message yet."

"Pretty sure?" Kane's massive shoulders bunched under the snug T-shirt. "How sure is pretty sure? If that went anywhere in Fuzzy Bunny's organization, you're as good as dead."

I ran my hands over my face and made fists in my hair. "Dead, I wouldn't mind so much. But I'm thinking I wouldn't be that lucky."

"No, you're probably right," Kane agreed slowly. "Captured and tortured, more likely."

"Don't say that!" Spider protested. He turned haunted eyes to Kane. "You wouldn't let that happen."

"Sorry, Webb," Kane said regretfully. "You know I'd do anything in my power not to let it happen. And you know it happened anyway, last time."

"Anyway," I interjected, trying to cheer up the

discussion, "Pretty sure in this case means almost certain. Ninety-nine percent. But that's why I have to go back into the sim tonight and make sure there are no other bombshells lurking in those files. It was just dumb luck that I got to that one before anybody opened it. Who knows what else is in there. That could have just been one of many."

There was a short, dejected silence. Guess I hadn't cheered the discussion up that much.

"All right," Kane said. "I hate to say it, but you're right. The sooner you get back into the sim and read those documents, the better. Tell me when you're ready."

I rose. "I'm just going to go and pee again first. Just in case."

A short time later, I stepped back into the virtual network. The food had helped, and the sim only wavered slightly as I headed for the virtual file room. The image stabilized as Kane appeared, too.

"Thanks for being here," I told him. "It really helps when you hold the sim still."

He grinned. "Just don't think about pigs."

A faint but pungent odour drifted to my nose, and I glared at him. "Stop that."

We stepped into the file room, and I buried myself in the documents again.

After an interminable time, I laid aside the last one with a sigh. "All clear." The file room wavered, walls melting like hot candle wax.

Kane stepped quickly over and grasped my arm. "Let's go."

My eyes burned. Kane flung a glass of ice water in my face, and I gasped and sputtered. "What the..."

He dragged me along the virtual corridor. "Your

eyes were on fire," he muttered. He forged through tall reeds and reeking swamp. The path in front of his feet stayed solid, but I sank up to my waist, the saw-like edges of the reeds slashing my skin. His grip bruised my arm as he dragged me bodily along.

"Come on, Aydan, help me out here." He pulled me out of the swamp with a sucking sound and placed me on the path ahead of him. "Walk." I squelched forward, expecting a solid path with all my might.

I stopped dead. Apparently, I had also expected snakes. Lots of them.

"Oh, for..." Kane shouldered me aside. His flamethrower belched fire and smoke. The snakes burned and shrivelled. He turned back to me, and before I could react, he slung me over his shoulder and ran for the portal. We stepped through just as blackness filled the void.

I sprawled on the sofa and cursed feebly until the pain subsided a bit. Then I flung an arm across my face and groaned for a while, just for variety. Finally, I shut up and hauled myself into a semblance of sitting position.

"Well, that was fun," I croaked. "Let's do that again soon. Not."

Kane was massaging his temples, too. "Not," he agreed. "Do you think you're in the clear?"

"Yes. But I don't know for how long. I wonder how long it'll take before whoever it was realizes that their message never arrived."

Kane shrugged. "No way to tell. Is there any way you can set an alert if that file gets re-sent?"

I laid my head back on the sofa and frowned at the ceiling. "I think so. If I go in again and just..."

"No. You're done for the night. So am I. I was

having trouble holding it at the end, too," Kane said. "We can't take the chance tonight."

Spider spoke up hesitantly. "I think I can do it from the external network interface. While you were busy in the sim, I was analyzing the file, trying to figure out where it came from. I could probably modify your program."

"Do it," Kane ordered.

I looked at my watch and groaned. "It's nearly midnight. You'd better take a break, Spider."

"No," he grinned. "I want to get in and play with that program. I'm used to being up half the night gaming anyway."

I squinted at him. He did look fresh as a daisy. I rubbed my aching forehead. Oh, to be twenty-six again.

"Let's go," Kane broke into my dull thoughts. "We've got one more stop to make before I take you home."

"Will the festivities never end?" I dragged myself up off the couch and plodded after him out the door.

On the main floor, Kane stopped at another heavy steel door and stooped for the retinal scan. I watched him warily. "Is this another time delay?"

"No."

The door released, and I followed him into a room lined with lockers of various sizes. I gazed around. "A changing room?"

"Not exactly." He pulled a piece of paper out of his pocket and consulted it for a second. Then he moved to one of the lockers and swiped his security fob across its prox pad. The door unlatched, and he reached in to extract a carton about the size of a shoebox. He carried it over to a small counter and opened it.

"For you." He turned and handed me a pistol.

CHAPTER 33

"Uh." I regarded the small black gun open-mouthed. "What...?"

"It's a Glock G26. A Baby Glock. For concealed carry." He delved into the box again. "Here's a concealed waist holster, and an ankle holster. You should use the waist holster whenever you can. It's easier to access. But the ankle holster is easier to conceal in the summertime when you're not wearing a jacket."

He pointed out features as he spoke. "It's a 9mm. Ten-shot magazine, standard Glock safe-action trigger, and the sights are good. It's an accurate gun for its size, but you'll notice it kicks a bit more than the full-size model. You're strong, you shouldn't have any difficulty with it."

I gazed blankly up at him. "I don't have a permit for this. And it's illegal to carry a concealed weapon."

Kane reached into the box again. "Your permit. And your concealed carry license." He handed them to me.

"But... I didn't think there was any such thing as a concealed carry license in Canada."

"Officially and practically, no, not for the general public. But they do exist. For people like you and me."

"But..." I tried to get my tired brain to process the new information. "But... what am I supposed to do with this?"

He gave me a wry smile. "Typically, you'd use it to

shoot somebody who was trying to kill you. That's been happening frequently enough that Stemp agreed you should carry."

"But... what if I shoot somebody?"

"That's the general idea," he said patiently.

"But..." I stopped. I was starting to sound like a broken record. I shook my head vigorously in the hope of kick-starting my brain.

"What I meant was, what if I get it wrong? What if I shoot somebody who isn't Fuzzy Bunny? Like, what if I'd been carrying this a couple of nights ago, and I shot Bill Harks? He's just a local guy, not a spy. There'd be all kinds of trouble. You couldn't just cover that up."

"Bill Harks was trying to kill you," Kane said. "Your primary objective, in fact, your orders, are to stay alive. At all costs."

"I don't think he was trying to kill me," I argued. "It wasn't like it was life or death."

"Aydan." He frowned down at me. "I saw the video. That kick he landed on your ribs, if it had been full-force the way he'd planned, and if it hit you in the head? You could easily have died. Or been brain-injured."

He looked into my eyes. "Your responsibility is to stay alive. If you'd had this gun a couple of nights ago, your responsibility would have been to shoot Harks if you couldn't scare him off. To disable, if possible. To kill, if necessary. Let us worry about any cover-ups that need to be done."

"But what if I get it wrong? What if I shoot some poor shmo who just happened to be in the wrong place at the wrong time?" I gazed up at him. "I can't do this."

"Aydan, I know you can. I've seen you do it."

"That was different," I mumbled. "I knew they were

Fuzzy Bunny. You were there to tell me."

Kane put his hand on my shoulder. "Aydan, I know you won't make a mistake. I'm not afraid you'll shoot someone by accident. I'm more worried that you won't be prepared to shoot someone when you need to."

I stood for a few moments trying to absorb the magnitude of what he was saying. My mind steadfastly refused to deal with it. I sighed. Okay, stick to practicalities for now. "I'll need to practice with it. Do I just go to the store and pick up ammo?"

"No." He smiled. "The whole point of carrying a concealed weapon is that nobody knows you have it. We'll issue you ammo. Just ask whenever you need it."

"Okay, I'll need a box for tomorrow, then." Other than the prospect of having to shoot somebody, I was actually pretty excited about the gun itself. I love guns. This one was a little beauty.

"I've never seen a handgun this small before." I grinned up at him. "Is there a firing range I should use, or should I just take it out to the back forty?"

"There's a firing range downstairs in the secured area, but if you've got a safe place on your farm, you could use that. Just take another gun with you so that you can explain away gunshots. Remember, nobody can know that you have this."

"Right." I thought a bit more. "So when do you want me to start carrying it? And when should I carry it?"

"As soon as you feel comfortable using it, start carrying it. And carry it with you at all times." He grinned. "Take it to bed with you, too. It's a little more effective than a crowbar."

"Yeah, but you don't get a second chance," I argued.

"If I'd had this when you showed up at my place, it would've been game over for you."

Kane sobered. "You're right. This is dangerous. That's why there are only a handful of these licenses in existence. I know you well enough to believe that you won't make a mistake." He repacked everything into the cardboard carton and handed it to me. "Come on. I'll take you home."

When we pulled up in front of my house, Germain stepped onto the front porch, hands on hips.

"You're out long past your curfew, young lady," he teased as I trailed up the steps.

"Yeah, where were you when my date wouldn't let me come home?" I groused. I raised a hand to Kane as he drove away, and followed Germain into the house.

"Long day," he commented.

"Yeah, but we managed to skirt disaster for another day."

His sharp eyes skimmed over the cardboard box tucked under my arm. "About time. What did you get?"

I glanced pointedly around the room.

"The bugs have been removed," he reassured me. "Cameras, too."

"How about the phone tap?"

His brows drew together. "I didn't know you knew about that. It's still in place."

"Good. It can stay. Just in case I get more calls from my secret admirer."

He snorted. "Good plan. I won't mention that you know about the tap."

"Thanks, Carl. You're the best."

He grinned at me. "So what'd you get?"

I popped the lid open and returned his grin. "Baby

Glock."

"Aw. It's adorable."

We traded cheerful banter for a few more minutes, until I yawned hugely. "I'm done. If I don't sleep soon, I'm going to turn myself inside out."

"Okay. Sleep well. Unlike me."

I laughed. "Thanks for watching out for me."

"You're welcome. Good night."

Mindful of Germain's presence, I decided on shorts and a tank top for nightwear. Just in case. I dragged myself into bed and knew no more.

I opened my eyes to Kane as he bent over me in the silver moonlight. He smiled as I reached to pull him down. He lowered himself on top of me, and my breath caught at the sensation of his hard body against mine.

I kissed him hungrily, moaning as his fingertips lightly traced my collarbone. He trailed his lips down to the hollow of my neck. His hands found my breasts, and I moaned again as my breath came faster.

He moved slowly against me, and I opened my legs to him, pressing up. Now that was an amazing hard-on. My hands locked onto his perfect ass and I urged him closer, begging for more.

He whispered my name, and I answered with another moan as I searched for his lips again.

"Aydan."

I ran my hands up over his massive shoulders. God, I could sink my teeth into those muscles. I traced my tongue over one of his bulging biceps, nibbling my way up to his neck.

His voice changed, more urgent as he spoke aloud. "Aydan."

I pulled him closer, panting with need.

"Aydan!"

I jerked awake with a yelp.

"Sorry." Germain stood silhouetted in the doorway. "You were having a nightmare. I didn't want to come close enough to get punched this time."

I groaned and flopped back on the pillow. "Thanks. I'm okay now. And I haven't woken up punching for a while."

"Good to know. Good night again." He withdrew, swinging the door shut behind him.

I lay seething in the bed. These dreams were so damn realistic. Must be some kind of hangover from the sim. Goddamn, I was horny.

I groaned again and pulled the pillow over my face.

The phone rang.

I resisted the urge to press the pillow down until I smothered. Another ring. I jerked the pillow off my head and slammed it onto the bed. The clock read three-thirty. The phone rang again, and I snatched up the receiver.

"What!"

"Die, bitch."

"Fuck you, fuck everybody who looks like you, and fuck your mother twice!" I slammed the phone down.

I sighed at Germain's tap on the door. "Aydan? Everything okay?"

"Fine. I'm unplugging the phone now."

"Good idea. I'll pick up next time. That might deter your caller."

"Thanks."

I burrowed back under the sheets and tried to relax.

I was just rolling out of bed at seven o'clock when I heard the phone ring in the kitchen. Hell, let Germain get it. I was on my way to the bathroom when he tapped on the bedroom door. "Aydan, it's for you. Do you want me to take a message?"

"No, that's okay. I'm up. I'll just plug in the phone and take it in here. Thanks."

I shuffled back to sit on the edge of the bed. "Hello?"

"Hi, Aydan, it's Tom. I hope I'm not calling too early. You said you were a morning person."

"No problem, I was up. What can I do for you?"

"I was calling to make sure you were okay. I tried several times yesterday evening, but you weren't home."

"I'm fine, thanks. It took a little longer to resolve the problem at work than I'd expected."

"Okay..." He hesitated. "Was that John who answered the phone? Are you safe there?"

I sighed. "No, that was Carl."

I didn't bother to fabricate an explanation for a man answering my phone at seven o'clock in the morning. I was pretty sure Tom could figure one out all by himself.

"Oh." There was a short pause. "Okay. As long as you're all right."

"I'm fine. Thanks for checking in, and I'm sorry for the bother yesterday."

"No bother. Any time you need help, just ask."

"Thanks, Tom. 'Bye."

I thudded the receiver against my forehead. Any other woman would be thrilled to get this kind of attention. Hell, who was I kidding? Any other time, I'd be thrilled to be getting this kind of attention. But right now, it was a huge pain in the ass.

I growled my way into the bathroom and bared my teeth at my reflection. Surrounded by men, and no hope of getting laid in the foreseeable future. I snarled and stepped into the shower.

CHAPTER 34

I'd just finished putting the breakfast dishes away when Kane tapped on the screen door.

"Come on in," I told him. "I'll just grab my waist pouch, and then I'm ready to go."

"No, your first priority today is target practice," he countered.

I grinned at him. "Aw, gee, sucks to be me. I was hoping to get a chance for that today."

He smiled back, but his eyes were serious. "Go get your guns, then. I'll tell the sentries to expect gunfire."

I headed downstairs to liberate my old .22 rifle and a box of shells from the gun locker, and grabbed the box that held my new Glock. By the time I got back upstairs, Kane was waiting on the front porch.

My heart lifted as we strode toward the back corner of my quarter-section. The air was already warming, and the birds were singing their little hearts out. I could even appreciate them this morning.

Kane surveyed the area as we approached the small corner that I used for a firing range. "What's beyond that knoll?" he asked.

"Don't worry. Nothing but empty pasture for miles. No roads, no human habitation. And I always shoot into the knoll as a backstop anyway."

"Perfect."

I set up a target, and walked back to the rock that I used to mark my firing line. I stood for a moment, cradling my .22 while I looked out over the farmland and breathed the sweet air.

"What?" I shook myself out of my reverie when I realized Kane was watching me intently.

"You were a million miles away."

I gave him a half smile. "No, just a few decades."

He raised an encouraging eyebrow, and I explained. "I always used to shoot with my Dad on the farm when I was a kid. Just like this, outside on a nice day in the middle of nowhere." I stroked my hand over the .22's stock. "This was his gun. He got it when he was sixteen. It's my favourite."

"Good memories."

"Yeah." I turned away to exchange the .22 for the Glock. Bittersweet memories. Hard to believe it'd been nearly ten years since he died. I concentrated on loading up the Glock's clip, and clicked it into place.

I turned to face the target and laughed. "This really is a baby. It's so little and light!"

"Try it."

I took aim and squeezed off a shot. A solid kick, as Kane had warned, but not unmanageable. I hit the target high and to the right.

"Hmmph." I took a few more shots, getting used to the sights. My shots moved closer to the centre, grouping nicely. "That's better."

I shot the rest of the clip and reloaded. Then I laid the Glock aside and picked up the .22.

Kane eyed me quizzically.

"I need to come back to it. So I know I can pick it up fresh and be accurate on my first shot."

He nodded, and I shot a few rounds with the .22, its familiar action feeling like an extension of my own body.

"New target." I headed downrange and pinned up a fresh one.

When I got back to the firing line, I bent and picked up the Glock, then turned rapidly and took three quick shots.

"Nice." Kane shaded his eyes with his hand as he surveyed the three closely spaced holes near the centre of the target.

"Good enough," I agreed. "I'll keep practicing with it, but I'll feel comfortable carrying it now."

"Okay. Try the holsters, then."

I fiddled with them until they fit as well as I could manage. It was a warm day already, so I decided to go with the ankle holster. I reloaded and eased the gun into the holster gingerly.

I looked up at Kane's raised eyebrow. "Carrying a loaded gun is so totally against all the gun-safety protocols that have been drilled into my head all my life. And I feel really uncomfortable with no external safety. I'll probably shoot my own foot off."

"Glocks have a safe-action trigger. The safety's built in."

"Clearly you underestimate my ability to fulfill Murphy's Law."

He laughed. "It'll be okay. You'll get used to it fast."

"Maybe." The unaccustomed weight dragged at my ankle on the walk back. Just like the unaccustomed responsibility dragged at my heart.

When we got back to the house, I glanced up at Kane. "Do I have time to clean them before we go? It's against my religion to not clean a gun after I use it."

He checked his watch and frowned. "Mine, too. But we really have to go. We have a meeting with Stemp in half an hour."

"Shit, why didn't you tell me? I could have quit sooner."

"I'd rather you took the time you needed to get comfortable with the gun."

I shrugged. "Okay. But if lightning strikes me dead for not cleaning my guns, I'm holding you responsible."

"Guilty as charged," he agreed. "Put your rifle away and let's go."

"My dirty rifle."

He sighed. "Yes. Come on."

My heart rate sped up while I feigned a relaxed posture in the meeting room. Spider looked distinctly anxious. His knee bounced rhythmically while he frowned into middle distance. Kane sat immobile, looking calm as always. I really had to learn that trick.

"What's up, Spider?" I asked as casually as I could.

"I called Stemp because..." he began. His head jerked up as Stemp entered the room. Stemp's expressionless eyes inspected us each in turn as he closed the door behind him and made his way to the table.

"Webb," he said without preamble.

"We have a problem," Spider blurted out. He turned apprehensive eyes on Kane and me. "I tracked the origin of that document you found, Aydan."

"And?" Kane inquired levelly.

Spider twitched a shoulder. "From what I could tell... It originated here in Silverside. At the internet cafe."

Kane's face was controlled as he met Stemp's gaze. "Were you able to pinpoint the sender?" he asked.

"No."

"So we have a leak."

"So it would seem," Stemp agreed. "Is there something you'd like to tell us?"

My mouth dropped open. I couldn't believe he was directing the not-so-veiled accusation at Kane. Kane gave me a warning glance as I sat forward abruptly.

"Obviously, it's the first I've heard about it," Kane said calmly. "But we have a fairly limited pool of suspects. There are only a few people who have sufficient security clearance to know about the network key, and about Aydan's ability to use it."

"Yes," Stemp agreed. "So what were you doing at the internet cafe on Monday evening?"

Kane sat slowly back in his chair, his face impassive. "My home computer died. I went to the cafe to check my email."

"I see." Stemp's flat eyes surveyed him.

"Don't be ridiculous," I burst out. "If Kane wanted to rat me out to Fuzzy Bunny, he could have done it at any time in the past four months. At Harchman's he could have snatched me and the key together and delivered us to Fuzzy Bunny in a nice, neat package. He wouldn't wait until now and send an email."

"Unless he was smart and organized," Stemp said. "And unless he intended to keep working as a double agent over the long term."

"That's bullshit, and you know it!" I glared at him. "There are always a bunch of people in that internet cafe. Who else was there on Monday night?"

"There were lots of people there," Spider put in quickly. "I was there gaming until nearly two."

"And did you see anyone else with a top-level Sirius security clearance?" Stemp asked.

"N...no." Spider's face fell. "But I was pretty involved in the game. I could've easily missed somebody."

"You have a top-level clearance, too." Stemp's voice was silky.

Spider's mouth fell open as he gazed aghast at Stemp. "Uh... yeah..." he whispered. "But..." He straightened up in his chair, frowning. "But I'd never do anything to hurt Aydan!"

"Stop!" I stood up from my chair and held back the urge to yell. "Stop flinging wild accusations around. I trust these men with my life."

"Yes, and how many times have you nearly died?" Stemp inquired expressionlessly.

The bottom dropped out of my stomach. "You can't be serious."

Kane broke in. "Aydan, we have to ask these questions. To everybody. We obviously have a leak. That means that somebody we trust has betrayed us. No matter who it turns out to be, you're not going to like it."

"Fine, then," I growled. "Let's ask the questions. What were you doing Monday night, Stemp? How did you know Kane was at the cafe? Did you happen to pop in there for a while?"

Stemp leaned back in his chair and surveyed me with his inscrutable eyes. "Actually, I did," he admitted finally.

"Because..." I prodded.

"I was transacting some business that I prefer not to do from home."

"What sort of business?"

"The sort of business that doesn't concern you."

"Oh, really."

"Really."

I glared at him. "I'm done here. I have work to do. And I need my team to help me do it."

"Very well." Stemp rose. "I will continue to investigate. Meanwhile, I suggest that you trust nobody, and be prepared to use your new weapon. At any time. Against anyone." He gave Kane a hard stare and left the room.

I kicked my chair back and stalked around the table, fists clenched. "What a prick!" I turned to face Spider and Kane. "I trust you guys more than anybody in the world. He's so full of shit!"

Kane rubbed a weary hand over his face. "No. He's not. There are only a handful of people who know what you can do. You know all of them personally. You've trusted all of them, until now. You're wrong about one of them. There's no way to sugar-coat that."

I did a quick mental inventory of all the people I'd worked with. Kane was right. I liked and trusted them all. I couldn't believe one of them would betray me. Except John Smith.

"What about Smith?" I asked. "Did you see him on Monday?"

Spider shook his head. "I didn't even see Stemp. I could have easily missed somebody else, too. I wasn't paying attention."

"Aydan," Kane said gently. "Just because you don't get along with Smith doesn't mean he's the mole. In cases like this, it often turns out to be the person you trusted the most."

I dropped back into the chair and buried my face in my hands. "I hate this. And I don't believe I'm wrong about you guys. Or Germain. I'd stake my life on you three. For what it's worth."

"Thanks, Aydan, that's good to hear," Kane said, and Spider nodded agreement.

Kane met my eyes. "I hope you're right."

CHAPTER 35

Back in my office, I scanned Spider's tired face. "How did it go last night?"

He rubbed his eyes, and I could read the strain in his shoulders. "It went okay. I altered your program, so if that specific file shows up again, we'll know. But I couldn't do anything to watch for any other files or variations on that file because of the encryption. It's actually pretty useless."

He met my eyes with a worried gaze. "There are some more files in the listening program this morning. You should look at them as soon as possible."

The anxious knot in my stomach clenched a little harder. "I'll do that right now."

I leaned back on the couch and stepped quickly into the virtual network. My heart beat a little faster at the sight of the small stack of files. I was just reaching for the first one with trembling hands when Kane stepped into the virtual file room. I twitched at his sudden appearance, my nerves strung tight.

"Sorry," he said. "I'm going to work in here again. Let's hope I don't need a bucket this time."

"Let's hope," I agreed, and opened the first file.

Much later, I laid down the last document with a sigh of relief. "That's it. So far, so good."

Kane looked up from his virtual terminal, his face clearing. "That's a relief." He looked at his watch. "You should take a break. It's nearly noon."

"Not quite yet. I have an idea." I dissolved into invisibility and was floating into the network structure when Kane shouted my name.

I snapped back to the file room, my heart pounding. "What?" I scanned wildly, but couldn't identify any threat.

Kane took a deep breath and let it out slowly. "Don't do that."

"What? Don't do what? Jeez, you scared the piss out of me."

"Don't just vanish without telling me what you're going to do. Last time you did that, you were gone for three hours and I had to carry you out in a bucket."

"Oh." I sucked in a deep breath of my own, trying to calm down. "Sorry. I'm going to try to modify my little program. I'll need to be invisible so I can check the connections. I don't think it'll take long."

"Give me your hand. Just in case."

"Okay." I felt his hand close around mine as I stretched my invisible, virtual self into the network.

It was easier than I thought. I felt Kane's grip tighten spasmodically as I popped back into existence beside him, grinning.

He let go of my hand and surveyed my face. "I take it that went well."

"Yes."

"Good. Then let's get out of here. You need lunch, and you can tell us about your changes."

"Sounds good." I smiled to myself as we walked to the portal. Regular meals had never been a priority for Kane. I was touched that he would pay such careful attention to my needs. Then again, it was his job.

I stepped out of the portal and swore my way through the pain.

When I straightened and opened my eyes, Spider was watching me anxiously. I sighed and cracked my neck. "I'm good. Where's Kane?"

"He just left to take the key down to the secured area. He'll meet us in the lobby."

I massaged my forehead. "I am such a massive pain in his ass. He must be ready to shoot me himself just so he can go back to his regular job without being saddled with a neurotic civilian."

"You're not neurotic." Spider smiled at me. "And this is his regular job."

I hauled myself to my feet and followed him to the door. "Not quite the excitement he's used to, though, I'm sure. Sitting around watching me stumble through the network."

"That's been far too exciting lately, if you ask me," he said wryly. "Boredom is a pleasant change for a guy like Kane."

"I guess."

Walking back from The Melted Spoon, Kane turned to Spider. "Webb, will you get the key for Aydan? I need to stop off at the cafe and check my email again."

"Sure." Spider frowned. "Your computer's still down? Do you want me to have a look at it?"

"No, I didn't want to bother you with it, so I took it to the repair shop. They said it would be ready later today. Thanks, though."

"No problem."

Kane strode off toward the cafe, and Spider and I continued on to Sirius. I sighed as we retrieved our security fobs. "I'm so glad I don't have to go downstairs anymore."

Spider smiled at me. "I'm glad, too. I'll go and get the key. See you upstairs."

In my office, Spider leaned forward eagerly. "I see some changes in your program. What did you do?"

"Well, you said the file was sent from the internet cafe, so I set up the program to watch for anything else that comes from there and goes to Fuzzy Bunny. If it catches anything, it'll send you an email alert flagged as urgent. At least that way we'll know if our traitor tries again."

As I spoke, Spider's phone buzzed. He glanced absently at it, then did a double-take as his eyes widened. "I just got an alert!"

"Shit!" I dove into the network and folded space to get to the file room. I snatched up the file that awaited me and scanned it at light-speed. "Shit!"

My virtual consciousness rocketed down the tunnels, tracking the file.

Much later, I oozed back down the connection toward the Sirius servers. Slithering back into existence in the virtual file room, I watched Kane pace. After a few seconds, it occurred to me that it might be helpful if I was visible.

With an effort, I concentrated. I wasn't quite fast enough. Kane altered direction and attempted to stride right through me. I let out an involuntary grunt at the impact, and we both sprawled on the virtual floor.

"Aydan?" His hands shot out, feeling across the floor as he gazed blindly right at me.

"I'm here."

He jerked back as his searching hand landed on one of my invisible boobs. "Sorry." A faint flush crept up his neck. "I can't see you. Take my hand."

If I hadn't been so tired, I might have had some fun with that, but I just wasn't up to it. I put my hand in his, and he gripped it tightly. "Let's go."

"I just need to do one more thing in my program first."

"Aydan, you're still invisible."

"I know. I'm too tired to change. And I need to be invisible to work in my program anyway."

"Why? You don't need to hide in our network," he argued. "Come on, you can do that later."

"I don't know why it works that way, but I have to be invisible. I can't do it otherwise. Just keep holding my hand. I'm not going far."

"Aydan!"

I ignored him and stretched lethargically into the network structure again, tweaking my program. I worked slowly and carefully, afraid to make a mistake out of sheer exhaustion. Finally, I backed away, barely breathing. It was a delicate setup, but it should work.

I tried to snap back into the file room, but it was more like the sluggish retraction of an earthworm in cold ground. Minus the slime. My imagery mercifully left that part out.

"Okay, I'm ready to go," I whispered.

"I still can't see you." Kane's grip tightened. He skimmed his other hand up my arm to find my shoulders, and lifted me to my feet. "Can you walk?"

"Yeah. Hold on." I focused the last of my concentration, and managed a ghostly image of myself.

"That's better." I read the relief on his face. "Let's go."

I concentrated on putting one foot in front of the other. I was dully surprised when we stood in front of the portal. Kane gave me a gentle push, and I stepped through into my aching head.

As the pain subsided, I slowly unwrapped my arms from over my head and uncurled. Thank God for the couch. I sprawled with my face mashed into the cushions for a few seconds, trying to gather the energy to sit up.

"Aydan?" Spider asked. "Are you okay?"

"Fine," I mumbled into the upholstery.

Kane's turn. "Can you sit up?"

"Probably." I sighed deeply. Motes of dust shot into my airways, and I immediately convulsed, coughing. I tumbled off the sofa onto my knees and clamped my hands around my throbbing head while I hacked and gasped.

At last, I wiped the tears from my eyes and looked up at the two worried faces above me. "Strategic error," I croaked. "Do not inhale the couch."

I dragged myself back up and propped myself in the corner of the sofa. "Jesus, has this thing ever been vacuumed?"

"I don't know," Spider said uncertainly. "Are you okay?"

"Peachy."

"What happened?" Kane demanded.

"I inhaled some dust..."

"No. In the network."

"Oh." I made an attempt to round up some organized thought. "My program caught another file outbound from the internet cafe. It was another report on me. Apparently our guy decided to try again. So I had to go and find it and get rid of it in Fuzzy Bunny's network."

"Did you get it in time?"

"Yes. And then I went in and altered my program. It's still watching for any traffic between Fuzzy Bunny and the internet cafe, but now it'll hijack the file and bring it here. I set it up so that the program will grab the file just before it arrives at its destination. That way, it'll look to the sender as though it went through. Unless somebody does a detailed trace on it."

"Good." Kane sat back in his chair, his shoulders easing.

Spider pulled out his phone. "Let's see if Germain saw anything."

"What do you mean?" Kane asked.

"As soon as Aydan disappeared in the sim, I called Germain to go over to the internet cafe and see who was there. See if we could catch our guy in the act."

Kane leaned forward abruptly. "And?"

"And, I'll call him and see." Spider dialled. "Hi. Any luck?" His brow slowly furrowed. "Oh. Okay. Well, thanks."

Kane's eyes bored into Spider. "Well?"

"Well, it took him about ten minutes to get over there after I called him," Spider said slowly. "There were several people working at the terminals. Nobody he recognized as a Sirius employee. I guess he didn't see you. But Stemp was leaving just as Germain got there."

"No, Germain wouldn't have seen me," Kane agreed. "I just went in, checked my email, and came straight over here." He opened his notebook and started to sketch. I recognized the layout of the internet cafe.

"When I came in, these terminals were occupied." He marked off several of the seats. "Stemp was there when I came in. He sat here." He wrote 'Stemp' on one of the seats.

"These ones, I didn't recognize the people, so they weren't high-level Sirius employees." He jotted a quick physical description beside each seat. Once again, I marvelled at his ability to observe without appearing to pay attention. No wonder he was the top agent in the service.

"Here, here, here, and here, were people in costume." He glanced at Spider. "Some of your World of Warcraft buddies, I expect. An elf here and here." He added their descriptions.

"Oh, sounds like Red Eakins and Tim Moorcroft," Spider put in.

"Okay." Kane added the names. "These other two wore rubber masks, the kind that cover their entire heads."

"What did they look like?" Spider asked.

Kane lifted a shoulder. "I don't know what your characters are called. Trolls, maybe. Ugly, wrinkled, kind of pig-like."

"There are about six guys that I know who'd wear a mask like that for their characters. Don't worry, it'll be easy to figure out who was there. I can just check the game record," Spider reassured him. "But nobody who works for Sirius has time to play during the day. The only guys who play during the day do shift-work or whatever."

"So Stemp was the only high-level Sirius employee there." I spoke into the silence.

Kane shrugged. "It could be sheer coincidence. Our guy could have come and gone, after I left and before Germain arrived. It wouldn't take much time to send a file." He stood. "Come on, Aydan, it's time for you to go home.

Webb, do you mind taking the key back down?"

"Sure."

I handed Spider the tiny box and trailed thoughtfully out the door behind Kane. I really didn't like Stemp. And I sure as hell didn't trust him.

When I stepped outside, a chilly wind was sweeping heavy clouds across the sky. I shivered and rubbed my hands over my bare arms while I trotted to Kane's Expedition. Damn, I'd wasted two beautiful, sunny weeks trapped underground. Now that I was aboveground again, the weather turned to crap. Murphy's Law.

I spent the evening catching up on my bookkeeping entries for some quarterly clients and doing some minor web updates for Spider's Webb Design. Kane stayed until Germain arrived to relieve him at eight. Rain pounded down outside, and I pitied the two guards who'd drawn the night's outside duty.

I went to bed early, and had another vividly erotic dream about Kane. As I lay there in wakeful frustration, the phone rang.

Fine. Gotta get the obligatory threatening phone call, too. Fuck my life.

I let Germain pick up.

CHAPTER 36

Morning was cool and overcast. I decided to give the waist holster a try, since it would be concealed by my sweatshirt. I squirmed uncomfortably at the breakfast table and met Germain's quizzical glance.

"How long did it take you to get used to carrying your gun?" I asked. "This just feels wrong."

He chuckled. "I was pretty much used to it after the first time it saved my life."

"Yeah, I could see that."

"But seriously, you'll gradually get used to it. You'll get to the point where you feel naked without it."

"Hmmph." I pulled at it again, trying to find a comfortable position. The doorbell rang, and I got up to let Kane in.

"Ready to go?" he inquired.

"In a minute." I grabbed my jacket and waist pouch, and put on my hiking boots in deference to the muddy ground outside.

Kane glanced over at me as we pulled into Silverside. "Stemp wants another meeting this morning."

"Do you think he's our leak?"

Kane blew out a breath. "I'd be inclined to say no. Webb and I spent several hours last night digging into him.

But we didn't come up with anything definitive."

"You were there half the night again? How much overtime do you guys do in a year?"

"What's overtime?" His lips crooked up. "This isn't a job, it's a way of life."

"I guess it is, isn't it?" I said slowly. He was on call, 24/7. Lives depended on it. God, I wouldn't want that responsibility.

I wondered if he had time left for any hobbies or life of his own. He worked ridiculous hours, and I knew he spent a lot of time working out, practicing martial arts, and target shooting. He was a deadly marksman in addition to his skills in unarmed combat. Being a lethal weapon really was a lifestyle. Once again, I thanked my lucky stars he was on my side.

When we tapped on the door to Stemp's office, he looked up sharply from his desk. "Ms. Kelly, come in. Kane, wait outside."

I glanced nervously at Kane, but his face was inscrutable as he took up a position at parade rest outside the door.

I stepped inside and obeyed Stemp's command to close the door.

"Please sit."

I stepped forward slowly and took a seat in the chair facing Stemp's desk. His face was as unreadable as always, half in shadow from the light of the window. I wondered why the hell he always kept the lights off in his office. Like being in a cave. Or a snake burrow. That'd be appropriate. I dragged my attention back to him as he spoke.

"Our mole made another attempt to communicate with Fuzzy Bunny yesterday."

"Yes." I wondered if I should mention that I knew he'd been there at the time.

"I was at the internet cafe during the time that the file was apparently sent."

"Oh."

Interesting. He admitted being there. I shut up to see what else he'd tell me.

"I was placing surveillance cameras in the cafe so that we can monitor activity there. But I wanted to warn you again to be ready to defend yourself without hesitation. Against anyone who threatens you, even if it's someone you know and have trusted up to this point."

"I'll keep that in mind."

He stood. "Are you carrying your weapon?"

"Yes."

"May I see it?"

I frowned up at him. "Why?"

"It has come to my attention that some of the Glock 26 magazines had a defect that causes them to jam. I want to make sure that your gun is in top working condition."

I eased it out of the holster and held it out reluctantly. He came around the desk and took the gun, carrying it over to the window to stand with his back to me. I heard him eject the clip, and he took a moment to examine it in the bright indirect daylight. He pushed the magazine back into place as he turned, and stood silhouetted against the window.

That just pissed me off. It was an obvious power trick, to make me look at him backlit so that I couldn't read his face. I stood and walked over to stand beside him, holding out my hand.

He returned the gun without comment, and I stowed it back in my holster.

"Remember to stay alert," he reminded me.

I nodded, and he watched me for a few more seconds. Snake eyes. Creepy.

"Please send Kane in on your way out."

Back in my office, I took out the Glock again. I ejected the magazine partway and pushed it into place again, just to make sure it was properly seated. Then I worked the slide to chamber up a round, and tucked it carefully back in my holster.

I sighed. I really didn't want to have to use it.

I wondered how long Kane's meeting would be. Spider was nowhere to be seen, so I dialled his extension.

"Hey, Spider," I greeted him when he picked up. "Do you have time to get the network key for me this morning?"

"Um…" he said. "I'm… I can't right now."

"Okay." I frowned. "Spider, are you feeling all right? You sound like you've got a cold or something."

"Yeah…" he said huskily. "Maybe… I'm coming down with something."

"Well, I hope you feel better soon. Take care of yourself, you've been working too hard lately."

"Thanks," he croaked, and hung up.

Poor guy. He sounded awful. But maybe it was a good thing he didn't have time to bring me the key after all. At least he wouldn't spread his germs to me.

On the other hand, it didn't leave me very much to do. Without the key, I couldn't decrypt anything.

Hmmm. But I could at least go into the network using my Sirius security fob and see if there were any new files piled up in my listening program. And it wouldn't hurt my head. That'd be a nice change.

I leaned back on the couch and stepped into the network.

There were a few more files piled up in my program, and I eyed them with annoyance. I could open them, but I couldn't read them. I made myself invisible and tried to check my program, but it resisted my efforts, too. And I was afraid to try too hard in case I upset its delicate balance.

I wandered aimlessly out of the virtual corridor and headed for the portal. Surely Kane had to be finished soon.

I re-entered my physical body and started slightly at Kane's closeness. He had an odd expression on his face that smoothed away almost instantly as he stepped back.

"Sorry," he said. "I was just going to wake you from the network."

"Good, I'm glad you're here," I told him. "There are a couple more files in my listening program, but I need the key to be able to read them."

"Mm," he said. "Leave them for now. I just got new orders from Stemp. Let's go."

"Go? Where?" I rose and followed him out of the office.

"New site."

"Okay." I frowned at his receding back. "Will we need to take the key?"

"No."

In the truck, I glanced over at his expressionless profile. As usual, his body language was relaxed, his face composed. But I could have sworn he was mad or upset about something. He kept his eyes on the road, so I couldn't tell for sure.

I sighed and leaned back in the seat as we drove out of Silverside. He'd tell me when he was ready.

Meanwhile, I could enjoy the drive. He steered the Expedition out into the country, and I watched the watery sun gradually win its battle against the clouds. The patchwork of fields kept me fascinated, with the vivid yellow of canola in bloom beside the blue-green of oats and the warm yellow-green of wheat. The wind swept across the fields in endless waves, and I caught myself smiling at the sight.

Out of the corner of my eye, I saw Kane glance over and quickly look back at the road. Something was definitely bothering him.

"Anything you want to talk about?" I asked.

"No."

I sat in silence while we drove out of the farmland and into more rolling, treed terrain. Kane turned the truck off the highway and made a series of turns on the back roads as we wound deeper into the uninhabited area.

I hadn't seen another vehicle in miles, and I breathed satisfaction. I had no idea where we were going, but the trip was wonderfully relaxing.

A few minutes later, Kane pulled into an overgrown driveway, and the Expedition bounced down a rutted track. He stopped to engage the four-wheel drive, and we churned our way along the muddy trail. At last, he pulled over and stopped, and we both got out.

The sun was warm in the clearing sky, and the birds sang in the silence of the deserted area. I stretched happily and peeled off my sweatshirt in the heat.

We walked a few hundred yards toward a stand of trees, and I puzzled over where the heck we were going.

More spy stuff. They probably had some top-secret installation out here in the middle of nowhere.

"Wait here," Kane instructed, and I obediently halted a few yards from the edge of the trees. I turned to gaze out over the rolling, open land behind us as I soaked up the sun.

"Aydan." Kane's voice sounded strange, and I turned to look at him as he stood just in front of the forested area.

I frowned at him. "Is everything okay?"

"No."

Something in his voice sent a chill down my spine. "What's wrong?" I started toward him.

"Stay there." He drew his gun and pointed it directly at me.

Adrenaline surged through my veins. "John... what's going on?" I held my voice as steady as I could.

"Aydan..." He stopped and swallowed. "I got new orders this morning."

"Oh..." My stomach turned to lead and my head threatened to float away. "From Stemp?"

"Stemp." He stopped again and took a deep breath. His gun never wavered. "And Briggs."

"Oh. So it's official." I was proud that my voice was still steady.

"Yes."

I took a deep breath of my own. One of my last. Too bad it had been rainy last night. I would have liked to have eaten one last meal of fresh peas.

"Do you need me to pass on any messages for you?"

"No, just notify the usual authorities that I'm dead. Everything's in order." My heart hammered furiously, as if trying to cram in as many beats as possible before the end. "Oh. There is one thing."

"If it's within my power, I'll do it."

A shaft of sunlight bathed him, and I could see his eyes clearly at this distance, dark with anguish. His gun hand was still rock-steady.

"Just a message. Tell Stemp..." I stood up tall and tossed my hair back. I refused to die like a snivelling coward. I gave Kane a vicious grin. "Tell Stemp he's a stupid asshole. I never would have betrayed the team. Or the country."

Kane's voice was hoarse. "I know."

His finger moved to the trigger. I tried to keep my legs from shaking. Wouldn't want to fall down before the bullet hit me.

He wouldn't miss. He never missed.

The sound of the shot made me flinch.

CHAPTER 37

I stared at Kane in shock. He'd missed.

He stared back at me, wide-eyed.

Then he pitched forward onto the ground and lay still.

I stood rooted to the spot, unable to understand. A movement in the underbrush caught my eye, and I stared blankly at Stemp as he stepped out beside Kane's body, gun in hand.

Caught in icy paralysis, I gaped at him helplessly. I was vaguely aware that my entire body was shaking. I swayed on my feet as my brain lurched into gear and delivered comprehension in a horrific flood.

Without thinking, I yanked the Glock from its holster and delivered three quick, smooth shots. I knew I wouldn't miss.

Stemp smiled.

My mouth fell open again, and I resisted the idiot urge to peer into the barrel of my gun to see what was wrong with it. I'd seen the casings eject. I knew I'd fired three shots. I knew they were good shots. At such close range, I couldn't possibly miss.

"First rule," Stemp said smoothly. "Never let anyone else handle your weapon. Second rule. If for some reason you must let someone else handle your weapon, check it over thoroughly afterward."

"You..." I tripped over my unwieldy tongue. "You swapped magazines. Gave me blanks. You fucking prick. I'll kill you..."

His gun jerked up as I lunged toward him.

Beyond fear or reason, I kept coming. His expressionless mask slipped as a berserk roar ripped from my throat. Even a bullet wouldn't stop me. I would tear him limb from limb with my bare hands. Redness suffused my vision.

Hard hands clamped onto my arms and shoulders. I flung them off, roaring and punching and kicking. I smashed my gun butt into a face. Folded a knee with a violent kick from my heavy boots. I was vaguely aware of impacts, but I felt no pain. I kept swinging, fighting my way toward Stemp. He would die today.

A heavy weight smashed into my back, and I slammed face-first into the mud. I spat out grass and dirt while I struggled and kicked against the relentless grips on my arms and legs. More weight crushed me. I couldn't draw a full breath. My arms and legs were completely immobilized. I tried to roar defiance, but only a wheezing sound emerged.

I wrenched my head up out of the dirt as Stemp's feet appeared in front of me. He squatted and looked into my face. "Very impressive. It took five men to subdue you. You must have been very fond of Kane."

"You... cocksucker..."

"Ease off," Stemp said. "She can't breathe."

The weight in the middle of my back lightened by a few pounds, and I gasped a lungful of air. Then I tried to lunge at Stemp again.

He jerked back a step. "Too bad he didn't feel the

same way about you. I was surprised. I really didn't think he'd kill you. And I really didn't think you'd stand there and let him."

"You gave the order, shithead. You set him up. He thought he was doing the right thing. I thought he was doing the right thing." I tried to get at him again with no success whatsoever. The men held me completely helpless. I spat at him instead. "Die, you fucking bastard!"

Stemp sighed and squatted down to my eye level again. "You're right, I set him up. And I set you up. It was enlightening. I know now that you won't hesitate to use your gun to defend yourself. That's good. And I know you're loyal now. Too bad I can't say the same for Kane."

A fresh flood of rage engulfed me, and I gave a titanic jerk. I got one arm free for a second, before the three men on top of me scrambled back into place and pinned me again. I let out a shriek of pure frustration.

"He was loyal, asshole! What the fuck did you want? You gave him the fucking order. He was going to carry it out!"

"I know that's what it looked like," Stemp said regretfully. "But he was the one who betrayed you to Fuzzy Bunny. He was at the internet cafe when both of the files were sent. He had intimate knowledge of your skills and capabilities."

"That's stupid!" I struggled fruitlessly again. The pain was starting to sink in now. I could feel every sharp knee and elbow digging into me. "If he was working with Fuzzy Bunny, he never would have killed me. They need me alive. If you hadn't shot him..." I gulped as the enormity of the loss finally hit me.

Kane was dead.

I clamped down with all my self-control to hold my voice steady. "If you hadn't shot him, he would have killed me."

"No. He wouldn't have," Stemp said. "That was a tranquilizer gun he was pointing at you."

"What?" I couldn't draw a full breath. A loud buzzing filled my ears.

Stemp leaned down to look in my eyes. "I set this entire thing up. I told all staff with sufficient clearance that your project was to be terminated today. They all knew that you would die. I wanted to force Fuzzy Bunny's hand. Today, here, would be their only chance to acquire you alive. I set up perimeter guards in advance. I had snipers ready. I was waiting for Fuzzy Bunny's operative to appear. And the only person who appeared was Kane. Carrying a tranquilizer gun."

My world went black.

CHAPTER 38

From a hazy distance, I watched Stemp stride over to Kane's body. He rolled the body over, and the horrible slackness of Kane's heavy muscles tore my heart.

Stemp reached into Kane's pocket and withdrew his keys. He tossed them to one of the men who'd dragged me to my feet. "Here. Take his Expedition. He won't be needing it." He eyed the two injured men lying on the ground. "Load them up and take them to the hospital. Take her, too, and get her checked over just as a precaution. Then take her back to Sirius for debriefing."

I didn't remember much about the trip back to Silverside. At the hospital, I sat dumbly while Linda cleaned most of the mud off me and Dr. Roth pronounced me cut and bruised but basically uninjured. Unlike the men I'd hit. One shattered cheekbone, one dislocated knee. Lots of bruises. I wished I hadn't hit them. They were just doing their jobs. So much suffering.

I passively climbed back into the vehicle for the ride over to Sirius Dynamics, and allowed the armed men to escort me up to the second-floor meeting room. I might have gathered a few stares on my trip through the hallways. It didn't matter.

My entire body throbbed with an ache that was more than just bruises.

I slumped in my chair in the meeting room, staring

into middle distance while Stemp and Briggs talked at me. I didn't absorb much. They'd discovered that the threatening phone calls and shots had come from Bill Harks's brother, who was now in custody. They were discontinuing my twenty-four hour guard. I would continue to carry my Glock. John Smith would be my new handler. All this was highly classified. Yada, yada.

I sat unmoving, waiting for it to end. At last, I realized the room was silent. Stemp and Briggs were looking at me expectantly.

"What?" I mumbled.

"Do you have anything to add? Any questions?"

I blinked slowly. Nothing much mattered.

No, dammit. One thing still mattered. I sat up straighter. "You're wrong. I know you're wrong. Kane was no traitor. You killed an innocent man."

General Briggs's face softened. "Aydan, we understand what a terrible shock this has been. But the evidence is all here. We can't come to any other conclusion."

I sighed. Briggs was a decent man, and a good commanding officer. Kane had liked and respected him, and I knew the feeling had been mutual. I could see the pain in his eyes, too.

"Maybe you can't come to another conclusion. But I can. You're wrong." I cut him off as he began to speak again. No point in arguing. It wouldn't bring Kane back. "Who will deal with his funeral arrangements?" I resisted the urge to fold over myself at the sudden pain in my gut. "Who'll notify his father?"

God, this would kill his dad. Both sons dead. All his children. Kane's younger brother, murdered at only twenty-three, trying to save a mugging victim. And now Kane himself, shot in the back.

"The chaplain will contact his father."

"When?"

"As soon as possible."

A new wave of pain washed over me. Arnie. He'd be devastated. He and Kane had been friends since childhood.

I stood. "I have an important errand to run. It will take the rest of the day, and possibly tomorrow. I'll also need time off to attend Kane's funeral, if there is one. I'll let you know when I'm available to work again."

I turned and left the room without waiting for dismissal. Outside the room, I grabbed the arm of one of the men who'd brought me in. "You're going to drive me home. Now."

"Uh..." He glanced around helplessly. Briggs caught his eye through the open door and nodded. "Okay." He followed me down the hallway.

At home, I showered the last of the mud off, wincing a little at the new set of bruises and scrapes. The pain was distant, though, part of a dull and constant ache. I shrugged and put on fresh clothes.

I carefully reloaded my Glock with live ammo, and loaded up a couple of extra clips while I was at it. A hard lesson. I'd never make that mistake again.

I strapped the holster to my ankle, and threw the waist holster into my small backpack along with some overnight things. I ate the last of the leftovers from my fridge without tasting them.

As I drove away, I tried not to remember how much I'd enjoyed my last drive with Kane.

Almost two hours later, I pulled over at the side of the road just outside Calgary city limits. I eased my stiffened body out of the driver's seat and stretched slowly and painfully. I'd driven the highway in a stupor. I couldn't remember much of the trip, but apparently I hadn't hit anything big. There were no dents in the car, and nobody had honked their horn at me.

I needed to be alert in the city traffic, though. I tried to force my numb brain to concentrate. I strode back and forth as briskly as I could for a few minutes to get some circulation going before getting back behind the wheel.

Half an hour later, I pulled into one of the visitor's parking slots at Arnie's condo unit.

Inside the main doors, I hovered beside the security call panel. I couldn't bring myself to press the button that would ring his apartment. My eyes welled up, and I dropped my head to blink rapidly while I pretended to scrounge in my waist pouch.

The secured door opened as a man came out. "Oh. Here you go." He politely held the door for me, apparently thinking I was looking for my keys. I mumbled thanks as I slipped into the hallway and headed for the stairs.

Outside Arnie's door, I stood again for a long moment, gathering my courage. At last, I watched my hand rise to knock at the door.

I stood waiting numbly, but no answer came. I knocked again, and then again. First I couldn't start. Now I couldn't stop.

Finally, I realized he wasn't there. I leaned forward to beat my aching forehead gently against the door.

"Oh, God, Arnie, where are you?" I begged.

What if he was out on some investigation, gone for

days?   I thumped my forehead a couple more times. Suddenly, I stumbled forward as the door was wrenched open from the inside.

"What the fuck!" Hellhound bellowed.

I'd clearly caught him at a bad time. Or, more precisely, in the middle of a really good time.

He was barefoot and shirtless, his jeans only half done up. Bright red lipstick was liberally smeared on his neck, and smudged lip prints tracked their way down his stomach to disappear inside his pants.

His scowl vanished. "Aydan! Hi, darlin', listen, now ain't a good time. Can I call ya…"

He trailed off, his eyes widening as he looked more closely at me. "Aydan…? Are ya okay?"

I took a deep, tremulous breath, trying to steady my voice. It came out as a tiny quaver anyway.

"No."

I bit my lip, trying to hold back the tears.

"Aw, darlin', come inside, I'll call the police…" He reached to draw me in, and I held back as I heard a light female voice call his name.

"I don't need the police." I took his hand. I didn't know how to tell him. "Arnie, I have bad news."

He went very still, searching my face. The fear rose in his eyes.

"Kane?" His voice was a hoarse whisper.

I could only nod.

"How bad?"

I knew he'd read the answer on my face already, but I had to say the words. "He's dead. Arnie, I'm so sorry." My voice abraded my throat like hemp rope yanked across a raw wound.

His face closed down, expressionless except for the dark wells of pain that were his eyes.

"I'm so sorry." I put my arms around his rigid shoulders and held him. He turned his face into my hair and we stood in silence.

"Arnie?" A tousled blonde head popped out the door. "Hey! What the hell? You creep! What, you thought you could do her in the hallway while I wait in the bedroom?"

I pulled away far enough to meet her eyes. "I'm just a friend. Arnie's had some very bad news. His best friend has been killed."

"Oh." The tiniest of lines appeared on her botoxed forehead. "Well, come back to bed, Arnie. I'll make it all better."

I stepped back and squeezed Arnie's hand. The loss in his eyes made mine fill with tears.

"I'm sorry. I'll go now. I'll call you later." I touched his face, wanting to take away his pain and knowing it was impossible. As I turned to go, his hand tightened on mine and he spoke, his voice rough with suppressed emotion.

"Don't go."

He turned and stepped back into his apartment, towing me by the hand.

The tousled blonde head proved to be attached to a small, curvy, naked body. She let out a squawk of outrage as we stepped inside. "What about me?"

"You can stay if ya like, Naomi." Arnie sank onto the couch and put his head in his hands.

"Well, there's not much point in staying if you're just going to sit there," she said tartly. "I can find plenty of other men who can get it up for me. And better-looking ones than you, too."

Unreasoning rage washed away my numbness. I took a step toward her. All my unfulfilled violence toward Stemp distilled itself into two words.

"Get. Out."

The tone of my voice was enough to frighten even me. The blonde squeaked and backpedalled, and then scuttled into the bedroom. Arnie stood and came around to look in my face. He opened his mouth as if to speak, but closed it again and stood in silence.

When Naomi reappeared a few minutes later, she was dressed. She'd apparently spent the intervening time summoning up her inner bitch. She stopped in front of me.

"Who the hell do you think you are? This isn't your home. I'll stay if I want to."

She had taken a cheap shot at a man I cared about. A man who had just been mortally wounded. I could tear her apart with my bare hands. I had a vivid memory of the feel of my fists against flesh. I took a single step toward her, redness tingeing my peripheral vision.

Arnie stepped between us. "Aydan," he said softly. "It won't help."

"Arnie, are you going to let her talk to me like that?" Her voice was the irritating buzz of a mosquito. I took another step forward, but Arnie didn't budge. I could still see her beyond his shoulder. Crush her.

"Naomi," Arnie said quietly. "Ya better leave now. 'Cause I don't think I can hold her if she comes for ya."

"Fine." She flounced out and slammed the door.

Arnie took a slow step back. "Aydan?"

"She hurt you. Nobody hurts you because of me. Not ever again." The voice that came from my mouth wasn't mine.

He reached slowly for my fist and held it, stroking it gently. "She can't hurt me, darlin'. I don't give a shit about her. Only the people ya care about can hurt ya."

The tremors started then, rolling through my body in long waves. "I couldn't save him, Arnie. I was supposed to die, not him. I couldn't save him."

"Aydan..." He put his arms around me and lowered me gently to sit on the couch. He sat beside me, and I held him with all my strength, ignoring the pain from my cuts and bruises.

"How did it happen?" he whispered.

"He was shot. Doing his duty. Shot in the back. By someone he trusted." I couldn't hold my voice steady, and I didn't try. "Arnie, I swear to God I tried to kill the fucker. I would have killed him with my bare hands. But they knocked me down and sat on me. I couldn't move... I'm sorry..."

Grief and fury choked me.

"Shhh, darlin'." He stroked my hair, and we sat in silence, just holding each other.

Finally, Arnie pulled away. "I'll hafta call his dad."

I looked into his haunted eyes. "You don't have to tell him. He'll know by now. The chaplain was going to notify him."

"I hafta call him anyway. He's... I'm Kane's executor. An' we'll hafta make arrangements for the funeral."

He was just getting up when the phone rang. He turned a stricken face from the call display. "It's him. Aydan, I dunno if I can do this."

I didn't know how to help, so I took his hand and

held it as he drew in a deep breath and picked up the phone.

"Hello?"   He sank into his chair, his knuckles whitening on the receiver. "Yes, sir, I just heard. Yeah. From somebody he worked with."

There was a pause while he listened.

"They wouldn't tell ya what happened?"

Ice filled my veins. If Stemp even breathed the word 'traitor', I would hunt him to the ends of the earth. Arnie gazed at me with anguished eyes.

"He died a hero," I said firmly.

"Sir," Arnie spoke hoarsely into the phone. "I dunno what the official word is gonna be. But his... partner... she says he died a hero. An' if she says it, ya know it's true."

"No, sir, I wouldn't expect anythin' less."

"Yes, sir." He rummaged for a pen and paper, and scribbled furiously for a few seconds.

"Yes, sir, 'course I'll be there."

His shoulders slumped, and he covered his face with a shaking hand. His voice was a rough whisper when he spoke the last words.

"Thanks... Dad."

CHAPTER 39

Arnie hung up the phone and sat in silence for a few moments. Then he spoke without looking up, his voice even.

"Aydan, could ya go out an' pick me up a case a' beer?"

I knew for a fact that his fridge was always full of beer. I made for the door immediately. "I've got some errands to run. I'll be at least an hour."

"Thanks, darlin'."

I closed the door softly behind me, and made it out to my car before I broke down completely.

It was close to eight o'clock by the time I pressed the call button again. I'd picked up the beer and driven aimlessly the rest of the time, in a state of suspended pain. When Arnie opened the door, his cat, Hooker, made a determined dash for freedom. I scooped him up and carried him inside while Arnie took the beer.

"Hey, big guy," I murmured as I cuddled the furry body. "Where were you earlier?"

"I put him in the bathroom," Arnie explained. "Naomi said she was allergic."

"Mm." I still couldn't think about Naomi without wanting to destroy her for her callousness. I massaged Hooker's scruff, and my eyes threatened to fill with tears again when he squirmed up to squeeze his paws around my neck, purring mightily.

Arnie turned away and made his way to the kitchen carrying the beer. "D'ya want one?" he called from the kitchen.

"I better not." I changed my mind. "Yeah. Yeah, I do."

I gave Hooker one last cuddle and put him down as Arnie handed me a cold one. He eyed me searchingly, and then put a gentle arm around my shoulders. "Come an' sit down, darlin'. Before ya fall down."

He guided me to the couch and eyed my trembling hands. "When did ya eat last?"

"I don't know. Around four or five, I guess. I don't want anything." I took a deep swallow of beer.

"Ya sure? I got some leftover pizza in the fridge."

"No. Thanks."

"Okay." He sank into his chair and drank off half his bottle in a long swallow. When he leaned his head back and closed his eyes, the lines of pain in his face wrenched my heart.

I poured another generous dose of beer down my throat. I knew it wouldn't help, and I didn't care.

Arnie's eyes opened again, and he came to sit beside me on the couch. He took my hand, turning it over to inspect the three-day-old scabs and the fresh cuts and scrapes. He traced the bruises up my arm, barely touching me.

"Can ya tell me what really happened?" He searched my face. "Somebody beat the hell outta ya, looks like a few days ago. An' then there's fresh stuff here. Aydan, tell me who did this to ya. Lemme help ya."

I sighed and leaned my head on his shoulder, taking comfort from his closeness. "The guys who beat me up a few days ago are in jail."

"Guys?" His hand tightened on mine. "How many guys?"

"Two."

"An' how many today?" His voice was very quiet.

"Three."

"Tell me who they are."

"I can't. I don't know who they were. And it wasn't their fault. They weren't trying to hurt me, just hold me."

"Three guys to hold ya? Brave guys," he spat.

I raised a tired shoulder. "That's what it took. There were actually five. I sent two to the hospital. I was completely out of control. But it didn't matter. I was too late anyway." I hid my face in his shoulder.

"Aydan, I can see how much punishment ya took. I know ya would've saved him if ya could. "

"Yeah." I choked up again, and tipped up my beer for another long drink to hide it. Down almost three quarters of the bottle in just a few minutes. I should slow down.

Arnie set aside his empty bottle. "Ya want another?"

"No, not yet."

When he returned with his fresh beer, he put his arm around me again, and we sat in silence for a while. I swallowed the last of my beer. "Was that a funeral date you were writing down earlier?"

"Yeah. It'll be in Winnipeg, on Saturday at one o'clock. I'll see what I can get for flights, but I'll prob'ly go out Saturday mornin', come back Sunday or Monday."

"I'll see if I can do that, too. Will it work for us to

share a rental car?"

"Yeah, if we can get the same flights." He thought for a moment. "I'll be stayin' with Kane's Dad. You could prob'ly stay there, too."

"No, I wouldn't want to intrude. I'll get a hotel." I looked up at his strained face. "John never mentioned his mother. Is she...?"

"She died. Sixteen years ago. Aneurysm." He opened his mouth as if to say more, but shook his head and drank off a few inches of beer instead.

"How's his Dad holding up?"

Arnie tipped up the bottle again and lowered the level of his beer to the halfway point. "He's tough. He's a tough ol' man." He gulped another long swallow. "But he's hurtin'." He took another slug. His second beer was almost gone.

"I can't imagine what it must be like to lose both your children," I said. "I don't even want to think about what he's going through."

Arnie pulled back to look at me. "Ya knew about Dan?"

"Yes, I saw his picture at Kane's and asked about him."

"Oh. Ya were at Kane's place?" His shrewd eyes searched my face. "Were you two...?"

"No." I pushed down the regret. "I was over at his place to look at some documents when we were doing that mission at Harchman's."

He eyed me seriously for a few moments. "Well, darlin', he trusted ya, then. He never took anybody to his place."

"I know." I swallowed hard and tried to take another

gulp of beer before realizing my bottle was empty.

Arnie went to the kitchen and returned with two more beers. We each took a long drink and sat in silence again.

When I glanced over a few minutes later, Arnie's third beer was almost gone, and I started to get concerned. I'd never seen him pound them back like this before.

I gestured to his almost-empty bottle. "You okay?"

"Yeah." He leaned his head back. "Just thinkin'." He absently drained the bottle.

"Ya know, darlin', I got two blood brothers, but Kane's... John was my real brother."

"I didn't realize you had brothers. I guess I never asked. Sorry."

"Yeah. Two brothers an' a sister. I ain't seen Don and Jim in... Christ, ten, fifteen years. More, prob'ly." He sighed. "Kathy, the last time I saw her was thirty years ago. Shit, thirty years ago, this year. I dunno if she's still alive. Prob'ly not, but I keep lookin'..."

He raised his empty bottle and squinted at it. I handed him mine, and he took another deep swallow.

"What happened thirty years ago?" I prompted gently.

"Nothin'." He shrugged. "That was just the last time I saw her. I'd joined up with the army, an' I told her I'd got a mailbox for her so I could send her money. She was hooked on drugs, livin' on the street. Guess she was prob'ly in the sex trade. Dunno how else she coulda paid for her shit. Hell, I was only eighteen. What'd I know."

He slumped lower on the couch. "But my cheques never got cashed. Next time I got out on leave, I went lookin' for her, but she was gone."

He sat up a little straighter and looked me in the eyes. "Kathy was a good person. She tried to take care of me when we were kids."

He slouched down on the couch again and drank some more beer, staring off into the past.

"But it was John an' his folks that saved me," he finished quietly.

He drained the bottle and headed for the kitchen again. "Ya want another?"

"No, thanks."

He brought back two bottles anyway, and handed me one as he sprawled back onto the couch beside me.

Arnie drank off a couple of inches as if they were water, and I decided it might be smart to keep him talking just to slow him down.

"How did John and his parents save you?" I asked.

He turned and examined me, his eyes searching mine. I'd felt that expression on my own face often enough. He was trying to decide if he could trust me enough to tell me.

"I'm sorry," I told him. "I didn't mean to pry. If you don't want to talk about it, that's okay."

He blew out a breath and leaned his head back on the couch, closing his eyes. After a moment, he spoke. "Yeah. Ya know what, darlin', yeah. Tonight, I wanna talk about it. 'Cause somebody else should know what they did for me."

He took another long swallow of beer. "My fam'ly was fucked up from the start," he began. "The ol' man was shitfaced mosta the time. Mean sonuvabitch. Beat the hell outta my mom, beat the hell outta us kids. When I was about five, he was whalin' on me, an' Mom tried to stop him. An' he killed her. Beat her to death right there on the spot."

I clutched his hand, barely able to comprehend the horror. "Arnie, I'm so sorry."

"Cops came, but they were too late," he continued as if he hadn't heard me. "We ended up in a foster home. Jim was the oldest, he was thirteen then. Mean sonuvabitch just like the ol' man. He's pretty much in jail for good now, far as I know. He ain't on my Christmas card list."

The beer bottle sloshed again. "Don, he got married, beat his wife an' kids. I kept tryin' to get 'em both to get help. Last time I went, Don'd been drinkin', an' he got mad."

He absently rubbed the jagged scar on his forearm. "Sometimes, ya gotta know when to give up. Ain't seen him in years." He tipped the last of the beer down his throat and reached to take mine out of my hand.

"Kathy, now." His eyes softened. "She was nine when Mom died. She was always tryin' to take care of me. Lookin' out for her baby brother. All she wanted was for somebody to love her. She started goin' with this asshole when she was thirteen. He got her hooked on drugs. She never had a chance. Poor kid. Never had a chance."

He stared across the room. I sat in silence, overwhelmed by his pain, letting him take his time.

He came back to his story with a sigh. "An' then there was me. They put me into grade one the next fall, an' that's where I met John. We were buddies right from the start. His mom used to invite all the kids over. Guess she felt sorry for me, an' I ended up spendin' mosta my time over there."

He shrugged. "They gave me a bedroom at their place, 'cause I was there all the time anyway. Treated me like I was one of their own kids. Got me into hockey with John an' Dan. Helped me with my homework. Got me music lessons, for chrissake."

He leaned his head back on the couch and stared at the ceiling with a twisted smile. "John and me, we were always pushin' each other. I was more into partyin' than studyin', but I got good marks 'cause I hadta beat John. He'd bug the shit outta me when he beat me on a test."

"I was gettin' into the party scene pretty good by the time we graduated," he continued. He raised the beer bottle in an ironic toast and had another swig. "Dunno where I woulda ended up if John hadn't dared me to join the army."

He gave a faint, humourless chuckle. "So I hadta do it. He was always buggin' me, 'Ya can't take it. Bet ya quit before I do'. Next thing I know, I got my twenty years in. Kept me outta trouble. Mosta the time."

He grinned, then sobered again. "I stayed in a year after he got out, just to prove the point. An' when I got out, John's the one that got me into bein' a PI."

He took another drink of beer. "When I was kid, I swore I'd never be like the ol' man. An' I ain't," he said quietly. "John an' his folks, they saved me."

I gently pried the bottle out of his hand and used the beer to swallow the enormous lump in my throat. As an afterthought, I poured the rest down as well. Then I sat and held his hand in silence.

A couple more beers and some rambling reminiscences of Kane later, I pulled Arnie up off the couch and guided him into the bedroom. I got him undressed and into bed, and then crept in beside him. His arms closed around me, and within seconds he was snoring softly.

Sleep eluded me for a long time.

Kane stood in front of me, his clothes plastered with mud. He raised his gun and pointed it directly at me. Then he fell, his body collapsing bonelessly. His outflung arm bounced as it hit the ground. The gun slid out of his slack fingers to lie on the muddy grass. Stemp smiled at my screams. His gun pointed at my forehead, and his finger tightened on the trigger.

"Aydan! Stop, darlin', shhh, it was just a dream."

I opened my eyes to Arnie's anxious face hovering above me in the semi-darkness. "Aydan. It's okay. It was just a dream."

I curled into an aching ball of misery. "No. It wasn't."

He sighed and curled himself around me, stroking my hair.

I opened my eyes to see Arnie watching me in the morning light. "Mornin', darlin'," he murmured.

"Good morning. How's the head?"

"Been better. Been a long time since I tied one on like that."

"Go back to sleep," I told him.

"Can't."

"I'll get you some aspirin." I rolled over with a groan and sat up slowly. Every inch of my body hurt.

"Stop, darlin', you're in worse shape than I am. I'll get the aspirin. You stay here."

He rolled out of bed and returned in a few moments with the pills and a glass of water. As he came around my side of the bed, he froze.

"Aydan, what the hell's that?"

I followed his gaze to the nightstand. "Glock G26."

"Yeah, I can see that. I meant, what's it doin' here?"

"It's not officially here. You never saw it."

He sat slowly on the edge of the bed and handed me the water and pills. "Darlin', ya know ya need a permit for that." He leaned closer to examine it. "That's a concealed holster, too. Ya do know that's illegal, don't ya?" He eyed me with concern.

"I have a permit. And a license to carry a concealed weapon. And you never saw that gun, because nobody is supposed to know I have it. Which is the whole point of a concealed weapon."

He looked from me to the gun, and back again. "Back in March, Kane told me you were a civilian. I wondered about that." He paused. "I told Dad that you were Kane's partner 'cause I didn't know what else to say. But ya were, weren't ya? Ya really were his partner."

"No. I'm just a civilian. We were just working together on this one thing."

He frowned, and I could see him considering and discarding possibilities. "But Kane got the gun for ya?"

"Yes."

"So maybe he knew he wasn't gonna be around to protect ya?"

I almost doubled over at the sudden pain. I barely managed a whisper. "Maybe."

"Aw, darlin'." My pain was mirrored on his face as he took my hand.

Suddenly, I just couldn't think about it anymore. I put the glass on the nightstand and pulled him to me. I kissed him hard, ignoring the pain from my bruised lips.

"Arnie, I'll understand if you're not in the mood," I whispered. "But I really need to forget about everything for a while. If you can."

He kissed me back gently. "But you're so beat up. I can't even touch ya without hurtin' ya."

"I don't care. You can't hurt me more than I'm hurting already."

He looked deeply into my eyes. "Well, now, darlin', I guess that's true."

His hands moved softly over my aching body. When we lay together afterward, the pillow was damp with tears.

The drive back to Silverside seemed even longer than the previous day's trip, and it was not improved by the knowledge that I'd have to do it again the next morning. Early.

When I got back to the house, I found a message from Spider on my answering machine. It sounded like his cold was worse. His voice was so hoarse that if he hadn't said who it was, I would never have guessed.

When I called his cell phone, he picked up on the first ring. "Aydan?"

"Yeah, hi, Spider," I said dully. "Sorry I missed your call."

"Aydan..." His voice broke. "What... Where are you?"

"I'm home now. I went down to Calgary to tell Arnie about Kane."

He seemed to be having trouble holding his voice steady. "I'm... glad you went to him. Stemp said you'd gone on an errand and you'd be back today. I..." He paused again.

"There's another file in the system. I got an alert."

Slow nausea crept through my stomach. "When?"

"Yesterday morning about eight o'clock."

Kane was still alive at that time. I refused to believe he'd sent it. "I need to see it. Are you in today?"

"Yes."

"I'll be there in half an hour."

Sitting in my office at Sirius Dynamics, I stared blankly across the room. I couldn't believe Kane would never come through that doorway again. His reassuring presence gone from the sim forever. Who would pour me into a bucket and carry me out? Who would fight his way through swamps and snakes, and pull open the bars of the cage for me?

I sucked in an unsteady breath and blew it out slowly as I reached for the phone. This wasn't helping. I'd always taken care of myself. I'd just have to get used to it again.

As I dialled Spider's extension, he appeared in the doorway. I surveyed him with horrified sympathy as I hung up the receiver. His eyes were reddened and deeply shadowed, and his shoulders sagged as if their own weight was more than he could bear.

"Oh, Spider." Without even thinking, I went to him and held him. He buried his face in my shoulder and sobbed like a child. I swung the door shut with my foot to give him some privacy, and my own eyes brimmed with unshed tears while I stroked his hair and let him cry it out.

When he finally subsided into hoarse hiccups, I guided him to the couch and sat beside him with the tissue box. At last, he turned a ravaged face to me.

"I thought you were going to die," he whispered. "And then Kane..." He buried his face in his hands. "This is awful," he quavered. "I hate this."

"I know." I rubbed his back gently. "I hate it, too."

"Stemp said he was a traitor." He spoke without looking at me, his voice muffled by his hands.

"Stemp's a liar."

"Really?" This time he did look at me, his face reflecting the dawning of desperate hope.

"Spider, I believe with all my heart that Kane was loyal. I don't have any proof, but that's what I believe. Let's prove it."

"How?"

"I don't know. Let's look at that new file for starters."

"Okay." He handed me the network key and opened up his laptop. "I'm glad you believe... believed in him, too. I know it doesn't matter now, but..." His voice quavered into silence.

"It matters," I told him fiercely. "It still matters."

The new file turned out to be exactly what I'd expected. It was marked urgent, and it said that I would be executed at the dump site yesterday morning. I spoke to Spider through the network interface.

"Well, this is actually good news."

"Why?" He sounded thoroughly dejected.

"Because now we know for sure that our leak is somebody with a top-level security clearance. You only found out that I was supposed to be executed yesterday morning, right?"

"Yes... Just about an hour before you called me yesterday. The memo was there when I got in. That's why I was in such bad shape, and I had to pretend I had a cold because everybody had strict orders not to discuss it or let you know anything was going on."

"So there wouldn't have been time for our leak to talk to anybody else. He'd have to have sent this message himself. And Stemp said he'd put surveillance cameras in place at the internet cafe the day before yesterday. All we need is those surveillance records."

"Right!" Spider's voice regained some energy. "I can get those."

"Now?"

"No, I'll have to find out from Stemp where the records are being stored."

Ugly suspicion reared its head. "Don't bother, then, Spider," I said as casually as I could. "We can get them later. Right now I need a break and a snack. I'm coming out."

I stepped through the portal slowly, but the pain still made me swear and whimper. When I finally straightened and let go of my head, I avoided Spider's concerned gaze and dragged myself to my feet.

"Come on, Spider, let's go to the Melted Spoon."

"I'm not really hungry," he demurred. "I'll just wait here for you."

Shit.

I sighed and let my shoulders sag. It didn't require much acting skill. "Spider... I'm sorry to be a pain, but I could really use some company." I let my voice tremble a bit, and he looked up with instant sympathy. I knew I could count on his soft heart.

"I'll come with you, then. I could use a walk. I'll just

drop the key off downstairs on the way."

At our table at the Melted Spoon, I pulled out a pen and scribbled on a napkin. "Spider, I was thinking about making some changes to my program. What do you think about this?"

I pushed the napkin over to him, and he frowned at it for a second as he read my note. He met my eyes cautiously. "I think that might work." He reached into his pocket and withdrew his scanning device. I held my breath while he activated it.

"Clear." He leaned forward over the table. "Why the note? What's going on?"

"I was afraid we might be bugged or under surveillance at Sirius. Or here."

"Surveillance for sure at Sirius, that's company policy. Probably bugs, too, and the network is monitored."

"I'm afraid to discuss anything about this leak while we're inside Sirius. If it's somebody with a high-level clearance, they'll be able to listen in on everything we say."

Spider's eyes widened. "You're right. Crap. Oh." Comprehension dawned on his face. "That's why you told me not to bother with the surveillance records."

"Yes. Can you hack them instead?"

He sat back smugly in his chair. "I can hack anything."

I laughed. "Anybody else, I'd accuse of boasting. You, I believe. How soon can you get them?"

"Gee, I just happen to have my laptop with me." He set it on the table between us.

"You always have your laptop with you," I teased him. "It's a permanent part of your body."

"Uh-huh." His fingers flew across the keyboard, and

my heart eased a bit as the sparkle came back into his eyes.

I sipped my tea and nibbled my muffin quietly while he worked away, utterly absorbed. I was just draining the last few drops of lukewarm tea when he straightened.

"Here we go." He turned the screen so we could both see, and brought up a surveillance record. "This is from yesterday morning, starting at seven A.M. when the cafe opened."

We watched the fast-forward intently, and my heart plummeted as Kane's massive shoulders temporarily blocked the camera. "Stop there!"

Spider punched a key and we exchanged a sick look as he rewound and then played the record forward. We watched Kane sit down at a terminal. He worked for a few minutes, and then stood and left.

I realized my hands were shaking. I peeled my tongue loose from my dry mouth. "What time was that?" My voice came out in a whisper. I didn't really want to know.

"Seven-thirty." Spider's voice was full of relief. "Too early. The file wasn't sent until eight-ten."

"Oh." It came out sounding like a sob, and I quickly added, "Good. Keep going. Go a little slower now. This is our critical timeframe."

"This is starting at eight o'clock. I'll run it at regular speed." His fingers flew across the keyboard again, and we exchanged glances as the video ran. He paused it at the eight-twenty mark, and we stared at each other wordlessly.

"Shit." I rubbed the frown wrinkles out of my forehead. "What are the chances that three top-level Sirius people would be there at the same damn time?"

I peered at the screen again. "Can you tell what they're doing?"

"No. But I think Mike Connor spends most of his waking hours there. He was just getting into World of Warcraft when I met him in March, and he's been going crazy on it ever since. But we investigated him in March, and he came up clean."

"Well, I don't believe Germain would rat me out," I said firmly. "It's got to be Stemp, dammit, I know it! He's such a slimy sonuvabitch!"

Spider turned an anxious face to me. "He's the director. It can't be him."

"Well, it's got to be somebody. And I don't trust him any further than I can throw him. A lot less, in fact. He'd lie to you as soon as look at you."

"Yes, but..." Spider's voice trailed off. "But I just don't dare think of the ramifications if the director himself is corrupt."

"Better start daring," I said grimly.

"But he put the cameras in himself," Spider argued. "He'd have to be an idiot to go in there and send that file when he knew he'd show up on the video."

"That guy's so twisty, he could make it look like anything he wanted." I rubbed my forehead again, feeling the precursors of what promised to be a whopper of a headache. "Well, until further notice, we'll have to consider Stemp, Germain, and Connor under suspicion."

Spider's face fell. "I really hate this."

"Me, too. Let's go, we've already taken too long a coffee break. We don't want to draw suspicion ourselves."

As we walked back to Sirius, I turned to Spider. "Hey, Spider, can you sneak me one of those scanning devices?"

"I thought you didn't want one."

"Changed my mind."

"Okay."

After a couple more hours in the network, my headache fulfilled its potential, and I groaned as Spider and I walked down to the main lobby to turn in our security fobs. "God, I'm not looking forward to a two-hour drive tomorrow morning."

"Oh. Are you going..." Spider gulped. "Are you going to the funeral?"

"Of course. I fly out tomorrow morning at eight-fifteen."

"Germain and I got a flight at eight. Do you want to ride down with us?"

"Depends, when are you coming back?"

"We leave Winnipeg on Sunday at two-thirty."

I sighed relief. "In that case, yes, I'd definitely like to ride with you. I leave at one-fifty, so I'll just hang around the Calgary airport until you guys get in. Oh, and can I ride with you in Winnipeg, too? I was going to bum a ride with Hellhound, but he went out this afternoon, and he's not coming back until Monday."

"No problem."

"Thanks, Spider, you're a lifesaver."

"Can we pick you up at five tomorrow morning?"

"That'll work."

I trailed into my stuffy house and opened all the windows before I went scrounging for some semblance of nutritious food. I nibbled without enthusiasm, and eventually wandered outside to my garden.

I stood in the moist, aromatic soil and held back tears while I ate fresh peas.

CHAPTER 40

Emotionally and physically exhausted, I crept into bed early, hoping to get a decent sleep before my early morning. At last, I found a position that didn't aggravate my bruises too much, and drifted away.

Kane's anguished eyes burned into mine. He raised his gun, black in the bright sunlight. His expression changed to shock as he fell slowly. His limp body sprawled in the mud. The gun slipped from his lax fingers, the sunshine picking out the logo on the barrel as it settled in the grass. Stemp stood over Kane's body, firing into it again and again while I screamed.

I bolted upright as the last scream ripped from my throat. Panting with physical pain and overwrought emotion, I curled down again, rocking with grief. Stemp was the leak. He had to be. I knew it.

My mind wouldn't let go of the vivid imagery of the dream. Ridiculously green grass, the logo on the pistol, Kane's eyes. I whimpered and scrubbed at my face. How long would I have to dream this, over and over?

I remembered the look in Kane's eyes. Nobody could fake that. Stemp had to be lying. In the darkness, the image hung in front of me.

Suddenly, I sat up, my mouth dropping open. Stemp

was lying. I knew it for certain now. That hadn't been a tranquilizer gun in Kane's hand. It was his Sig Sauer P226. My memory jogged by the detail in my dream, I could remember the pistol lying in the grass after it fell. The Sig logo on the barrel had been unmistakeable in the bright sunshine. Kane was no traitor.

I curled up and cried.

I was still awake when my alarm went off at four A.M. I groaned my way into the shower, and dressed slowly in the blouse and slacks that I would wear to the funeral. I threw some clothes into my small backpack, and carefully weeded through everything, checking for anything that could be construed as a weapon by the airport security.

When I heard the crunching of tires on gravel at five, I closed up the house and climbed into Germain's SUV. Both men's faces looked drawn and tired in the dim light of the dashboard panel. We exchanged subdued greetings, and then fell silent as the highway unrolled in front of us in the gray light.

At the airport, Germain offered to drop us at the departure area, and I gratefully accepted. I was only carrying my small backpack, but I still felt too stiff and sore to walk for very long. Spider joined me as we stood by the check-in, waiting for Germain to park.

I looked up at his pale face. "Hey, Spider, I remembered something last night."

"What?" he asked listlessly.

"I know for sure now that Stemp was lying. He said Kane was going to shoot me with a tranquilizer gun and take me to Fuzzy Bunny, but it wasn't a trank gun in Kane's hand."

"Are you sure?" His brow furrowed. "What does

that really mean?"

"I'm positive. And what it means is that Kane really intended to shoot me."

Spider's eyes widened with horror. "Kane was going to kill you? And you're still coming to his funeral?"

"Yeah, of course." I took another look at his face. "Hey, Spider, that's a good thing. It's good that he was going to kill me."

"Aydan, that's awful," he wailed. "That's not a good thing at all!"

"No, no, it's good. It means he was following orders. He wasn't a traitor! And there's more. Right after those guys took me out, I was lying there with my face squished into the dirt, and Stemp said 'I didn't think he'd really kill you.' What does that tell you?"

Spider shook his head in bewildered dismay. "I don't know. What?"

"It tells you, he knew Kane didn't have a trank gun in his hand. He knew Kane was holding his Sig. And then, a few minutes later, Stemp lied to me and told me it was a trank gun. He's a filthy, disgusting liar. And a murderer."

Spider's mouth dropped open. "Then we're in serious trouble. And you're in serious danger."

I twitched an impatient shoulder. "Same old, same old. That's not what matters. What matters is that we were right. Kane died a hero. And when we finally nail Stemp's ass to the wall, Kane can rest in peace."

"Do we tell Germain?" Spider whispered. "Here he comes."

"No, not yet." I turned to greet Germain. I believed in him, but I wasn't quite ready to share my theories. I needed more time to think about our next step. I had a lot to occupy my mind on the two-hour flight to Winnipeg.

By the time we sorted out the rental car paperwork and left the Winnipeg airport, we had just enough time to stop for lunch before heading for the chapel. We ate without much appetite, and Spider and Germain carried their bags into the men's room to change.

They emerged a few minutes later, Spider in a dark suit that made him look even paler, and Germain in an impeccable dress uniform, his usually cheerful face grim and withdrawn. The drive to the chapel was very quiet.

I clamped down hard on my emotions as we entered the lobby. Kane had been a brave man. The least I could do was show a little courage of my own. A few men stood around the lobby, most of them in uniform. I glimpsed General Briggs, but fortunately not Stemp. As we made our way toward the chapel doors, I realized with a shock that Hellhound was standing near the entrance.

Somewhere in the back of my mind, I'd known he wouldn't be wearing his usual jeans and T-shirt, but the imposing man in the immaculate uniform made my jaw drop. He'd never be handsome, but his stern, ugly face had a stark magnetism.

His expression softened as I came up to him. "Hi, darlin'." He folded me into his arms, and I pressed against him for a few seconds of comfort. As I drew away, he turned to the ramrod-straight uniformed man beside him. "Sir, this's Aydan Kelly. John's partner. Aydan, this's John's dad."

I recognized Kane's intent grey eyes as they surveyed me from his father's wrinkled face. He extended a hand. "Doug Kane. Pleased to meet you."

I accepted his firm handshake. "I'm so sorry for your

loss."

Bleak eyes met mine, but his face was composed. So like his son. "Thank you."

I turned away before my eyes welled up.

I managed to hold it together for most of the short service. I avoided looking at the urn at the front of the chapel. Such a small resting place for such a big man. Germain sat stiffly to my left, his dry-eyed face etched with hard lines. On my right, Spider wept openly and unabashedly.

As the service drew to a close, the chaplain stepped away from the pulpit, and Arnie stood and made his way to the front. He leaned down to the microphone. "Ya know I ain't much for words. But I gotta say goodbye to my brother somehow."

He stood tall and straight, and began to sing 'The Wings That Fly Us Home' completely unaccompanied, his voice strong and sure. I gulped helplessly at the lump in my throat and held my head high, but I couldn't stop the tears that ran down my cheeks.

After the interment at the cemetery, I drifted away from the group. I was gazing blankly out across the headstones when I sensed someone behind me. I turned to see Arnie's uniformed bulk.

His face was still stern and emotionless, but his eyes broke my heart. I reached to touch his cheek, and he closed his eyes and leaned into my palm for a just second.

When he spoke, his voice was controlled. "You're invited back to the house. It's just gonna be a few friends."

I cleared the huskiness from my throat. "I wouldn't want to intrude. I have to go back with Germain and Spider and find a hotel anyway."

He reached for my hand. "I'd like ya to be there."

I stroked his strong fingers. "Then I'll come. What's the address?"

"You can ride with me." He moved back to the group, and I turned and stood alone for a few more minutes.

When I heard footsteps approaching behind me, I expected Arnie again. Instead, Doug Kane came up beside me and we stood quietly watching the dispersing group around the grave.

He spoke without looking at me. "Arnie tells me you were with John when he died."

"Yes." I didn't know what else to say. "He was doing his duty. He died a hero."

"You can't tell me any more than that, can you?"

"No." It sounded so final. I had no comfort to offer. This should never have happened. "I'm sorry," I stammered finally. My voice came out in a whisper. "I'm sorry I couldn't save him."

The grey eyes turned to assess me then. "Arnie says you fought through five men to help John."

"I didn't get through. And it was too late anyway. I'm so sorry."

He took in my scrapes and bruises. "Nobody could have done more. And John told me you saved his life twice before. You gave me my son for a little longer."

"He told you that? I didn't think he would have discussed..."

"No details. He just said that he was working with a new partner, and that he thought very highly of her."

I stood in silence, fighting for control.

"I hope you're coming back to the house," he said.

I managed to find my voice. "Thank you, I will.

Arnie invited me earlier."

The piercing grey eyes appraised me again. "You're fond of Arnie, aren't you?"

"Yes. He's a good friend."

"He's a good man." He rocked back and forth, heel to toe. "He's fond of you, too, I can tell." He glanced quickly at my face. "Don't hurt my boy."

My throat closed up. "I'll do everything in my power not to," I said huskily. I'd caused the death of one of his boys, just through my own existence. God help me.

His face softened. "I believe you. But I need to tell you something to keep you from getting hurt, too."

He sighed and rocked heel to toe again. "You need to understand that Arnie will never give you a committed relationship. He's been hurt too badly to offer that to anyone. Don't fool yourself into thinking that he will."

I gazed at him, touched that he'd care enough to protect me as well as his adopted son. "Arnie and I had that conversation," I told him gently. "I don't want that from him, or from anybody. All I want from him is what we have now."

His smile was like the sun coming out, his steady eyes framed by a maze of wrinkles. "Then I'm glad he has you."

At the house, a handful of men reminisced in the living room, chuckling over stories of John playing hockey, winning track and field competitions, and chasing girls. I discovered he'd gotten his love of all things automotive from his father, who'd owned a speed shop after he retired from the army. We chatted easily about cars, and as the guests gradually drifted away, I realized that the afternoon was gone, and it was supper time.

I rose. "I should get checked into the hotel. I'll just give Germain a call and ask him to pick me up."

"You're welcome to stay here," Doug Kane offered courteously.

"Thank you, but I wouldn't want to trouble you," I told him.

"No trouble," he assured me. The lines crinkled around his eyes, so much like John it wrenched my heart. "Especially if I'm correct in my assumption that I wouldn't need to make up another bed."

Faint heat rose to my cheeks. You never really get over the idea that parents shouldn't know about your sex life. But what the hell, I wasn't embarrassed about my relationship with Arnie. I grinned back at his adopted dad. "True."

"Stay?" Arnie slipped his hand into mine, and I looked up into his desolate eyes again.

"Okay. I'll just have to get my things from Germain. I left my backpack in the rental car."

"I'll take ya over to the hotel to pick it up. It's time ya ate anyway, so we can get some supper on the way." He turned to Doug. "Come along with us. Ya gotta eat somethin', too."

Doug shook his head. "I have too much food in the house already. I'll eat here. I'll see you kids later." He winked at Arnie. "You make sure you get in before your curfew, boy."

Arnie's face twisted in a bittersweet smile. "Yessir."

Later, as we lay in bed, I stroked Arnie's face and brushed a kiss across his lips. "Hard day."

He sighed. "Yeah." His arms tightened around me carefully, mindful of my bruises. "Thanks for stayin'."

"Glad to. I needed some comfort, too."

He turned his face into my hair. "It's not like we really did a lotta shit together," he mumbled. "We were both busy. Sometimes we wouldn't see each other for months. But I always knew he was there, ya know?"

"I know."

I held him until he relaxed into merciful sleep at last.

Kane stood beside the bed, his clothes coated with mud. In the dimness, I saw his smile, the laugh lines crinkling around his eyes. I reached for him. My dream-self knew it was a dream, yet it was vividly real.

He leaned down to kiss me, and his lips were hungry on mine. "Aydan," he whispered. "I want you." I pulled him closer, gasping at the sensation of his hands running over my naked body. My hands slid under his dirty T-shirt to caress the hard muscles of his chest. Then the T-shirt was gone, and he was pulling off his jeans.

When he lowered himself on top of me, the touch of his skin burned like fire against me. I wrapped my arms around him as I kissed him furiously, pulling him closer. I pressed against him, desperate with the need to feel him inside me.

His eyes widened, and his body suddenly sprawled limply on top of me. Terror drove through me at the horrible laxity of his muscles.

I struggled to push him over onto his back,

whimpering frantically. At last, his body flopped over under my efforts, his massive arm slithering loosely over his chest. His eyes stared sightlessly as I began CPR, sobbing with the effort. I knew I was too late. He was already dead.

"Aydan, wake up, darlin'." Arnie's hands were gentle on my shoulders. "Shhh, Aydan, it's just a dream."

"I couldn't save him. I couldn't save him." I wept helplessly against Arnie's chest while he held me in the darkness.

CHAPTER 41

In the morning, I said subdued goodbyes to Doug Kane and Arnie, and gratefully boarded the plane for a couple of hours of solitary introspection. I had a measure of relief now that the funeral was over, and I could settle down to a level of functional numbness.

By the time the plane landed, I'd mapped out the beginnings of a strategy to trap Stemp.

When we pulled into my yard a couple of hours later, I turned to Spider. "Hey, Spider, I'm having some computer problems. Can you come in and have a look?"

He eyed me tiredly for a few seconds before the subtext got through to him. "Oh! Sure, no problem."

I turned to Germain. "Thanks for the ride. If you want to head out, I'll run Spider home when he's done."

Germain agreed, and Spider and I went into my house without speaking. Once inside, I held a finger to my lips as I retrieved the scanner he'd given me and quickly scanned for bugs.

"Clear," I said, and he sighed relief.

He cocked a quizzical eyebrow at me. "I'm assuming your computer is fine."

"Yeah. I wanted to talk to you in private before we got started at Sirius again. I've been thinking about Stemp. Is there any way you can snoop on what he's doing at the internet cafe?"

Spider raised an eyebrow. "I have many ways. What exactly did you have in mind?"

"Can you tell if he's the one that's sending the messages to Fuzzy Bunny?"

"Not unless I catch him in the act of doing it. I'd have to snoop on his actual session."

I sighed. "Too bad. That would've been too easy, wouldn't it?" I thought about it for a moment. "I guess we'd better check and see if my filter has caught anything more. If it has, we can cross-check the surveillance footage again..."

My voice trailed off as an idea occurred to me.

"What?" Spider demanded.

"Can you bring up the surveillance records from here?"

"Sure. I just..."

"Happen to have your laptop with you," I finished for him, and he smiled as he pulled it out of his bag.

"Of course. What are you looking for in the surveillance?"

"I wonder how often Stemp goes to the internet cafe."

Spider shrugged. "Let's find out." His fingers flew over the keyboard.

In minutes, we were looking at surveillance records. As we fast-forwarded through them one after another, I turned to Spider to see my growing smile reflected on his face.

"Well, well. A creature of habit. Isn't that convenient," I mused. "So, what are you doing tomorrow morning around eight o'clock?"

"Same thing I'll be doing at one in the afternoon. And nine at night." Spider's predatory grin was incongruous on his boyish face. "Hacking into Stemp's internet session."

We reviewed the last of the records, and then Spider shut the machine down. "Interesting. The man's like clockwork. Same times, even on weekends. I guess that explains why he was in the surveillance record before. When you do something habitually like that, you just keep doing it, and nobody pays any attention."

I grinned at him. "Except us. Let's go to Sirius and see if there's anything new in our filters."

At Sirius Dynamics, I idled my way through the deserted building on my way to my office while Spider retrieved the network key from the secured area. On a Sunday evening, the only sign of life was the bored guard in the security wicket.

I wandered through the door of my office, turning over strategies in my mind. I jerked to a halt with a yelp of surprise when I realized I wasn't alone.

John Smith stood up from behind my desk. The solid wall of his body odour hit me from six feet away. I surveyed him with distaste, wondering if that was still the same shirt he'd been wearing three weeks ago. I thought the pattern of food stains looked familiar.

"Ms. Kelly," he greeted me warily.

"What are you doing in here?" I demanded.

He ran a hand through his lank, thinning hair. "Since I've been assigned as your handler, I was checking over the structures that you've created in the network. I wanted to be prepared for tomorrow morning." He frowned. "Why are you here tonight?"

"I've missed several days of work. I wanted to check my filters to see if there's anything urgent."

"I didn't see anything there," he said. After a short

pause, he continued. "I'm impressed with your program. It shows a surprising level of sophistication."

I held back my instinctive retort at the patronizing compliment. At least the guy was making an effort to be pleasant. He was probably hoping to get off on the right foot.

Because the last time he'd pissed me off in the network, he'd gotten my right foot in a place that had caused him considerable discomfort.

I smiled. "Thanks."

Spider appeared in the doorway and halted uncertainly, looking from me to Smith.

"Webb," Smith greeted him.

"Hi." Spider glanced at me. "Um..."

"We're going to be a while, if you want to leave," I told Smith. Subtle, that's my middle name.

"As your handler, I need to be here," he disagreed. "In fact, going forward, I need to be present at all times when you're in the network. You'll need to provide me with a schedule of your planned access times."

Shit. That was going to throw a wrench in the works. I didn't like him. I didn't trust him. And I really didn't like the way he smelled. I tried to sigh and hold my breath at the same time. The resulting grunt was unbecoming.

"Fine. Spider, let's get started." I plopped down on the sofa and waited while he set up his laptop. We both ignored Smith as he took a seat at the desk. As soon as Spider gave me the nod, I stepped into the network.

I took a deep breath of the untainted virtual air as I headed for my program. With determination, I tamped down the wave of self-pity that threatened. Trading Kane for Smith was like trading an Audi R8 for a manure spreader.

I shook myself and firmly focused my attention on

the job at hand. Kane was out of the picture. Suck it up and get on with life. I managed not to tear up only because I knew Spider was monitoring me.

As Smith had informed me, my filters were empty. The good news was that nobody was trying to talk to Fuzzy Bunny. The bad news was that nobody was trying to talk to Fuzzy Bunny. I sighed. I would have preferred to see something there. I was positive Kane hadn't betrayed me. But a bit of proof would have been really welcome.

I double-checked the program to make sure that it was working. It was, and I made my way back to the portal with a sigh.

I barely noticed the soft impact against my head when I folded over to swear and clutch my headache. As the pain subsided, my stream of profanity was drowned out by angry shouting. I hurriedly dragged my eyes open to see Spider and Smith squared off in front of me. Spider's fists were clenched, his eyes blazing in his flushed face. I slowly registered his words.

"...dare you! Keep your hands off her, you pervert!"

"I wasn't." Smith backed away slowly, his hands raised placatingly. "I wouldn't, I was just..."

"Is there a problem here?" Germain stepped into the room, his sharp eyes assessing the combatants. I breathed a silent sigh of relief. Germain was about half an inch taller than me, but the breadth of his powerful shoulders made him look short and square. I'd watched him spar in practice with Kane only a few weeks ago. If there had been a problem earlier, it was officially over now.

"Aydan, are you okay?" he asked. "What's going on?"

I straightened up and let go of my head. "I'm fine. I

don't know what's happening."

"He was... He was *fondling* Aydan while she was in the network!" Spider blurted out, his face scarlet. He glared at Smith. "You're sick!"

"I wasn't!" Smith's face was reddening, too. "I was just going to massage her temples."

Germain frowned. "Aydan? What happened?"

I stared at him as faint nausea rose in my stomach. "I don't know. You know I can't feel anything with my physical body when I'm in the network. It takes a pain stimulus to wake me."

The nausea intensified as I realized that Smith could literally have stripped me naked and had sex with my real body while I was in the network, and I'd never have known unless he actually caused me pain. I was sure he hadn't done that, but the thought of it was horrifying. I shuddered violently before I could stop myself.

"Webb," Germain snapped. "What did you see?"

"Aydan was coming out of the network, and I was just going out to take the key back to the secured area. I realized I'd forgotten to set up our schedule for tomorrow, so I came back in, and he was standing in front of her, running his fingers through her hair..."

"I wasn't!" Smith barked. "How stupid do you think I am? If I was going to assault her, I wouldn't do it when I knew she was coming out of the network and I'd be sure to get caught!"

"So you've given this some thought," Germain said evenly.

"No! Jeez!" Smith's eyes darted around the room as if looking for an escape route. "I'm her handler. I read up on Kane's reports, and he noted that massaging her temples helps relieve her pain on exiting the network. I was just trying to help!"

Spider opened his mouth to retort, and I could see that this would only devolve into a 'yes-you-did, no-I-didn't' argument. I stood up and put my hand on his arm. "It's okay, Spider, thanks for looking out for me."

I turned to Smith. "If you were just trying to be thorough, I appreciate it, but for your own safety, you shouldn't come near me when I'm in the network. It can be quite disorienting for me to exit, and I sometimes have violent and unpredictable reactions."

I met Smith's eyes. Clearly, he'd gotten the message. He took a step backward as his angry flush drained away. "But... what if you stop breathing again?" he stammered. "Who will resuscitate you? Should I just stand here and watch you die?"

"You don't need to worry about giving Aydan mouth-to-mouth," Germain said quietly. "Webb has completed his emergency training. He'll be with Aydan at all times when she's in the network from now on. He'll deal with any medical emergencies that might arise. Isn't that right, Webb?"

"That's right," Spider agreed, his young face hard.

Smith threw up his hands. "Fine! Jeez, I'm just trying to do my job!" He detoured widely around Germain as he stormed out.

"Man, does that guy ever wash?" Germain asked.

I fanned the air in front of my face. "Apparently not. Thanks, Carl. I'm glad you were here."

His normally humorous face was sober. "You're welcome. But you should definitely take precautions. It didn't occur to me how vulnerable you are when you're in the network. Everybody else wakes up at the slightest touch."

I shuddered. "It didn't occur to me until now, either. I've always been with you guys, and I trust you. It never even crossed my mind."

"Well, thanks, that's good to hear." Germain gave me a tired smile. "Take care. See you later." He strode out the door.

I sighed. "I've had it for tonight."

"Is it okay if we start at nine tomorrow?" Spider asked.

"Actually, I have to be at the Greenhorn at ten," I told him. "Do you want to meet after lunch? I could be here by..." I thought for a second. I wanted to make sure he had enough time to eavesdrop on Stemp's session at the internet cafe.

"How about two," Spider broke in. "I need to spend some time over at the office..." His voice wavered, and we met each other's eyes miserably. The office that he'd shared with Kane.

"Okay, two o'clock it is," I agreed, trying to avoid the thought. "Come on. I'll wait for you in the lobby and then I'll drop you at home."

"Thanks." He trudged out the door, his shoulders sagging.

I had the same dream about Kane again and woke up screaming. Sex and death. I knew it was only my subconscious mind replaying my husband's final moments, but I felt very alone as I lay shivering in bed.

In the morning, I dragged myself into the shower. The bruises and scrapes were still tender, but the stiffness was gone from my muscles. I stood for a long time in the hot spray, wishing it could ease the ache in my heart.

I had an hour before I needed to leave for the Greenhorn, so I carried my guns out to the firing range for a bit more practice in the morning. I deliberately concentrated on drawing the Glock quickly to make fast, smooth shots. If I got another chance, I wouldn't waste it.

At the Greenhorn Cafe, Jeff and Donna hovered solicitously, concerned about my injuries. I passed them off as slow healing from my run-in with Bill Harks, and they seemed to believe me. I hated to lie to them, but their concern warmed my heart. I left with a full stomach and the comfort of friendship.

I had time to kill before meeting Spider at two o'clock, and it was another beautiful, hot day. I parked at Sirius with the intention of waiting there, but on impulse, I decided to treat myself. I wandered over to the ice cream shop in the next block and took my place in the lineup. I'd just taken a seat at one of the sidewalk tables when I spotted Mike Connor strolling along the sidewalk toward Sirius.

I waved at him, and he did a double-take. Consternation filled his face as he made his way rapidly to my side. "Aydan! How did you... How are you holding up?" He examined my bruises. "Are you okay?"

"Fine, thanks, Mike," I assured him, touched by his obvious concern. I could see why he and Spider had hit it off so well. They were both so gentle and warm-hearted. We chatted pleasantly for a few minutes before he strode off. I finished my ice cream cone and headed for Sirius.

Spider and Smith were already waiting for me in my office, and I drew in a deep breath before entering Smith's noxious aura. At least he saw no need to follow me into the network, and I settled down to my decryption with relief.

I'd only been working for a few minutes when Spider's tense voice interrupted me. "Aydan! I just got an alert!"

I dove for the filter program and quickly decrypted the message. A peculiar mixture of fury and relief and fear filled me. That motherfucker Stemp had killed an innocent man. A good man. Kane was definitely in the clear now. But I was in serious danger, and I didn't have Kane to watch my back anymore.

I spoke through the network interface. "Our guy's at it again." I bit off a more detailed explanation. "Spider, could you please ask Smith to let Stemp know right away?"

"Sure." There was a pause, and then his voice came through the interface again. "Aydan, I need a break. I'm going to go over to the Melted Spoon. Want to come?"

"I'll be right there." I folded sim-space and stepped out the portal, holding my head together with both hands. By the time I'd finished swearing, Spider was jittering in the doorway.

Anxiety scuttled down my back on icy feet, and I stood a little more briskly than I would have under normal circumstances. I swore some more as I staggered into the coffee table and bruised my shins.

Spider eyed me with concern. "Are you okay?"

"Fine. Just stood up too fast. Let's go."

I didn't have to tell him twice. He strode down the hall at a pace I'd never seen him use before. In the lobby, I turned in my security fob while I waited for him to emerge from the secured facility. When he did, he made a beeline for the exit, and I had to remind him to drop off his own security fob before leaving.

Once on the sidewalk, he set a hurried pace for the Melted Spoon. I hadn't realized how fast those lanky legs could move. "What's the hurry?" I panted as I trotted beside him.

I got the distinct impression that he was grinding his teeth. "Stemp," he gritted. "He showed up late today at the internet cafe, wouldn't you know it? He was just getting started when I had to leave to meet you."

He shot through the door of the Melted Spoon and had his laptop open on the table before his butt hit the chair. His face was intent while his fingers flew.

Trying to maintain some semblance of casual behaviour, I went up to the counter and ordered us each a cup of tea. I sipped mine while Spider sat engrossed. Finally, he glanced up with a wolfish grin. "Ha! Katya!"

He ducked back behind the screen. At last, he resurfaced with a sigh, rubbing his eyes.

I gave him a raised eyebrow. "What language was that?"

"Bulgarian."

"Say what?"

"Katya. That's the name of Stemp's contact. In Bulgaria. That's who he contacted this morning and this afternoon."

"Bulgaria?" I frowned at him. "Does that mean anything to you?"

"Maybe," he said slowly. "Fuzzy Bunny does a lot of business in the eastern bloc countries. But it wouldn't make sense for Stemp to be contacting them there, when we're here."

He smiled, and I recognized the look of the hunter. "But he's definitely hiding something. He went to a good deal of effort to cover his tracks to Katya, whoever she is. If it is a she."

"We'd better get back," I told him. "Smith is going to wonder what the hell we're doing. Let's talk while we walk."

He packed up his laptop, and we meandered down the sidewalk toward Sirius. "Spider, this latest message was a request for Fuzzy Bunny to contact Stemp," I told him.

His jaw dropped. "Stemp, specifically?"

"No. I mean, our guy. I'm just sure it's Stemp."

"If you're sure it's Stemp, why did you tell Smith to tell him you'd detected a message?"

I shrugged. "Because if he sent the message himself, and if he knew we were monitoring the network, he'd be suspicious if I didn't."

"But why would he do that?" His brow furrowed. "Aydan, it doesn't make sense."

"Well, he'd have to, wouldn't he? He wouldn't want to arouse suspicion if he wanted to stay in his position as director."

"But... Aydan, he told everybody that Kane was the traitor. If he wanted to maintain that story, he wouldn't send another message that he knew we'd catch."

I groaned and hugged my aching head. "I don't know why he's doing what he's doing, but he's a lying slimeball. And he murdered an innocent man. That's all I need to know."

Spider paced along beside me frowning. "You didn't mention the contents of the message to Smith."

"I didn't want to give anybody more information than necessary. Because I have an idea."

"What?" He eyed me with interest.

"I think Stemp..." I caught Spider's eye. "Okay, *our*

guy, whoever he is, will get suspicious if he doesn't get a response. But this could really work for us. What if we pretend to be Fuzzy Bunny? Tell him this method of contact isn't secure anymore, and set him up to communicate with us directly? Only he wouldn't know it was us, he'd think he was talking to Fuzzy Bunny."

"A sting!" Spider grinned at me. "That's brilliant! I love it!"

"Okay, then." I grinned back at him as we walked into Sirius. "Let's do it."

I pulled up short when we came face to face with Stemp in the lobby. Pure red rage surged through my veins at the sight of his reptilian features, and I gulped it back, holding onto control by its ragged edges. I felt my fists clench and my shoulders bunch as I took a single step toward him, my eyes locked on his detestable face.

"Aydan...?" Spider's quavering voice barely penetrated my consciousness. I brushed his restraining hand off and took another step.

Stemp stood his ground, watching me expressionlessly. Another step. He was only about an inch taller than I was, and I glared directly into his eyes from close range.

"Looks like you were wrong about Kane." I was fighting so hard to restrain myself that it came out barely above a whisper. Apparently the menace came through loud and clear, though. His impassive face never changed, but his eyes twitched sideways just a fraction.

Do it, asshole. Make a sudden move. Give me a reason.

We stared at each other in silence.

"Maybe," he said at last, his voice almost as quiet as

mine.

"Aydan!" I became dimly aware that Spider was tugging on my arm, almost whimpering. "Aydan, come on. Let's go."

I spared him a glance, and as soon as our eye contact was broken, Stemp took a couple of slow, smooth steps backward. Then he turned and casually walked away.

I stared holes in his back, my breath hissing through my clenched teeth.

"Aydan, stop. You're scaring me," Spider pleaded.

"Sorry." The word rasped from my constricted throat. I swallowed again and tried to unclench my muscles. Violent tremors shook me.

"Come and sit down." Spider tugged me gently toward one of the reception chairs.

I sat stiffly and stared into middle distance while I imposed yoga breathing and struggled to calm down.

"Everything okay?" Germain eyed me with concern on his way through the lobby.

Great. Of course I had to make a spectacle of myself when everybody was coming back from lunch. Although come to think of it, he must have taken a late lunch, too.

"Fine." I managed a more civilized tone this time. I stood carefully and made my way to the security wicket to pick up my fob, avoiding his gaze.

CHAPTER 42

After a couple more hours of decryption, I took my aching head down to the lobby to turn in my security fob for the day. Then I loitered outside on the sidewalk, waiting for Spider to appear.

I was foiled when he came out the door deep in conversation with Mike Connor. I raised a casual hand. "See you tomorrow, Spider."

"Oh, hold on," he replied. "Before you go, I want to talk to you for a minute."

"I guess I should get going," Mike told him. "World of Warcraft tonight?"

"Um, no." A faint flush appeared on Spider's cheeks. "I, um, have plans."

Mike surveyed him quizzically. "What kind of plans? Remember, we've got that big campaign tonight. It'll be great. Can't you do your other stuff tomorrow?"

"Actually, um..." Spider studied his feet. "I'm seeing Linda tonight."

Connor's face split in a grin. "Linda Burton? Good luck with that. Half the guys in town are chasing her."

Spider raised an awkward shoulder. "Actually, she asked me."

Mike's jaw dropped. "You lucky..." He glanced quickly at me and apparently decided to save the guy talk for another time. "Okay, well, that's a good enough excuse, I guess. See you tomorrow." He tossed off a jaunty salute and strode away.

Spider turned to me, still slightly pink. I decided to let it lie. "I have an idea for our sting," I told him quietly as we strolled down the sidewalk. "I have to go to Blue Eddy's and Up & Coming tomorrow, so I'll have time to sneak into the phone store and get a couple of disposable cell phones. We can set those up as our communication channels."

"That should work," he agreed. "How are you going to send the message?"

"I thought I could make it look like it came from Fuzzy Bunny if I generated it from just outside Fuzzy Bunny's firewall. Our guy provided contact information, so it should work."

"Perfect." He paused. "I'll dig into Katya some more tonight if I have time."

I patted him on the shoulder. "Don't make it a priority. Have fun with Linda."

He blushed. "Thanks."

That night, I dreamed of Kane again. As before, he stood beside my bed, looking down at me.

I knew he was dead. I tried to stop the dream, but he stooped and took my hand.

"Aydan."

Giving in, I pulled him closer. At least I could have a few short moments. I pushed the sheets aside and kissed him deeply as I placed his hands on my breasts. I felt his indrawn breath against my lips. "Aydan. Oh, God."

I tugged at his T-shirt, running hungry hands over the taut muscles underneath. He stood, and I reached for him.

"Please..." The word wrenched out of me.

Please don't go. Please don't die this time. I willed the dream to continue with all my might.

He groaned. "Aydan... Goddammit..." Then he was stripping off his clothes. His weight pressed me onto the bed. His demanding mouth found my lips, my throat, my breasts. Fierce heat overwhelmed me.

"Please..."

I spread my legs for him and clamped my hands on his perfect ass to pull him closer. We both cried out when he pushed inside me, huge and rock-hard. The intoxicating almost-pain made me arch against him, my nails raking across his back as he began to thrust.

Wild with need, I drove my hips up to meet him. His bulging biceps and shoulders were hot steel under my teeth. I dimly realized that I was screaming abject pleas for more, harder, while he pounded into me. My orgasm was so sudden and intense that I utterly lost myself.

I had known how the dream would end.

When his body jerked and shuddered and went limp on top of me, I didn't try CPR. I couldn't bear to look into those sightless eyes again. Instead, I held his slack, still-warm body close, rocking him gently.

When I woke in the greyness of early dawn, the loss was so profound that I curled into a ball and wept hopelessly.

At the sound of the voice behind me, I snatched my gun from under the pillow and sprang from the bed in a single motion. As I whirled to aim with tear-blurred eyes, my brain caught up.

Kane's voice. "Oh my God, Aydan, I'm so sorry!"

I blinked stupidly, clearing tears from my eyes while

the gun wavered in my grip. Kane lay in my bed in all his glorious nakedness, his expression anguished as he repeated, "I'm so sorry!"

"Wha...?" I shook my head vigorously. "You're dead," I quavered.

"I know I deserve that..."

"What? No, this is another stupid dream. I know you're dead. I saw you die. I went to your funeral. You're dead. This is a dream." My gun shook uncontrollably.

"It's not a dream. I'm not dead."

"Yes, you are." My heart refused to believe otherwise. Soon I'd wake up, and the pain would be too great.

"I was captured and drugged. I don't know how long I've been held. I don't even know what day it is..."

My gun dropped to my side as I stared at Kane open-mouthed. "It's... Tuesday morning. You mean... this is real? You're really alive, and we really just..."

I checked in with my body.

Oh yeah. No mistaking that feeling.

We'd really just...

I grabbed for a tissue to wipe at the trickle running down my leg.

"I'm sorry." His voice vibrated with emotion. "I can't tell you how sorry I am..."

I dove onto the bed and smothered him with kisses, floating in the blissful sensation of his living body against mine. "Thank God, oh, thank God! You're alive..." I kissed him some more. "You're alive, ohmigod, I have to tell Arnie and your dad right away..."

"Aydan, stop." He held my shoulders and looked into my eyes.

I surfaced from my joy to register how upset he was. "What's wrong?"

"Everything's wrong. Goddammit, I can't believe what an idiot I am. Criminally stupid idiot."

"But what...?"

"Aydan, how can you stand to look at me? I broke into your house in the middle of the night and raped you, for God's sake."

"What? No! Jeez, no, you didn't. What part of me screaming, 'Oh, God, John, harder' sounded like rape to you?"

"Oh." A sheepish look crept over his face. "I guess... I'm still a little foggy. I woke up, and you were lying there bruised and crying, and I thought... All I remembered was coming in here and you were naked... and..." He took a deep breath. "God, that was mind-blowing."

I cuddled up to him. "That's more like it."

"But, Aydan, this is bad. This should never have happened. Damn drugs, messed up my judgement, I should have known better..."

I looked more closely at him in the dim light and realized his eyes were dilated and unfocused. The first shiver of concern shook me. "Are you okay? What did they give you?"

He shook his head vigorously and ran a hand over his stubbled face. "I don't know. Some kind of long-acting drug. Not a hallucinogen. Maybe a barbiturate. They shot me with a trank gun each time so I was out when they injected me." He gestured to his forearm, and I could see the needle marks in his skin.

"I still don't understand how you're still alive. I heard the bang. I saw the blood. I know what gunshots sound like. Trank guns just make a little 'phhtt' sound."

He blew out a long breath. "Sirius has developed a special-purpose trank gun that mimics real ordnance. You're right, the propellant for the actual trank is virtually silent, but the gun shoots a blood-coloured paint pellet, along with a blank cartridge for sound, and the casing from the blank gets ejected so it looks real. It's for undercover use, for when you need to appear to kill somebody. It doesn't hold up under close scrutiny, but if you just need a gunshot and a falling body, it works."

"But why would they keep you drugged?"

He sat up and rubbed his face again. "I don't know. Maybe to make it harder for me to escape. Or they might have been planning to interrogate me or apply some kind of psychological leverage. They'd want to lower my inhibitions and impair my judgement. Make me easier to influence."

He groaned. "I'm trained to withstand those effects, but I guess I let my guard down when I saw you. I should have known better. I'm sorry."

"Why are you sorry? Is there something you need to tell me? Do you have a sexually transmitted disease?"

"What? No!" He frowned at me. "No, I'm clean." He paused. "How about you?" he asked cautiously.

"No, I'm clean. It's all good."

"What about... Could you get pregnant?"

"No. No chance. I had a hysterectomy ten years ago."

"Oh." He eyed me uncertainly. "But... I still owe you an apology. I could have hurt you badly, losing control like that." His hand reached as if to touch my arm, but stopped. "You're covered with bruises. I must have hurt you. I'm so sorry."

"Trust me, I wasn't paying attention to any bruises." I tugged gently at his arm. "Relax. Now that I know I'm not dreaming..." I grinned at him as I lay back on the pillows. "Come a little closer."

He swallowed hard, his eyes locked on me. "Aydan, we can't," he said hoarsely.

"Why not?" I swung astride him and leaned forward to kiss him, letting my nipples trace lightly across his chest. I felt another magnificent hard-on growing under me as I slid slowly against him.

He groaned. "Aydan, I have to get out of here. It's a miracle they haven't found me already. You'll be in danger, too, if I'm here..." His hands cupped my breasts despite his words as he began to move under me. "Damn drugs... Damn fool... Aydan... have to... stop..."

Even my lust-clouded judgement had to bow to reality. I didn't know exactly what time he'd arrived, but he'd been in my bed for at least an hour and a half, probably more. Too dangerous.

I sighed deeply and got off him.

He rolled out of bed without looking at me, and started rapidly pulling on his clothes. I flopped back on the pillow and watched. I could've looked at that body all day long. Among the other things I could've done to that body all day long.

"Aydan, get dressed." Kane was still looking away from me. "I need to get up to speed with what's happened, but it's too dangerous to do it here. I'm going to hide in the woods down by the creek for now. I need you to come and brief me."

I grinned as I crept out of bed. "I'd rather de-brief you."

"Meet me down by the creek." He made for the door without looking back.

Struggling to overcome the lassitude caused by a head-banging orgasm and a gigantic emotional roller-coaster, I stumbled brainlessly around the bedroom. Eventually, I got all my clothes on, in the proper order, and tucked the Glock into my waist holster.

On my way through the kitchen, I snagged a handful of cereal bars, and lifted a small backpack out of the closet as I went out.

The dawn light was turning from grey to rose by the time I arrived at the woods around the creek that divided my land from Tom Rossburn's to the south. I stepped into the cover of the trees, and stood still, listening.

A movement caught my eye as Kane stepped out from behind a small thicket of diamond willow.

I looked up at him in the pink light. "Come on, I have a spot where I like to sit."

"Does anybody else know about it?"

"No. It's a good vantage point, you can see out without being visible."

"Good." He motioned me forward, and I led him along the game trail. When we reached the smooth fallen log tucked into the underbrush, he grunted approval and sat down beside me. I handed him the cereal bars and the backpack.

"What's this?" he hefted the pack.

"Survival gear. I wasn't sure what your plans were, but I'm guessing you don't have your gun or any equipment."

The laugh lines crinkled around his eyes as he sorted through the items, smiling. "Aydan, you're amazing. Did you just pack this?" He strapped the hunting knife onto his belt.

"No, I had it by the back door."

"It's a joy to work with a professional like you."

I shifted uncomfortably on the log. "I'm not a professional. That's the kit I carry in my car in the wintertime. I just never got around to unpacking it."

"Of course," he agreed, straight-faced. "Thanks. This will hold me until I can get to one of my caches."

"How did you even get here?" I asked. "It's ten miles out of town."

He shrugged. "I lay low after I escaped yesterday afternoon. As soon as it was dark, I cut cross-country on foot. I wasn't trying to set any speed records, so it was an easy trip. That doesn't matter, though." He eyed me intensely. "Tell me everything that's happened."

I tried to gather my thoughts into an organized narrative. The memory from the dump site was still so vivid that I clasped my hands together to hide their trembling.

"Stemp shot you in the back." The words choked out of me, my throat constricted by rage and remembered pain. "He said you were dead. I tried to kill him. I couldn't get to you..."

"Slow down." He took my hands and held them gently between his own. "Stemp shot me? So it was a setup," Kane muttered. "It felt like it to me, but..."

"Yes." The words burst out. "He lied, the filthy fucking scumbag! I'll kill him! I'll kill him slowly so the bastard suffers like he made everybody else suffer..."

"Aydan, stop. Tell me what happened after he shot me."

I took a deep breath. "I'm sorry. I just... He hurt so many people..." I clamped down on my emotions. "He shot you," I said levelly. "He told me you were dead. I tried to shoot him, but he'd tampered with my gun. Switched the clip out for a load of blanks. I checked it after he gave it back to me, but I didn't pull the magazine all the way out to look at the bullets."

"Then what happened?"

"I completely lost it. I tried to get at him, but his guys knocked me down and sat on me." My hands clenched with remembered fury. "I'd have torn him apart with my bare hands if I could have. I tried..."

"His guys? Who? How many?"

"I don't know who they were. They were wearing combat gear, and they came back to Sirius afterward. I presume they were on government payroll. I felt really bad about the two I put in the hospital when I realized they were just doing their jobs."

Kane's eyebrows went up. "You put two in the hospital? How many were there?"

"Five to start with."

"You took on five trained soldiers. And sent two to the hospital." He eyed me quizzically. "Tell me again how you're just a bookkeeper."

I sighed. "I'm just a bookkeeper. It wasn't like I did some big ninja thing. They weren't trying to hurt me, just hold me. I was fighting for all I was worth, and they just sat on me."

He frowned at me in silence for a few more seconds. "So Stemp set this up using department resources," he said finally.

"Yes. He told me that he'd set the whole thing up to draw out Fuzzy Bunny's operative. Said he had guards and snipers set up, but that nobody showed up except you. And he said you were a traitor, that you had a trank gun and you were going to take me to Fuzzy Bunny, so he'd killed you." I realized I was babbling, and took a deep breath. Anger overtook me again.

"Filthy liar," I ground out. "He lied to me, he lied to Briggs, he lied to your dad. And he made me lie to Arnie. I had to tell him you were dead. Your funeral was on Saturday." I broke off. "We need to tell all of them right away."

"Don't tell anybody I'm alive."

I bolted upright. "But, John, what about your dad? And Arnie? You should have seen them, it nearly killed them..." I broke off at the pain in his eyes.

"Aydan, Stemp obviously wanted me out of the picture for some reason. Now that I've escaped, he'll pull out all the stops to find me. I might not get out of this alive. The funeral's over. If I survive this, there'll be plenty of time for good news. If I don't, then at least they won't have to go through it twice."

I subsided. I had to agree with that, as much as I hated it. "But what will you do? How can we nail Stemp?"

"First, tell me the rest. He told you I was dead, and that I was a traitor." His voice was level, but his eyes blazed. "Then what?"

"I didn't believe it. But I was so... in shock. It was all a blur. I didn't have any proof. He and Briggs debriefed me, and I went down to Calgary to tell Arnie in person. But then I realized that Stemp had lied."

I looked up at him and clutched his hand tighter. "I knew he'd lied. Because I remembered seeing your Sig in your hand. You were really going to kill me. I was so glad. I knew you weren't a traitor."

"Aydan, only you would say you were glad I was going to kill you. You're insane."

"Well, no, I meant..."

His lips silenced me.

CHAPTER 43

A long, tender kiss. He pulled away at last, holding my face between his palms. "Aydan, I wasn't going to kill you. I couldn't."

"But..." My mind reeled dizzily. "I saw your finger on the trigger."

"I didn't say I wasn't going to shoot you. I said I wasn't going to kill you." He sighed. "I was sure it was a setup. I caught sight of one of the snipers as I drove in, so I knew we were being watched. And I knew..."

He smiled and stroked my hair back from my face. "I knew that you'd stand there and take a bullet because you thought it was the right thing to do. I was counting on it, that you'd stand still and let me shoot you. It was a tricky shot, but makeable. If I hit you in the upper chest, it would look like a mortal wound, but you could survive. I was planning to put you into a body bag and rush you off for treatment. It was risky, but it was the only thing I could think of. I have some medical contacts who owe me some favours. And you'd have been free of this."

"Oh." I didn't know what to say. I'd truly believed that he would follow orders, no matter what. "Thanks," I finished inadequately. "I... Thanks." I swallowed hard. "Where was I?"

"You realized Stemp had lied."

"Right. So I was sure he was the leak, because he

was at the internet cafe every time a contact was attempted with Fuzzy Bunny. And now I know it, because he's been holding you all this time."

Kane frowned. "That doesn't necessarily follow."

"What do you mean? How the hell could it not?" I threw up my hands. "He was at the cafe when the messages were sent. He lied to Briggs. He abducted you and held you drugged. He faked your death. What more do you want?"

"Do you have direct proof that he contacted Fuzzy Bunny?"

"Um." I surveyed my feet. "No... but he's been making frequent contact with someone in Bulgaria. Spider's tracking down his contact."

"Bulgaria?" Kane scrubbed his hand through his hair. "That's... interesting. Let me know what you find out. But in the mean time, don't assume that Stemp is the leak. I'm not sure it adds up to that, and you don't have any evidence. We need more information."

I eyed him with frustration. "I'm sure it's Stemp. He's such a slimeball."

"Slimeball or not, we need proof."

"Fine." I sighed. "Spider and I are working on it. I'll keep you posted. Which leads me to my next question. What are you going to do? How can I contact you?"

"I'm going to lie low for now. I'll probably stay around here for a while. Don't be surprised if you find food missing from your fridge."

"How can I contact you?"

"It's best if you don't, unless there's an emergency. I'll contact you. But if you need to talk to me, leave your hoe lying in your garden, and I'll come in at night. If it's an emergency, fire three shots."

I grinned at him. "Excuse me while I go put my hoe out in the garden. You can come in at night any time."

He took a deep breath, and his eyes heated up. "That's not a good idea," he said huskily. "Too risky."

He stood. "You need to go back to the house now. You'll be due at Sirius soon. I'll get set up here." He turned away, and I barely heard his mutter. "And by the time you're back, maybe these damn drugs will have worn off."

"Wait, one more thing."

Kane half-turned back to me. "What is it?"

I grinned at him. "You just fucked my brains out. The least you can do is kiss me goodbye."

"I... That's really not a good idea, either." He stood frowning at me for an instant before he pulled me into his arms. I'd been half-joking, but at the touch of his lips, I realized that now I had a chance I could have lost forever. A chance I might still lose if Stemp found him.

I'd tried to protect Kane by keeping my distance. When I'd thought he was dead, I'd only regretted what I hadn't done. Life was too short.

I ran my fingers through his hair and pulled him closer to tease his lips with my tongue. He groaned, and heat flashed through me when he deepened the kiss. His hands slid down my back to pull me against him.

I lost my breath at the feel of the thick, unyielding ridge in his pants. Lust drowned me and I groped at the button on his jeans with a shaking hand.

"Aydan, stop," he mumbled against my lips. "Too dangerous..."

"Please..." I managed to fumble the button undone. "Please, just once when I know you won't die. When I know I'm not dreaming." I eased the zipper down.

"God... Aydan... stop..." He grabbed my hand.

"We might not get another chance." I circled my hips, rubbing against him, feeding my need. "Please," I panted. "Now. I want you now." I closed my teeth on his neck, licking and nibbling.

He groaned and wrenched my jeans down while I slid my hand inside his pants. Breathless hunger suffused me when I freed his erection from the confining cloth. The last time I'd seen something that big and hard, it was black silicone.

Then my back was pressed against the smooth bark of a tall poplar. His hands clamped under my ass and he lifted me bodily. When he drove deep inside me, the forest echoed with my wild cries.

We pressed against the tree, sweating and shuddering. I dropped my head onto his massive shoulder and gasped out the last waves of mindless ecstasy. His rigid muscles vibrated under my hands. After a few more breaths, I slowly unlocked my legs from behind his back to lower my feet tentatively to the ground. My quivering knees barely supported my weight.

He held me close as he buried his face in my tangled hair, kissing my neck. His lips searched across my jaw to find my mouth in a long, sweet kiss.

At last, he pulled away, gently disengaging himself. He steadied me when I wobbled and smiled down at me, the lines crinkling around his still-dilated eyes. "Amazing. You're amazing."

"Now that's what I call a goodbye kiss," I gasped. "Holy shit." I gave him a breathless grin as he zipped up his jeans.

"I have to go." His fingertips stroked my cheek, and he brushed another light kiss across my lips before he turned quickly and disappeared into the forest.

I tottered over to the log and collapsed onto it while I panted some more. When I was finally capable of standing again, I floated back up to the house.

I trailed into the bedroom to shower and change, and grinned at the sight of the churned-up bed. I straightened it, wincing a little. Kane was a big, strong guy, and he hadn't been holding back. Despite my earlier reassuring words to him, my bruises ached deeply.

I smiled. He was alive. And maybe I could look forward to a rematch when I was in better shape to enjoy it.

My smile persisted until I sat down at the breakfast table and started to think things through. Then the magnitude of the situation finally filtered into my brain.

I was euphoric that Kane was alive, but I couldn't tell anybody, and I couldn't show my happiness in any way. I somehow needed to gather proof of Stemp's betrayal. Producing Kane alive would land Stemp in a lot of trouble, but it wouldn't prove that Stemp was the leak to Fuzzy Bunny.

I blew out a breath and made fists in my hair. Back to our original plan. Time to set Fuzzy Bunny up.

In Silverside, I slipped into the tiny electronics store and picked up a couple of disposable cell phones before heading to Blue Eddy's for my regular eleven o'clock session. After lunch, I avoided conversation other than the usual pleasantries at Up & Coming. I didn't want to deal with any awkward questions about Kane. Lola didn't know that he was officially dead, and I didn't want to have to lie to her.

I took a few moments to devise a strategy before meeting Spider at Sirius Dynamics. It felt wrong to keep him in the dark about Kane, but I had to agree with Kane's reasoning. After a short internal debate, I decided that silence was the safest course of action. It would prevent me from blurting out the good news, and Spider would assume that I was submerged in gloomy thoughts.

As I walked into my office, I realized with a jolt that keeping silent would be easier than I'd anticipated. I'd forgotten that Smith would be present for our afternoon session. His stench pervaded my office, and I bit my tongue to keep from asking him if he'd ever considered changing his shirt.

My filter hadn't captured any further communications with Fuzzy Bunny, so I made a substantial dent in the decryptions during the afternoon. When I emerged from the network and let go of my pounding head, Spider gave me a small smile.

"You're making some progress."

"Finally." I rubbed my aching eyes. "Too bad there's no way of knowing if any of those files are valuable until I get into them."

He shrugged. "They're all valuable to some extent. Even if there's no actual intel in them, it helps to see the internal structures and systems Fuzzy Bunny uses. And you never know what's going to turn out to be important down the road."

"I guess you're right." I sighed and looked at my watch. "I'm starving. Do you want to go over to Eddy's for supper?"

Spider caught my eye. "No, I've got some work to do tonight over at the other office. Let's grab something quick at the Greenhorn instead."

I tried to conceal my sudden interest. Maybe he'd made some progress of his own. "Okay. I'll meet you in the lobby after you take the key back down to the secured area." I followed him out of the office and did my best to look bored while I hovered in the lobby.

At the Greenhorn, he leaned across the table. "I've been digging into Katya. I'm not sure if this is going to help us or not."

I glanced quickly around the tiny restaurant. A couple of other tables were occupied, and we could be easily overheard. "Can we talk at the office?"

He nodded and clammed up, but curiosity got the better of me. "Did you find a lot of information?"

Spider shook his head. "No, just bits and pieces. It looks as though there's been some professional-quality covering up. I'm not even sure what it adds up to, but it's definitely interesting."

I held back my questions with difficulty while I bolted down my meal without tasting it. Spider seemed equally disinclined to dawdle, and we were on our way to his office a few minutes later.

His shoulders sagged as he unlocked the door to the small converted house that he and Kane had shared. Sympathy choked me, and I bit my tongue to keep from telling him that Kane was really alive. Instead, I focused on the knowledge that the sooner we could nail Stemp, the sooner everyone could stop suffering.

Spider sank into the chair behind his desk in the former living/dining space. He glanced over at Kane's empty desk and ran a hand over his face briefly before unlocking a desk drawer to withdraw several sheets of paper.

"Let's go to the meeting room," he mumbled as he stood.

We sat at the small table in one of the converted bedrooms, and he carefully scanned the room with his handheld scanner before speaking.

He pushed the papers across the table to me. "Here's what I've discovered so far. Stemp used to be a field agent, but he switched over to administration five years ago, and quickly got promoted up the chain into his current director's position. But about seven years ago, he was part of an op that took place in Bulgaria. That's the only time he was officially there."

Something in his voice made me prompt, "But..."

I recognized the hunter's smile. "But... unofficially, he's travelled to central Europe several times since then. A few times within a year of his first visit. A couple of times a year, after that. There's no record of him visiting Bulgaria again."

"But..." I prompted again. I didn't mind playing straight man. I could see there was more coming.

"But..." Spider's smile turned predatory. "He slipped up. I found little things here and there. A credit card receipt. A phone record. I can't place him in Bulgaria with each trip, but I'm willing to bet he went."

I leaned forward, rapt. "So who's Katya?"

"That's why I'm willing to bet he went. Because I hacked into each of his sessions again today, and guess what?"

"What, what?" I demanded. "Jeez, spit it out already!"

He blushed. "It seems that Katya is his lover. And has been for some time."

I sat back slowly in my chair. "Oh. But what does that mean? Did you find any links between Katya and Fuzzy Bunny?"

"No." Spider slumped back in his chair, too. "I can't find any connection at all. I dug into everything I could find. I found out where she lives, and she works at the Sofia Technical University, but that's all."

"Shit. So we're no further ahead on proving anything."

"No. Unless we can show that Stemp has been secretly meeting with Fuzzy Bunny operatives over in Europe, there's no connection there." He sighed. "I'll keep digging."

The sound of the doorbell made me jump.

"Oh, that'll be Hellhound," Spider said as he stood.

I quickly folded the papers and stuffed them into my pocket as I looked at my watch. "At eight o'clock at night?"

"Yes, he said he needed something from Kane's desk." The animation drained from his face as he turned to leave the room.

I trailed him out into the office area as he opened the door. Hellhound gave him a nod as he stepped into the room. The tired lines in his face eased when he smiled at me. "Hi, darlin', what're ya doing here so late?"

"Um... just going over some work stuff with Spider," I mumbled. "I've been helping out with the overflow from his web design business."

True, though not relevant. I hate lying at the best of times, and lying to somebody I cared about was even worse.

Hellhound nodded absently and turned to Spider. "I

just gotta get a coupla things from his desk. I'm gettin' ready to clean out his condo, an' I need some paperwork an' the keys to his storage locker. I shoulda just got ya to bring 'em down when ya came, but I wasn't thinkin' straight then."

Spider heaved a sigh and waved a hand at the empty desk. "Go ahead."

I caught his eye. "Spider, there's just one more thing I need to ask you before I go."

"Okay."

He turned back to me, and I slapped my forehead. "Oh! I left those papers in the meeting room. Let's go and have a look, and then I'll take them with me."

He obediently followed me back down the hall, and I leaned close to whisper. "I got the phones. I'm going to generate a message to our mole first thing tomorrow morning. I'll set him up to call one of the phones. If he actually calls, I'll tell him to watch for an ad online at Craigslist for further instructions."

Spider nodded. "Perfect. You'd better disguise your voice, though. Don't forget, all of our suspects know you."

"I was thinking of doing a recorded message. I can run it through my freebie sound-processing software to distort it."

"That'll work." We looked at each other and sighed simultaneously. "Good luck," he added.

CHAPTER 44

When we returned to the office area, Hellhound was just getting up from Kane's chair.

"Got everything?" Spider inquired.

"Yeah." Hellhound picked up a file box from the corner of the desk. "I'll get outta here so ya can lock up."

"Me, too," I seconded the motion as I followed him out. Spider flipped off the lights and turned to lock the door as we went down the walk.

Hellhound's Forester was parked in front of my car, and I nodded toward it. "What, a nice day like this and you're not on your bike?"

He opened the rear door to slide the box in. "Nah. Hadta carry the file box. Didn't feel like tryin' to strap it down."

We both lifted a hand in farewell to Spider as he drove off. I turned to look up Hellhound. "How are you doing?"

My heart smote me at the sight of his face. I could erase that weary pain with a few simple words.

"I'm okay. Been better, but ya know how it goes."

I took his hand and stroked it, trying to remind myself how important it was to keep Kane's secret. What would it matter if I whispered the truth in Arnie's ear? I knew I could trust him to keep his mouth shut. But then there was Doug Kane. How could I tell Arnie the good news, but forbid him to relieve his adopted father's pain? And what about Spider? And what if Kane ended up dying after all?

When I looked up at him again, some of my struggle must have shown. His face softened as he misunderstood my troubled expression, and he stroked my hair. "Aw, darlin'. I was gonna head back tonight, but I think I'll stay at the hotel instead. Come on back with me, an' we can make it all go away for a little while."

I had a moment of discomfort as I gazed up at him. Despite my defiant thoughts of sampling the herd, it seemed a little sleazy to have sex with two different men within a day of each other.

Observant as always, he caught my hesitation. "It's okay if ya ain't in the mood. I'll just head on home."

His voice and expression were casual. If I hadn't known him, I would have thought he couldn't care less, but his eyes betrayed him.

Any qualms I might have had evaporated in the knowledge that he needed me tonight. I could offer him comfort, if only for a little while. And besides, we'd been lovers long before anything happened with Kane.

I squeezed his hand. "Let's go. Can I ride over with you? I don't want to leave my car at the hotel."

He frowned down at me. "Ya bein' watched here?"

I shrugged. "I don't know, but I'd rather not be seen at the hotel." I didn't bother to explain the consequences of my last appearance at the hotel. I knew he'd accept my preference without question. I slid into the passenger seat and held his hand as we drove away.

In the pink light of sunrise, I leaned over to kiss Hellhound one more time before I got out of his SUV. "Thanks for bringing me back."

He chuckled. "Well, I wasn't gonna make ya walk."

"That's good, because my knees are still shaking after this morning."

He captured my lips in a lingering kiss. His fingers slid through my hair and traced a feather-light caress down the side of my neck. I shivered at the brush of his whiskers and his deep growl in my ear. "Checkout time ain't 'til eleven, darlin'. An' I still got half a box of condoms."

I pulled away reluctantly and grinned at him. "You always travel with a whole box of condoms?"

"Hell, yeah. 'Specially if I might see you." His cheerful leer did my heart good. "I promise I'll put a smile on your face. Again." He bounced his eyebrows.

I slid out of the vehicle before I could change my mind, and leaned in the open door. "You always do put a smile on my face. Any other time, I'd take you up on that, but I have to do some important work stuff this morning. See you. Drive safe."

"See ya, darlin'."

I watched him drive away, and then steered my car toward home, still smiling.

I was only a couple of miles out of town when a movement from the back seat caught my eye. Adrenaline jolted through me when I realized the collapsible seat back was opening into the interior, and a dark-haired man started to push his head and shoulders through the opening.

I slammed on the brakes in horrified déjà vu. Kane's body thumped against the back of my seat as the car swerved wildly.

"Aydan, it's me! Keep driving!"

Kane righted himself in the back seat while I hyperventilated. I concentrated on steering the car, trying to loosen my deathgrip on the wheel. "Jesus, John, what the hell!" I stammered finally. "I damn near crashed the car!"

"Sorry," he grunted.

I drove for another mile or so before I calmed down enough to talk. "What the hell are you doing in my trunk?" I demanded. "I thought you were going to stay around the farm."

"Change in plans," he said shortly. "You've got guards in your yard now. Probably Stemp watching for me."

I glanced at his frown in the rear-view mirror. "How did you get away from the guards?"

"Stole Rossburn's truck and ditched it halfway to town. Walked in the rest of the way."

"How did you find me?"

"Followed you when you left Sirius yesterday."

I threw an incredulous glance over my shoulder. "Where were you? I didn't even see you."

He scowled and twitched a shoulder. "I'm a spy."

I put two and two together with a sinking sensation. If he'd been following me all evening, I had a hunch as to why he sounded so terse. His next words confirmed my suspicions.

"How's Hellhound?"

I met his eyes in the mirror. "He's suffering. Unnecessarily."

"But you made it all better for him last night."

I jammed on the brakes and pulled the car over to the shoulder.

"Keep driving," Kane growled.

"No." I twisted around in the seat to face him. "Get up here and talk to me. Say what you really want to say."

"I don't have anything to say."

"You're upset because I was with Hellhound last night."

"Who or what you do is none of my business. I don't have any claim on you."

I reined in my temper with an effort and kept my voice as non-confrontational as possible. "John, could we please just be honest about this? I'm sorry if you're hurt, but Arnie and I have been lovers off and on since March. He needed me last night." With heroic restraint, I managed not to add, 'Because of you.'

"Since March?" His expression closed down. He sat in silence for a few moments. "So all this time..." He took a deep breath. "I should have seen that."

"I'm sorry you had to find out this way. Bad timing."

He shrugged, his face impassive. "So all this time, you've been screwing him and coming onto me at the same time. What exactly do you want?"

I controlled my voice with an effort. "Go ahead. Say it."

"Say what?"

"Call me a slut. You obviously want to."

"No, I don't want to." His voice was hard. "I just want to know where I stand with you. Are you in love with him?"

"John..." I sighed. "Look, could you please come and sit in the front seat so we can talk comfortably? If you're going to ask questions like that, this is going to be a long, complicated conversation."

He crossed his arms obdurately over his broad chest.

"It's not complicated. Are you in love with Arnie? Yes or no?"

I clenched my fists in my hair and flopped back into my seat as I stared through the windshield. "No. I care about him, a hell of a lot. But I'm not in love with him. He's not in love with me, either. We're good friends. With benefits. That's all it'll ever be. That's what we both want."

After a few seconds of silence, I heard the back door open and close.

I blew out a long breath. Fine. Whatever.

I was reaching to put the car into gear when Kane opened the passenger door and slid in.

"You should keep driving," he said quietly. "It's too dangerous for us to sit here out in the open. Take the next turnoff to get us off the highway."

I nodded and followed his instructions. We drove in silence down the dusty gravel road for a mile or two. At last, he turned to me. "Aydan..." He paused and made a frustrated gesture. "I don't know what you want from me."

I kept my eyes on the road. "I don't want anything from you."

"Then what... Dammit, it's hard to believe I misunderstood your intentions when you had your hand down my pants and your tongue in my mouth!"

"Hey, you had your tongue in my mouth too," I reminded him.

"Aydan, dammit..." He stopped and took a deep breath.

"Anyway, you know damn well you didn't misunderstand my intentions," I interrupted before he could speak again. "But you told me flat out that you couldn't be anything more than friends with me. And then you showed up in my bed. Now you're mad because you changed the rules and I didn't read your mind."

"Aydan, I... You know this never would have..."

I nosed the car onto a deserted crossing and stopped so I could turn to face him. "I know. It never would have happened if you hadn't been drugged to the eyeballs. So let it go. It was just sex. It doesn't have to be some big thing. If you want to go back to the way we were, that's fine with me. If you want to go forward being friends with benefits, that's fine, too. Just tell me what you want. Don't expect me to read your mind."

"Are those my only options?" Kane asked quietly.

"What else did you have in mind?"

His fingertips brushed my cheek. "Was it really just sex for you? Could we be more than just friends with benefits?"

His hand dropped as he read my expression. His face closed down.

"John..." I took his hand and held it in both of mine. "What you're asking for... I don't have that to give. Not to you, not to anybody. I'm sorry."

His eyes searched my face. "Aydan, my life frequently depends on being able to read people accurately. And I'd be willing to swear that you love me."

I turned away to study the brilliant yellow field of canola in front of us. The wind ruffled its surface, bright blossoms caught up in a sprightly dance.

"Do you love me?" he prompted softly.

I answered without looking at him. "John, I don't like to use that word. It's too easy to misinterpret."

"What word do you want to use, then?"

I sighed and pulled my hands away to scrub at my

face. "I... There are two kinds of love." I met his eyes. "In
the first kind of love, you're willing to give your life *for*
another person. You know I feel that way about you. So yes,
I love you."

"There's a but," he said flatly.

"But I don't think that's what you're asking for. In
the other kind of love, you're willing to give your life *to*
another person. That kind of love comes with promises and
commitment and a future. It's... I can't offer that to anybody.
I don't have it to give. I just..." I struggled for words.

"Just what?"

"I... nothing." I took his hand again. "If I had that
kind of love to give," I searched his face, willing him to
understand. "If I could, you'd be first in line. But I can't.
And I don't think I'll ever be able to."

"But, Aydan, if this was over... If we weren't working
together..."

"That's not the reason. It's just me. I can't."

Kane sat in silence, frowning. "It's your other
undercover op, isn't it?" he asked finally.

"No! I don't have another undercover op. I'm just
fucked up, that's all."

"I don't believe that." He gazed into my eyes. "I
don't know what's holding you back, but I know you're worth
waiting for. If things change for you, I'll be here."

"Don't!" I slid down in the seat and held my head in
my hands. I'd been so careful to avoid attachments, and now
I had one that I'd never expected, staring me in the face.

I tried to soften my voice. "I don't want you to wait.
It's not fair to you. I can't give you what you want. You
deserve somebody who can."

He gently pulled my hands away to search my face,

his brow furrowed. "Aydan, I can see you're trying to do the honourable thing here, but…"

He stopped. Rubbed at his forehead and blew out a long breath. "I should have known you wouldn't make a promise you can't keep."

After a short silence, he gave me a twisted smile. "I wanted to believe that we could have something together," he admitted slowly. "But I see what you mean about promises and commitment. I guess I don't have that to give, either. I never know when I'll have to vanish for months at a time. I can't promise fidelity because I never know what role I'll need to assume when I'm undercover. As for a future, I could be dead tomorrow."

He paused. "I guess that second kind of love can't happen for people like us."

We gazed at each other for a few moments. "I'm sorry," I said.

"Me, too."

I gave him a hopeful smile. "Friends with benefits?"

He sighed and shook his head. "That wouldn't work. I couldn't pretend it was just sex for me. It would drive me crazy to think you might be with another man." He grimaced. "And if the other man was Hellhound, it would just feel… incestuous."

"I'm pretty sure it's only incest if you and I are related," I told him.

"That's not funny. You know what I mean."

"Does it have to be all or nothing with you?"

Kane nodded regretfully. "You saw how jealous I got. And we didn't even have a relationship, just a few drug-induced minutes together."

He dropped his eyes. "I'm actually quite

embarrassed about that," he mumbled. "I'm usually better in bed. A little slower, for one thing. More considerate. And I don't roll over and fall asleep right away. Or vanish in the woods."

I laughed. "You were drugged. I think you can be forgiven. Besides, if you'd been any better, I wouldn't have survived the orgasm. I wouldn't want it that way every time, but, holy shit, you were incredible."

He met my eyes with a grin. "I'm glad you thought so. Because you blew my mind. I've never lost control like that before."

"Are you sure we couldn't just try it again? Now that the drugs are out of your system? In the interests of research," I added virtuously.

His eyes darkened before he shook his head. "No, that would be a bad idea. Unless you want to have this conversation all over again."

"So, back to the way we were, then?"

He nodded slowly.

"Damn. Let me know if you ever change your mind about the friends with benefits option."

"You'll be the first to know." His lips quirked up in a smile that didn't reach his eyes. "Next time I'm drugged to the eyeballs, I'll drop by."

"You do that."

CHAPTER 45

I manoeuvred the car out onto the road again and steered back toward the highway. As I drove, I briefed Kane on our plans and gave him the information on Katya.

He frowned. "No connection to Fuzzy Bunny?"

"Not that Spider has been able to find so far. So we'll have to draw Stemp out using our sting."

"What exactly do you plan to do?"

I sighed. "I don't know yet. My first step is to see if I get a response to my message. If I do, I'll have to figure out a way to bring him into the open and make him do or say something that proves he's working for Fuzzy Bunny. And somehow record it." I rubbed the frown lines out of my forehead.

"Aydan, what you're proposing is incredibly dangerous," Kane said. "Your plan has to be airtight. Don't forget, this person is smart enough to have remained in a top-level security position unnoticed. And if it is Stemp, he has the full skill set of an experienced field agent, too."

"Thanks for the encouragement," I told him. "At least I have you for my secret weapon. Everybody thinks you're dead. Except Stemp. I can probably use that to my advantage somehow. I just have to figure out how. Which reminds me, how can I contact you?"

"Don't try. I'll plan to be in visual range whenever possible. If you need to talk to me, move your 'Support Our

Troops' magnet to the right side of your trunk. I'll make contact with you somehow."

"Okay. If you're going to hide in my trunk again, at least say something before you come through. You scared the hell out of me."

He laughed. "I will."

About a mile from the highway, he said, "Stop. Let me out here."

"Are you sure you'll be okay? Do you need anything?"

"I'm fine." The laugh lines crinkled around his eyes. "I managed to stay alive all by myself before I had you to take care of me."

"Sorry," I said sheepishly. "I know. I'm just..."

"Being a friend," he finished. "Thanks." He leaned over and kissed me lightly, and then slid out of the car. I watched him lope easily across the field and disappear into a ravine.

I steered the car thoughtfully home. That confrontation had turned out better than it might have, but it had left me feeling wary and off-balance.

I had assumed that a man like Kane would avoid personal entanglements and always put duty first. It was flattering but unsettling to discover I'd been wrong. And even though it hadn't been strictly my fault, I felt terrible that he'd been hurt. I really did lo... like him a lot.

I pulled into my garage and thumped my forehead against the steering wheel a couple of times.

As I hurried into the house, the flashing light on the answering machine caught my eye. I punched the button, and Tom's voice concerned voice floated out of the speaker. The timestamp was from the previous day.

"Hi, Aydan, I just wanted to let you know to be careful. My truck got stolen out of my yard, so make sure your garage is locked. And at dawn, I heard some kind of animal making noise down by the creek. There might be a cougar passing through."

I snorted laughter. First time I'd ever been called a cougar. But at least he hadn't identified the true nature of the noises. Good thing he hadn't decided to walk down and investigate.

I gave him a call to thank him for his concern and commiserate over his truck. He assured me that it had been returned undamaged, and warned me again about the cougar. I managed to sound appropriately serious.

By the time I'd showered and dressed and eaten and recorded my distorted voice message, I was late. As I trotted back to the garage, I thought I glimpsed a flash from my windbreak. Could have been a leaf catching the sun. Or could have been a reflection off a scope or a pair of binoculars. Apparently I was still under surveillance. I wondered if the cameras had been reinstalled. Shit. No way to find out without searching.

I called Spider to let him know I was running behind, and made my way as rapidly as possible to Sirius Dynamics. When I arrived slightly breathless at my office, Spider and Smith were both waiting, and I mentally cursed Smith's malodorous presence.

Spider held out the network key wordlessly, and I plopped onto the couch and stepped into the virtual void without speaking. My snoopy little program was empty. No further attempts at communication with Fuzzy Bunny. I decided that was a good sign. Our mole was waiting for a response. Time to give him one.

I spoke to Spider and Smith through the network interface. "I'm going to go in and double-check my program connections. I'll be invisible for a while."

"What should I do if you don't come back?" Spider asked fearfully. "I don't know if I can help you the way Kane..." his voice choked off.

"Don't worry, Spider," I comforted him. "I'll get back here one way or another. I shouldn't be gone long." As I faded into invisibility, I fervently hoped it was the truth. I hadn't realized before exactly how much I had counted on Kane to rescue me when things got hairy. Thank God he was still alive. For now.

I followed my shimmering thread of connection down the data tunnels to Fuzzy Bunny's firewall. Hovering outside it, I shaped a burst of data into the number of the disposable cell phone and floated it down the virtual pathways to its destination.

Here you go, mole. For a good time, call this number.

I snapped my consciousness back to the familiar walls of Sirius's virtual file room. My heart didn't seem to want to slow down, and I hovered invisibly while I tried to overcome my slightly queasy excitement. The first step had been taken. Now we had to play the waiting game. When I could fake calm again, I faded back into visibility and started decrypting the next file in the stack.

When the signalling blip stabbed me behind the eyes, I jerked involuntarily. I'd been completely absorbed in the document I was working on, and I blinked dumbly for a few seconds before I registered my surroundings again.

"What's up, Spider?" I inquired.

"Lunch time," he responded. "Come on out."

"Oh!" I glanced at the time and realized that in fact it was closer to one o'clock. I suppressed a smile. I guessed that Spider wanted to take a later lunch so he could hack into Stemp's regular one o'clock session. I stepped carefully through the portal and back into reality.

I sucked air through my teeth as I hugged my head. Jeez, the only thing that could improve this rotten experience was the addition of Smith's stench. Truly I was blessed. Not.

CHAPTER 46

At the Melted Spoon, Spider immediately set up his laptop and began to type. I drifted to the counter and ordered food for both of us. When I returned to the table, I put his sandwich beside him, and he abstractedly munched at it, his eyes riveted to the screen.

"There!" He swivelled the laptop around so that we could both look at the screen. "Look at this. Every time, he uses a different routing system to contact her."

He traced the line of complicated text above the session. "See how he's bouncing the message around to hide his trail? He spoofs an IP here, here, and here. And this explains why he always goes to the internet cafe instead of using his home computer. The IP addresses rotate more frequently, and he uses a different terminal each time. You weren't kidding when you said he was twisty. "

"And he apparently knows his way around computers, too." I rubbed at the frown lines in my forehead. "I don't like this. With his background, he's going to be really hard to nail."

We both watched as the online conversation progressed. I shifted impatiently in the hard chair. "They're not saying anything. It's all just 'How was your day' stuff." I blinked. "Oops. And pillow talk. Whoa. Too much information."

I glanced over at Spider's scarlet face. "Is this their

usual conversation? Could they be using a code?"

He averted his eyes from the steamy exchange on the screen. "If they are, I haven't been able to figure it out. I've been running some decryption algorithms on it, but I'm not getting anything." His eyes narrowed in sudden thought. "Maybe you could decrypt it. If you were inside the network."

I sat up with sudden hope, and then slouched back into my chair. "But I couldn't, because the Sirius network is all monitored."

"That's true, but you're invisible." Spider grinned at my expression as I thumped my fist against my forehead.

"Shit, you're right. Lucky one of us has a functional brain. So all I have to do is sneak into the tunnels while he's online. It never even occurred to me to try, because I don't have a clue about hacking into computers from the outside."

He swivelled the laptop back in front of himself again. "That's it, they're done." He blushed again. "I mean... the session is ending."

I hid a smile. "I guess we'd better get back, too. Maybe I'll manufacture a reason to work late tonight. Say, around nine o'clock."

"Sounds like a plan."

We were halfway back to Sirius when my butt vibrated.

I snatched the disposable phone out of my pocket. "Bingo! We got a bite. I bet Stemp's still on his lunch break. First he talks to Katya, then he calls us." I showed Spider my teeth. "I can hardly wait to nail that bastard. It's his turn to suffer. And he will. Oh, he will."

Spider's eyes were wide as he took a step back. "Um, Aydan, you're scaring me again."

"Sorry." I attempted to convert my expression to something a little closer to neutral.

"Now what?" he asked cautiously.

"Now we reeeeeeel him in," I grinned.

"How?"

"In my phone message, I told him to watch Craigslist for an online ad for a pink and blue Fuzzy Bunny brand teddy bear." I wiped the phone off thoroughly with the tail of my sweatshirt and dropped it into a garbage bin as we walked by.

"What are you doing?" Spider demanded. "What if he calls again?"

"He'll get the same message, unless the phone dies in the mean time. And if he manages to trace the phone, he'll find it in the dump."

I kept walking, and he caught up to me after a few paces.

"I told him the ad would contain a link to a web page with instructions," I continued. "It'll look like a 'Page not found' notification from Fuzzy Bunny's server, but I'll hide the instructions in HTML comments so they won't be visible to browsers. I told him to view the source code to read them. As soon as I know he's viewed the page, I'll take it down."

"Speaking of twisty…" Spider squinted at me warily. "I thought you said you were a bookkeeper."

"Jesus, Spider, not you, too!" I yanked a handful of my hair.

"What?"

"Never mind," I told him as we walked up the front steps of Sirius Dynamics. "Let's talk after work."

"Okay…"

The hesitation in his voice made me demand,

"What?"

"Um. Actually, I'm having dinner with Linda." His cheeks were pink, and he didn't meet my eyes.

I laughed. "Okay, Romeo. Can you make it to your office for eight for a planning session? Or is this going to be an all-night thing?"

His flush deepened. "No! I mean... Yes, I can be there by eight. Linda's on the night shift tonight, and she starts at eight."

"Okay, I'll tell Smith we'll be here at nine."

Spider eyed me as we signed for our fobs again. "Do you have to?"

"Might as well. We've got nothing to hide, right?"

Comprehension filled his eyes. "Oh. Right, of course."

At eight o'clock, I pulled up outside the shared office. There was no sign of Spider, so I leaned against my car. While I waited, I casually moved my trunk magnet over to the opposite side. I was pretty sure I was going to need Kane's help with the next steps.

At ten after eight, Spider's car swung rapidly around the corner and pulled up with a jerk behind mine. He scrambled out of the driver's seat, his lanky limbs awkwardly uncoordinated in his haste.

"Sorry I'm late," he panted.

Clearly the date had gone well. His normally tidy short hair was mussed, and he was smiling in spite of his apologetic air. With an effort, I restrained myself from making a smart comment, and followed him up the walk and into the office.

By ten to nine, we had a plan. Spider hovered nervously while we walked toward our cars. "I still don't like it, Aydan. It's too dangerous. I won't be able to do anything to help you, you know that. You need somebody like..." His voice trailed off. "...Germain," he substituted determinedly. "You should ask him to help."

I bit my tongue. I couldn't tell him that Kane would be there to cover our backs. And I didn't want to involve Germain at all. He was my backup plan if things went seriously sideways.

"Remember, Germain's still on our suspect list," I reminded him. I didn't believe for a minute that Germain was the leak, but it made a good excuse.

Spider's shoulders sagged. "I guess you're right."

At Sirius, I held my breath through Smith's offensive aura and dove into the network. "I'm going to go invisible and check my program," I lied. My heart pounded. Point of no return.

I faded into invisibility and stretched down the data tunnels.

CHAPTER 47

I slipped my fake web page onto a convenient server, and then created a convoluted trail, ping-ponging through various connections to lead to it. Then I burrowed into Craigslist and placed my ad.

It was frighteningly easy.

I suppressed a shudder as I realized the sheer potential for disaster. I could go anywhere in cyberspace. Read any document, browse through any server, drift through firewalls as if they didn't even exist. And I didn't leave a trace.

I had a fleeting thought that it might have been better if Kane had actually killed me. Nobody should have that kind of power. And what if there were other network keys out there? Other people who could do what I could?

I wrenched my mind away from the thought. If there were, Fuzzy Bunny apparently didn't know about them. And so far, they didn't know about me, either. All I had to do was catch Stemp, and I'd be home free.

Yeah, I'd just keep telling myself that.

I hovered in the virtual data tunnel, sifting the data streams almost unconsciously. Waiting for the right one.

I almost missed it. I'd grown so accustomed to watching for communications with Fuzzy Bunny that Stemp's convoluted signal barely registered as it whisked by. With a shock of adrenaline, I hitched my consciousness to the final data packet and used it to trace the pathway he was using this time.

When the connection stabilized, I sank my virtual fangs into the data session and drank deeply.

About fifteen minutes later, the connection broke up, and I snapped back into Sirius's virtual file room, suppressing the urge to vent my frustration with foul language. Absolutely nothing incriminating. And if it was encrypted, I couldn't crack it. It still just looked like banal conversation to me. Hadn't even gotten any cheap thrills this time.

I faded into visibility again. "Everything looks fine," I said as casually as I could. "I'm coming out, unless you can think of anything else I should be doing here."

"No, come on out," Spider assured me.

When I straightened and pried open my aching eyes, Mike Connor was leaning against the door frame, chatting to Spider while Smith looked on sourly. Smith had been none too pleased about our nocturnal activities, but when we'd assured him that his presence wasn't required, he'd obstinately insisted on attending.

I got up and trudged for the door. "That's it, you guys, I'm heading home."

They all trailed me down the hallway, and my head throbbed as Connor regaled Spider with a blow-by-blow description of his latest World of Warcraft escapades. Once again, I envied Spider his youthful energy as the two of them made plans to head over to the internet cafe for the rest of the evening.

I'd intentionally left my car in a dark corner of the parking lot in case Kane needed to get into it, but now it didn't seem like quite such a smart idea as I strode over to it, trying to look confident. I knew Bill Harks was still in jail, but I didn't know who else might be lurking in the shadows. I cursed my idiocy. I should have gotten Mike and Spider to walk me to my car.

My shoulders were up around my ears by the time I slid rapidly into the driver's seat and locked the door behind me. My back prickled. If Kane could hide in the trunk, who else might? I didn't dare look while I was still in the parking lot, in case Kane was in there; but I was also afraid to drive off into the country without looking, in case somebody else was in there.

My hands were clenched around the steering wheel in an agony of indecision when I finally brained up. Jeez, I must be more tired than I thought.

"John?" I spoke out loud, hoping for an answer.

"I'm here," came the soft reply from the trunk.

The air hissed out of me in a long sigh as I slumped with relief. "Thank God." I started the car and drove away, wiping my palms on my jeans.

"You can come out now," I told him when the darkness of the open highway wrapped around the car.

I heard movement in the back seat, and then Kane spoke from behind me. "You shouldn't park in such a secluded area at night."

"Tell me about it," I sighed. "That only seemed like a good idea. I was trying to make it easy for you to get in the car."

He chuckled. "I'm a spy. I could get in your car in broad daylight if I wanted to."

"Oooh, big talk," I teased him. "Confident much?"

I could hear the smile in his voice. "Yes."

"Good. Because I'm going to need you for this next

part."

"I'm not sure I like the sound of that," he said slowly. "What do you have in mind?"

"I've set myself up as bait. I'll need you to watch my back."

"You what?" There was a distinct edge to his voice. "Aydan, I warned you how dangerous this is. Your first responsibility is to stay safe. Not..." His voice was rising, and I heard him take a deep breath. "Not put yourself at risk," he finished evenly.

"No choice. It's already done." I sounded more confident than I felt.

"Aydan, goddammit..." There was a short silence. "All right. Tell me what you've done."

"I've relayed a message to Fuzzy Bunny's operative, and told him that he is to snatch me and bring me in." I heard a faint sound from the back seat that sounded like grinding teeth, but Kane didn't interrupt me, so I continued.

"It's perfectly safe," I assured him. "You know they need me alive."

"But not necessarily unhurt," he grated.

An involuntary chill ran down my spine. Hadn't thought of that. "True," I admitted reluctantly. "But I'm pretty sure they'll want me in good shape. Anyway, I told their mole to call when he had me, and he'd receive instructions on where to drop me."

I handed the second disposable phone over my shoulder. "There's a recorded message on here that gives the location of the drop site. The real Fuzzy Bunny doesn't know anything about this. So I'm perfectly safe. Even if our guy manages to snatch me, which he won't because you'll be there, he can't get me to Fuzzy Bunny. Worst-case scenario, the phone rings, and you'll know you can just show up at the drop site and pick me up."

"That's fine as far as it goes," Kane said. "But how am I supposed to watch your back? Don't forget, I can't necessarily shadow you constantly. I'm still officially dead. I can't take a chance on being seen."

"I thought you were Super-Spy. What happened to that?"

"Aydan!" His growl raised the small hairs on the back of my neck. "This isn't a game."

"Ya think?" I regretted the smart-ass comment as soon as it left my lips. "Sorry. I know," I added. "And don't worry, I have a plan."

His heavy sigh ruffled the back of my hair. "I always worry. It's my job."

"Well, don't. I've got it covered. I'm going to advertise my vulnerability at a convenient time and place, so you'll only have to show up there, not actually follow me. I'm pretty sure he'll go for it."

"How?" he asked cautiously. "Remember, you're not dealing with an idiot here. He'll smell a setup a mile away."

"I think I can get away with it, with the wonders of modern email. Tonight when I get home, I'm going to email Spider to meet me at the park tomorrow evening at nine-thirty, for a private memorial to you. I'll tell him that I'll be there a few minutes early because I'm setting up something special, and that he can come a little later. And then I'll accidentally send it to the group. Immediately followed by an 'Oops, please disregard' message."

After a few seconds of thought, Kane grunted grudging approval. "That could work. The park's never busy even in daylight, and it's abandoned by that time of night.

He'll think you'll be alone in a secluded area. And there's lots of cover for me to hide in."

"Yes. And Spider will actually be in place before I ever get there, also hidden. He'll be recording everything that happens so that we have the evidence we need."

"Oh." The approval wasn't quite so grudging this time. "Good thinking."

"Thank you."

"Stop here."

I pulled over. "Do you want me to take you back to town?"

"No, I'll work my way back on foot. I've set up a base in that ravine a couple of miles out of town."

"Do you need anything? A blanket or something? It's chilly tonight."

Kane laughed as he got out of the back. "No, Mom, I'm fine. Thanks." He opened the driver's door and leaned in. "I have everything I need in that kit you gave me. Those mylar blankets work for both warmth and shelter."

Then he gently raised my chin and gave me a long, soft kiss.

"Have you changed your mind about the friends with benefits thing?" I asked when I could catch my breath.

"No. But the next time I see you, you'll be in danger. It's a good plan, and I think it'll work. But just in case." He kissed me again, and faded into the darkness beside the road.

I drove the rest of the way home convinced that I was an idiot. For many reasons.

At home, I sent my accidental email and its follow-up, and then jittered my way into bed. I was definitely an idiot.

I didn't sleep well.

The day dawned cool and cloudy, and I sighed relief. I'd be able to wear a sweatshirt and use my easily-accessible waist holster. At least something was going well. Maybe it was a sign.

I groaned at my hollow-eyed reflection in the mirror and shuffled into the shower. By tonight, it would be over. One way or the other.

"Idiot," I mumbled.

At Sirius Dynamics, the morning crept by. Spider seemed as antsy as I was, and I hoped that Smith hadn't noticed anything out of the ordinary.

As I swore and groaned my way out of the network at lunch time, I questioned my sanity yet again. I could always call off the whole thing. But then Stemp would get away with his betrayal, and everyone who cared about Kane would suffer longer.

I let out a final heartfelt groan and straightened. When I squinted my eyes open, Germain was standing just inside the doorway. His face was pleasant and open as always, but I sensed tension in his posture. He smiled, his eyes crinkling in their usual cheerful lines.

"Hey, Aydan, can you join me for lunch? You, too, Webb, if you want."

"Sure, where do you want to go?" I matched his breezy tone.

"Let's go over to Blue Eddy's. I could use a beer."

"Sounds good to me. I could use a beer, too."

Boy, could I. I tried to hide the trembling of my hands as I stood up.

"I'll take the key down and then meet you in the lobby," Spider offered, and we all walked out, leaving Smith sitting at the desk. I felt a pang of sympathy for the man. Did he have any friends at all? But I wasn't feeling sympathetic enough to endure his stench while I ate, and I had a feeling Germain's invitation had specifically excluded him, anyway.

My surmise was confirmed when we relaxed at our usual table in Blue Eddy's. Germain glanced casually around the bar, and then leaned forward, pitching his voice just below the level of the music.

"Aydan, about your memorial in the park tonight..."

Dismay rushed over me. He had been Kane's right-hand man, and I considered him a trusted friend, too. I hoped he hadn't been hurt that I hadn't invited him to my fake memorial.

"Could you consider doing it another day?" he asked quietly.

"Um... why?" My mind raced furiously. How could I justify not inviting him? I needed him to be far away from the park, just in case things went desperately wrong. If Kane was killed and I was captured, I needed an experienced field agent to retrieve me. Spider and I had planned to hold Germain in reserve as our backup plan.

"I don't think it's safe for you," Germain said. "You realize that you emailed everybody that you'd be alone and unguarded in an isolated area. If Fuzzy Bunny's operative is looking for an opportunity, you've just handed him one."

"Oh..." I said weakly. Shit, shit, shit. Think! "Um... I would, but, um..." I seized on the first excuse that came to mind. "Today would have been, um, a special day for us. It has to be today."

An unreadable expression crossed Germain's face, and then he reached for my hand and held it.

"Aydan," he said gently. "Kane would have wanted you to be safe. He wouldn't have wanted you to take a chance like this. And it won't matter to him now, whether you do this today or tomorrow or next week."

I gulped down the shame of lying to the pain in his eyes. "But it will matter to me," I said softly.

He gazed at me unhappily. "Aydan..." He sighed and squeezed my hand. "Just be careful, then, okay?"

"I will. Thanks, Carl." The guilt threatened to strangle me, and my voice emerged as a choked whisper. Stemp would suffer for this. For causing these good men pain. For making me lie to them. He would suffer.

Germain released my hand with a sympathetic look as our food arrived. We ate in silence, the men with their stoic grief, and I with my tortured conscience.

CHAPTER 48

By the end of the day, my head was pounding even before I stepped out of the virtual network. When the wave of extra pain hit, I swore violently and clutched my skull.

"Aydan, stop!" Spider's agitated voice penetrated my misery. I cracked open one eye and realized that he had both hands wrapped around my head.

"Stop," he repeated urgently, and I desisted from beating my head against the couch. I let out a prolonged whine as I slowly uncurled.

"Are you okay?" His worried face hovered in front of me.

"Fine." I massaged my temples tenderly, trying to hide how much my head still hurt. Poor Spider. He really didn't need any more stress right now.

"No, really, I'm fine," I repeated. "Just a long day, that's all." I stood slowly and carefully. "I'm going home for a while. I'll see you tonight."

"Okay..." His distress was plainly visible on his face, and the guilt surged back stronger than ever. I was afraid of what might happen tonight, but I didn't think I was as worried as Spider was. I fervently wished I could tell him Kane was alive. It would change everything for him.

As I stood wrestling with indecision, Mike Connor poked his head in the door. "Ready to roll, Spider?"

"Yeah, just about," Spider replied. He turned to me,

his face still troubled. Then he wrapped his arms around me and hugged me tightly. "See you later," he said tremulously.

I hugged him back. "See you later."

He glanced back at me one more time with anxious eyes as he went out the door.

Promptly at nine o'clock, I pulled up in front of the park. My hands shook, and my stomach toyed distastefully with my supper. I leaned back in the seat and took a few long, even breaths, trying to slow my pulse.

There was no reason to be worried. Nothing bad could happen. Kane was there. And the mole couldn't deliver me to Fuzzy Bunny because they didn't even know he was doing this. Plus, they wanted me alive. Really, they did.

My heart stepped up the pace, and I blew out a shaky sigh and picked up the shopping bag from the passenger seat. I'd packed some candles and other props into it, hoping to look as though I was convincingly absorbed in preparing for the memorial.

I gulped down my fear and strode toward the clearing Spider and I had selected. I knew he would already be in place with his video camera, so I deliberately avoided glancing in that direction.

I was just kneeling down to reach into my bag when I heard the sounds of a violent struggle. Underbrush crackled and snapped, and the sound of heavy impact and male grunts of pain and effort made me rocket to my feet.

Kane! I dashed toward the noise.

When I burst through the bushes, Kane and Germain were locked in combat.

Shock and horror rooted me to the ground. Germain

was the traitor? I had trusted him with my life.

My mind whirled while they battered each other. I'd seen them spar before, but the speed and violence of a real fight was appalling between the two men I'd liked and trusted.

My paralysis broke, and I lunged toward them. "Stop!"

They both froze for a fraction of a second, and in the silence, another voice spoke behind me. "Yes. Stop."

I whirled to face Stemp. He sidestepped, looking for a clear shot, his gun already searching for Kane.

"No!" The word tore from my throat, and I flung myself between them.

"Aydan, don't!" Kane voice sounded almost simultaneously.

I backpedalled rapidly, still staying in Stemp's line of fire until I backed into Kane. "Run!" My voice didn't seem to be working right. I spread my arms to make myself a bigger target. "John, get the hell out of here!"

"Stay where you are." Germain's voice was hard as ice. I saw with horror that he'd picked up his gun from the ground and was pointing it at Kane, too.

Heart pounding, I shifted my position to try to cover Kane from two angles. I shoved against him with my back. "Go!"

"Aydan, no." His hands closed on my shoulders as he tried to move me out of the way.

Germain's face twisted. "You knew he was alive. You lied. You sat there beside me at his funeral, and you knew he was alive."

The betrayal in his face stabbed me in the heart. "Carl, I swear I didn't know. Stemp knew. He lied to us all."

"Shut up." Stemp jerked his head. "And move."

"You won't shoot me," I quavered. My legs shook uncontrollably.

"I won't kill you. Of course I'll shoot you if necessary." His gun drifted downward. "You don't need your knees to decrypt files."

"Drop it!" Germain's gun snapped around to point at Stemp.

There was a soft thud, and a small canister tumbled onto the ground just inside my peripheral vision.

And all hell broke loose.

A ragged chorus of men's voices bellowed, "Aydan, run!"

I gasped a breath and immediately doubled over, gagging and coughing. My eyes seared with scalding tears, and I pawed wildly at them. Shots rang out. I heard the heavy thud of bodies hitting the ground, but I was completely blind.

I staggered helplessly sideways, trying to escape the choking agony.

An arm closed around my shoulders. "Aydan, come on. Hurry, we've got to get you out of here!"

I stumbled along beside my rescuer. Tears and snot poured down my face, and my stomach lost the battle with supper as I hunched over, vomiting and choking.

"Come on! Hurry!" The arm around my shoulders was insistent. I blundered along as best I could, still blinded.

At last, I heard the sound of a vehicle door. "Come on, let's get you in here. Step up. No, higher."

"Mike?" I mumbled.

"Yes, I'm just putting you in the ambulance. Sit here." He swivelled me around and lowered me onto a soft surface. The stretcher, I assumed. The door closed behind us as I gasped and choked.

"You're going to be all right," he assured me. "Here."

He handed me a cool, wet cloth, and I mopped at my face uselessly. The stinging pain didn't abate, and more tears poured down.

"What about the others?" I gasped.

"There's another ambulance coming," he said firmly. "Our first priority is to make sure you're safe. Hold on..."

I heard him answer his phone. Alarm flared into his voice. "Hang on, we're coming!"

The ambulance rocked with his rapid movement, and I heard him rush forward to the driver's seat. "Aydan, I'm sorry, we have to go. Spider has collapsed, and there are no other ambulances available."

Fresh terror pierced my heart. "Go, go! Hurry!" I choked.

I barely managed to keep my balance as he accelerated. "Wait, where are we going?" I demanded. "Spider's in the park."

"No, that's why I was here." Connor's voice was strained. "He got delayed. He was worried that you'd be alone in the park, so he told me to come and let you know he was going to be late. He's still at home."

"What happened?"

"I don't know."

I scrubbed frantically at my face. The burning was starting to dissipate, and I finally managed to squint my eyes open. My heart hammered in my chest.

"Any word on the others yet?"

"I wouldn't know. We're shorthanded tonight, that's why I'm alone." He swerved around a corner. "Tonight, of all nights."

"Did you see anything?" I persisted. Three shots. I was sure I'd heard three shots. And bodies falling. Oh, God.

"Aydan, I'm sorry, I couldn't see anything. I barely got you out." He sounded so stressed that I shut up and worried in silence instead, still dabbing at my eyes and nose. At least I could breathe and see again.

We slid to a halt in front of Spider's small, newly-purchased bungalow. Connor leaped from his seat and began to rummage in the back. "Aydan, I'm sorry to ask you, but can you walk yet? Can you help me?"

I sprang up despite my still-wobbling legs. "Yeah, come on, let's go!"

"Hurry. He's in the bedroom." Connor was flinging equipment into a bag as he spoke, and I didn't wait around. "I'll be right behind you," he called as I ran up the sidewalk to the front door. Unlocked. Thank God.

I burst through the door, shouting Spider's name. No response. A wild glance around the small house revealed a hallway to the left, and I sped down it, glancing in doors as I went.

In the last bedroom, Spider's lanky body sprawled motionless on the floor. I dove into the room and skidded to a halt on my knees beside him. His colour was good, and I gasped a breath of sheer relief when I felt his steady pulse. I heard Connor's feet pound across the hardwood floor in the living room.

"In here!" I called, my eyes still glued to Spider. He was unconscious, but at least he seemed to be breathing well. What the hell could have happened to him?

I heard Connor behind me at last, and moved aside so that he could kneel beside his friend. When he didn't, I spared him an urgent glance. "Come on, hurry up."

"Aydan, we've got another problem."

The tone of his voice sent a chill down my spine. "What?" I demanded, on the verge of snapping completely.

"The house is on fire."

CHAPTER 49

"*What?*" My voice rose in a panicked shriek.

"Come on, we have to get out, now!" As he grabbed my arm, I smelled the first whiff of smoke.

"Help me." I grabbed Spider's arms. "Get his legs."

"No, we have to go. Now!" He yanked my arm. Already the smoke smell was getting stronger.

I recoiled, jerking my arm away. "No! Come on, we have to get him out!"

"Leave him. There's no time!"

I gave him a single incredulous glare and seized Spider's arms. I was dragging him toward the door when something in Connor's voice stopped me. "Aydan. Leave him."

I turned to face Connor and my mouth dropped open at the sight of the gun in his hand.

"Mike?" My voice felt lost in my throat. Dark smoke was beginning to collect on the ceiling, and my eyes started to sting again.

"Move." He jerked the gun.

Horrified comprehension flooded me. Three shots. Three bodies falling. And Connor hadn't been affected by the tear gas.

"Mike, no!" I couldn't believe it. I had to be wrong. "What are you doing?"

"What do you think? You're going for a ride. Webb's

going to take the fall. And I'm going back to work at Sirius tomorrow morning as a dedicated employee. Move it, or I'll shoot."

I gaped at him for another second before desperate defiance took over.

"No. You won't shoot me. You need me alive." The smoke was getting thicker. I couldn't seem to suck enough air into my lungs as I panted with terror. My throat prickled and burned.

"True. I'll shoot him instead." He pointed the gun at Spider's head.

"No!" I fell to my knees beside Spider, trying to block the shot.

"Then come on. Now!"

I doubled over, rocking. Tears slid from my stinging eyes again. "Just let me say goodbye." I turned my back on Connor and bent over Spider as if in the throes of grief. And carefully freed my baby Glock from its holster. The one thing Connor didn't know about.

"Hurry up." Connor coughed. The room was beginning to fill with smoke now. "That attached garage is full of accelerant. The whole place'll go up in a few minutes."

Okay, I could hurry up. I spun on my knees and took two smooth shots. I knew I wouldn't miss.

Connor's body began to topple, two dark holes in his forehead, but I was already turning back to Spider.

I grabbed his wrists and dragged him toward the door. Thank God for slippery hardwood. A lungful of smoke made me double over coughing. My eyes teared up again and my nose ran.

I almost threw up again as I shoved Connor's flaccid body aside to make a way for me to drag Spider past. The smoke was so thick I had to bend double to breathe and see where I was going. By the time I reached the living room, I was coughing uncontrollably. My knees gave out and I sprawled beside Spider on the floor, gasping and retching.

Stay low. I crept forward on my belly. A few inches. Pull Spider behind me. A few more inches. Thank God for hardwood. A few more inches.

In the heat and darkness of the smoke, panic engulfed me. I was lost. Completely disoriented. Even lying prone, I couldn't see more than a few feet in front of me. I pushed my face to the floor in a desperate search for clean air as my breath wheezed in my constricted throat. The distant crackle of flames spurred me on. I dug my toes into the hardwood and pushed forward another inch.

A bolt of agony shot through my outflung arm as it was crushed under someone's boot. Then strong hands pulled at my grip on Spider's wrist. A muffled voice bellowed in my ear. "Let go! Let go!"

"NO!"

The coughing started again. Hard hands gripped my bruised arms and legs.

Coolness on my face. Warm lips on mine.

"Come on, Aydan, breathe!" I caught a glimpse of Tom's tense face before I jerked into a ball, coughing helplessly.

"Clyde," I gasped between paroxysms.

"The man who was with you?"

I nodded, still choking. An oxygen mask materialized out of nowhere and covered my nose and mouth.

"We got him. Is there anybody else in there?"

I yanked the mask aside. "Don't go," I gasped.

"Accelerant."

Tom's eyes widened, and he turned to shout at the scurrying figures in the driveway. They fell back a few paces, only seconds before the garage window shattered and enormous tongues of flame shot out.

A bulky figure loomed up out of the darkness, and I recognized Wally Nodell's handlebar moustache. "Where the hell are the paramedics?" he demanded. "We have to get this guy to the hospital. He's not waking up."

"Inside," I croaked. Sick horror spread over Tom's face. "Already dead." I squeezed his callused hand. "You couldn't... have helped."

"Don't talk. Just breathe." He held the mask over my face.

Wally spun around. "You. You." He jabbed his finger at two of the men. "Bring the stretcher. Tom, you'll drive. Take him first." He jerked his thumb at Spider's still form. "Come back for her, then get back here ASAP. We're going to need everybody we've got."

I struggled into sitting position. "I can ride in the front. Save you a trip."

Tom started to shake his head, but Wally overrode him with a nod. "Do it." He strode away.

"I'm okay," I reassured Tom. My eyes and throat still burned, but the coughing had subsided.

He helped me carefully to my feet and lifted my arm over his shoulders while he supported me with an arm around my waist. "Take it slow," he cautioned.

By the time we'd made our way around to the front of the ambulance, Spider's stretcher had been loaded into the back. Tears streamed down my face, and I wasn't sure if they were from smoke or tear gas or emotion.

I trembled helplessly in the seat. The tears wouldn't stop. Kane, Germain, Spider. They might all be dead or dying. My mind refused to deal with any of it. I wrapped my arms around my body and folded over as slow numbness descended.

"Aydan, stay with me!" Tom's hand shook my shoulder.

"I'm okay," I mumbled. "Don't worry."

"Aydan!"

"I'm fine."

When we arrived at the hospital, I pulled myself upright and opened the door. By the time my feet touched the ground, Tom was already beside me. I looked up into his blue eyes, and collapsed into him.

I could've stood up if I'd wanted to. I just didn't feel like it. Besides, I needed a hug.

His arms were tight around me, my bruised ribs screaming at the pressure. He lowered me gently to the ground, shouting something, but I didn't notice what he was saying. I just kept holding onto him until they pried me loose and loaded me onto a stretcher.

I opened my eyes to Hellhound's ugly face. He smiled and stroked his hand over my hair. "Hey, darlin', how ya doin?"

I smiled back, the sight of his homely features warming my heart. "I'm okay," I whispered.

Sudden fear drove through me as memory returned. I bolted upright. "Spider! Is he..."

"He's gonna be okay, darlin', he's just a little groggy still. Ya saved him."

"What about Kane and Germain?" The question slipped out before I could stop it, and I cursed myself for the spasm of pain that twisted Arnie's face.

"Aydan, John's dead," he said softly. "Ya know that. Ya went to his funeral, remember?"

I clutched his hand. "I'm sorry, Arnie, I know. I just..."

"It's okay, darlin'. Why don't ya lie down for a bit." He pressed me gently back onto the pillow.

I held his hand tightly. "What are you doing here? I thought you left yesterday. How long was I out? What day is it?"

"It's okay, ya were only out for a little while," he comforted me. "It's still Thursday. I tried to leave yesterday, but the goddam piece a' shit timing belt shredded about twenty miles outta town. Hadta get towed back here an' wait for the fuckin' belt to get shipped up from Calgary so the garage could fix it. I been at the hotel."

"But how did you find me here?"

"I was over jammin' at Eddy's tonight when a coupla the guys got the call an' hadta drop everything to go to the fire. Somebody said they saw ya gettin' pulled out. Ya know how that kinda shit travels in a small town."

He leaned over and kissed me. "Ya had me worried there, darlin'."

I grinned at him. "You know you don't have to worry about me. Only the good die young..." My voice trailed off at the sudden sick realization that it might be true.

We exchanged a twisted smile.

Urgency hammered at me. Those shots in the park...

"Arnie, do you know if Dr. Roth is working tonight?"

"Yeah, she was in here a few minutes ago."

"Would you mind getting her if she's not too busy?"

"Sure thing, darlin'." He rose and left.

A few minutes later, Dr. Roth stepped into the cubicle and pulled the curtain closed behind her. I motioned her closer to the bed, and her eyes sharpened as she bent down.

"What is it?" she asked softly.

"Have you heard from K... Germain?" I whispered.

"No. Should I have?"

"Oh, God." I squeezed my eyes shut. "Somebody needs to go over to the park right away."

By the time I reopened my eyes, she was already texting, her face grim. "Where, exactly?"

I described the clearing as best I could as her fingers flew. "Should we send a tactical team? Ambulance?"

"I... don't know. It might be too late for that. But I don't know." I buried my face in my hands.

"Don't worry." She patted my shoulder. "Just rest. We'll deal with it. I'll keep you posted."

As she whisked out of the cubicle, Hellhound returned to his post in the chair beside my bed. I clung to his hand, and he eyed me with concern. "Darlin', it's okay, you're safe now."

He stroked my hair, and I loosened my grip with an effort of will and tried to relax against the pillow. "I know. Thanks."

I let my eyes gradually drift closed and feigned sleep while I strained my ears for sounds outside the cubicle.

Long minutes later, my eyes flew open at the soft swish of fabric. Dr. Roth stood at the foot of my bed, a troubled expression on her face. I smiled up at Hellhound. "Thanks for coming, but you don't need to sit with me. Why don't you go back to the hotel and get some sleep?"

"You might as well," the doctor agreed. "She's in no danger, but we'll hold her overnight just as a precaution."

"I can stay if ya want," he offered.

"No, that's okay. Go back and get some rest."

His shrewd gaze flicked between the doctor and me, and comprehension filled his eyes. He nodded and rose. "See ya in the mornin', then, darlin'." He frowned slightly as he squeezed my hand. "Take care." He shot Dr. Roth a suspicious glance as he left.

She bent over the bed to whisper. "There's nobody at the park. Nothing but signs of struggle and an empty tear gas canister."

"Any blood?" I didn't really want to know, but I had to ask.

"No."

My breath went out of me in a rush of relief.

"What happened?" she demanded.

"Stemp and K…" I bit off what I was going to say. Kane was still officially dead as far as I knew. Please, God, don't let him really be dead.

"Stemp and Germain were there. Somebody tossed tear gas, I heard shots and bodies falling. Then Mike Connor snatched me."

She stiffened. "Mike Connor? The paramedic?"

"Yes. He was a sleeper agent for Fuzzy Bunny."

She jerked upright and snatched out her phone. "Where did you see him last?"

"He's dead."

Her shoulders eased and she stared down at me, frowning. "Where's the body?"

"Inside the house. Probably burned beyond

recognition by now."

Her frown deepened. "You set a fire to cover your tracks?"

"No. He set the fire. He planned to leave Clyde Webb inside."

"You need to be debriefed as soon as possible." She turned and swished through the curtains before I could stop her.

CHAPTER 50

I spent a miserable night, dozing and waking at the slightest sound. Dr. Roth still hadn't managed to track down Germain by the time she left at the end of her shift. Worry gnawed at me while I tossed and turned.

At six A.M., I caught myself looking at my watch for the umpteenth time. I groaned and rolled over, resisting the urge to bury my head under the pillow. I had to get out of there and start looking for Kane and Germain.

Despite my momentary lapse of faith when Germain had turned his gun on Kane, I still believed he was one of the good guys. I knew exactly what it was like to discover an apparently dead man still living and breathing. Hell, I'd pulled my gun on Kane, too.

The swish of the cubicle curtains made me jerk upright. Cold fear pulsed through my veins at the sight of Stemp's expressionless face. He was flanked by two armed men, their eyes darting alertly around the cubicle, hands hovering near their weapons.

"Get dressed," Stemp said flatly. "You're being discharged."

Frantic half-formed plans darted through my brain while I gaped at him. Safest to stay here and make a big fuss. No way I was going with him. I was just opening my mouth to scream when he spoke again.

"Now. Or he dies." He twitched the curtain aside to

reveal another large man holding Spider by the arm. The gun was only visible because I knew to look for it. The busy hospital staff would never notice. Spider's face was bone-white.

I slowly swung my feet over the edge of the bed, yanking the gown down in an attempt at modesty. I'd half-expected Stemp to make me strip while he watched, but he nodded shortly. "That's better. We'll be right outside. Don't try anything."

He withdrew and pulled the curtain across. I tottered to the locker, my heart pounding in time with my shaking legs. By the time I'd dressed slowly, my mind was still devoid of any useful strategy. If Stemp was here and Kane and Germain were nowhere to be seen, then my plan was utterly destroyed. Stemp and Connor must have been working together. Why hadn't I thought of that?

My stupidity had cost Kane and Germain their lives. Would probably cost Spider's life. And ultimately mine, after hours or days or weeks of torture.

I swallowed hard and clamped down on terror.

"Hurry up." Stemp's voice was hard.

The cubicle wavered, and I realized I was hyperventilating. I leaned heavily on the bed and tried to slow my breathing. That worked for a few seconds until the swish of the cubicle curtain made me suck in a startled breath again. Stemp glowered at me. "Let's go."

His hard hand wrapped around my arm, crushing the aching bruises, and he ushered me briskly out of the hospital and into the waiting van.

When the van stopped at Sirius Dynamics, I was surprised. I was even more surprised when we all entered the lobby, and Stemp retrieved our security fobs from the wicket. Spider was still being held, but the guard in the wicket didn't seem to notice as the other men blocked his view.

As Stemp approached the door to the secured facility, my heart picked up the pace yet again. The door opened, and he waved us all inside. Three big armed men. Spider, Stemp and me. I was gasping for air before the door even closed.

Crammed into the enclosed space, I grappled for control while the adrenaline surged through my system. When the door released and Stemp moved forward, I stumbled on shaking legs and would have fallen if the two men hadn't grabbed my arms. Stemp eyed me impassively as they half-dragged, half-carried me down the stairs.

Instead of our usual right-turn toward the labs, Stemp turned left down a concrete corridor. I managed to get my legs under me, but my captors kept a firm and painful grasp on my upper arms. Spider walked stiffly ahead of me with his escort.

We passed several glassed-in rooms, featureless except for benches bolted to the walls. As we arrived at the last one, my distracted brain finally processed what I was seeing. Our armed guards stood aside and raised their weapons. Stemp punched a code into the keypad and the heavy tempered-glass door slid open.

Kane and Germain stood tensely as Spider and I were shoved inside. The glass door slid closed, and Stemp leaned against it from the outside. He regarded us with his habitual indifferent expression. "Now, we're going to talk."

I don't know how long we would have stood staring at him if Spider hadn't collapsed to the floor.

I fell to my knees beside Spider in desperate fear, but

he was already sitting up, gaping at Kane as if he was seeing a ghost. Which, in his mind, he was.

"You're... alive...?" he whispered.

"For now," Kane snapped. He glowered at Stemp. "What do you want?"

"Information." Stemp turned his reptilian gaze on me. "We'll start with you. Who's your contact at Fuzzy Bunny?"

"I don't have a contact at Fuzzy Bunny," I quavered. I swallowed hard, cursing my trembling and trying to steady my voice.

"Then what were you doing at the park, setting up a fake memorial to a man you obviously knew was still alive? Getting ready to fake your abduction by Fuzzy Bunny? Who's your contact?"

I glared at him and stayed silent. He locked eyes with me, and neither of us moved or spoke.

After a few seconds, he glanced over at the armed men. "Fine." He punched the code to release the door again. "Put her in the time-delay chamber. Lock both doors." His eyes glinted dangerously at me. "Just start screaming when you're ready to tell me what I want to know."

I jerked my chin up and stiffened my knees in an attempt to hide my violent tremors.

"No!" Spider scrambled to his feet as the men approached. "I'll tell you."

"Spider, don't." The harsh voice that came from my throat made him twitch, but he stood his ground.

"It doesn't matter now," he quavered. "It won't make a difference anyway." He turned to face Stemp. "We were trying to trap you. Aydan was the bait, and I was supposed to be hiding to video you when you kidnapped her.

She was pretending to do a memorial..." He swallowed hard and turned an agonized face to me. "You knew he wasn't dead. How could you...?"

"Spider, I'm sorry!" My voice tore my aching throat. "Stemp lied to me. I really thought John was dead. I didn't find out he wasn't until yesterday, and..."

"I ordered her not to tell," Kane interrupted. "Direct order. No argument."

"But... Why?" Spider turned pleading eyes to Kane.

"Stop." Stemp's voice cut through the conversation. "Why would I take her?"

"Because you've been secretly working for Fuzzy Bunny," Spider blurted out.

Stemp's poker face cracked into astonishment. "What? Are you crazy? What the hell would make you think that?"

I took a step toward him, and the armed men jerked their weapons up and backed outside the cell. The glass door slid closed again. "Oh, I don't know. Little things," I grated. "Like kidnapping and drugging a federal agent. And faking his death."

"That was necessary." Stemp's mask was in place again. "I couldn't afford to waste time once I realized we had a leak. I had circumstantial evidence that pointed to Kane. When he didn't make a move at the dump site, I had to make a snap decision before he shot you. Holding him did two things. It eliminated him as a suspect, and it left you in a position where I could plausibly use you as bait. Again." He eyed me. "Except you beat me to it."

"Do you have any idea what you did to all the people who care about him?" I snarled. I realized I'd surged toward the glass when the armed men on the other side jerked their weapons up.

He shrugged. "It was necessary," he repeated. He turned to Kane. "How did you escape?"

Kane's expressionless cop face was firmly in place, too. "You should have checked those restraints more frequently."

"What were you doing at the park?"

"I'd made contact with Aydan early Tuesday morning." A faint flush rose on his neck, and I guessed he was remembering exactly what that contact had been like. I knew I was. "She told me her plan, and I was there as backup. Which would have worked if Germain hadn't jumped me."

"Yes, what were you doing there?" Stemp inquired as he turned to Germain.

Germain glowered. "Trying to protect Aydan. I thought she was out there all by herself." He shot me a look.

Guilt suffused me all over again. "Carl, I'm so sorry I had to lie to you..." I began.

He shook his head. "It's okay. You had to."

I swung around to face Stemp again. "So what the hell were you doing there?" I ground out.

"Waiting to see who Fuzzy Bunny's operative was, of course," he replied smoothly. "When I saw your email, I couldn't believe you'd been stupid enough to set yourself up in such a vulnerable position, but I chalked it up to you being a dumb civilian."

He eyed me sardonically. "Clearly, I misjudged you. Regardless, you'd solved a problem for me. I'd been trying to figure out a way to use you as bait again, and you set it up for me as neatly as could be. So I took advantage of it." He shrugged. "I had video surveillance equipment set up, too."

"If you needed a trap, why didn't you just ask me?" I demanded.

"Would you have done it?"

I sighed. "Of course. Well, before I found out you'd lied and kidnapped Kane, anyway."

"But what happened at the park?" Spider broke in.

"I got there early as we'd planned, and I was just starting to pretend to set things up when I heard fighting."

"That was when I jumped Kane," Germain said. "I'd never believed he was a traitor, but when I saw him alive, I thought he'd faked his own death and he was trying to abduct Aydan."

"And I thought you were attacking me because you were the mole," Kane put in. "Sorry," he added. "I didn't believe you'd turn, either, until you showed up there."

"Why were you trying to shoot Kane?" I snapped my gaze around to Stemp. "You knew he was innocent."

"I didn't know that, actually," Stemp replied dispassionately. "A message to Fuzzy Bunny was sent the morning that you went to the dump site. No further messages were sent while I had Kane in custody. The day he escaped, another message went to Fuzzy Bunny. Then he appeared in your trap. What would you have thought in my place?"

"So you were going to shoot me to get me out of your line of fire."

"Yes. I thought your judgement was... biased... when it came to Kane. I realized afterward that you had known in advance he was alive and you'd expected him to be there. That changed things."

"So why are we in the cell and you're outside?" Kane grated.

"I had a contingency plan in place." Stemp nodded to the armed men. "They brought us back here to sleep off our tranks. Too bad the tear gas got them, or they could have nailed Connor right there."

"That's what the shots were." Comprehension finally filtered through to me. "You were tranked. All of you. He lobbed the tear gas so nobody could see, and then it was like shooting fish in a barrel. He needed you alive so he could shuffle off the blame and continue working as a double agent."

Spider had been following the exchange open-mouthed, his head swivelling back and forth. "What happened to you?" I asked.

"Mike and I were gaming over at the cafe. We needed some props, so he drove me home to get them. Then I woke up in the hospital."

"He drugged you and set your house on fire," I said gently. "He was Fuzzy Bunny's agent."

"But..." He gazed helplessly at me. "Linda told me at the hospital that my house burned down." He gulped. "Completely. My new house." His voice quavered a little, and I reached to hold his hand. "Why would he do that?" he asked.

"Spider, Connor was setting you up."

"Yes," Stemp agreed. "Smith intercepted a plain-text message to Fuzzy Bunny that was sent from your laptop yesterday evening, saying that you had captured the asset."

"He planned to make it look as though you'd abducted me and then been killed in a fire," I told Spider. "He tricked me into going over to your house by telling me that you'd collapsed. He lit the fire to force me to leave you."

"But you wouldn't." Spider squeezed my hand.

"Linda told me the firefighters said you dragged me out. You wouldn't let go even when you couldn't go any further. They had to go in with their new breathing masks, the smoke was so thick."

I smiled at him. "Of course I wouldn't leave you."

A snort from the other side of the glass interrupted us. "This is all very touching," Stemp said. "May we get back to the point, please? Dr. Roth said you killed him and left the body to burn in the house."

I felt Spider's jerk of shock.

"Yes, that's true," I said quietly. "I'm sorry, Spider."

Stemp gave a brisk nod. "Well done." He surveyed me. "I presume you lost your gun in the fire? You didn't have it on you at the hospital."

"I dropped it when I was dragging Spider."

He reached for the keypad again, and the door slid open. "I'll arrange for a replacement. You can pick it up by end of day. Kane, Germain, you can retrieve your weapons from the storage locker. You're all free to go. Get back to work." He turned and walked away, trailed by the three guards.

CHAPTER 51

We all stood frozen for a few moments. My brain steadfastly refused to comprehend what had just happened.

"That's... that's it?" Spider's eyes were wide. "Just like that?"

Kane's lips quirked up in a humourless smile. "That's how Stemp operates. Instant action. He was an excellent field agent."

I opened my mouth, but nothing came out. It seemed as though I should be doing a dance of joy, but no emotion penetrated the shock. I'd been wrong about Stemp. I'd been wrong about Connor. So desperately, dangerously wrong. I'd come so close to losing these three men who meant so much to me.

I hugged them fiercely, each in turn. When I stepped back, I returned their smiles and turned to Kane. "We have to go to the hotel."

Spider blushed, and Germain's eyebrows went up. "Why?" Kane asked warily.

"Because Hellhound's there. You've got a reunion to go to."

In the hotel lobby, I stopped Kane. "Just give me a few minutes to tell him. It'll be a hell of a shock."

He nodded, and sat in one of the lobby chairs while I

made my way up to Hellhound's room.

I tapped on the door and waited. There was no response, and I pressed my ear to the door to hear soft snoring. I knocked a little louder, and was rewarded a few seconds later when the door opened to reveal Hellhound's bleary face.

His brow furrowed, and he scrubbed a hand over his face. "Hi, darlin'. What're ya doin' here?" He shook his head and blinked sleepily. "Come on in."

I slipped in the door and closed it behind me. He pulled me into a kiss. "Still pretty early, darlin'. Ya comin' to bed?" He began to tow me in that direction.

"Not right now."

His eyes sharpened at my tone as he snapped fully awake. "Aydan, what is it?"

"I have some news. I think you'd better sit down."

He scanned my face as he sank onto the bed. His hand tightened on mine, and sick expectation filled his eyes. "Tell me."

"It's good news," I hastened to reassure him.

"Then why'm I sittin' down?" he demanded. "Jesus, Aydan, ya ain't pregnant are ya?"

I recoiled. "Christ, no! Bite your tongue, man!"

He slumped in relief.

"That can't happen," I added. "I've been fixed. We're safe even if a condom fails."

"Good." He took a deep breath. "Jesus. Then spit it out, darlin'."

"Kane's alive."

He searched my face and pulled me gently down to sit beside him. "Aydan, ya saw him die, remember? Remember we talked about this at the hospital?"

"No!" I took his frowning face in my hands. "I mean, yes, I remember we talked about it, but I was wrong. They lied to us. They lied to us all. He's alive. He's downstairs."

His face went slack. I gave him a little shake. "He's alive."

A knock at the door made me jump. "I'll get it." I left him sitting silently on the bed and opened the door a crack.

Kane stood in the hallway. "Is he here?"

At the sound of his voice, I was rocked by a bellow from behind me.

Kane grinned and stepped into the room as Hellhound lunged. "Ya fuckin' asshole! I oughta kick your fuckin' ass! Ya goddam sneaky spyin' sonuvabitch!" He seized Kane in a rough embrace and pounded him on the back.

I slipped out the door to the sound of Kane's laughter. "Jeez, put some pants on! I don't want to get hugged by some ugly naked hairy bastard..."

I left them to what would undoubtedly be the first of many joyful reunions for Kane. I had business elsewhere.

I strode into Stemp's office without knocking and closed the door behind me. He glanced up, unsurprised, as I sat without invitation.

"I've been expecting you," he said.

"I don't doubt it." I met his snake-like eyes. "Because you've managed to hurt quite a number of the people I care about. And I promised that you'd pay. I keep my promises."

He leaned back in his chair, the faintest smile playing about his lips. "Let's cut the crap. We both know you won't do anything to threaten national security. We both know you'll keep on doing the decryptions and putting your life on the line no matter what. We both know you can't harm me. So drop the empty threats."

All the pain he'd caused, dismissed with a shrug. Just collateral damage.

Rage poured through my blood, burning like strong liquor. I channelled it, shaped it, narrowed it into a white-hot beam of pure hatred.

I held my voice steady with a supreme effort. "You're right, of course." I sounded almost conversational. "I can't hurt you physically, and I'll keep on doing the right thing for the country. But I think you need to understand the kind of pain you've caused."

"Is that so?"

"Yes." I leaned back in my chair, too. "How's Katya?"

He was good. If I hadn't known to watch for it, I would have missed the tiny flicker of his eyes. "I'm sorry, I don't know anyone named Katya."

"You didn't get to talk to her this morning, did you?"

There was definitely a flicker that time. He stretched nonchalantly and linked his hands behind his head. "I don't know what you're talking about. Are you finished?"

"That's a nice apartment she's got in Sofia, over on Dianabad. Nice and close to her work at the university."

He shifted in his chair, but said nothing.

I shrugged. "I thought you might be interested to know what would happen to her if Fuzzy Bunny found out about your relationship. But I guess you don't know who I'm talking about." I made as if to rise.

"Sit." Suddenly I was looking down the barrel of his gun. He was fast. I hadn't even seen him draw.

I leaned back again. Slowly and carefully. "Let's cut the crap." I spat his words back at him. "We both know you won't shoot me."

"What have you done to Katya?" He was holding onto his imperturbable mask, but I could see it crumbling.

"Don't you wish you'd talked to her this morning? I thought you should know what it feels like to discover that someone you care about is gone forever. No chance to hold them one last time. No chance to say goodbye."

"What have you done?" I could read the anguish in his eyes now.

"How does it feel?" I asked him softly. "Imagine what Kane's father went through when you told him his son was dead."

Stemp's face twisted, a shocking change from his usual emotionless facade. His knuckles whitened on the gun as he surged forward over the desk. "What have you done to Anna?"

I frowned. "I don't know who you're talking about."

"Don't play games with me! What have you done to my daughter?"

As I stared blankly up into the tortured eyes of a man who'd lost his child, my stomach churned with slow nausea. I hadn't known they had a child. He'd been in Bulgaria for the first time seven years ago. She'd be about six years old. Maybe younger. My throat closed up.

"I'm sorry," I whispered.

"*What have you done to my daughter?*" His voice was raw agony, the gun shaking in his hand.

He understood Doug Kane's pain better than I ever could. I couldn't believe I'd done this to him. Making him suffer wouldn't atone for the pain of the people I cared about, it only made things worse. More suffering in the world.

"I haven't done anything," I told him shakily. "Katya is fine. Anna is fine. Nobody knows they exist. I'll never tell anybody they exist. They're safe. I never said I'd done anything. You just assumed."

I sucked in an unsteady breath. "I thought I wanted you to suffer, the way you'd made others suffer. I was wrong. It was petty and vicious, and I'm sorry. I would never, ever try to hurt a person by hurting somebody they love."

He sank back into his chair, breathing heavily. We watched each other in silence.

At last, he drew a long breath. "Why stop torturing me so quickly? You warned me you'd make me pay. You would have killed me without a qualm if you'd had bullets last week."

"I thought it was necessary last week. I'll do what has to be done, but I can't... won't... cause unnecessary suffering."

"Neither will I." We met each other's eyes again, and his face composed itself into its usual emotionless mask. "That was stupid," he said.

"Yes. It was. I'm sorry."

"I didn't mean it was stupid of you to want me to suffer. That, I understand." He put his gun away. "I meant it was stupid of you to admit that you hadn't hurt them. And it was stupid of you to admit you'll behave honourably no matter what. You just gave up all your leverage."

I slouched down in the chair and rubbed my aching

temples. "Leverage is useless if you don't have the balls to use it. I obviously don't."

"That's not necessarily a bad trait," he said quietly. "But you realize that your knowledge of my weak spots gives me another reason to make sure that your project, and you, get terminated as soon as possible."

I blew out a long, exhausted breath as I got up and turned toward the door. "You don't need another reason to kill me. This is just a reason to enjoy giving the order."

His voice stopped me as my hand touched the doorknob. "I won't, you know." He sounded very tired.

I turned to face him. "Won't what?"

His weary eyes met mine. "I won't enjoy giving the order. When the time comes."

I thought that over for a few seconds, and gave him a short nod. "Thanks."

I let myself out.

A Request

Thanks for reading!

If you enjoyed this book, I'd really appreciate it if you'd take a moment to review it online. If you've never reviewed a book before, I have a couple of quick videos at http://www.dianehenders.com/reviews that will walk you through the process.

Here are some suggestions for the "star" ratings:

Five stars: Loved the book and can hardly wait for the next one.

Four stars: Liked the book and plan to read the next one.

Three stars: The book was okay. Might read the next one.

Two stars: Didn't like the book. Probably won't read the next one.

One star: Hated the book. Would never read another in the series.

"Star" ratings are a quick way to do a review, but the most helpful reviews are the ones where you write a few sentences about what you liked/disliked about the book.

Thanks for taking the time to do a review!

Want to know what else is roiling around in the cesspit of my mind? Visit my blog and website at http://www.dianehenders.com.   Don't forget to leave a comment in the guest book to say hi!

About Me

By profession, I'm a technical writer, computer geek, and ex-interior designer. I'm good at two out of three of these things. I had the sense to quit the one I sucked at.

That's how I currently support myself. To deal with my mid-life crisis, I'm also writing adventure novels featuring a middle-aged female protagonist. And I'm learning to kickbox.

This seemed more productive than indulging in more typical mid-life crisis activities like getting a divorce, buying a Harley Crossbones, and cruising across the country picking up men in sleazy bars. Especially since it's winter most of the months of the year here.

It's much more comfortable to sit at my computer. And hell, Harleys are expensive. Come to think of it, so are beer and gasoline.

Oh, and I still love my husband. There's that. I'll stick with the writing.

Diane Henders

Since You Asked...

People frequently ask if my protagonist, Aydan Kelly, is really me.

Yeah, you got me. These novels are an autobiography of my secret life as a government agent, working with highly-classified computer technology... Oh, wait, what's that? You want the *truth*? Um, you do realize fiction writers get paid to lie, don't you?

...well, shit, that's not nearly as much fun. It's also a long story.

I swore I'd never write fiction. "Too personal," I said. "People read novels and automatically assume the author is talking about him/herself."

Well, apparently I lied about the fiction-writing part. One day, a story sprang into my head and wouldn't leave. The only way to get it out was to write it down. So I did.

But when I wrote that first book, I never intended to show it to anyone, so I created a character that looked like me, just to thumb my nose at the stereotype. I've always had a defective sense of humour, and this time it turned around and bit me in the ass.

Because after I'd written the third novel, I realized I actually wanted to publish them. And when I went back to change my main character to *not* look like me, my beta readers wouldn't let me. They rose up against me and said, "No! Aydan is a tall woman with long red hair and brown eyes. End of discussion!"

Jeez, no wonder readers get the idea that authors write about themselves. So no, I'm not Aydan Kelly. I just look like her.

Bonus Stuff

Here's an excerpt from **Book 4: Tell Me No Spies**

I suppressed a curse as I furtively shifted the concealed holster to a more comfortable spot at my waist and rearranged my sweatshirt over it. A tension headache pounded sullenly at the base of my skull.

The vibration of my phone made me start, and I snapped a glance over my shoulder before I snatched it up.

I could barely hear the whisper on the other end. "Aydan, can you stall him for a few more minutes?"

"How long?" I hissed. "What's wrong?"

"We just need a few more minutes to get everybody into position."

"I'll try." I punched the disconnect button with more force than was absolutely necessary. Why the hell did I let myself get sucked into this?

I knotted my fists in my hair and tugged, but quickly desisted at the sound of the door latch releasing. Trying to look relaxed, I leaned back in the chair and stretched my legs out. The security guard glanced my way, and I gave him a quick smile, heart thumping.

At the sound of footsteps behind me, I turned my smile toward my quarry as I stood. "All finished?"

"Yes." He stretched, grimacing. "Long day." He made for the door.

"Hang on a second," I blurted.

"What?" He shifted from foot to foot, obviously eager to leave.

"Um..."

Goddammit, what could I say to stall him? My mind was completely blank. The silence began to stretch. His forehead creased ever so slightly, and I saw his eyes dart toward the door. Think, think, dammit!

Absolutely no inspiration came to mind.

Shit!

I did my best sheepish laugh and slapped my forehead. "Forgot what I was going to say. Sorry, you're right, it's been a long day."

He let out a short laugh and turned away again. "See you."

As he disappeared out the door, I whisked my phone out and hit the speed dial. Still attempting nonchalance, I wandered out of the building, raising a farewell hand to the security guard as I left. The phone rang interminably at the other end while I muttered "Pick up, dammit, pick up!" When I finally heard the whisper on the other end, I snapped, "He's on his way!"

"Crap! Can you get here before him?"

"I'll try."

When I was sure nobody was watching, I launched myself into a silent sprint toward my car.

I lunged into the driver's seat and swore violently as the door slammed on my long hair and nearly dislocated my neck. I wasted precious seconds opening and closing the door to free myself. The tires chirped on the still-warm asphalt when I stomped on the gas.

Minutes later, my car skidded to a halt in the gravelled alley and I dashed through the twilight to let myself in the back gate. I spun at the last second to catch it before it banged behind me, then flew across the yard. As I reached the top step, the door of the darkened house opened, and a disembodied hand yanked me inside.

My eyes hadn't adjusted to the dimness, and I allowed myself to be towed rapidly through the house. A jerk on my arm made me duck behind the sofa just as the scrape of the front door key sounded, loud in the listening silence.

End of Tell Me No Spies, Chapter 1 excerpt

CPSIA information can be obtained at www.ICGtesting.com
Printed in the USA
LVOW091011020412

275750LV00001B/5/P